Warning: this story contains graphic descriptions of intense sexuality sensuality brutality sexual assault strong language and shocking violence to suggest and interpret an authentic representation of these events which may cause extreme mental imagery. Reader discretion is advised.

MOONSHINE
Taming a Werewolf
Book One

by Tracy Godwin Sr.

Cover art by Kemono Inukai

Copyright 2020 Tracy Godwin

Table of Contents

Ch 1. You Don't Know, what you Don't know

Ch 2. From the Beginning

Ch 3. The Talk

Ch 4. On the Road

Ch 5. Nde

Ch 6. Frying Pans and Fires

Ch 7. Out of the Fire and Straight into Hell

Ch 8. Dog Soldiers

Ch 9. Destiny calls, Fates merge

Ch 10. Who are You? What are We?

Ch 11. No Second Chances

Ch 12. Answers

Ch 13. Taming werewolves

Ch14. Werewolf and were-animal College

Ch 15. Can't Say I'll Miss You

Ch 16. Present Day

Ch 17. Fates Kiss

Ch 18. Epilogue

Tristan

Movies never get it right. They all form the assertion that it's the moonshine (full moon), alone that forces the change, and they are all wrong. It is also when there is no moon, during a new moon cycle, when the night is at its darkest; that is when the tragedies of my life of horrors take place. It is known, to my kind, as black moon. Black moon is when a werewolf is truly, at the mercy of the night.

During the days of a black moon, even an ascended elder werewolf must focus on not losing control, constantly at risk of losing themselves in the moment and getting lost in a murderous rampage. With all untamed and adolescent werewolves, completely out of control, and at their worst with no hope of recompense.

Although adolescent werewolves are out of control during moonshine and black moon both; no elder werewolf is ever afraid of the moonshine. Moonshine is when we are strongest and have full control of all our capabilities. Able to choose to make the shift from man to monster or not to make the shift at all. During a full moon (moonshine), if we are in human form, we have all the strength and abilities of our werewolf counterpart. Same as, as a werewolf, we keep all or most of our faculties from our human side.

If you take your best adrenaline rush ever and multiply it by five hundred times, you will begin to have a minor understanding of the rush a werewolf, in their human form, experiences during moonshine. The same is true when we are fully shifted from a human to a werewolf.

Some of the ancient lore has truth to it. Though it's been so muddled thru the ages, it's no wonder, that the true history and legends of the werewolf have been lost to time; with what remains, being nothing more than chilling bedtime stories for children these days.

There are many fallacies and downright jokes pertaining to the history and legends of the werewolf. The biggest fallacy of them all is that to make the change from human to werewolf and back again is an unbearable, agonizing and excruciating pain that is worse than death. Hah! Quite the contrary, to be sure. It is the most intense ecstasy and euphoria imaginable. It is as exhilarating as a hundred orgasm's rolled into one.

The biggest joke is the claim that silver bullets kill us. Silver is a strength, not a weakness. Being riddled with bullets in general, can slow us down, but it is by no means a sure thing.

Many a time I have awakened to the reality of my deranged existence. The taste of blood, or actual blood, still in my mouth. Entrails, skin and hair packed under my fingernails. The smell, still fresh in my nostrils, of human parts and innards that no human was ever meant to smell—let alone recognize. Awoke to find bullets lying beside me where they had fallen, as my body pushed them out during my transformation back to a human form. Healing itself as it does so, barely ever leaving a scar.

And even if there was a scar, it didn't stay but a few hours or days, and then it was gone forever. Leaving no trace of the horrible savageries I had indulged in… or been condemned to. Countless times, I have sifted through the bullets and kept the silver ones. My collection of them is impressive, I must say.

My Uncle J.R. always told me, *kill the head, the ass will die*. That statement stands true for every walk of life, werewolves included, except on extremely rare occasions.

Not to mention that damaging or severing a werewolf's head is damn near impossible, to be blunt about it. Requiring uncanny skill and strength, coupled with almost magical weapons from an ancient time, long past.

An incredibly old wiseman, as old as time, told me of the ways I could be killed, but those are very few and far between. There are only two ways, he was certain of, and after all these years, so am I.

The first is, only a werewolf can kill another werewolf. The second, is fire. Burn the body to ashes and they will not come back. But then again, who wouldn't that kill?

The remaining few, require a combination of factors and is not always successful. Except, for one other way that I will not speak of now. Suffice it to say, that for a werewolf, to be killed and/or die permanently, are very separate affairs.

It's been many years since I've seen or felt the old wiseman's presence. Even so, I remember him well. Without him, I would have never made peace with and accepted what I have become. Just as, without him, I would have never survived it in the first place. I was thinking of him. As the night began to take on a life of its own.

Chapter One

You don't know, what you don't know

Tristan–The vibrance of the city was abounding with its usual night-time activities. Indulging in their pleasures and delights, the people were festive and growing wild. The full moon was beginning to rise over the land from behind the mountains. Inspired to shine upon the city, giving off an inconceivable vibration from its light. A daunting and cosmic force that would cause the city to modulate into a frenzy. The same as it has done throughout the eons. Playing its games on all the creatures of the Earth since a time unimagined.

Be it merriment, mayhem or murder, the moonshine will extract its toll for the part it plays in the ecstasies of human beings. The same as it does with all of Earth's creatures.

Just exactly, how does the Earth's rotation combine with the Moon's charm; to shape the lives of human beings for good or evil?

Is it controlled by: destiny, coincidence, synchronicity, happenstance, luck, chosen path, seekers discretion, paranormal manipulation, enlightenment, damnation, roll of the dice? What mechanisms are responsible, for turning the gears of such things? So that they align with a person's life, ambitions, ego or fate....

Ah, yes, fate... let's not forget fate. For she is the lady who cuts in to dance with whoever she wishes, whenever she chooses.
She will change the music, the tempo, or the entire reason for the dance at her slightest whim. She has command over them all, and she can intervene at will, for good or bad. Who, if anyone, can ever know what drives the whims of fate?

Fate and destiny, often wrap themselves within each other, like an insulated communications wire. Blocking out all other overtones and sounds to create a one directional current, that no matter how you attempt to proceed: up, down, around, over, under, left or right, this way or that; you find yourself travelling down a path that has been chosen for you, from which, there is no escape.

The vibrations of the Earth, Moon and stars that triggers their ignition is the very spice of life; the sauce for the goose, which is always the one thing, you don't yet know, and have no way of figuring out until it's in your face. Only then, becoming aware that it could ever happen to you. Until that very moment, you don't know, what you don't know.

* * * * *

On this night, I play the part of the messenger, delivering the truth of fates kiss to an unsuspecting soul. A soul that will become; either, a willing or unwilling lover, of a destiny of dark and (most likely), fatal design.

The irony of it all is that it was a bite, more than a kiss, that fate had delivered. A bite he had gotten from ending up in the wrong place, at the wrong time. If left to deal with what has happened to him on his own; he will become the night stalking, homicidal rage of evil that is believed to be the epitome of all werewolves, condemned to be a plague upon the Earth and all her inhabitants, or destroyed, to prevent it.

If he decides to accept what has happened, and can be tamed and trained, there is hope for him. Hope of powerfully dangerous, becoming controllable.

Useful, for the good and betterment of man and Mother Earth. Sometimes with and sometimes against, the species that presently reins over her living surface and plight.

Kind-of-like, a dysfunctional superhero. Though there would never be credit, acknowledgement or celebration of his deeds or passing. After this night, if his recruitment is even possible, the world would forget he ever existed at all; except, for the ones of whom he is of a kind now... and some few humans... strangers really.

A hard thing to embrace when one finds out they've become immortal.

Call me dysfunctional if you want, but I have no regrets of the hand I've been dealt. So far so good, knock on wood.

* * * * *

When I found him, he was in a little bar just off the beaten path of most of the revelers of the night. A small place but well to do none-the-less. He was on the bottom of a bottle of Patron, tequila. With nothing but a shot glass as his drinking apparatus.

"Celebrating?" I asked him.

"Not quite," he replied somberly, "this is more to acknowledge loss... and to forget...."

As he looked up and saw my face, he said, "You again... Is it merely simple coincidence that keeps us running into each other, or is there a greater design at work?"

I shrugged and said, "Mind if I join you?"

He motioned a hand for me to have a seat. I called to the server, "Can we get another bottle over here and an extra shot glass—please?"

We toasted a few shots and became a little more acclimated to each other's presence with small talk. After a short while, I asked him, "Care to talk about it?"

"Care to talk about what?"

"Whatever it is that has you here collecting bottles of Patron and in such a melancholy."

"I need to talk about it to someone. But it's classified military bullshit."

I dropped a Majestic level clearance badge in front of him.

He picked it up and read it aloud, "Tristan Jonas, Majestic Level Clearance.

"A bona fide M.L.C. having shots with me. Pleased to make your acquaintance, my lord," he said and smiled.

We both laughed, then he said, "My name is Thomas.

"This is the second time, in so many days, I've seen one of these. I didn't get such a good look at the first one. Until recently, I thought this level of security was just a myth, now I've been exposed to proof of its existence twice in so many days."

I told him, "Well, that A-1 in the top corner means—the only level higher is God himself coming down and having a shot with us.

"Don't hold on to it too long. It has its own build-in defense mechanism. After another minute or so, it will melt away completely. Killing anyone other than me with the poison it will release as it melts to prevent anyone from having it too long—

should they get their hands on it. Taking your life in seconds and leaving no trace at all of what killed you. Other than symptoms of a mass heart attack...."

Thomas handed it back and said, "I've stepped into a world of shit, haven't I?

"I've seen something that can't be unseen and exposed to shit that must have a lid kept on it at all costs. And so, it's by design that we sit here now together, isn't it?"

After another shot, I said to him, "Tell me what happened to you, Thomas."

"I would guess a man of your clearance status would have a copy of my report on his desk."

"I probably do but I rarely sit at the fucking thing. Besides, I would like to hear it from you. Not to mention it might help you to talk about it. Forget my credentials. Tell me as you would to a person without a clue of who you are. Because that's—basically—the truth of it."

"I'm Captain Thomas A. Bremen. Army Rangers, security counter-sniper. I've supervised missions all over the world that my team and I have successfully completed without losing a single man. Our last assignment took place right here in the states.

"Have you ever even heard of such a thing? We had no earthly idea why we were being sent in to take out nonmilitary targets in our own country. Only that we were to take 'em out—burn the bodies and leave no trace but ashes. Then we were to scoop up those ashes, to the last speck, and bring them back with us." His face went blank; his eyes stared as if in a trance. He continued,

"When the fighting began, we exhausted all our ammunition on an enemy that never fired a shot. When the dust settled, all my men were dead. Ripped apart in ways—that looked more like—savage animal attacks...than anything a human would do.

"I managed to end up the last one alive. I could hear them breathing... all around me....

"One of 'em rushed me... I emptied half a clip into it... and it just, kept, coming."

Thomas looked around as if he were about to be attacked again. Then he took in a long drink of silence before continuing,

"It grabbed hold of me; sank claws into my flesh that were as long as bear claws.

"I could barely see it even as it attacked. I thought, at first, it was a bear. But, when it grabbed me, and tore me open with its teeth and fangs...I sensed malice in the damn thing.

"Malice that animals don't have... not even rabid ones. This fucking thing had a human characteristic about it."

He grabbed the bottle of tequila and up ended it, to calm his anxiety. I could see in his eyes; he was reliving the trauma as he spoke. After another swig from the bottle, he continued,

"As it bit into me, I grabbed it around the back of its head, stuck my pistol in its ear and capped five bullets into it. The damn thing eased its grip and flung me over the edge of the ravine we were next to. That ledge was well over twenty feet away—I don't give a damn...!" He took in another drink of tequila. He looked as one utterly subdued, lost in an astral projection of memory. I didn't need to be a mind reader to know he was struggling with the playback in his head. I didn't expect him to go on... but he did.

"The fall put me out cold. When I came to, I was on a stretcher, being hoisted into a medevac chopper; all my wounds were already tended to. I was told there was no trace of a body. Not the one I put so much led into, nor any others.

"The only body count... was of my men....

"I was told by the medic; the site had already been cleared when they found me. Even my wounds had already been cleaned and dressed.

"Wounds that should've had me crippled for life that are already almost fully healed; with me feeling like I could outrun a cheetah-on-cocaine...."

He up-ended the bottle again, wiped his chin with the back of his hand, and said, "I wasn't even allowed to see what was left of my men. Not even to say a final farewell.

"I know someone knows what-the-hell it was...hit us that night—god-damnit! And I fucking wanna know!"

He slammed his fist down on the table. His look over at me, was as abrupt, as his next words, "Why are you here? To debrief me and decide my future...?

"Well if I am to be lobotomized... at least, tell me what it was that hit us that night."

I didn't respond, and after a short stare-down, he asked me, "Who do you report to? Who are your superiors?"

"I have no superiors that I answer to. There's a few, you would call superior, that I work with from time to time, but they answer to me. My team consists of myself and two others, Paris and Trudy. We—"

He cut me off, "Girls?"

"Yes, girls!" I retorted.

"You sure your name isn't Charlie? What happened to your other angel?"

We laughed. Then I said, "You'll throw rocks at Charlie's angel's when you've seen my two!" He laughed even harder. I poured the last of the tequila equally into our shot glasses. We did our last shot and I said,

"Come with me, Thomas. I will tell you what you want to know, but this isn't the place to do it.

"Besides, you're gonna want and need proof of what I tell you, and that definitely can't happen here."

With his curiosity peaked, we paid our tab, and he followed me out the door.

* * * * *

As we stepped up to my car, with a look of surprise, he exclaimed, "*A MERCEDES-BENZ SLS AMG GT*! Who bank rolls your operation?"

"I do, or rather, we do. Paris, Ariel and I are a team. And our bank roll, as you call it, belongs to all three—"

"Ariel? Who is Ariel? I thought you said your other team member was named Trudy."

"Trudy is a nickname. Her real name is Ariel."

Then he asked, "Besides being your team members, who are they to you?"

"My wives…for lack of a better term," I told him.

"Wives? What are you… Mormons?"

I soundly retorted, "Oh-so—you think that's fuckin funny!"

The look in his eye was at once apologetic. I smiled and held back a laugh, saying to him calmly, No…we're not Mormons….

"Let's just say, our rhythms merge like guitar-bass-and-drums…. We're not just a-trio…we are The Trio….

"It's a long story…a story you will get to hear when we get where we're going. If you can shut up—long enough—with all these stupid fuckin questions."

"Where are we going? The fucking Batcave?"

With a chuckle I replied, "Maybe… just get in the car…where we are going… ain't just around the corner."

We drove for an hour, deep into the countryside. After leaving the main road, we made our way down a private driveway and approached the main gate.

After a thumb print and voice recognition, the gate opened, and we went ahead thru it. When the house came into view, he said,

"Hey man, I was kidding about the Batcave, but now I'm not so sure. What the fuck…? You really don't exist on a government salary, do you?"

"You can bet your ass on that poncho!" I told him.

He laughed another contagious laugh, one that I, quickly joined him in.

It took us a long minute to make our way thru the house to the back patio where I suspected the girls were. Being a history buff himself, Thomas was struck dumb by all the décor. "These artifacts are the genuine article, aren't they?

"They must be worth millions! Why do you even trouble yourself with missions and bullshit for the government?

"Why aren't you kicked back with your two wives? Touring the world and munching the cheese."

"I assure you," I replied, "what we involve ourselves with… is way above any government knowledge or pay grade. And I've seen the world more times than I can count.

"When you have lived as-long-as I have, you need something to occupy your time and keep your interest peaked.

"Plus, no one else is qualified to take on the *missions*, as you call them, that we take on. Except for the girls and I."

With a bewildered tone, he said, "Lived as long as you…? You can't be that much older than me… if I'm not the actual elder here…."

I didn't respond. I just kept walking to the back of the house. Only giving him a sly smile over my shoulder as I did so.

We walked onto the back terrace; the girls were there. They were naked and drinking Mai Tai cocktails. They weren't expecting me to come home with a guest.

Though you would have never known it by their demeanor or lack of surprise. Nor did they feel the need to jump up and go running for clothes.

Thomas, his mind now completely blown, rattled off, "Butt-naked—and sippin on—Mai-Tai's...! Until this very moment, I thought that to be only a statement of jest.... I now stand corrected."

He stood there glowering at the girls with his eyes about to pop out of his head. Their expressions never changed. They just stared back, trying to get a read on him.

Ariel got up and walked over to him, donning a robe as she did so. When she got within an arm's reach of him, she sniffed the air as one does to someone with cologne on.

Then, she went off on me.... "So—we're bringing home stray's—now?

"Are you fucking bent...? You know—too-damn-well—what must happen if this goes south...! He can't be let loose to run amuck...! And we ain't having—no young pups staying—here.... Pissin-in-shittin all over—everything—

"What got in your head—that made you bring-hm here? You—fucking—tool...."

"Damn-it Jim.... if you'd hold-on just one-damn minute—"

"And fuck-you-n-your—stupid shit...you know I don't like Star Trek...."

Now, I had really pissed-her-off.... I decided to stop fucking with her—and said,

"I have a good feeling about him. Plus, there's something about him that reminds me of someone—"

"Oh yeah? And just who—the fuck—might that be?"

I answered her with a tone as mocking as hers, "It just might—the fuck—be me...!"

Trudy stared at him a moment longer, then walked over and grabbed me by the back of the neck. She pulled my face closer to hers and gave me a long, sensual tongue kiss.

After our kiss, without moving her body or releasing my neck, she turned her head to look over at Thomas again.

As she stared at him, she said, "If he ends-up having to die... I'm going to fuck him first—

"He can consider it his last meal."

I exclaimed, "Oh no—the hell—you're not! That's simply out of the question!"

Ariel and Paris exclaimed together in one voice, "Oh yes—the hell—we are!"

With Ariel following-up, saying, "Whether—you—like it-or-not buddy boy...."

I was in the doghouse—now....

Paris started in, "Do you need to be reminded of all the pussy you've gotten because of us?"

"I wouldn't say—I got it because of you. Just because you were there doesn't mean—I wouldn't have got it had you not been there—"

Ariel retorted, "Ok mister smart-ass.... Keep that up, and you'll never get laid again...."

Thomas, not missing a beat, quickly chimed in. "All of a sudden, I'm feeling a need to-fit-in here...."

The four of us fell into a good laugh. Then he asked,

"Now, what's this shit about having to die...you guys aren't a bunch of cult followers who believe you've found a sacrifice, are you? Tell me I'm not—caught-up—in that shit!

Ariel told him, "No one here is gonna harm you...not yet anyways. As for cult shit... that's baby stuff...compared to what you've stepped into—yo.... And I'm not talking about us...or this place. Actually...we're your salvation—"

"Stop-it.... Before you freak-him-out. I didn't bring him here for you to tease—

"Come-on Thomas...let's go to the den where we can talk and be a little more comfortable."

The girls went to put on clothes while the two of us made our way to the den.

I said, "Ok, Thomas, time for those answers, but you might not like them.

"You and your men weren't attacked by other men. It didn't become clear to me at first, but after giving it some thought... I think I figured it out.

"There were good guys already there that night to handle things. Someone sent you and your sniper team in to take out good guys and bad guys alike.

"The problem was you were out gunned from the jump street. You had no business being there at all. Someone, in your ranked hierarchy has their own little secret agenda, and when I find the motherfucker's—I'm gonna snap their fucking spines!"

"Out gunned? They never fired a shot...! We were attacked—by something... something—big... and powerful.... And whatever or whoever they were...they didn't mind a shit-load-of-bullets in their ass—either!

"We never even got off one round with our rifles. They hit us while we were still dug in like tics.

"They snatched us out of our positions as if we were kids playing hide-n-go-seek. I've never been spotted and plucked out like that in my entire career... and neither had any of my men. Not to mention their wounds... if you can call them—wounds....

"Their bodies were ripped and torn like what dogs do to—couch pillows. Ghastly—and—horrific lacerations....! Guts everywhere...like they had—food-fights—with them!

"I have never...seen or met, or even heard of men or soldiers, or even stark raving lunatics...capable of such wonton violence and butchery—"

"You were not attacked by men... you were hit by Werewolves."

He stared at me long and hard, straight in my eyes, trying to see where I was coming from. I waited for him to speak. Finally, he gave a little chuckle and said,

"Ok, ok. You had me for a minute. Where's the camera's? Is this supposed to be... some-kind-of—*Interview with the Vampire*—shit...?"

I smiled at him and said, "Well, there are no vampire's close by—that I know of. But in the spirit of the beloved writer of the *Vampire Chronicle's*...and her character *Loui, we can't begin like this—*"

Paris and Trudy came into the room. Scantily dressed but dressed none-the-less. Paris, as she was walking over to us, asked me, "Well, does he think it's some big joke on him...? or that you're a fucking—nut...."

"Undecided.... But he did ask if he was on candid camera...and made a pun about vampires...."

Paris told Thomas, "Vampires...! Oh-no—sweetie...right genre...wrong monster. There be werewolves here...!"

Thomas gave her a crazy look. Dumbfounded, as to what to say to her statement. I spoke up,

"This is why I've decided to cut to the chase. He gave me the idea when he made me think of what Loui did in *Interview with a Vampire*, when the reporter didn't believe him."

"*Oh Loui...my love...! Don't go away—and leave me...!*" said Ariel. Jokingly reciting words from the movie.

"HaHa, very funny... But I'm thinking... let's just show him what he won't be able to discount, discredit or disbelieve...."

Paris rolled her eyes, and said, "I bet—the usual bet—that he loses consciousness—before you're halfway through the shift...."

"You're on! The usual bet...."

Ariel muttered, "So-much-for—not—freakin-em-out...."

Then said aloud, "Well— I guess this will be the test, let's get this show on the road. This ought to be good either way. Just-sit-back and relax—Thomas—ole-boy. You're about to have your cherry popped...."

Thomas asked, "What's the usual bet...?"

"Oral sex...given by the loser...." Paris casually replied.

"A win-win situation really." I stated.

Thomas acted as though he was to be the butt of some big joke, at his expense. The first sign of him getting nervous, since we'd met in the bar, was when I started taking off my clothes.

"Don't worry—my new-found—friend. This isn't about sex or dicks...." I told him.

His tension subsided a little. A good thing! Given what he was about to bear witness to....

* * * * *

Ariel–Regardless of Tristan's first reaction to what I said earlier, Thomas is a gorgeous man. As gorgeous as Tristan—almost...but-no-cigar....

They will both be present for what Paris and I have planned. If he survives the next few minutes—that is....

I've seen strong and healthy men: in complete control of all their mental faculties, have a heart-attack and die, on the spot, at seeing what Tristan was—fixin—to show Thomas.

If he can make it all the way through this, without at least passing out, it will say a lot for his own mental abilities.

Tristan sat down in his chair as though he was settling in for a good storytelling.

He closed his eyes for a moment. When he opened them again, they were no longer the color they were before. His eyeballs were solid black.

Thomas instantly drew his head up and back with a look of bewilderment. I don't know what was going thru his head, but we had his full attention. He was no longer throwing zingers either. Finally, he had—shut-the-fuck—up....

Tristan's eyes changed color again, seeming to glow red.

He bared his teeth, sucking in a breath between them.

The look on his face, was one of pure ecstasy. His knuckles went white as they gripped the arms of the chair. His penis went fully erect; and after another moment, he began to spontaneously ejaculate, as one long—continuous orgasm coursed through him. No semen, only blood.

Tears of blood started from his eyes. Blood began to spew from every orifice of his body and out from under his fingernails and toenails. Followed by mucus and Saliva...*the Drool*...as Tristan calls it. To see it happening, looked like it was terribly painful. But to see his expressions, you could easily tell...he was feeling no pain. He was completely capsuled in an enduring...orgasmic state. The look of ecstasy and euphoria on his face was even more extreme than a few seconds ago and kicking up a notch with each passing moment. Thomas was frozen in place, still speechless.

Tristan began to shake violently now. So much so, the convulsions shook him out of his chair and onto the floor...rolling onto his back—involuntarily. His mouth opened, and he began to expel one extremely long breath as his toes, fingers and nails began to morph and grow.

His feet began to deform and swell, stretching and growing in an oblong way. With his big toes seeming to stay put as the rest pushed out backward and forward. Making his big toes look more like weird thumbs, for a second.

The sound of his bones stretching and growing, as they changed their structure and density, was—really—unnerving. A sickening crackle, like someone crushing pretzels and bubble-rap at the same time.

Watching him change, may have been gross and repulsing for the uninitiated…but…call me crazy…it was turning me—on…. One of the little side effects of being a werewolf…is an—insatiable—overindulging—sex drive….

The balls of his feet were now his actual feet. With the rest of his foot stretched so far back…his heels and ankles were now more like—backwards facing knees…than they were heels and ankles anymore….

His hands still looked like hands, but his fingers and nails were now excessively longer, with a diabolical look to them.

The palms of his hands were swelling into more like the pads of a dog's paw…or wolf…pun intended.

Tristan rolled over now onto his feet and hands. Like a person on their hands and knees, except he was now on all fours like a crouching tiger—with its belly to the ground.

Both his hips made a loud and revolting pop, as they dislocated and shifted their position in his body. His entire body continued to grow, stretch and swell.

He began growing hair instantly in some places, losing it completely in others.

The only part of his body that wasn't transforming was his genitals. The sexual organs stay fully human on a werewolf….

His teeth were—now—fully transformed and fanged. With canines longer than my middle fingers, over three inches easy.

His ears grew backwards to a point that looked more like evil elf-ears than natural wolf-ears. His moans and groans leveled-up to grunts and half growls.

His head started to misshapen; his jaws and face began to push out from underneath his eyes. For a moment, his normal voice came back. Not speech…only a long moaning sound like a man getting off on oral sex.

His mouth now fully formed…opened and closed spasmodically. Like a dog that's trying to hock something up, from its throat. Finally, he vomited up a large amount of blood and bile, produced by the rearrangement of his inner organs. Now…the blood from him was no longer red … like what was pushed out of him by the drool…no-no….

This blood was bright pink; filled with what looks to be crystals, shimmering like diamonds dancing with sunlight....

Even—puked up—from a freak of nature, it catches the eye.... If you want an explanation...of how that works, that makes sense... I promise to have Tristan explain later. But I am babbling now, and we are missing it—

His tail bone had punctured the skin, and grew out into a tail, complete with blood, meat and skin. Much shorter than your average wolf tail but functional—all-the-same. Hair now covered it completely.

For those enlightened in such things, a werewolf's tail is a distinguishing factor. No two are alike. The individual's tail can determine age, level of advancement.... Shit...! I'm doing it again, aren't I?

His arms had grown out much longer than their normal length. Making it so that as he lifted himself up more onto all fours, his shoulders were higher, than his hips. His posture, in a small way, resembled a gorilla poised on their knuckles. But not as short in the hind legs.

His legs were taller...not as stocky, but much more powerfully build than his human legs.

His facial expressions were fiendish and wicked. Especially his eyes. Tristan is the only known werewolf to ever exist with red eyes. He is also an ascended elder, as are Paris and me. I'll have him explain that later too.

It's done. The shift is complete. Tristan stands upright on two legs and lets out a blood curdling howl.

A sound that is both human and wolf...intermixed into a screaming-howl. It's more like a howling-scream—to be exact. Tristan, Paris and I all agreed... scream-howl rolls off the tongue better. But...in fairness of correct observation; it starts with an abominable wolfish howl... and ends in a scream...of human quality. Accursed and detestable in its tone and volume. Definite and definitive in its effect to strike terror within all beating hearts. It even gives—me—goosebumps, at times. A scary fucking thought... considering, I'm a werewolf.... It's not the last thing you want to hear before you die....

With Tristan on his hind legs, it became easy to see he was, now, well over seven feet in height. Every sound, expression and movement he made was menacing and ferocious in its bearing and nature. Tristan is one bad-ass werewolf...bar none...!

* * * * *

Narration–Paris cried out, "He's losing it...! His sanity's slippin...! He's gonna boil over.... Thomas...stay with us."

His mouth began to open and close involuntarily, trying to form words, "I, I, I," was all he could manage. Without realizing it, he started up from his chair.

Paris and Ariel yelled to him, "No! Don't move!"

It was too late. The werewolf turned toward him, its demeanor now a grim and dark malevolence. Shining teeth like a wolf about to attack... only far more intimidating. It let out a spine-chilling roar that was felt in the bone.

Thomas, now in Stark Terror, pissed himself as he tucked his feet under his ass in the chair, and began to cry like a frightened child without its parents.

The werewolf stepped over to him and put its face next to his. Sniffing him for a second, then went nose to nose as it shined its teeth full in his face and sounded-off a hair-raising and god-awful growl.

That was all poor Thomas could handle. With his senses now fully flown, he gave up staying conscious for any more of this appalling and dreadful experience. His eyes rolled up into the back of his head, and he slid out of the chair onto the floor, as his body went fully limp.

* * * * *

Thomas was out for the rest of that night, all the next day and night, and all the following day. It was close to midnight when he finally stumbled out of the room, they had put him in.

Upon seeing Tristan, still trying to rub the blur of sleep from his eyes, Thomas said, "So, you are real. This place is real. And that wasn't just a nightmare last night, was it—"

"You mean the night before last? You've been out for almost forty-eight-hours," Tristan replied.

"I'm not surprised. I needed some good sleep. I've been unable to sleep hardly at all since that night by the ravine.

"Your approach to helping me get that sleep was a little extreme though. Xanax would have done fine. And how did I get into these clothes?"

"You pissed and shit yourself when you passed out. The girls cleaned you up and put those clothes on you. Then tucked you in real nice."

"The girls huh? Great.... That's just the first impression I wanted to give them. Cleaning a grown man of his own excrement as he lay unconscious. Wish I'd thought of it sooner...." He put his head in his hands, unable to look at Trudy or Paris.

Tristan told him, "That wasn't our first impression of you. Our first impression was watching how you handled what we exposed you to like a champ. Most do much worse their first time out—

"Consider us quite impressed that you lasted as long as you did—without getting yourself mauled, at the very least. Everyone else, who has been exposed to the same has either died or gotten themselves killed."

Unconvincingly he said, "Well that makes me feel better.

"Was there anything else impressive about me? Say, maybe... when you were putting these clothes on me?" forwarding his questions to the girls.

Tristan smiled and rolled his eyes.

Saying so, in the third person, as if Thomas wasn't there, Ariel said, "He's nowhere near the length and girth of Tristan, but he is well endowed." Not wanting to blow his head up too big, she told him, "I'll work wit-it *Yo*... but if it's a foursome...you might have to go first." They all laughed hard at that statement.

Thomas was handling all of it very well. The girls were beginning to see what Tristan saw in him and why he had brought him to the mansion.

Though it was far from daybreak, they all decided that a good breakfast would hit the spot. Werewolves do not have to eat much people food, but it doesn't hurt them. What they eat as werewolves, sustains them without any further need.

It's like a supercharge. Except for human flesh. Human flesh is forbidden.

Eating human flesh, as a werewolf, will take you to places you do not want to go if done too often. Tristan admitted once; to the remembrance of enjoying eating the heart of an enemy or two, but he didn't give an exact count.

After breakfast, they made their way back into the den. Where Thomas had his brush with a werewolf in his face...up-close and personal...for the second time in his life.

The servants had cleaned-up everything, as though it never happened. They knew the goings on there, and were lavishly rewarded, to the point of spoiling, for keeping their secrets.

After a few minutes of teasing, Tristan began, "Now, where were we? Before we were sidetracked the other night...ah yes.... I was there that night. We had gotten intel, there was to be a meeting—involving some heavy hitters.

"We've had surveillance on that pack for some-time; trying to find who is funding them...and giving them their orders. They are extremely dangerous, but also naïve and stupid in their youth.

"I couldn't save or help your men. I showed up too late to know you were there or what was happening at first. I did see you get attacked. Saw how you fought back...and was impressed—to say the least. Yet, I couldn't risk letting them know we were there and ruin months of surveillance.

"I thought you were dead for sure anyway... after the mauling you received ... followed-up by your flight off the cliff. My personal cleanup crew cleaned the sight. When they found you still alive, they promptly informed me. I couldn't believe you were still breathing! I thought to myself, this is one impressive motherfucker—"

"Even a simple bite from a werewolf, is usually fatal. Let alone the ghastly wounds and blunt-force trauma you suffered. I had them dress your wounds after I decided to save you from certain death—"

"Why do I get the feeling, that when you say, *you decided to save me*, there is more to it than just bandaging my wounds and getting me to a hospital?"

"Probably, because there is. I used my clearance level to keep you off the military brass's radar. I also had my people keep you protected and list who came and went from your room while you were being treated. The list they gave me, in conjunction with what you know, might help us figure out why you were even there that night and who's behind it. Now—"

"Wait a minute... If a bite is usually fatal, how come, I'm alive?"

Tristan was quiet for a moment, then avoided answering his question directly.

"If I hadn't done anything, you would've died. With everyone thinking your wounds got infected and gangrene took your life. After seeing your will to survive, I figured, it would be a shame—to let you die.

"But the life you knew... is dead....

"The only way you go on living: is if you can accept and embrace what has happened, cut all ties to your past, and are able to be tamed and trained, to control what you are."

"And that is...?" He asked

"You...are a Werewolf...my newfound—friend....

"If left unchecked, you will maim and murder and commit acts of unspeakable and savage atrocity.

"We will either tame you or kill you. Sending you right where you were headed when I found you... to meet the grim reaper.... And trust me.... I've killed for a lot less."

Tristan felt a brief pause was in-order. Thomas sat in silence. He'd been listening intently, to Tristan's tale of what he saw, and knew of that night, but now, he found himself lost in thought. Pondering the intrinsic values of his life, fading to the extrinsic.

Tristan's thoughts were on seeing a werewolf being born. Thomas was the first-ever that he'd decided on condemning to this precious curse. Rather than letting him die or killing him because he thought it—more humane. Compassion, for the first time, since the passing of this precious and sinister gift on to him, had crept back into the human side of his existence. But he wasn't ready to tell him, he had died, and was reborn to this world, not only as a werewolf, but also, as his son.

Less-is-more was his thinking, as he was blasted out of his thoughts at hearing Thomas form words again.

"Just exactly—how many are on your side of this *chessboard of death* and destruction?"

Chessboard of death! Ariel's thoughts were catapulted back in time; to the day she heard the only other person use that phrase in her entire existence, of close to two-hundred years. A man she hadn't seen since her youth, not in the flesh anyway. Then a voice, not her own, spoke aloud in her mind. It said, **Reincarnation**.... No one noticed, she was now completely oblivious to them and their conversation, as Tristan spoke.

"How many of us are there? Infamously, we are known as and called, *the Trio.* Our call-sign is *Trio-One,* which is...me—of-course, Ariel, Paris... and maybe...you....

"In a fucked-up sort of way, it's like when the three musketeers meet D'Artagnan.

"We also have men and women signed-on to us through our Majestic connection. A small battalion of special-ops forces, doctors, scientists....

"Usually, we just kill everything. You're the first we've tried to save—"

"And how many oppose you in this insane game of blood-lust and debauchery?"

Tristan grinned slightly, as he looked over at Thomas, "Debauchery...nice name-drop.... A defining word for werewolves.

"Werewolves in general are more populous now than any other time in existence. Since the most ancient knowledge, of the first times, was scribed to tell of their existence. Probably legions in number."

Trudy and Paris came into the room with four glasses and an incredibly old bottle of scotch.

As Trudy opens the bottle, Paris asks, "If you could only use one word to describe his mental and emotional condition, what would it be?"

"Undaunted." Tristan told her.

Trudy was quick to rebut, "I'm sure he isn't finished asking all his stupid fucking questions. Next, he'll probably ask if one of us is little red riding hood."

As Thomas opened his mouth to speak, Trudy put her hand up, with her palm facing Thomas, turned her face away from him, and said, "If you even look my way and say one word—motherfucker...! I'm gonna crack this fuckin bottle over your fuckin head!"

Paris butted in just then with a babying voice, "What's the matter Red? Did you lose your hoody and need a little nap... in grandma's bed?"

Trudy tried not to smile, but she was soon grinning from ear to ear. Chuckling now, she told Paris, "Will you shut the fuck up?" All four of them were enjoying the teasing.

Ariel poured double-shots and made a toast, "***To the thrill of the chase!*** The sauce, for the goose!" After Cheers, they did their shot. "I think I feel most alive...when something is trying to kill me," was her follow up comment.

The first of many, as they delved further into the bottle, opening a second before they were finished. Surprisingly, the conversation drifted off into social content and getting to know each other, minus werewolves. It felt good to play, at just being human.

* * * * *

The next morning, everyone stirred at the same time and unanimously decided breakfast sounded good again. Without anyone really saying anything or playing director, they just fell into cooking breakfast. Everyone effortlessly falling into a rhythm. Taking up a chore towards completion of their breakfast without getting under foot of each other. Even as they were introducing a young pup to the family, he was already in sync with the pack.

After more light conversation over breakfast and some hot showers, followed up with fresh clothes. Thomas and Tristan went for a walk. They walked a few miles to where an overlook on the back of the property allowed them to see the Pacific Ocean and the city of Pismo Beach. Even given the distance they were from the coast; the Pacific, with her bluest of blue waters, stretched to the north, west, and south from horizon to horizon. As they settled into a comfortable spot for admiring the view, they began talking again about current events.

The reality that this was not a hoax, had started to sink in for Thomas. He shied away from any serious questions, at first.

"So, why did you choose this part of the world to call home? Is Pismo your hometown?"

"No... we just like it here. And since this was where you went when you left Nevada, it sufficed," Tristan told him.

Thomas replied, "I had to get out of that Nevada high desert. I had been here before and enjoyed myself, so this is where I came. How many of these little hovels do you guys own?"

"As you prove yourself trustworthy, you will gain more and more access to our life and lifestyle. For now, it's enough to know that you don't have to worry about money ever again."

"Ever again huh? Now, that's one hell-of-a perk!

"Are you ever going to tell me how I'm still here after being fatally bitten by a mythical creature?"

"In time… There is much more you need to understand and make peace with first.…" Tristan told him.

Thomas changed the subject. "When I watched you change…. Man—what a total mind-fuck that was. But now, as it plays back in my head…I can't stop thinkin…I've heard sounds…like you made… somewhere before—"

Tristan interrupted, "*American Werewolf in London*, the opening scene. When they are tracked and attacked on the moors. The grunts and growls before they are attacked, and all the howling-screams… are as close, to the real thing, as you can get…as you now know. The howls from a distance are also spot on."

Thomas looked as one who's having an epiphany. "That's it! Not as dramatic as when it's in your face… but., that, is, it! How does that happen?"

"I don't know.… The best we can figure is, either someone knew a werewolf or had encountered one, and was able to replicate the sounds. Another sublime example is *The Howling*, the first one. At the end… when the woman does the first scream as she starts to change. That is an authentic scream-howl. It's only a split-second before it fades to bullshit but it's there. We always say it backwards, it's actually… a howl-scream. It starts in a howl…ends in a scream.

They talked for hours about everything and nothing. When they got back to the house, it was after dark.

As they kicked off their hiking boots and slipped into some house-slippers, Thomas asked in a whisper,

"Were the girls serious about having sex with me?"

Tristan chuckled a little and said, "Maybe, probably, who ever really knows with those two. I wouldn't get ahead of yourself though. Remember… their words were… *if you end-up having to die*.…

"The common phrase is…*two is company, three's a crowd*…

"The girls always say…*three is company, four's aloud*…!

"Look at it like this…. They are Siamese when they please, you will have to leave when you don't—please….

They both laughed and entered the house, which smelled of the aroma of steaks for supper.

* * * * *

After supper they found themselves up on one of the roof decks where they had a telescope for moon gazing. Tristan had filled an—*uncommonly old and authentic*—American Indian peace-pipe with some good *sweet-leaf* Kona. They'd opened another bottle of that good Scotch whisky—and as the Trio puts it, *they were feeling kinda right, we've merged the rhythm*. Hours passed as they gazed up at the Moon and stars, answering and laughing at more of Thomas's stupid questions.

"What about Vampires? Ever meet any?"

They all fell instantly silent on him. It was Tristan who answered him,

"Do not invoke or evoke their name. I have never met one that didn't see us, and every other form of life on this planet, beneath them. Which makes everything their food and property to hear them tell it. We've had run-ins but no real disputes, so far."

Ariel chimed in, "There's not many things like sex with a cold-blood!" Her and Paris high fived that comment. Thomas looked at Tristan for a response,

Tristan shrugged and said, "What can I say, I've yet to meet a female Vamp or Dhampir that wasn't drop dead gorgeous—pun intended.

"The sex is most definitely transcendent. Especially, if you're with one that can bite you without trying to suck you dry. If they bite you… right as you're climaxing…there's nothing else that even compares. And to answer your next question… it takes a lot more than a bite and a little blood loss before you're in trouble."

"What's the worst part of becoming a werewolf for a night and changing back?"

Paris answered him, "Like a dream for some…a nightmare for most…especially for those without a grip on it…

"Bien que, aube brise un nouveau jour pour tous les loups garous"

Thomas translated, "Though, every dawn breaks a new day for all werewolves."

Paris nodded and smiled as she said, "I'm impressed....

"but a bath is the only thing, which clears—my—head. Waking up from the shift, always feels, to me, like I've been covered in syrup all night while running around naked in the woods... then passed out before I've had a chance to wash it all off. Add that feeling to a bad night on a black moon, and it makes for one shitty morning until you've had a proper bath."

Ariel looked at Thomas and said, "You—know.... It's kind of like after sucking dicks all night—then getting up the next morning and starting your day without washing your fucking face and brushing your teeth."

Thomas quickly retorted, "I wouldn't know... because I don't suck dicks! Now if you want to talk, pussy...."

Ariel quickly covered her mouth with the back of her hand and gave him a look of surprise. She then, just as quickly, changed the look in her eyes with a flash of her eyelids, turning them into bedroom eyes. She then straightened her index and middle fingers and pulled them across the bottom of her nose as if to smell them, and said,

"I'm a woman who doesn't care much for multiple choice. When confronted with such *A*, *B*, questions, I usually choose *C*... all of the above."

Her facial expression lost its look of seduction. She walked over and sat down next to Tristan, humming a tune to herself. Thomas's next questions were bomb shells.

"When will I start to feel this? When will I make my first change?"

Paris spoke up again, "It's different for everyone. By the third black moon or moonshine...without a doubt...."

He cocked his head sideways, "Moonshine or black moon?"

"A full moon or new moon." She told him.

He then asked, "Is the fucker that bit me, like, my father now?"

Ariel didn't miss her chance at stirring things up, saying,

"No...Tristan is your father now... If you care to look at it in those terms."

Boom! There it was. In his face now. All eyes on Tristan.

Ariel, with a shit eating grin, watched him squirm. Tristan walked over towards her, reaching in his pocket as if to give her something. Only to pull out an empty hand and shoot her a bird that touched the tip of her nose with the tip of his middle finger. Tristan tried to find his words.

"Um…ok…um…yea… well, you know…you see…no wait…hey…! fuck!" Tristan was at a loss for words.

Paris came charging to his defense, saying,

"Well, just being scratched or bitten is one thing, but with the severity of your wounds—it took two werewolves, of the same blood-line, to feed you blood—to ensure you didn't die. So, as you say hi to your new father…give a little shout out to your new mother." Paris pointed to Ariel.

Ariel started laughing, saying, "Don't even give me that mommy-daddy bullshit! You know that's not how it is at all! Mom and dad don't even make the list.

"If anything, we are the blood-donors that made you. Real mothers…give birth to babies…. You're…more like a test-tube, without the tube—"

Thomas threw his hands up, "Ok-ok-ok, you know what, I think we can come back to that one…let's move on…shall we? Let's just slow this way the fuck down….

"Ariel, you're right, sometimes I do ask stupid, fucking ill-timed questions."

"I'm always right, yet everyone is always so amazed when they figure it out," she quickly proclaimed.

He smiled at her, and for the first time since he arrived, she allowed him to look directly into her beautiful green eyes. As did she, finally look deep into his.

What she saw, wasn't a man full of undaunted confidence in his ability to assess, adapt and conquer. It was a man on the brink of losing his sanity. Here was a man: trained to kill, day or night, and get restful sleep when he slept. And how to do both, extremely well…without remorse. He was a leader back in the world of men. A commander in his own right. Now, knocked off his perch…back down to novice.

Being told: if the killing he's already responsible for wasn't enough, it was about to become a whole lot worse, with no rhyme or reason to it. He had been trained a killer, now he just wasn't sure what being a killer meant. Or these people, he was now forced to let mentor him; were they deranged, psycho lunatics, or saints in wolf clothing?

What he saw, in her eyes, infected him with their seduction and depth. Not a sexual arousal or dreamy infatuated crush. Something even more intangible tugged at him. Her eyes... became far off and deep, as they called to him without sound, and pulled at his reason, to such a degree, he realized, she could see into him.

She was doing it now. Seeing right into his deepest self that even he was barely privy to. No need for confessions, she now knew everything. He could just drop the façade and let go of the wheel. For the first time since he could remember, he was going to have to trust someone else to be in charge for a while.

Thomas felt as if he was in an astral projection into another realm of dimension. His chin started to quiver. His eyes began to water, and the expression on his face now matched his deepest and purest inner thoughts. Thoughts that Ariel had just seen in him. She began to let her guard down and let Thomas into their inner circle.

His faced dropped into his hands, in an attempt, to hide his eyes from her, but she was in his head now.

He looked up at her again as a whisper planted itself deep inside his head. He knew it was coming from Ariel.

Without speaking a word aloud, she told him, "Don't be frightened by what you have seen, or thoughts of your future, of being a werewolf. Fate has not been so unkind to you. She allowed us to find you. You will soon understand how this is a comforting thought. Find your patience young one. For a window has closed on you, but a door has been opened in its place. Allow yourself to let go and be sucked into its vacuum. Knowing you are not alone."

He was completely enveloped now in her trance and essence. She began to walk towards him. Her stride was slow, long and sleek as she approached him, like a she-panther.

Yet, the emotion pouring off her, was more akin to a little girl bringing a flower to a grieving man. Dropping slowly to one knee as she reached his side; she caressed the edge of his ear, and with her actual voice, said to him softly, "besides, it's not a bad thing to realize you don't have all the answers. It's only after this happens that we start asking the right questions."

She shut her eye lids down over her eyes with a sensuality that only a woman is capable of. As she opened them again, he was snapped back from across the gulfs within her eyes, to the reality of time, no longer on pause. Still not able to take his eyes from hers, he said,

"There is a whole lot more to you than meets the eye, isn't there?"

With a smile that was now in her eyes as well as on her lips, she replied, "Oh, you have no fucking idea...."

They shared a little laugh together as if they were alone in the room. Then she asked him genuinely, "better now...?"

"Yes... How did you do that?"

She rose from where she had been kneeling beside him, saying, "All I did was free your mind from all the turmoil that was overtaking it. Free your mind, your ass will follow."

"Wise words from an extraordinarily wise lady." He retorted kindly.

Ariel put her hands up as a praising angel would and said, "Oh my god... he can be taught. The prosecution would like to take a short recess to consider this new evidence... I'm beginning to think little—*White Fang*—over here, just might survive all this after all."

With the voice, tone and posture of a smart-aleck, snot-nosed kid, he told her, "Oh yeah, well if I call myself—
White the Fang... I think that sounds pretty dope.... And my call letters will be *W T F*...! So-fuck-you!

They all laughed uncontrollably. After they settled down, Thomas asked, "How about we start with how you three came to be what you are? You know, like, from the beginning...?"

Tristan told him, "Ok, from the beginning.... I need you to know though...that none of us have told this story before or even spoke much about the past amongst ourselves.

"Werewolves are not Vulcans. We can be very emotional and even a little sentimental at times. So, there may be some emotional baggage that comes to the surface.

"You know, somebody really should roll some video for this. The similarities with *Anne Rice's* books are uncanny.

"They used a tape recorder; we're videoing our story for youtuber potential…. True irony at its purest—"

Tristan paused in thought and then, jokingly, said to Thomas, "Thomas man, if you haven't read all her books, I highly recommend that you do before the human side of you disappears to the point of not being able to read any more."

Thomas looked up at Tristan, wide-eyed and thought-filled, Tristan smiled and told him,

"I'm just fuckin with you—man… Ok, from the beginning….

Chapter two

From the Beginning

Tristan–My full name is – Tristan Elijah Jonas – I was born in – 1835... —the timeline for all this though, begins in 1864.

I was a southern boy just turned twenty-nine; I was born in Florida and raised there by my parents and grandparents.

They taught me how to survive off the land: how to live with respect for myself and others, and especially, how to protect and care for Mother Nature.

My mother was more Native American, in her ways, more than anything else.

My grandmother was a pure-blood Apache Nde. Loving mother nature was paramount to my entire family, and still is to me, to this very day.

We did not believe in the slave trade. Though, from the outside looking in, it appeared, we had many slaves. Everyone, we bought, was free the moment they stepped onto our property.

They were given lodgings and paid a fair wage, and when they had paid back the cost of freeing them, all obligation to us was satisfied. Those that stayed on, received an education and training; each to their own abilities and desire, in operations of, every part, of owning a cattle/horse ranch and farm. Among other ventures that my family were involved in.

With the *War of Northern Aggression* in full swing; it was dangerous times in the south for all slaves and white folk, alike, who were sympathetic to the freedom of all men and women.

I was no coward, but I was not about to kill my northern brothers for a cause I didn't believe in. Nor was I going to fight against my southern brothers—no matter how wrong they were.

My family had land on New Providence island, in the Bahamas. The freed men and women, who chose to go there, were sent to help tend it. My grandfather and father still called them the Baha Mar Islands, so named by Christopher Columbus. They both decided, it was time to go, so they packed up everything and everyone, Africans included, and made their way there.

I decided not to go with them. It was time for me to strike out on an adventure of my own. Island life was something I had come to appreciate, and I planned on returning to enjoy its many delights, but I wanted to see mountains, desert and California. Growing up in central and southern Florida and the Caribbean had its pleasures; to this day, I feel more at home there, than anywhere else in the world. To realize that truth though, required adventure. I saddled up, stocked all the provisions I could carry and bid farewell to my family.

* * * * *

Setting aside the devastation being caused by the military; the burning, raping and murder of civilians was out of control across the south. Travel was arduous and dangerous. I helped everyone I could, and I hid when I couldn't....

Several times I was forced to kill to keep from being killed, by people and animals alike.

I argued with myself as to why, I just didn't turn around and head for the islands. Some nights I cried myself to sleep, from the memory of the atrocities I'd seen.

Yet, some part of me, kept screaming; that I was on some sort of mission, in as much as it was an adventure. A fated rendezvous with destiny. All I knew for sure and kept telling myself; was that to turn back, would be the act of a coward. This fact would win the argument every time.

At times, I posed as a simpleton to augment the arguments of the many, who were loyal to their slaughter, in the name of the *war between the states*. With all of them wondering, why I wasn't on a battlefield, or as enthusiastic about the butchering of tens of thousands as they were.

There were days; when I was able to smell the stench of death ahead, could hear a battle in front of me. So repugnant were both...I knew it was better to avoid it altogether. I would leave the beaten paths and travelled roads. Traveling sometimes deep into the wilderness or skirted the coastline along the Gulf of Mexico.

I had one horse, and I didn't trade or swap for any reason. If we had to hold up on her account, we were hold up. Her name is Sarah—

Thomas interrupted me,

"Is? What the fuck do you mean… is?"

"I meant – was – it was – Sarah—"

"Man—I fucking swear – if you—demented—fucks – got—werehorses – tucked away—on one of your little—getaway hideaway's – well that's some fucked up—dysfunctional shit – and that's all I'm gonna say about it…"

The girls and I looked back and forth at each other. Trudy saved the day, saying to Thomas,

"That's it – for you—that's all-he-wrote—fuckboy—

"You've lost your talking privileges—

"Speak again—without being asked somethin – and I'm gonna—knock you out and—fuck-start you with a strap-on…. Tristan, please continue—"

I was in Texas when the first of fate's kisses exposed me to the dragon's breath. It was the first time on my journey, I thought I was really going to die. Most importantly, it was the day I first laid eyes on Paris and Trudy.

The day our lives became forever entwined with one another, and the current drama of death and lust began its march into reality.

For days, the trees had been giving way to an arid landscape of scrub and bush. A fine thing: given the days spent crossing the biggest swamp I'd ever seen in my life….

The fact I made it out of that swamp at all, was a gift from God. Only thing I can say for certain about Louisiana swamps, is the same as I always say about Florida. You don't call an Alligator ugly, until you're across the river and well on your way.

One morning found me headed from San Antonio to Fredericksburg. There was a gunsmith and knifemaker there that I wanted to visit. After seeing him, I made my way north to see the *Enchanted Rock* mountain. An entire mountain of pink granite. An amazing sight that was worth the detour.

For a southern Florida tropic's native, this land was awe inspiring. It was becoming more and more unfamiliar to me.

I was, without doubt, officially out of the swamps and forests and coming into the desert land. Even the sky over the open ocean, don't seem as big as the sky in Texas.

I rode thru the day at a slower pace than usual, taking in the new scenery. The last light of the day was almost gone. The stars were beginning to shine their night-light upon the land.

Smoke had been rising in the waning twilight just ahead of me. I could see the glow of fires as I got closer to the top of the last ridge. As I crossed over the top of the ridge and started down into the valley, it became all-too clear to me what was happening. It was a ranch that was burning. The sounds of gunfire made it known that bandits were the cause.

The light of the fires made the surrounding dark my camouflage. I could hear men laughing and dying. Women were screaming. Animals, of all sorts, waling in agony to escape the fires.

Just as I made it to the edge of the fire light, I heard a scream. Then came a volley of pistol shots. A moment of pause. Then, the blasts of both barrels of a double barrel shot gun, echoed out from its source.

Why I didn't even hesitate, to consider the danger, wouldn't become clear for some time.

I pulled out one of the three Henry repeater rifles, I'd just bought in Fredericksburg, from its case. Tucked my spare pistol in the back of my belt. Undid the tether on the holstered pistol at my side and strapped on the belt that held my knives....

* * * * *

Paris–My name was Paris. Just, Paris. I'm an orphan who somehow managed to survive the streets of Paris, France.

Until I was found by an American couple who took me in, and raised me, as their own, here in America. I remember the attack on the ranch. It's been so many years, yet it plays back in my head, from time to time, like a horror movie.

I was tending to the horses. Brushing 'em out and giving them their feed for the evening. Dozens of riders were approaching the main house. It wasn't long before we realized what they had come for... to rape...murder...and loot—in that order.

The first exchange of gunfire killed four of them and two of their horses. Five ranch hands lay dead or dying. Including

Charles, the eldest son of the owner of the ranch and my adoption father. I watched from the barn as some rode their horses into the main house; the others split- up and went in different directions—burning and killing, as they went.

When they had scattered and I thought it safe, I ran out from where I was hiding, to Charles's side. I rolled him onto his back and supported his head in my arms. He looked up at me...barely able to breathe. With a voice that was barely a whisper, he said to me,

"Paris, I failed you... They caught us off our guard. I will always be watching over you girls. Don't let them get to the boys or Trudy. Find Jenny. Sav, sav, save them..."

The air left from his body; he died in my arms. I couldn't stop the tears and pain in my heart. He was my father. The only one to want me and take me from the streets of Paris and give me a last name, love and a home. I was determined to make good on his final wishes... or die in the attempt....

I placed his head gently on the ground and kissed his cheek as a final farewell.

As I did, I was swept up with sadness and pain. I raised my head to the sky and screamed! As hard and as loud as I could...! Looking down at him again, through my tears, I told him... "I love you, father.... I will probably be joining you directly, not before I get some payback though, and fulfill your dying wishes—"

With no time to mourn, I grabbed his pistol and big hunting knife he always kept on his side and forced myself up and away from him. Just leaving him there like that was the hardest and most painful thing I had ever had to do up to that point in my life.

*****

Narration—She stopped her story just then. Wiping tears from her eyes, she hid her face in her hands and began to cry the hardest cry Ariel and Tristan could remember ever seeing from her.

Thomas's eyes even watered at the sight of her in so much pain. He wondered if this was the first time, she had allowed these, obviously suppressed, memories of her father to the surface.

Trudy went to her side and lifted her face out of her hands. As their eyes met, Trudy felt the pain and sadness pouring from

Paris's heart. She knew Paris had never let it out before, and neither had she. Paris said to her,

"Oh Trudy… it hurts… it hurts so much." Trudy lost her control and began balling her eyes out, right along with Paris. They just held each other and cried, so awfully hard.

Tristan, wiping tears from his eyes, at the sight of his two lovers in such pain, said to Thomas,

"You see…? Your arrival here is already proving itself a great thing. The healing process begun here tonight has been over a hundred and fifty years in its coming. Finally, they remember they still have human in them after all…."

Ariel and Tristan both wanted her to stop for a little while, but she refused. Telling them that this was something she needed to do. After a good cry, she continued with her story.

* * * * *

Paris–As I looked around, wondering how and what to do, I realized the only things not burning was the house and hay barn. There was screaming and crying, gunshots and laughter—coming from everywhere and nowhere.

I ran to the side of the house that was easiest to climb up to a second-floor window. Before climbing up, I peaked in through the kitchen window on the bottom floor. Three of them had the missus of the house on the table. Two were holding her down. The third, a large bearded faced man, drove his fist in her face, her eyes rolled up in her head, as blood splattered about. He ripped her clothes up as he dropped his own trousers. It was horrible to watch them laughing as he took advantage of her helplessness.

Two more entered the kitchen with Jenny, who was Charles's wife, and my adoption mother. She was already naked and bleeding. They threw her to the floor onto her stomach and pulled her up onto her hands and knees. One worked his way violently inside her from behind and began brutalizing her… while the other forced himself in her mouth—holding a knife to her throat. I knew I couldn't save them… and that I had to get the children out.

I climbed up the lattice work and pulled myself through the window at the boys' room. My heart sank. Both had their throats cut. Cut so violently…it was little more than skin that kept their heads attached to their bodies.

Trudy...! I had to find her.... I didn't even try to mask my steps. I ran straight to her room. Tears were running down my face again. The boys' nanny was lying on the floor with her head bashed in and cut from her privates to her breasts.

Trudy was gone... I heard her scream. Then, Jenny screamed out, long and loud, "*No!*"

Rage took me! I no longer cared about living or saving anyone. I wanted blood! That was my only thought. I ran down the stairs, jumping from the last five or six steps to the floor. As I entered the kitchen door, the scene playing-out was one of madness.

The lady of the house was senseless as she was being raped. Blood and semen ran down her face and legs. The two with Jenny, were a half step in front of me on the floor, still ramming her from both ends. One of the two that was holding the missus down let her go, to have his way with Trudy. While the one who brought her in, held her down. The man about to rape her, said,

"You just thought you were gonna sneak away, didn't ya? Let's see how much you like having a master little lady. Nothing like a little anal when you miss your mom."

She screamed again as he drove himself inside her. The one holding her mother by her ear and ramming himself down her throat, looked up and saw me just as I reacted.

I stepped forward and drove my blade in the back of the head of the one, on his knees, with his back to me. At the same instant, I shot the one in the back that was raping Trudy.

My second shot...hit between the eyes of the one that was holding her down across the table. He dropped instantly.

As for the one that was raping her, the wound to his back didn't kill him, but it stopped him long enough, for Trudy to get away and run out the door.

The two men at the big table, looked up from the missus and over at me. The one raping her, stopped and turned toward me. I aimed and fired...blowing off part of his manhood onto the floor.

The one facing me, on his knees, had pulled his gun and aimed for a kill shot. Just as I was gritting my teeth to take a bullet, he cried out in agony. Jenny had bit him. She had bit his cock completely off and spit it on the floor. As he screamed, he fired his pistol. What would have hit me square in the chest, grazed the inside edge of my breast, went in under my collar bone and out the back of my shoulder. Lodging itself in the top of the door jam, behind me.

The pain was unbelievably extreme. I fired my pistol as I was hit, but it went wide, missing any possible targets. The one on the floor, shot Jenny in the back of the head; Jenny and the one with my blade in his skull, fell over together onto the floor, ripping the knife from my hand.

The pain in my shoulder was not allowing me any kind of grip on it. I dropped my pistol and grabbed the pistol of the man with my knife in his head.

Bullets flew now, all about me. I emptied my gun, hitting nothing. The gunshot I took, blinded me with pain to the point where I couldn't think. I somehow turned…and ran back the way I came. None of them, were hurt bad enough to die, and two were coming across the room, as I burst out the front door.

As I ran out the door, I saw Trudy. Caught by another one of the bandits. He had one fist wrapped in her hair and the other around a double barrel shotgun. My burst through the door startled him. As he turned to look at me, her response was instant.

She pulled his knife from his side and drove it, straight up under his chin, into the roof of his mouth. As he dropped, she grabbed the shotgun. She aimed straight at me and yelled, "Get down!"

As I dropped to the ground, she fired both barrels. The whistle of buckshot over my head was an unnerving sound.

As was the splatter and shatter of meat and bone as two loads of buckshot hit their mark.

The blast of both barrels knocked her backward off her feet and flat on her ass. The men chasing me out of the house had become jammed up at the door, trying to hurry out all at once. Their faces and throats were rearranged by buckshot.

As they were falling to the ground, I was on my feet. My head was spinning from the pain in my shoulder. While the intensity of the chaos all around me was taking its measure upon my sanity.

Trudy was already on her feet. Blood was running down her legs. "Are you ok?" I asked her.

With tears in her eyes and crying, she exclaimed, "No! But I'm alive and we need to move!"

We made our way towards the only building not burning, the hay barn.

"Where are the rest of the men that came with those bastards?" she asked me.

I told her "I don't know. Just keep moving. I am out of bullets and you emptied both barrels."

Trudy said, "Father and grandfather keep a couple of saddle bags full of supplies in the barn behind the hay bales."

We made our way into the barn. Ducking behind the hay as we grabbed the saddle bags. One was filled with bandages and medicines. The other had ammo: an extra loaded revolver with holster, bullets, shotgun shells and two hunting knives, attached to belts. I started reloading the shot gun as Trudy hurriedly strapped one of the knife belts around her naked body and the other one to mine. As I handed her back the shotgun, she asked me,

"Is mother dead"?

Not looking up at her I said, "yes."

"And father…our brothers?"

I looked up at her and could not bring myself to say yes again. I looked away in tears. She knew the answer without me saying it.

As I forced myself to look up at her again, I expected to see fear and sorrow in her eyes, but it wasn't there. Rage was all I saw…. Raw, malicious rage.

I made her turn around so I could see where she was bleeding from. Her ass was swollen and bleeding, but she would be alright. The right side of her face was bruised heavily around her eye. Trudy grabbed the saddle bag with the medical supplies and tended my shoulder.

There was a gun fight taking place from, what seemed to be, the helps quarters. The sound of men dying was demoralizing. We could not tell where anyone else was, or who may still be alive. Most of the buildings on the ranch yard were on fire. The bandits had set fire to just about everything. The smoke was so thick, coupled with the dark, we couldn't tell what was going on around us.

"Your shaking like a leaf on a tree," I said to Trudy. She looked into my eyes, and said,

"Yes…. And – my nipples are hard – and my pussy is wet… and I am going to—kill every—last one—of those slimy fucks – for what they've done to us!"

I Started to ask her something, but forgot what it was, realizing I was dripping wet too.

At that moment, we heard more shots. They were awfully close. A man dived into the barn onto his belly. A gun in both hands. He rolled over onto his back and aimed his guns at the entrance. Before we could react, two of the bandits rounded the corner and he fired at them. Two shots rang out. One hitting a man in the throat while the other man got it in the knee. As he dropped down onto his other knee from the pain, a third shot rang out. With the bullet passing right through his teeth and out the back of his skull.

The man lying on the ground turned and looked at us and yelled, "I'm not with them, obviously… I won't hurt you ".

POW!! POW!! The first bullet dusted his face with dirt from where it hit the ground in front of him. The other went through his forearm. Forcing him to drop one of his guns.

As he raised his other arm to defend himself, pow pow pow! Three bullets sank into him, one in the hip, one in his thigh, and one under the collar bone of his right shoulder. We ducked behind the hay bales as the shooter entered.

It was the one that had been holding the missus of the house for the others. He told the stranger,

"You son of a bitch! I don't know how you managed to kill my friends. You and those damn women. But I get the last laugh. I'm gonna let you die slow so you're still alive long enough to know I fucked them both to death as you died."

He started laughing, and we both heard his gun hammer cock back. We looked at each other square in the eyes, and knew we were thinking the same. We both stood an aimed our guns. He looked at us startled. The man on the ground rolled to one side just as we fired. I got two rounds off. Both hitting their marks. Trudy fired both barrels, hitting him square in the chest. The blasts put her on her ass again.

At the same instant he was shot, the bandits gun went off from shock-reflex. Grazing the stranger across his back as he rolled to one side. Then two more shotgun blasts rang out. As the bandit practically split in half at the waist, the missus of the house came into view. She had already pulled a revolver from its holster at her side and aimed at the stranger's head. I screamed, "No! He's not with them!"

She drew the gun back as she looked at us. Tears rolled down her face as she spoke, her voice crackled, full of emotion. "I prayed they hadn't gotten you two in their clutches"

We went out from back of the hay bales and Trudy ran straight to her grandmother and clasped her arms around her tight. I stooped over the stranger to see if he was still alive. Our eyes met for an instant. For an instant, that felt like eternity. My mind raced with images of familiarity in those eyes. ***Recognition of past lives with this soul,*** who looked through the eyes of this face, I had only now seen for the first time. Everything started spinning and all went black as I fell over on top of him.

*****

Tristan–I left my horse where she was on the slope. I was making my way hurriedly down towards the chaos when I saw the first of the bandits. He had shot a dog, only wounding it. He was taking a better aim to fire again from atop his horse when the dog leapt at him, grabbing him by his leg, just above his ankle.

The dog was either, not hurt that bad, or to enraged to feel it or care. The suddenness of the dog's attack not only spooked the horse, but also startled the man. He screamed out in pain as his bones were—most likely crushed—from the force of the bite. He tried frantically to take aim to shoot the dog again but was too late.

I dropped to the ground, aimed my rifle and fired. The bullet hit him at an upward angle, under his right eye. His hat was blown from his head. Followed by a spray of blood and brains as the back of his head blew apart.

As his horse reared, it threw him to the ground. The dog let go of his hold, ran under the rearing horse and leaped on the man. Ripping his throat out with the first snap of his jaws.

Not realizing he was already dead or just a vengeful act, I couldn't say. I remember thinking... *that was the meanest dog I'd ever seen in my life.*

Another man with a torch in his hand rounded the corner of a building. As he did, he saw the dog mauling his companion. He drew his pistol and aimed it at the dog. He fired a shot and missed, hitting the ground under the dog's belly.

I jumped up and started running toward him. Because of the fires blazing so fiercely, I was still invisible. The dog had seen him and was moving toward him. Teeth bared to a savage snarling froth.

He aimed and pulled the trigger again, only to realize he was empty. He dropped the torch and tried to reload his gun. The dog was too close to allow that, and he quickly gave up trying. He dropped the gun, pulled out his knife and grabbed the torch back up... bracing his legs for the dog's attack.

By the time all that took place, I was close enough to throw one of my knives. Not knowing how many more there were or where they might be, I chose stealth over gunfire. At the same time the knife sank deep in his throat, the dog leapt on him. It was a grisly scene watching that dog tear his face apart. I remember saying a little prayer for the dog—that he didn't cut his tongue on my knife. One thing I knew, right then, was I liked that dog. He was committed, and had no hesitation following thru to his convictions. A born killer, through-and-through.

Not wanting to get in a tangle with him myself, I ran around the building I was closest to. As I got around...back of the building, I heard the dog start barking and growling again. Staying as close as possible to the building, feeling the intense heat coming off the wall from the fire that was burning inside, I made my way across to the next building that was; somehow, free of fire. I made my way to the front corner until I could see what was going on.

At first, I couldn't see what the dog was on about. I surveyed all I could from where I was. There were shots still ringing out, but not close enough to concern me. As I made my way to a better vantage point and line of sight, the dog suddenly changed his attitude and ran towards someone.

After a moment, I could see that it was a woman. A woman dressed for bear: a revolver on her hip, a machete tucked in behind her gun belt and a shotgun in her hands.

A belt of shotgun shells lay across her shoulders and the look on her face was one of murderous intent. It was easy to see; she was just defending her home.

Not wanting to cross her path, 'til I figured out how to let her know I was here to help; I ducked back around the building and made my way around the back of it again. As I rounded the corner, I could see a man, well hidden from anyone who might be in front of him. He raised his rifle and aimed to fire. I knew it was the woman that he had in his sights. I drew my big bowie knife and with a throw that took all my strength, buried it to the hilt into his back—tip sticking out of his chest.

He fell to his knees, looking down at the tip protruding from his body. A look of astonishment was still on his face as his eyes rolled up in his head. He fell over, face down in the dirt. Dying without ever knowing where it came from. As morbid as it may sound, I'm still proud of that throw.

Another shot rang out, then another. Both splintered the wood of the building beside me, just missing my head. Out of the corner of my eye, I could see two men coming towards me. I ran out and around to the front of the building and turned to fire but instead of firing, I acted as though I was out of rounds.

Bullets whizzed past my head again. I turned and ran to the entrance of the building, dived into the entrance to the ground and pulled my spare pistol. Which gave me a gun in each hand. I knew they thought I was out of bullets and trying to reload. They would be expecting an easy kill. A deadly mistake.

As they came into sight, I fired both guns…killing one, wounding the other. As he fell to one knee, I fired again, hitting him in his mouth, killing him instantly. I thought I was hearing echoes of my own shots, until I felt the hits in my body. At the time, I didn't know exactly how many hit me. Try as I might, I still can't remember anything after that. Only what I was told.

Except, seeing the most beautiful creature. Bent over me and staring. How beautiful she was. She laid her head on my chest as everything went black. I was thinking, if I am dying, it can't be so bad. My guardian angel was already with me.

* * * * *

Ariel/Trudy–My name is – Ariel Gertrude Ross. Trudy is my nickname – short for Gertrude.

Tristan calls me Ariel—mostly – and Trudy—only when he's on about some-shit – be-it good-or bad.

While Paris—calls me Ariel –only when she's mad at me, or freaking-out—in general….

Tristan calls Paris – **Sexy-Voodoo,** and me – **Babysugar**. His premise being: the only thing sweeter than sugar – is **baby-sugar**, though he says both sparingly—these-days. Tristan has always been—and he—forever-will-be – our one and only ***Champion of Champions – Bar-none!***

The three of us—are closer and more entwined—than anyone—could-ever—even possibly—imagine.

More than friends – More than family….

Even though they—both—still call me—child – the little buggers—

Which-is—bullshit—because – Tristan-is-only—half a dozen years older than me – and Paris is even less—

I was twenty-four – when Tristan came into our lives….

I was born – one hundred and seventy-nine years ago – as of this year – 2019….

And I haven't aged a day – since my early thirty's – none of us have—

Of all those days – if any one of them was fated – it was the day—Tristan showed-up….

I lost my parents—that day – and both—my baby brothers….

At the time – I didn't have any idea of—what I would—later—uncover about my parents.

All I was left with—for a long time… was questions.

There is so much—I wish they would've told me – so I didn't have to find out the way I did….

My God! Sometimes—I wonder how I make sense—and peace—with this dark and costly gift—

But I regress… Oh, the day my grandparents' ranch was attacked….

Rape and murder are—so fucking—brutal.

Had those pricks had their way about things—that day – Paris and I would—both—be dead.

That was the first time in my life – I experienced true fear—and absolute rage—to such a degree.

It's hard to recall, how much time passed… while Tristan and Paris recovered from their wounds: days turned into weeks – weeks into months – and more months….

Even Jojo had recovered back to full strength….

Jojo is short for—dog – though I sound out the letters and say it fast – D-o-g….

And I spell it D'o-ji –instead of plain jane dumb old, dog.

My grandpa named him dog—and pissed me—off, so I re-spelled it to give it more style. Eventually, calling him Jojo – or Jo.

Jojo, is a huge black dog: who showed-up on the ranch—a year-or-so before Tristan, and the attack. Though we didn't know it then, we found out later he was a Tosa Inu.

Also known as a Japanese Black Mastiff. Two hundred pounds of fighting machine.

He was sketchy – you couldn't baby talk him – and if you did, he would—light your ass up….

Someone must have treated him—really—bad. He loved all of us though…for whatever his reasons.

If anyone got mouthy… or loud—with any of us—when he was around – we were hard-put to pull him from them.

He was shockingly violent – once he was on about something.

Jojo—is truly one of a kind: coyotes or any other dogs didn't stand a chance when he bared teeth – nothing has ever stood toe to toe with him – he even whipped a mountain lion once that almost ambushed my grandpa….

Jo proved that day—not only was he a badass – he could take a hell of a beating—and just—keep-on—going.

JoJo acted towards Tristan—the first time he saw him – as if he were his long—lost master—

Tristan loved him just the same—right—back—

Everyone knew not to get between them—

Or it was a bad day – all bets were off.

Tristan and Paris—were meant—for each other.

And they – were meant for me. It was love at first sight for them both – I *came* – a little later….

They are soulmates…. And I don't think—this was the first life they've spent together – that we've… —spent together – to be politically correct….

Paris and I had always been play-time lovers. Lovers to the point of being in love with each other—as we grew older.

None of us – knew just how entwined our lives would become.

Nor that they were stuck with me – and I with them.

Today—the three of us are still in-love – and wouldn't have it any other way….

Like it or not – the three of us are soulmates – just didn't know it then.

They were not aware of me—the first time I caught them—making love in the hay barn.

I watched them the first time – just—honey-dripping—with desire—

They are both—so beautiful....

Seeing them together—was so erotic and arousing – I barely touched myself—and had an orgasm, so amazing—I almost yelled out.

The second time – I took off my clothes – and I walked up to them

Tristan was wide eyed—not sure what to say—or do.

Paris—pulled me down onto the blanket with them—and stuck her tongue in my mouth – and her hands elsewhere.

Tristan stared for a second—or so – and then his lips was on my skin....

My hand—shot straight to his manhood – *Oh my goodness!* I thought....

We kissed: nibbled – sucked – and licked—each other from head to toe.

He gave us both orgasm after orgasm with his tongue—

We all laughed—when he jizzed on himself—watching Paris and I together....

But he was up again in no time – and when I pushed him down on his back and straddled him—he wasted no time.

He pressed himself up against me, slid up to my top button. Then slid back and—

I gave out a long moan – it was like we had done this before.

We instantly moved in perfect unison: his hands on my hips—as he slid back and forth – as we—moved up—down – and back.

Paris whispered to us, "Oh my God – just watching—the two of you – I'm about to cum—"

She moved over toward us – we both fondled each other as we tongue kissed.

She straddled Tristan's face—

A moment later—I yelled out – and that was the catalyst.... They both—sounded off too—

All three of us were cumming—at the same time....

We had *merged our rhythms*.

I remember thinking—how I couldn't wait—for him to do it—again....

The three of us made love to each other all night. Grandpa almost caught us the next morning – butt naked—

Sleeping all cuddled up together on top of the hay bales....

The three of us have been in love with each other ever since – Madly in love – Fierce love – Forever love....

Any one of us—would kill and die—for the other two without hesitation.

Killing for someone you love is easy—

But dying?

Well now—that – is just—something else—altogether – That's true love....

Take-it-or-leave-it. – that's what it is – and what it's—all about....

Cum—blister—or bleed – that's how that shit works—

And I wouldn't test us – If I—were you....

Many have – and they all came to the—very same—conclusion.... Don't Fuck with Us!

If my grandparents knew we were all fucking... they never let on about it....

They knew—Paris and I were inseparable – and that her and Tristan were head over heels in love.... Gave no signs—to anything else....

It seemed no surprise to them—when the day came that Tristan said... he was ready to continue his journey west—and asked if he could take Paris and me with him—

Chapter three

The Talk

Tristan–She is so full of shit! Her grandparents said, *No-way is she going to California with you.* They freaked that I had the audacity to even ask. She pitched such a fit, they almost begged me to take her along. Ariel-Trudy: has always been spoiled, always got her way… and if I have my way about it, she always will. Her and Paris both….

After my wounds healed, I stayed on to help protect the Ross's interests. It was a year or so, give or take, that I had been on the Double R (RR) Ranch, when we got the word, *THE WAR WAS OVER!!*

The RR ranch was so named after the old man, Richard Ross. Richard and Julia Ross became my second mom and dad. Yet even after I showed him: that I wasn't lazy or broke, that I had a nice cache that would fund our touring indefinitely, should we choose to see the world and live on room service till we die, he still had concerns.

"I don't know—Tristan. The war is over, but this country will be a dangerous place for some time before it calms itself of all that has happened. Just between us, my granddaughters are a handful. Those two Phillies are spoiled rotten, headstrong and mean as hell. I've caught those two little coochie-bumpers more than once—with their tongue in each other's—ass…. I gave up trying to stop them. They are and always will be, inseparable.

"And don't go to bed tonight thinking that I'm not akin to all three of you sneaking around here, having sex on every square inch of the property!

"Which tells me, they've got you wrapped around all 10 fingers and toes. Don't you go and tell them that I know about it or said any of this either. I don't want them acting funny around me or the missus. Understand?

I said, "My lips are sealed. As far as the girls are concerned, my life is the highest price I can pay for their protection, and I will pay it proudly and happily to see them safe. I already bear scars for them...."

The ole man looked at me with a sense of pride he didn't try to hide. "Tristan, since you've been here, you have proven yourself to me more than once. There is no one living that I trust more than you. But I've never heard of a man successfully keeping two wives happy that are as free spirited as those two are."

I looked at him bewildered, "two?"

He told me, "To love either one of them... is to take on both.

"You had better square with that here and now.

"Those two are wrapped up in each other. Like corn in shuck. With no more to really be said about it.

"A sentence will start in Paris's mouth and end in Ariel's. You are by no means a stupid man. I know you've noticed this. Given all the time you spend with them.

"It's as if there's one soul, in two different bodies. Don't ever make the mistake of saying this out loud around them, but as you well know, they're not blood sisters.

"But after watching them all these years...it doesn't take a wizard to realize their destinies are intertwined and have been—since the day they were born.

"They surprised me the day the ranch was attacked. I never would have guessed, they were capable of the retaliation, that they inflicted on those men.

"Under such extreme conditions of rape and murder... happening before their eyes...to people they love...to themselves.

"Ariel raped.... Paris shot...both seeing their mother and grandmother being raped, their mother and father murdered. People they knew, respected and loved being killed all around them.

"Yet, they managed to escape their attackers and kill six or seven of them... Quite spectacularly I might add. Then, instead of running and hiding, they made their way to my stash of weapons in the barn—and armed themselves to the teeth. Ready to get back—at it—as if it were all just another day on the farm.

"All that from two young girls, barely women, that before that day, had never killed anything in their lives."

"I've seen trained men buckle under lesser extremes."

"You don't need to be a seer, to know the sadness in their hearts at the loss of Charles and Jenny.

"But I've never seen a tear, from either of them. And everything else that happened that day…it's as if it didn't happen. I know of people who have lost their minds after being subjected to such brutality.

"And… There is something else I've noticed that's peculiar.

"They are both, dreamy eyed in love with you.

"Not just some school-girl infatuation, either.

"They are ape shit crazy about you, and yet, there isn't an ounce of jealousy between them, that I can fathom. Not to mention that on top of all that….

his words trailed off.

He looked me in the eyes with a dread look. I could feel that he was about to tell me something very deep…maybe, even secret. He had a dead serious look on his face that I hadn't seen from him before. A look of dread and fear, which I pretty much knew, didn't exist in the man.

Just as quick as that look came…it went. We sat in silence for some time before he spoke again. "I give up trying to make sense of it. Let's just leave it at, they are both connected in a way I have never been able to fully reckon…"

I said, "Hold on a minute. In the year or so I've been here, I've come to know you well. You were about to divulge something to me. Something that scares—the hell out—of you. And I didn't think that was even possible."

The look returned to his face. He looked me in the eye again, wanting to say it. Still, something stopped his words.

Then he continued as though I hadn't asked the question at all, saying,

"Trudy has a wild spark in her. She's like a young and free Mustang pony. She could burn the world down today, without ever giving a slightest thought—to what she's gonna do tomorrow. She is very smart and extremely clever. With a sarcastic and provocative wit about her—most men can't handle.

"Paris has got more intelligence, in her little finger, than any other human being I know. A truly keen mind. She hides it superbly from the world. If she had been born a man, she could have run for president and took it by a landslide. She could run a small country as their queen. Tell that girl what you need to have happen and she'll figure out how to do it. And both of 'em can shoot—like no tomorrow...."

He looked over at me with a shit eating grin. Then he laughed out loud and said, "I sure hope I'm around to hear the tale that's about to unfold on your little *Menage a Tois.*

"If there's a man alive with the belly to go up against those kinds of odds and come out on top, my money is on you—Tristan Jonas—"

He laughed, loud and jolly.

I tried to hold it in but couldn't. I broke out in a full belly laugh, right along with him. The conversation drifted off from there. We spoke of everything and nothing for the ride back to the ranch. As we reined in the horses in front of the barn, the old man said to me,

"Tristan, before we go wash up for supper, I want to show you something. Also, I wanna give you something."

I followed him into the barn. Passing through and out the back, we made our way to a small circle of brush-patch. He pushed his way into the middle of the patch. Moving aside a bit of brush, he exposed a hole in the ground that I mistook for a gopher hole. He reached in and pulled up hard on some sort of lever. Turning it a quarter turn this way and that, as if it were some sort of sequence he was performing.

The ground in front of us moved down a foot or so, and began to slide back, exposing stairs cut into the solid rock.

"Holy-shit! I blurted-out. "From what sorcery was this conjured up?"

He smiled and said, "Don't ask me, this is Charles's contraption, or was, anyway."

There was no musty smell. No cobwebs or dust on the walls that lined the stairwell. The air escaping the entrance from below was clean. Which meant that whatever this was, it was well used and—most likely had—air shafts cut into it. Venting fresh air from the outside.

At the top of the stairs was a polished metal disc that was attached to some type of multi-hinged mechanical arm. Making it adjustable in all directions. The old man pulled it up out of the entrance and positioned it so, that as the sunlight hit it, its beam of light shot down the stairwell, reflecting light onto another identical disc, at the bottom of the stairs.

"Come on," he said, "we don't have long before we lose the sunlight."

We traversed the stairs down for some distance. I could see that it was dimly lit in the room that we were about to enter. At the bottom of the stairs, on the wall, hung lanterns. He lit up two and handed me one.

"Where does this bit of genius with the sunlight come from?" I asked him.

"A neat little trick my son Charles brought back from his travels to Egypt." He replied. "This cellar was his personal study. You're the first person to set foot in here besides Charles and myself. But then—of course—only a fool would let himself believe those little snoops I call granddaughter have never been in here."

The room was carved clean out of the granite bedrock. The walls and roof were pink with red streaks running through it. It looked smooth and sparkled like diamonds from all the quartz imbedded in it. There were shelves with books and scrolls that looked ancient. All sorts of artifacts, statues and things scattered about, that I had no clue, as to what they were.

A large table with chemistry equipment was set against a back corner. In the opposite corner was a large steel cage. I didn't even try to guess its purpose. I was like a child, realizing for the first time that the world was a much bigger and grander place than my playroom and crib.

In the center of the room was a worktable with leather bound books stacked upon it. They looked fresh and new, as though they were recently written and freshly bound. On the back wall, centered so that it was in front of the center table, hung a magnificent tapestry. With a map of the world woven into it. A map of the world far more detailed than any map I had ever studied. It was exceedingly old, yet it showed Antarctica clear as day. A continent only recently discovered by the modern world.

"What is this place... and what are all these things?" I finally asked him.

"Charles collected all these things from his travels all over the world. He loved the ancient world and going to all these different places to study and learn about them. It was one of his true passions.

"Charles told me that in these books was knowledge that the ancient civilizations knew about and has been lost to time and forgotten. Knowledge that the modern world is only now starting to rediscover. Knowledge that will change the world to an unrecognizable place from what it is today once it is fully realized. With some of it best kept secret for now. That mankind was better off without its rediscovery for at least a couple of more centuries.

"Only then, if the world is able to overcome war and hate for one another and adopt a more peaceful existence than we are capable of today. He said that the power of such knowledge unleashed upon the world before these changes can take place, would destroy us all and most of the world with it.

"To tell you all this is not why I brought you down here. And I have a lot to tell you, so pay attention and try to keep up."

He smiled and gave me a slap on my back as he gestured me to follow him. He led me over to the tapestry. Moving it aside, he exposed a passage. It led down at a gradual slant for some distance and opened into another chamber. This room was smaller than the first

The sparkle of the rock face was far more intense in this lower chamber than in the upper level.

In the center of this chamber was an object that looked to be made of solid steel. It was in the shape of a pyramid. It was dark and smooth with a dull green glow that seemed to emanate from its core.

Richard said, "A perfect four- sided pyramid."

I rebutted, "No, it has eight sides. See the slight inward slant to the middle of each side?"

Richard squinted his eyes as he raised his lantern, then exclaimed,

"Well I'll be! Your right! Charles never pointed that out and I never noticed. It's so slight it's almost imperceptible.

"Well, anyway… it measures out to forty-eight point one inches tall, and seventy-five point six inches wide at its base, on each of its sides. I forget the rest of its measurements.

"Charles said it was a perfect scale to the great pyramid in Egypt.

"He also said, that this one, is older than the big one. That the big one, was a replica, scaled up.... It once housed this thing—and another one, just like it—once upon a time.... They were called the ***Twins of the Nine***....

"I've never heard of the big ones having eight sides. A curious thing that makes one wonder. According to Charles, the pyramids themselves are much older than Egypt."

A low, deep hum was coming from it, rebounding off the walls. Causing a vibration, I could feel in my bones. At each of its four corners, was a large, tall, slender clay pot. With what looked to be copper tubes coming out of them. Each tube ran underneath the pyramid and appeared to be attached to it from there.

The feeling coursing thru my body was exhilarating. I was at once addicted to its vibration. I took a step towards it for a closer look.

He tapped me on the shoulder and cautioned me against it with a shake of his head, and said, "Another time, lets head back up."

As we made our way back to the upper chamber, I asked him, "What in the hell is that thing? And what are those pots connected to it?" He didn't say anything until we were back in the first room and had sat down in one of the chairs at the table. Gesturing me to do the same as he slid out the other chair for me. As I sat down, he began.

"I don't pretend to understand all of this. Consider it fortunate that I'm able to explain any of it.

"Charles was always fascinated with ancient times and things from the forgotten past—as he called it.

"He and Jenny had been gone for some years, traveling in the old countries. Collecting these things, you see here. These books you see here on the table are the translated texts of all those books and scrolls on that shelf. Most of them anyway.

"One day, we got a letter from them. Saying, they were returning home and that we were grandparents now. That Jenny had given birth to a little girl, and they had adopted a little girl, orphaned on the streets of Paris.

"When they finally returned home, Charles spent months pouring through these old writings. Though he never said so at first, I knew he was searching for something...almost in a panic at times, spending days and nights trying to figure out some ancient code.

"When I was finally able to get him to tell me what he was looking for, I understood his apprehension. He told me, that in their travels, Jenny had contracted a rare blood disease that no modern doctors could cure her of. And that Ariel was born with it as a result. He had learned from an old shaman that the ancients knew of this sickness and that there was no cure, but in these scrolls, manuscripts and tablets was a way to suppress it—so that it would not take their lives. If he could find it, they would live out their lives, free of its suffering and die old and gray one day. As god had intended.

"Then, out of the blue one day, he said there was something he must do, and they left. Two years later he returned and told me, he had bought a ranch in Texas where all of us could live out our days. He handed me a deed that was in my name. He begged me to come with him here.

"Said that it was the only way to save his family. He also said we didn't have to worry about money ever again...for generations to come.

"After we arrived here and had settled in, he showed me this place. How it was constructed, I know not. Only that there was something about the magnetic properties of this rock that made them special. Also, that—that contraption down there created an electromagnetic sphere around this place for tens of miles in every direction. It even draws energy from the *Enchanted Rock* mountain that's only about seven miles away from here.

"The red streaks you see running through all this pink granite is from deposits of iron oxide in it. It's the perfect proportion of iron to granite that is one of the key factors in all this generating the extreme power it does.

"The field generated by that thing, in conjunction with all the surrounding pink granite, would keep whatever it was in Jenny, the boys' and Ariel's blood dormant forever. If they stayed within the confines of the sphere or weren't outside of it for too long.

"He had also learned on his latest journey, that there is a cure. The problem is it's in a book, that he procured, that is written in a forgotten language that will have to be deciphered, before its mysteries can be unlocked, and its knowledge fully explored and understood. The discovery of where the cure even is within the text, will be a revelation in and of itself alone.

"According to him, this book is tens of thousands of years old. It sets on that shelf over there."

He walked over and grabbed it off the shelf. Then brought it over to the table. "Even Charles never figured out how they had books ten thousand years ago, when the most ancient civilizations, documented to five thousand years ago, wrote on stone and papyrus. Let alone how they made it possible to exist for eons, perfectly preserved, usable and readable.

"It's written in the language of a race of men that once ruled the earth. He called them the Atlanteans. That glowing hunk of metal down there, also comes from there civilization.

"The clay pots surrounding it, are copies of some sort of ancient technology. He brought them back from Arabia, or his travels to the black sea... I can't recall which exactly.

"There is a much smaller version of them around here somewhere. They give off an electrical charge and somehow, when combined with that block of metal, the field of vibration you felt, along with the powerful magnetic field, is created. The field encompasses this place for many, many miles in all directions as I have already said. Coupled with the properties of the surrounding granite, magic happens.

"All I have to do for its care, is make sure those clay pots are topped off with a concoction Charles taught me how to make. It is a substitute for the properties of very acidic juices, such as lemon and grapefruit. Keeping the liquid mixture changed every so often is the only chore of its upkeep.

"I know how crazy this all must sound. I've often questioned Charles's sanity in all of this. Nothing has ever happened, that led me to believe, his wife and children ever were sick at all. Even so, I was sworn by my oath to him to never speak of it to anyone, especially Ariel and the boy's. God rest their souls.

"That thing down there, keeps all of us as healthy as the best hogs. Charged with energy enough for one to do the work of three. I'm sure you noticed a little pep in your step of late. Though you probably thought it was from—fucking—my granddaughters.

"Ariel has no clue of any blood disorder. That's the way Charles wanted it and that's the way it's been. Now that she has decided to leave with you and Paris, I think it's now necessary for her to know. She can decide for herself if she wants to take the risk or not. If she decides to go, at the first sign of trouble with her illness, no matter where in the world you are, you bring her back here. I ask you now for your promise.

Richard made me swear this. I did as he asked. He continued,

"Even Charles knew he couldn't keep Ariel here her entire life. We both hoped he would find the answers he needed to cure her before that time ever came. Now that he's dead, I suppose it's a lost cause."

"Charles told me that the power contained within this place and these ancient writings was so dangerous, if it ever fell in the wrong hands, the evil it could conjure would be unstoppable. For this reason, he would trust no others with his discoveries.

"More so, because of what lies beneath that glowing hunk of metal down there. The secret ingredient that is essential for all of this to work properly.

"Few men exist that could make sense of all this stuff, but what is underneath that thing, all men crave, kill, and die for. Gold! It's the perfect conductor for amplifying the field to such a large proportion.

"Down there are three hundred bars of the purest gold anyone has ever laid eyes on. They weigh in at fifty pounds each. It only takes half that amount to make that glowing hunk of metal and those four clay pots work, or so I'm told.

"Charles' thinkin was, at the end of the day, he is just a man, and when he stumbled upon so much of it, just sitting there undisturbed for so many eons, his figuring was, finders' keepers.

"I think that's what those men you helped us defeat were after. They were trying to make it look like a simple raid to keep suspicions down.

"Charles thought he had been thorough in his secrecy of it. Now, I'm not so sure. That's why I keep three times the men it takes to run this ranch hired on since that day.

"The one thing that plagues me…if they were after any of this? Why did they kill Charles before finding it?

"A big risk to take that anyone but him knew about this place. Let alone where it's hidden. He must've given 'em no choice. We may never know the truth of it."

All that Richard had just told me was unbelievably overwhelming. My head was swimming, trying to make sense of it all, and put it into proper perspective. I took in a long drink of silence, as my thoughts fought desperately to organize themselves into a clear picture, of the revelations that I had just been subjected to. Finally, I found my voice again.

"If this is all—so, then there is no way Trudy can go with Paris and me."

"Oh No!! He quickly retorted, "there is no way to keep her here now. This was inevitable. I've always known this day would come, so did Charles. We hoped he would find the cure before it came but... all we can do is hope that fate is kind.

"The fact that it's you, she is going with, makes me feel much better than her going off alone or with some jerk off.

"I consider your part in all of this to be a thing of great fortune. I know you will protect Ariel and Paris with your life. I also know, that taking your life is not an easy thing to do."

I said, "With god as my witness—"

He cut me off, "God... —is your witness—and so am I.... May he have mercy on me—for what I do to you—if you fuck this up!"

I took in another drink of silence as his words sank in deep. He got up and walked over to the bookshelf. After replacing the ancient manuscript, with a little effort, he pulled on one side of the bookshelf and it opened like a door on hinges.

There was another hidden room behind it. He waved me over as he stepped inside it. As our lanterns lit the room, he said, "You say you have enough money to fund you indefinitely? Well, welcome to the Ross reserve bank."

I almost passed out. The room was filled with statues and objects, big and small, made of precious metals and stones. There was a lot of smooth green stone that had a glassy surface appearance. There were precious stones and exotic materials I'd never seen before. Gold and silver ingots were stacked against one wall, from corner to corner, almost to my height.

Stacked on shelves against the back wall was American paper cash and coin. Legal tender, enough for two lifetimes of spending, with blatant disregard. I was speechless as he spoke again,

"Everything contained within these rooms belong to those two girls. When Julia and I leave this world, everything we own is also willed to them now. If my intuition serves me well, you are now a permanent part of their future. So, this is all yours too, now."

He walked over to a small table in the room. On the table was two blades, sheathed in the most beautiful and intricate leather cases. Both were forged from one solid piece of metal, from tips to pommels. One was huge in size. The other was the size of a large hunting knife.

He pulled the hunting knife from its sheath and handed it to me. It was made of the same metal that was below. A little over a foot in length from end to end.

The blade was dark in color. Resembling a clip point with a slight upward curve that was integral to the length of the blade. With the same greenish dull glow emanating from it.

The handles that sandwiched the full tangs, was made of what looked to be ivory but wasn't. As I examined them closer as to what they were made of, Richard said, "The handle is made from pearl."

It fit my hand as if it were made for me. The cross guard and pommel were of the same metal as the blade. The match in their design was uncanny. The blade was sharp enough to shave with. A close shave at that. There were markings on the blade at the cross guard. But what was most notable was its incredible lightness and balance.

The other blade, sizable to a machete, was made of the same materials as the hunting knife. With a leaf shaped blade, close to two feet of blade length. Just short of three feet, in overall length, give or take. The pommel was of an octagonal shape and larger than one would expect. More like a counterweight than an ornament.

The handle was also Pearl. The lightness and balance of this humongous blade was even more extraordinary than that of the smaller knife.

Taking it from me, Richard swung it at the end of a chain dangling off the end of the table. Cleaving thru it as easily as if it were a thin rope. He raised the blade to show me that the edge had not the slightest bit of damage to it. Smiling from ear to ear as he shook his head in bewilderment, Richard said,

"Those Tulwars over there are made of watered steel. One of the strongest steels ever made by a man for at least the last thousand years. I'd bet my bottom dollar that this stuff would cut right thru it. Though I'm not willing to test it on such beautiful swords."

He put the blades back in their sheathes and handed them both to me.

"I want you to have these. Take them with you and take good care that you don't lose them. As you can see, they are made from the same metal as that thing down there. Maybe they will help with Ariel, should she have trouble after she leaves here.

"Before you go, we will find a couple of those smaller clay pots laying around here, that are smaller versions of those big ones down there, and teach you how to charge them and connect the blades to them.

"Charles said that if Jenny or Ariel, or even one of the boys' blood disorder became active, it would wipeout the countryside, before anyone knew what was happening."

He looked at his pocket watch and said,

"Come on, let's go get some supper, and I wanna show you the sequence of turns it takes to open the entrance to this place. If done wrong more than three times, it'll set off a trap that will incapacitate everyone standing around it and kill the one trying to open it. If it doesn't kill everybody.

"I've never seen it work but, Charles never jested of such things. If he said, that is what'll happen, you can bet your ass it will."

After showing me how to work the opening, we made our way towards the house for supper. As we got to the front of the house he said,

"Oh, and one more thing. I want you to take that damn dog with you. He has imprinted on you it seems, and he will die protecting those girls. No matter what comes calling. Just consider him your loyal and trusty back up."

I laughed and said, "That was already the plan. Didn't know I needed permission to take him along."

"Give me a break, will ya…" He replied, with a smile.

With another slap on my back, we went inside and got ready for supper. We spoke no more of what he had shown and told me. Except for telling Ariel about her illness. Which we did right after supper.

After a first shock reaction, she seemed calm for someone being given such news. Her deliberations on the matter were nonexistent.

Cum, blister or bleed, she was going with Paris and I…. Half believing it wasn't even true by the time we all went to bed.

Chapter four

On the Road

Tristan–It was a couple of weeks—before we were ready to head out for the west coast. With a covered buck-board wagon, stocked with provisions, and our riding horses trailing behind; we said our farewells. And our fateful adventure towards a destiny as-yet-unknown—began....

We decided to stick to my original plan. Head for San Diego, then up to San Francisco. From there, we would all decide where to go next.

We set out—on the lower immigrant trail—to El Paso. The Comanche left us—alone. The reason being—the girls knew and were friends with most of the local bands. A few choice words in the Comanche tongue—got us through elsewhere.

On-average, we made good time. As many as fifteen to, and upwards of—twenty-five miles a day. Although, as often as not, we barely made five miles, in a single day. We couldn't help taking in the scenery and beauty—all around us....

There were plenty places along the way, to camp or rest: old campsites, used repeatedly by travelers, forts, stage-line outposts—and even—private residences, were open to a weary traveler. For the girls and I, the one thing of common value to any of those places was: water, occasional shelter from elements, and a soft bed—now-and-then....

We spent a few days in El Paso; then a week in Las Cruces, in the New Mexico territory. What a fun week that was.... The road from Las Cruces to Tucson in the Arizona territory was slow and uneventful.

A surprising thing, given it was the heart of Apache lands. The Apache Nation had been at war with the states since 1863. When the U.S. Army captured and murdered Mangus Coloradas, as he's known by the English-speaking world.

Da soda-hay was his name in the language of the Apache people. He was a tribal chief of the Mimbreno and Warm Springs Apache. He was also the father-in-law of Cochise, a Chiricahua warrior and leader. Mangus was a great chief, tribal elder and warrior. And a good man.

The incredible beauty of the region had all three of us mesmerized. Myself most of all. I couldn't shake the constant feeling of familiarity with the land, as though I had been here before; it called out to me....

* * * * *

It was in Tucson, when our first bit of trouble found us, and we weren't going to *beat the devil around the stump* on this one either.

We were at the Palace saloon, on what was known as whisky row—back then. The girls and I were on the ass end of a two-day bender and we were beach nut drunk.

Trudy was being her normal flirtatious self. She had a group of cowboys enamored with her beauty. All was well, until one of them grabbed her by the arm as she went to leave the table, trying to pull her down onto his lap.

With no results from asking, to be let go, she said, "Fella—you've gone from thorn-in-my-side to pain-in-my-ass real—quick." He just stared. Then she said, "Let me put this another way," and she slapped him across the face. He still didn't let her go. Now, she was really fired-up....

Paris and I both, knew what she would do next, and it wouldn't be pretty. That's when I decided to put my two-cents-in.... Though, there were some, who wished I hadn't.

* * * * *

Narration–Tristan rose from his table and was on the man before anyone knew it. He warned the man to let her go—but was told, *to mind his own god-damned business*. Tristan grabbed the arm of the man holding Trudy in one hand.

With the other, he slammed the man's face into the table and brought it up again just-as-quick. Knocking the man unconscious with a bloodied and broken nose for all his troubles. The sudden speed and tremendous force were abrupt—in their effect of shocking the entire saloon to—silence.

The man sitting next to him was on his feet in an instant. With the force of a sledgehammer, Tristan's knuckles met cheek and bone just below the man's eye. Peeling the skin to expose red meat resembling a large strawberry on the man's face, spinning him around like a ballerina. The man was out cold and crashing to the floor in an instant.

No one else at the table moved a muscle. Tristan turned and led Trudy to the bar while examining her wrist.

Another man, at the corner of the bar, stepped to Tristan, calling him out in the most childish of ways, trying to goad him into a confrontation. Tristan was given, for an instant, to knocking him out cold—like his two friends. But-oh-no. *That'd be—just too-easy for this—jerk-off.*

Tristan turned to the girls and said, "Do-you-know—what a fire-eater—with a paper-asshole is?"

They shook their heads; he told them, "It's a dead-man."
Tristan turned to the stranger; his eyes showing thoughts of deadly intent. The stranger's eyes showed doubt, as he instantly blinked.

Tristan saw-it but didn't care. He used it to taunt—the man. Saying, "You've the look of a man who done wrote a check—his ass caint cash."

The man didn't understand the insult. Tristan smiled, and look to the man's glass on the bar. Then looked back with an even bigger smile and said, "You should put a thumb—in your mouth, go back to your seat and practice—counting—to ten."

The man glanced at his friends, then back at Tristan. Tristan was now, thoroughly annoyed. Saying, "Now you're just being rude…." No response. Tristan, now showing real irritation said, "Well—aren't you—just a—simple—fuck—"

The whole room choked; the man instantly went for the pistol at his side.

Tristan drew and fired his revolver faster than anyone could see. Raising it no higher than his hip; he'd fired off a round with an amazing display of timed-response and superb hand to eye. Putting a bullet so close to the side of the man's face, he felt the heat of the bullet on his ear lobe, just as-much-as he heard its wiz. Causing the man to flinch.

Leaving a hole in the brim of the man's hat that was still smoking from the heat. Tristan's gun was back in its holster before anyone in the room could blink, his arm resting on the pistol-butt. Still staring the man down, with a calmness unnatural for the high stakes game being—played-out.

All bearing of a man sure of himself was gone from the stranger. Replaced with a realization that he had made a deadly mistake, and was now at the mercy, of the man in front of him. A realization that most men only experience when they're breathing their last breath.

The entire room was dead silent; not a whisper, or even a sigh, could be heard. No one in that room, had ever saw that kind of speed on the draw. Half of them were out-right confused as to what'd just happened.

It was Tristan, who broke the silence, "So... you're not as fucking-stupid as you look. Now that you have my full attention though... maybe —you were right. Maybe, my lack of conviction to put that bullet between your eyes is a sign of weakness. Or maybe, I meant to blow your brains out and missed—at almost pointblank range. Care to step into the street and do it again? By the book...?"

The sheriff stepped thru the saloon doors just then and exclaimed, "From this point forward, anything done—by-the-book, will be done by me. Now both you—boys, follow me over to the jail and acknowledge the corn. And as for you two little spit-fire fillies, that means you too. And if nare a one of you, even thinks of pulling any bosh, your gonna find yourselves in a whole-heapa-trouble—and don't try to say you ain't been-warned!"

Once at the jail, the sheriff's impetuous nature began to show. Realizing it was just a squabble amongst drunken patrons, he dismissed the cowboy with a final warning to go sleep it off. Not so with Tristan and the girls, he bid them stay a bit longer.

"You folks had better take care and stay alert from here on out. The bunch you went up against are part of a larger crew... that's been causing a ruckus all over town since the day they got here. They won't take kindly to being made fools of by a young buck and a couple of females. You can bet your bottom dollar... once your far enough out of town... the entire bunch of twenty or so will be on you like stink-on-shit...."

"As sheriff, I'll do what I can, but I have an entire town to watch over. I'm not a babysitter to be pussy footing around with every drifter that strolls into town and gets themselves in a pickle. So… good fortune be with you folks—. Now… get the hell out of my sight, and best pray we don't cross paths again under similar circumstances. Next time—won't be so civil—if you catch my drift."

As the trio made their way back to their hotel room, some-what sobered from all the ruckus, Paris asked, "Any ideas on what to do if the sheriff is right?"

Ariel spoke up, kicking a rock out of her way as she began to speak. "Fuck—those four-flushers—and that dumbass sheriff! Let 'em make the mistake of coming back for more. It won't just be Tristan they go up against next time."

Paris went off on her, "Are you off your rocker…? You have a fucking death wish? You just going to kill-em-all? Single handed? Just gonna walk up to the shit-house naked?

"Nope… you and Tristan are gonna help me… I say we grab all our stuff and head out of town right now—and make sure this whole fucking town knows it!"

Tristan watched the two of them squabbling, with a slight smile. He knew Ariel was still in her drink, and would think differently, after they'd gotten some food and a good night's sleep.

He also noticed how their demeanor had changed. Even though they were monkey-ass drunk, they both had become more alert and methodical in the way they now eyed their surroundings. Like a couple of mountain lions, ready to pounce on anything that jumped out at them. Though they were bickering, their eyes denoted the killer instinct, that old man Ross had spoken of that day at the ranch. He finally chimed in on their discussion.

"I say… we get some food, go up to our room, crack open that bottle we left up there, make a little love and get some good sleep tonight. It may be awhile before another restful night comes our way. As for these dickhead goat-ropers, I know you'll think of something Paris. Of that, I have no doubt. Now, let's go get some grub, and make bets on who walks bow-legged tomorrow."

The girls looked at each-other and smiled, then looked back at Tristan and said together in one voice, "Oh it's on!"

Paris then said, "A better bet, would be who wakes up last, with their thumb in their mouth." She stuck her thumb in her mouth, looked at Tristan and muttered, "Mom-ma."

Their laughter carried to both sides of the street as they started walking away from Tristan, shaking their asses unconsciously. He stared at them for a minute before catching up with them. They strolled down the middle of the street to the hotel as if there was no one else around for miles.

The love-making that went-on that night, would be recalled to memory for decades to come.

*****

The next morning, Ariel woke-up as Paris was returning. In a loud whisper, she got on to Paris. "Where did you go? Are you crazy? Going off by yourself? Tristan would be livid if he had gotten up and found you gone!"

Paris looked over at him, passed out still. Holding back a laugh, she said, "Maybe. If he wasn't still recovering from the ass-kicking he took from us—last night." At that statement, they both giggled. Their giggling woke him up. After a smile for them both and a full body yawn-n-stretch, he asked them, "What's the plan?"

As Tristan and Ariel wiped the sleep out of their eyes, Paris brought them up to speed on her plan.

Paris had snuck down to the stables and had a couple stable boys prep their wagon and horses, so they could head out as soon as they got down to the stables. Giving no one a chance to be ready to follow them.

She had deduced, that if they were to be attacked at all, it would be at night while they camped or in the early hours of the morning. She had also paid the two stable boys to hide in the wagon as the three of them rode it out of town. Letting everyone see them go. Once they were a good distance from town and sure no one else was around, they'd take their horses, tied off to the back of the wagon, and head out. Letting the boys take the wagon on till nightfall. Then set up a fake camp and leave the wagon. Returning on the wagon horses with no one the wiser.

The three of them, would high tail it south for a bit, turn east and ride most of the night. Making their way around to the east side of Tucson, giving it a wide berth. Then head north till they felt safe enough to turn west again. That should throw anyone, trying to follow them, off their trail.

Providing they didn't get turned around and lost. They resolved, that with a full moon to shine that night, their ride thru the wilderness of the desert should be easy enough. With little chance of getting lost in the dark.

The girls would also dress up as men before leaving the wagon. So, if they were spotted, from a distance, or even up close; they might be mistaken for men.

When she finished telling them her plan, Tristan looked at her with astonishment. "You pulled all this out of your ass? Since you woke up this morning? While we slept like babes?

"Are you sure you didn't leave a stone unturned between here and California?"

Paris smiled and said, "Just get dressed… and let's get some breakfast. We may be with nothing but hard-tack and no fire for more than a few nights."

Paris's plan was flawless. Except for the one thing she didn't predict. The walls had ears. Their entire preparation had been overheard and was being repeated, in its entirety to their adversaries, before they finished breakfast.

Knowing the lay of the land as they did, as Tristan and the girls headed west out of town, the cowboys headed east.

They planned to turn south and spread out half their number so there was no chance that Tristan and the girls wouldn't be spotted. Then a few of them would chase after them, funneling them into a place of their choosing, for an ambush.

As the cowboys rode east out of town that morning, they laughed and joked about what they were going to do to the women. While Tristan was made to watch, before they killed him.

As for the women, they would be given a few rides. Over and over, until they lost the fight in their eyes, then be killed as well.

* * * * *

The three companions, with their two stowaways, traveled west till around noon. Then, bidding farewell and thanks to the boys, rode south hard for a few hours. After a short rest for themselves and the horses, they mounted up and rode east thru the night, until they were sure they were well east of Tucson. Stopping a few hours before morning, to get a little sleep, before turning north and continuing onward.

The sun was still red on the horizon as it rose over the desert. They had just finished saddling the horses when they caught site of riders coming in fast and hard.

Paris shouted, "How?"

Ariel yelled, "We were betrayed that's how! Those fucking little bastards sold us out!"

Tristan interrupted, "No time for debate! Let's skin outta here! Now!

Like bats out of hell, they spurred the horses through the desert. Giving them full rein to run like the wind.

It wasn't long before they saw riders to either side and just ahead of them. They were riding fast and hard to come in alongside them. To cut them off while others closed in from behind.

A mile or so ahead was a canyon pass. Ariel yelled to the others, "If we can make that canyon before they get too close, we can take some high ground and hold them off."

"No!" Paris yelled back, "that's what they want us to do.

"There trying to corral us right into it. There is only a handful of them chasing us. The rest are in that pass, ready to ambush us."

Tristan told them, "She's right! Follow my lead! We're gonna let 'em think they have us fooled. When I say-so, cut a hard left and head up the slope… and pray we find cover before the whole lot overtakes us!"

Tristan was keeping just behind the girls, so that there was no way he would lose sight of either of them, as they all raced to stay alive.

One of the riders to their side was gaining ground fast, about to overtake them. Tristan knew he would try to rein in next to the girls, in an attempt, to trip them up.

He might be a clever cowboy of the west, but Tristan was a seasoned cowboy from the east. A Florida cracker through and through. No Florida cracker was ever on a horse without his bullwhip.

The man reined in next to Paris on her right side at full speed, then reached out to grab her. As he did so, Tristan licked out with his whip and caught him around his neck.

With all his strength, Tristan braced himself and hair-pinned his horse to the left. Snatching the man from his mount and under Paris's horse.

A hoof caught him just below his neck on his back. His spine was snapped by the horse's hoof, at the same time his face hit the ground, snapping his neck like a twig.

Tristan, wanting to make an example of him for all his pursuers to see, did not let loose with the whip. Instead, he dragged him behind his horse for thirty or so yards, until his body caught a rock, and his head popped off his shoulders, and rolled into some underbrush.

Tristan whipped his horse around and quickly regained his position behind the girls. Just before they reached the canyon entrance, Tristan yelled for them to make the turn.

He was so close to the rear of their horses; he was all but spitting the dirt they were kicking up.

They all made the turn together in such a tight formation, they looked to be one rider from a distance. Keeping that formation as they spurred onward for their lives.

They made their way up the slope only to find that there was no cover to be seen. As they topped the ridge of the slope and headed down the other side, praying for some cover to take advantage of, their plight went from bad to worse. Off to the side of them, they could see the rest of the riders racing out of the pass, at a full run, on fresh mounts. It wouldn't be long now before they were overtaken and rode down.

They flew off the slope onto flat ground, passing beside a large crag. As they passed it, Tristan spotted a dry, narrow ravine. He shouted to the girls to turn and head for it.

With an even tighter formation than before, they made another hairpin turn and headed for it. Riding like the wind.

Tristan hoped it snaked its way enough thru the crags to find a defendable position or exit.

The ravine was barely wide enough for two horses at a time. With sheer walls, a good twenty feet in height. That gave Tristan and the girls immediate advantage. Now, all their pursuers' numbers meant nothing. They had to enter and exit two at a time. Tristan was praying he hadn't just gotten them all killed.

He was desperate for something, anything, that would allow them some cover and a chance at surviving this predicament. If there was an exit to it, they could get to either side of it and catch their attacker's in a crossfire as they came out.

Only able to do so two at a time would even the odds for the girls and Tristan. If their pursuers were stupid enough to make such a deadly error. Either way, they'd be free of them. Tristan said, "Just a little help God…. Please?"

The ravine opened into a short gorge that came to a dead end. With only a couple of rocks on the ground, barely large enough to take cover behind, at its far side. But there were rocks to get behind, and that's all Tristan had asked for.

They jumped from the horses. Tristan snatched the saddle bags full of ammunition from his horse. They had enough ammo to put up a good fight. If they were to die today, they weren't going alone.

All three took cover behind the rocks as best they could and prepared for the worst.

The ravine opened at its end large enough to easily allow ten or more men, to charge straight at them, on horseback.

The distance from the opening to where they were—at Tristan's best guess—was close to two hundred yards. But they still had to enter the opening, two at a time.

The riders coming in after them must have known how the ravine ended. They had slowed their horses to a walk as the first few rounded the bend and entered the opening.

One of the cowboys, feeling the joy of victory in his grasp, yelled out to his soon-to-be victims. "Looks like you've made it easy for us!"

He'd begun to laugh when a shot rang out thru the ravine, spooking their horses. His laughter was cut short as a bullet caught him in his ear. Blowing off the other one and splattering his companions with his blood and brains as his head blew apart. The rest of them quickly removed themselves from the line of fire of the rifle that had just killed their friend.

"You see that? That was that young girl that took that shot! Nary a one of you sons-a-bitches—could have made such a shot as clean as that! Not from that distance…"

The rest of them dismounted and gathered just before the opening into the wider space. One of them suggested. "Let's just rush them. They'll panic. Taking away their advantage of being sharpshooters. Maybe even take 'em alive still. At least one anyway... if not all three."

Another man replied, "Are you stupid-or-somethin? You wanna just jump out and run at a firing squad? You dumb-ass! Those are Henry repeaters they have. They already proved they know how to use them. Not to mention that bastard's skills with a revolver. It's too narrow for all of us to go charging in there. Rushing them is suicide."

"Well they can't get us all." The other man replied.

"Well then, be my guest! I'll follow in behind ya."

"Well what do—you propose then? We just sit here and wait 'em out?"

Another man among them, offered up, "This is simple. A handful of us will run out on foot and stay on this end.

With all us firing, we keep them pinned down while three or four horse and riders rush-in on 'em."

With no objections to that plan, they began to position and ready themselves for the attack.

Tristan told the girls, "they are going to pin us down with an ass load of fire power from where they are, while a bunch of 'em rush in on horseback."

"How do you know that?" asked Paris.

"That's what I'd do...." Tristan told her, with a solemn tone, she wasn't used to from him. Then he said,

"We might take out a few of 'em but, not all. After a few goes at us, their plan might just work. This maneuver may be the end of us. We can't let them take any of us alive."

That was the moment that something snapped on in Ariel. In a low an eerie, guttural voice, Ariel said, "Not without a fight—"

Bewildered by the sound of her voice, Tristan and Paris looked over at her. She had dropped the rifle in her hands and began to back away from the rock in front of her on her hands and knees, resembling a crouching panther, more than she did a human.

Unconscious of her actions, she dropped her head down to look out of the top of her eye sockets, like a cornered animal that had turned to attack. Her breath came out in short huffing inhales and exhales. The sound she made as she did this, was a low and guttural grunt.

"Err, err, err...." Increasing steadily in its intensity. Her face changed from that of a woman in stress, to a wild inhuman frame of hate. Making her almost unrecognizable to her partners.

Tristan and Paris were completely taken back by her actions. The thing now possessing Ariel's body, startled and frightened them both. This was new, and it scared them.

Struck dumb by her unnerving actions, all they could manage to do was look on. Momentarily frozen in place.

Ariel no longer acknowledged their presence. All she could do now was feel, and that feeling... was pure, savage, unchecked rage; a cornered predator, ready to fight.

Bullets began whizzing by all around them, ricocheting off the rock face behind them. The charge came shortly following. Five of them came charging in at a full gallop, holding their fire to the last possible moment, to gain an advantage without risk of empty pistols before they could achieve a pointblank range, and maybe take them alive.

Ariel was primal in her bearing, as she lifted on to one knee, pulling the knife from its sheath at her side as she did.

Tristan's effort to get her attention quickly became screams of plea, "Ariel...! Trudy! Trudy! No! don't, don't you do it damnit...! Tr-u-d-y! God-Damnit!

Paris was almost in a panic; she looked at Tristan wide eyed and said, "What'll we do?"

Tristan, with his blood pumped and adrenalized, yelled, "We back her up! We rode in here together! We die in here together!"

As the five men reined-in their horses in front of the rocks, and began firing their pistols, Ariel's attack was simultaneous and abrupt.

From her squatted position, she made an astonishing leap onto the rock in front of her. Raising her arms above her head and waving them to make herself seem larger. Simultaneously letting out a primal, almost inhuman scream. It echoed thru the ravine, causing the horses to spook and rear up. Tristan and Paris instantly followed suit. Causing the same reaction from the horses in front of them.

As the horse in front of Ariel, spun on its rear legs to bolt away, she made another amazing leap onto its back, behind its rider. Driving her knife deep into the space where neck and shoulder meet. Holding the rider in his place with her grip on the knife.

The horse bolted towards their attackers. Ariel grabbed the pistol out of the man's hand and let out a war cry that panicked the horse even more, having a hair-raising effect on everyone that heard it.

She leaned in as the horse picked up speed and began firing the pistol in her hand, still holding the man in the saddle with the knife. He now became her shield, from the bullets that were riddling his body, from the other cowboys' trying to bring her down. The horse was hit half a dozen times but was too panicked to notice or slow down.

As she emptied the captured pistol, she tossed it, grabbed the pistol at her side, and opened fire again.

Tristan shot two of the men in front of him and jumped to the closest horse. Throwing the man upon its back to the ground, dying from a bullet in his throat. He spurred the horse onward, racing after Ariel, trying to provide her with as much cover fire as he could. Firing his rifle till empty.

Paris, now completely enveloped in the same emotional state of rage as Ariel, jumped to the horse in front of her, just as her companions had done, landing in front of its rider, instead of behind him. How the bullets he fired at her missed their mark, could only have been fates kiss to Paris.

As she landed on the horses back in front of the man, fingernails instantly clawed his eyes, sinking deep into their marks. He let out a scream in agony. A scream that was cut short, as she pushed his head up and back and ripped-out his throat with her bared teeth. Spitting out his Adam's Apple and slinging him to the ground with a display of strength unusually vigorous for a woman.

After spinning around in the saddle, she charged her horse after Tristan and Ariel. Their attackers had become the attacked.

Most of the cowboys still alive, shaken up by such guile and savage reprisal, retreated into the corridor of the ravine. Only two held their place, in a futile attempt to survive the onslaught they were now faced with.

As Ariel's mount raced passed one of the men, she dove from the horse and onto him, knocking him to the ground.

Before they hit the ground, she had already sunk her knife deep into his eye socket. Landing square on his chest, she quickly straddled his body. Letting out another blood curdling war-cry into his face, she slashed his throat, almost severing his head in the process. Turning her head from side to side in due process of her state of persona, looking for another victim.

Tristan dived on his victim the same as she had done. Coming up on one knee on top of the man. Firing the last bullet from his revolver into the man's face.

At that same instant, Paris reined in her mount beside Ariel and jumped down beside her sister, to see if she was alright. Ariel knew she was there but didn't acknowledge it.

As Paris put her hand on Ariel's shoulder, Ariel looked up at her with murderous intent in her eyes. A look that vanished without a trace as she realized who had touched her.

Seeing Paris's face and chest covered in blood, Ariel exclaimed, "Shit! Are you alright?"

Paris said, "I'm fine. It's not my blood."

As she helped her sister to her feet, Paris realized there was an awful lot of gun fire still going off, but no bullets were whizzing by them. The sounds of gunfire were coming from the corridor of the ravine, where their assailants had fled.

After a moment of pause to listen, Paris asked Ariel, "Now what do you suppose—that's all about?"

Ariel replied, "Got me by the ass…!" There's just no-telling with these dumb-bastards."

They looked over at Tristan, who was staring, back towards the other end of the ravine, frozen in place. Both the girls turned to see what had his attention.

The cowboy that had managed to survive their first retaliation, now lay face down in the dirt with an arrow sticking out of his back.

Looking over at Tristan again, they noticed he was gazing up at the cliff top. As they looked up, the reason for his slack jawed gaze became obvious.

Indians! Apache Indians! Their number so great, it was impossible to count them all. That was the reason for all the excessive gunfire. The Apache were slaughtering what remained of the cowboys. The big question now…. What were the Indians going to do to them…?

Chapter five

Nde

The girls made their way slowly over to where Tristan was standing, trying not to make any sudden moves. His thoughts were distracted for a moment from their newly evolving predicament. He surveyed their surroundings with astonishment. Then he looked back at the girls with even greater amazement.

All the raw and primal emotions that was pouring off them, only moments ago, was completely gone from their demeanor, as if it had never happened.

He said to them, "Well that was… vigorous…!"

Looking at Ariel, he said, "And you… from what corner of hell did you pull that from your ass?"

She looked into his eyes, her face an expression of calm. Showing no sign of the ferocity that erupted from her only moments ago.

"What do you mean?" Her voice clear and soft once again.

Given the abrupt change in her appearance back to her normal happy go lucky self. He half wondered if she even did know what he meant. As he pondered this for an instant, his thoughts trailed off, back to their newly developing situation. He told the girls,

"I wish you'd look at this—shit now…. Ain't this a bitch!

"Fate drops a miracle in our lap, only to turn right around, bend us over—and reinsert cock! I mean… what'd we do—to manifest such a day? It would have been better to be staked out for the crows!"

Paris interrupted his tantrum, saying, "Careful… that might just be where we end up before this day is over."

Tristan quickly responded, "And what a day we're having…."

He looked over at her. She could instantly see that he was struggling to make sense of it. Desperate for an answer that would explain how to get them through this day, with their lives intact. That's when Trudy intervened.

"I don't think they are going to kill us. If they were... why haven't they already? They wasted no time on those fuckers back up the canyon."

One of the Apache men atop the cliff called down to them, "Da'anzho ash"

"What did he say?" asked Ariel. Thinking out loud, more than she was asking an actual question.

Tristan said, "Apache blood flows thru my veins from my mother and her mother. They taught words and phrases to me as a child. He said, *hello friend*."

Both the girls, bewildered by his statement, looked back at him and stared.

With Ariel saying, "Aren't you just full of surprises."

Looking over to her and meeting her gaze, Tristan smiled and kindly retorted, "Look who's talking."

Tristan repeated the words but added an extra word, saying, "Aoo Da'anzho ash" (Yes, hello friend), back to the man who had first spoke them to him. Waving an arm side to side and above his head, as he did so. The man that had spoken those words, gestured for them to come out with a large arcing wave of his arm.

"Well, no sense beating around the bush," said Ariel, to her lovers. Continuing with a witty tone,

"If you're – One of the Boys – we may just live thru this day after all... But we aren't going to find out standing here amongst all this death and carnage.

"Let's grab our horses and get the hell out of here.

"We'll take all these other horses with us.

"I'm sure they would want them.

"Momma always said, *always bring a gift when you go to visit people. It's just the polite thing to do*."

They gathered up the horses and made their way out of the ravine, to meet what they hoped, were newfound friends. Or at the very least, not newfound enemies.

As they made their way out, Ariel said, "If they want all these weapons and shit... They can come down here and get them their selves."

* * * * *

Paris—*Nde*, sounds like In-day or Indee... That is what the Apache people call themselves. It means, *The People.*

The propaganda of their nature and the reality of it, are as different as night and day. True, if you were considered an enemy, you saw a side of them that was, at times, without compassion to say the least. But can you name one race or culture that didn't treat enemies in like fashion?

The Apache culture and their highly spiritual religious beliefs are a beautiful way of seeing our world and living in harmony with nature. Tristan, Trudy and I all agreed after our time spent with them. That if we had to sum up the Apache people and their way of life with only a few words, they would be, *Awe-Inspired Admiration.* For those of you who doubt my words. My suggestion to you is, find yourself among them as a friend and see for yourself.

The party of warriors that had found us, had been trailing the men that had attacked us. These men had attacked their hunting camp, many days past. In the night, while the warriors were out hunting, killing everyone in the camp. Raping their women before murdering them most savagely.

Even the children were murdered... all their throats slashed. Their only provocation, blind hate for the *Red Man.*

From the early 1600's, until 1865, history has recorded the slavery of, at least, half a million African Americans that entered the colonies and states thru those centuries.

With well over twelve million populating the Northern and Southern continents of America and the Caribbean islands, at the end of the war to end slavery in America.

Between 1500 and the turn of the twentieth century, over 100 million Native Americans of the north, central and southern continents of America, including the Caribbean and Bahama islands, were slaughtered or had perished through disease from foreigners. Some tribes and peoples now forever extinct.

It wasn't to enslave them, either. It was an attempt at genocide. That began with the arrival of Columbus and escalated into apocalypse by the time of Cortes and Montezuma.

To our fortunate favor, one of them spoke extremely good English. His name was Nantan. He became our translator, teacher and good friend.

He told us they had captured a handful of the cowboys that had split off from the main group, which were intending to set a trap for us, though they did not know that at the time.

When they found items in their possession that had belonged to members of their group, they knew these were the men they had been tracking. They killed them where they stood. Cutting their throats, the same way they had done to the children.

They had seen everything that had happened from the moment we were chased from our camp that morning.

They couldn't help laughing hysterically, when they spoke of what Tristan had done with his—*Strange Rope*—as they called it, to the man who tried to grab me during the chase. They had never seen a Bullwhip before, nor had they seen a man's head just pop off. They told us it had been a privilege, watching us fight off all those men, and that they had never seen white folk fight like Apache.

At first, they thought we were Apache dressed as white men. They were struck dumb when they realized that Trudy and I were females. Every single one of them were in complete awe of Trudy and I, some were even downright afraid of us. Saying, *we were possessed with the spirits of the wild creatures that kill and eat men.*

Tristan was completely infatuated with the Nde. Telling us that he was beginning to understand why he was so enamored with the land.

They invited us to return with them to meet their chief and tell *The People* our story around the fires. So that it would not be soon forgotten.

Tristan told them yes without even a look over to me or Trudy. We never called him out on it though. Given the fact, we would have said yes too, had we been asked.

They took us east, back the way we had first come into Tucson. We traveled for two full days and the better part of the morning on the third day. To arrive at, what we learned on the way, was more of a mountain hideout than a permanent encampment, though they were just as much at home there, as anywhere.

As long as they were free, they were happy. War or peace did not matter. Freedom was what was best in life…

When we arrived, we were taken before the chief and formally introduced. His name was Cochise. He was the leader of the Chiricahua Apache people.

Our story was told that night around the fires. The fact that Tristan had Apache blood had spread like wildfire among the tribe. To the Apache, there was no doubt of Tristan's Apache heritage. For them, it was easy to see he was one of them.

This fact and the telling of our story made us kind of, celebrities among them. But trust wasn't something lightly given. We would have to prove ourselves worthy of that respect before it was freely and fully bestowed upon us.

Cochise assigned a young girl, barely in her adolescence, with the charge of our welfare. An ingenious way of finding out who your guests are. How we treated, or mistreated her, said a lot about our true character and just how far we could be trusted. Just her not being afraid of us, spoke volumes.

Her name was Bina. It means musical instrument. Because she was always singing. She had beautiful singing vocals. Tristan fell in love with her instantly; he spoiled her rotten, as if she was his own daughter. He would have gone up against anyone and everyone to protect her.

A wickiup was prepared for us to use during our stay with the tribe. Everyone saw Trudy and I as Tristan's wives, a thing not frowned upon as it was in the states. Here, in the apache nation, having more than one woman wasn't uncommon. So, to them, it was only natural, that we were given just one wickiup.

Our presence among the people, and the story of our battle, spread all over the Apache nation, throughout all the tribes big and small. We had been with the tribe for a couple of weeks, when we were informed that a highly respected man, of the Mescalero Apache, was traveling to meet with us. It was said his father was a Mescalero Apache and his mother, Lipan Apache. Though it was rarely mentioned of a man of his status among the Mescalero. Not that it mattered in any way.

The purpose of his visit was known only to him. He was an old warrior and holy man of his people. His age being the reason it was taking so much time to make the journey.

The entire tribe was preparing for his awaited arrival. There would be much celebration during his stay with the Chiricahua.

When he finally arrived, he was taken before Cochise. They at once retreated into one of Cochise's lodgings and wasn't seen again the rest of the day.

A full moon was shining high above the desert when we were finally summoned to the wickiup of the chief. We were bid to sit with them in the middle of the room. Cochise spoke English well enough. The old man's English was a-little broken and slow, but we understood him.

The old man's full attention had been on Tristan since he had entered the wickiup. Even after Nantan came-in and sat down, there was silence for some time before the old man finally spoke.

Looking straight at Tristan, he said, "It is known to me... that you have said your mother... and her mother are one of the people... and daughters of this land. What is your grandmother's name?"

Tristan told him, "Her native name is, Sonsee-array. She told me it meant, Morning Star."

The old wiseman smiled and replied, "Let it be known... we are of one blood you and I... Tristan Jonas....

"You... are the grandson of my youngest sister. Which makes you my nephew... by your understanding of the nature of such things....

"I have heard of your prowess in battle... it makes my heart sing... to know the instincts of the people... are strong in you.

"I have also heard... of the ferocity... and violence... of your wives. A most impressive thing... given their delicate appearance and incredible beauty... especially so with them being white.... I am told... such a thing is rare in the white man's culture....

"I have not seen my sister for many years... and though I am curious to hear about her... it is not why I have made this journey. To meet you and your wives and acknowledge to all the people that you are my kin... is reason enough for me to have made such an exhausting journey... but this also... is not the reason I have come here....

"I am known among my people as... Wicasa Wakan, which means... holy man as you understand it.... My given name is, Tarak.... It means... Star... in your tongue.

"I have spent most of my years... interpreting the dreams and visions sent from the spirit world. It is they... who have sent me here.... In a vision... I was told to prepare for a journey... to speak with three... who are one.

"Tomorrow... we will go into the wilderness.... Where we will consult with the spirits... and hear what they have brought me here to tell you. Your wives will also come with us.... This concerns them... as much as it does you.

"The three of you coming here... was no accident. It is fate... that has brought you to the people... not just mere chance.... But enough talk on these matters for now.

"Tonight... we celebrate our meeting and make it known that we are of one blood. Cochise and I have spent many hours this day... deciding on names for you. You have your names of the white folk... This night you have been accepted into the people... as warriors.

"You will be known throughout all the Indian nations... as the adopted children of Cochise... leader of the Chiricahua.... You will also be known as blood kin of the Mescalero and Lipan people... who are my kin.... Now... Cochise will tell you your new names."

Cochise looked at Ariel and said to her, "Your name is, Dahteste... It means in your speech, warrior woman. The warriors who have heard it, say your war cry makes them afraid, and that you are fearless in the face of your enemies. For this, I have chosen this name for you.

He looked to me next, saying, "Your name is, Onawa. It means in your tongue, wide awake. For I have never met a woman, and few men, with a mind as keen as yours.

"Also, I want to tell you both that I have learned your birth names well. Repeating them many times to myself so that I may honor you by saying them properly. Ariel... Paris... I think that they are beautiful names, and my ears enjoy the sound of them, as does my tongue, as it makes them."

He then looked to Tristan. "From this day and forever, you will be known amongst the people as, Biminak. It means, slick roper. It speaks for itself. Everyone knows of your, bull whip, as you call it."

Tristan smiled from ear to ear and said, "Aheeiyeh, thank you. What has happened here this night, brings great joy to my heart, and I'll be forever proud of who I am now in the eyes of the Nde. From this day and forever, I will hold my head high as son of Cochise, leader of the Chiricahua. And, that I am the nephew of Tarak, elder brother to my grandmother."

Men... no matter what creed or color, they all must beat their chest and stroke their cocks. Prancing around like roosters in their best feathers and pumping each other up with words of grandeur. Trudy and I shared a look between us that said as much without ever saying a word. The celebration that ensued that night would not soon be forgotten.

* * * * *

Narration–The next day, Tarak led them into the mountains, accompanied by Nantan.

Nantan told them that the mountains were called, the *Chokonen* by the Apache, it means, Tall Cliffs. The People that followed Cochise were also known as the, Chokonen band of the Chiricahua. The Mexicans called them, *Sierra muy Penascosa*, in native Mexican tongue, it means, very rugged mountains. They were known as, the Dragoons by the U.S. cavalry. The Apache didn't use the term mountain range. They call them, *Sky Islands*.

The old man took them close to the summit of the tallest peak in the area. The place where the old man took them, was a sacred and hallowed place to the Apache people.

Once there, Tarak began preparing himself. As he did so, Nantan prepared for a fire in the fire pit they would all sit around, as Tarak called down the spirits.

Shortly after dark, they lit the fire. They threw herbs, and powdered potions into it, while Tarak recited rights that would protect them from dark forces and shield them from evil things.

Once the ceremony that connected him to the spirit world was complete, it didn't take long for him to begin reciting what he was being told.

To the girls and Tristan, it was as though an invisible person was whispering in his ear, and he was just repeating what he heard.

He spoke first of shortcomings that they each had that needed to be overcome, at all costs. So that they would not drown in the sorrows that would be conjured up if they could not.

They listened intently and without interruption. For the things he spoke of hit too close to home to be just a load of bull. None of them thought it nonsense. The goosebumps and hair standing up on the back of their necks and arms were too intense to dismiss any of this as trivial or whimsical. The very air around them was charged with a supernatural essence that was almost tangible.

Tarak paused his interpretations to rest for a moment. After a silence, he began the chants that would invoke the spirits who were the heavy hitters. They are the sanctified spirits, the Gaan. They were the ones that had called them to this place.

As Tarak's chants trailed off into silence, he slowly began to slip into some sort of trance. His eyes rolled up in the back of his head and when he finally spoke, it was with a voice that was not his own. The things that the old man told them, blew their minds. Nantan interpreted.

"All three of you are wielders of the light.... and the dark. Capable, at times, of going pitch black, to defeat great evil.

You will all prove that everything that comes from the dark, is not evil. You must remember this at all cost if you are to succeed against what you must face.

"The three of you are one. Three souls, one heart... Three hearts, one soul...

"The elder female... is the mind that guides. The male... is the body that protects. The young one... the soul that binds. It is emotion that combines the three of you into one and makes you strong.

"All three of you share a singular cleverness that makes you hard to defeat when your minds are focused as one.

"Any one of you, will kill and die for the other two... without question. You do not fear death, but you also, do not welcome it.

"When I say you, I am speaking of all three of you. *Body... Mind... and Soul.*" He pointed to each in turn as he said this.

"This life is not the first life you have shared. You have spent countless lifetime's together. One thing that has remained constant thru them all, is no matter whose hand is caressing destiny... the three of you have always been together, or ended up together, even when you weren't meant to.

"Your souls are so ancient; father time no longer keeps track of them.

"Throughout all existences, you have served the loving light. In recognition of this, you have been granted full autonomy and liberty to write your own destinies for each new lifetime. Except for this one.

"The bonds between you will be tested to their fullest measure on this journey you are about to embark upon. Any one or all of you, may not survive this task. None of your earlier lives have prepared you for what you must do.

"You have been sent here to this world, again, to retrieve a powerful magic. That in the dawn of time, protected the angels who once took a material form; to oversee and protect the growth of the foundations of this world and all its life sustaining resources, after its creation by the All Father... he who breathes life... and is the father of all living things, in this universe of wonder. The source of all things.

"Unclean powers that-be will attempt to steel this great magic... and transform it into a great evil that'll become a plague upon the earth. An evil that threatens the goodness of all the people of this world. If you fail, it shall be the end of all things that are good.

"Do not try to anticipate or discern when you will be confronted by this undertaking. It is your destiny... and it will find you. It will only serve to weaken you if you dwell upon its arrival. When you are, at last, confronted by it... you will know it for what it is. The powers and tools you will need to overcome this evil... fate will provide.

"Before you are compelled to leave this land and continue upon the path that has been chosen for you, you will be joined by one whom you have left behind, and now travels from a great distance to be with you. You must wait with the people for his coming.

"Another will cross your path, in time. He will be your guide... and teacher.

"The spirit of the animal resides within them both... and both... will be of great aid to you on your journey. You must not abandon either of them... and you must trust in them.

"When the night is at its darkest, the strength of your unity, will be the weapon that brings forth the light.

"For paradise is imprisoned in paradise... and the end times... never really are... the end times."

The old wiseman's eyes dropped out of his head to expose his pupils again. Nantan caught him as he fell forward, almost burning his hair and face in the flames. Nantan told the others that the old man must rest now.

They made camp there for the night. The trio agreed that they would not speak of this, not even to each other, until it was forced upon them. As they lay around the fire, staring up at the brilliance of the stars and the dark spaces that separates them, they couldn't help pondering what they had seen and had been told. They laid there quietly for hours, trying to absorb all that had been divulged to them this night.

Tristan thought to himself about what a mindfuck he had just been exposed to. As sleep finally came calling for him, his final thoughts were on who it was, that he, or they, had left behind.

* * * * *

When Tristan awoke the next morning, waking Paris from her slumber as he gathered himself. She said to him,

"Where is Trudy?"

He looked around, "Probably relieving herself. I'm sure she's fine."

He called out for her a couple of times with no response. Paris stood and started calling for her also. Tristan then said,

"Nantan and Tarak aren't here either. She must be with them."

Just as he finished his sentence, they both heard a faint voice coming from a little way's up a hill to the south of the camp. After a moment, Tristan spotted Nantan. He was waving frantically for them to come to him.

"Something's up, let's hurry!" Tristan exclaimed.

Grabbing a pistol from its holster, he tucked it in his pants, not wanting to waste time strapping anything on.

Snatching up the pair of Henry rifles they had with them, he tossed one to Paris and they both took off up the hill.

When they reached Nantan, he quickly put a finger to his lips, signaling them to silence. They made their way up the hill to where

Tarak was lying on his belly, looking out over a small plateau, just below them. The opposite side of which was a drop off, of no short distance. In the middle of the open field was a large pack of gray wolves, warming themselves and frolicking in the morning rays of the sun.

With smiles on their face, Tristan and Paris both watched the wolves, awe-struck at the sight of them. This would mark their first encounter with a wolf of any sort, let alone an entire pack. They were enticed by this unexpected scene before them, until Nantan pointed towards the opposite side of the wolfpack, to the edge of the cliff. Sitting a few feet from the edge, was Ariel.

Beside her was a huge wolf. Her back was to her onlookers. She was sitting with one leg tucked and the other with her knee in the air and foot flat to the ground.

She had her arms rapped around the wolf as though they were lifelong pals. The wolf was so big, her head only came up to his neck. Tristan and Paris were in shock, unable for an instant to even move.

Tristan started to stand up, to get a bead with his rifle on the wolf next to Ariel. Nantan grabbed his arm. Whispering to Tristan, "What you doing? No! Spook them and she will be in more danger. If, she even is, in danger…. I have never seen this before.

"The one she sits beside is the leader of this pack. He is like a ghost in these mountains. You only see him if he wants it to be so. Same as the others but more-so with him.

"They are born killers. Deadly in their ability to stalk and hunt. Silent as ghosts when they choose to be."

Tristan whispered back, "What the hell then? We can't just sit here and hope it all works out for her…they'll kill her!"

"If that, was what they were going to do… it would already be so. The pack is showing no interest in her. And as I have already told you, the one sitting beside her is their leader. They do his bidding and his alone. Only a handful of our best hunters have ever seen him at all. No one has ever gotten so close to him and lived. Somehow, she got herself in their mix. She is the only one that can get herself free. If they see, smell or hear us—it could be bad for her."

After what seemed an eternity to the watcher's, the wolf at Trudy's side rose and moved off towards the others.

Trudy stood up and followed, almost skipping, along behind him. Like a child playing in her own back yard with her pet dog, without a care in the world.

Practically biting a hole in his lip as he looked on, Tristan was ready to burst. Paris was not given to smiling anymore either, but their hands were tied. All they could do was watch this potential fiasco unfold, helpless to do anything to help her.

As the big one moved off a short distance from her, a few of the other's came running up to her and began jumping around her playfully. All four of the onlookers heard her laugh and watched her take off running, as the wolves chased after her. One of them tripped her up, sending her sprawling to the ground, with even greater laughter, as they jumped over and all around her. Completely infatuated with her presence among them.

It was easy to see the joy upon her face. It was as if she really was a child again. The wolves showed no malice of any kind. Most of the pack ignored her entirely, as though they were completely unaware of her presence.

Paris couldn't take it anymore. Before anyone could caution her against it, she called out, "Ariel, let's go—"

The entire wolf pack was on their feet, ears up, noses to the wind, sniffing the air for a scent.

Ariel thought she had heard her sister's voice but didn't acknowledge such.

The wind blowing in the faces of the watchers on the rock, was why the wolves weren't more startled. Unable to catch a scent or sight of them. They still showed no ill will towards Ariel.

Ariel did not respond to the calling of her name, but she did realize she should get back to camp before the others came looking for her. She picked herself up onto her feet, and brushed herself off, as she made her way over to the alpha wolf. He was standing now on all fours with his nose in the air, searching for any scent of danger.

Standing there as he was, made him even more impressive to look upon. A splendid example of gray wolf.

Ariel walked over to him and kissed him between his ears, and then stood staring in his face. With her face so close to his, she could have kissed his nose. All four of her witnesses atop the ledge sucked air between their teeth as she did so.

The wolf stared at her for a moment and then licked her from chin to eyebrow with a tongue that almost covered her entire face. She turned her back to him and started off back towards the camp, like a little girl in her own little fantasy land. The wolf pack watched her leave, unperturbed in any way. With some of them, still ignoring her all together.

The watchers backed away from their perch, bellies to the ground, being as quiet as possible, so as not to risk alerting the wolves to their presence. As they met up with Ariel, on the way back to the camp, Tristan was the first to speak.

"I've seen some really stupid stunts in my life… but what I just saw you doing beats them all."

"What…? They were nice, I wasn't scared. You guys were watching? Did you see the big one? My goodness—was he a big fellow. It was so amazing being among them like that…. Are all wolves so friendly?"

Nantan answered her, "Even those are not friendly. At least, not to anyone but you. I have never seen another get as close…and not be torn apart… or play among them like tame dogs."

Paris said, "Please don't do that shit again. My heart stopped…seeing you out there like that. Helpless to do anything without risk of getting you killed."

Tarak spoke to her in Apache. The tone of his voice and expression on his face denoted his distaste for her actions, nor did it take a genius of linguistics to tell of the sarcasm in his words.

Nantan said to Ariel, "You do not want to know what he said."

She replied back, not trying to hide her anguish, "I don't need to speak your language to perceive the meaning of—his—words. You can tell him for me… he can go fuck himself."

Nantan was taken back by her words, but Tarak demanded he be told what she said. Nantan, reluctant to do so, did as the old warrior bid him do.

After telling him and sharing a stare of astonishment, Tarak looked over at Ariel for a moment and broke out into a hysterical laugh, with Nantan joining in his laughter.

Never had they heard such an insult, come from a woman. Tarak, after wiping the tears from his eyes from laughing so hard, looked at her and said,

"I can die now in peace... knowing I have seen... and heard all there is to see and hear... after watching and speaking with you this day. The courage... and defiance in you is rare... indeed."

Ariel and the other two joined in their laughter. Ariel walked over to Tarak and kissed him on his cheek. She walked along beside him, arm in arm, as they made their way back to camp. Once there, they gathered their belongings and made their way back to the stronghold of Cochise.

* * * * *

Weeks passed by with no real excitement to speak of. Ariel wanted to find the wolves again but was warned against it; she was told it was too dangerous for the members of the tribe, who might come across them, and try to interact as she did. Not to mention, the same danger for her wild friends, should they begin to get too close to other people, of other tribes, not so inclined as her to play with them.

Ba'Cho Izdzaa was the nickname given to Ariel. It means, *Wolf Woman*. Now she had her given name, *Dahteste,* and her nickname. She was fast becoming a legend in her own time among the Apache, and tribes other than just the Apache, such as the Kiowa and Navajo, as were they all.

The everyday happenings in and around the encampment took place as they normally did. Tristan was picking up the language more and more. The lessons taught to him as a child had stayed with him through the years and was serving him well, in picking it up now.

Paris was learning even faster than he was, without ever hearing a word of it spoken before that day in the desert.

Tristan had a larger vocabulary. But if they had both been starting from scratch, she would be his better.

Paris spent most of her time among the elders, talking and absorbing all the knowledge she could from them. Tristan and Ariel spent most of their time learning: to shoot a bow, practicing Apache stealth, tomahawk, warclub and knife fighting....

They awakened one morning, to a large commotion taking place at one end of the camp. Tristan, standing in front of their wickiup, asked one of the warriors passing by what was going on.

The warrior told him that all the dogs of the camp were attacking some animal that was ripping them apart. A rabid dog or wolf, and the men were trying to kill it. Before all their dogs, were smitten with rabies or killed outright.

"My wolves!" exclaimed Ariel, as she took off in the direction of all the noise.

Whatever it was, there was a savage fight taking place. Both, Tristan and Paris, ran after her to see for themselves just what the hell could be putting up such a fight, against every dog in the camp, without going down at the first onset of attack.

As they came up to the edge of the battle, all they could see, at first, was that it was big, black, and ferociously defending itself against its attackers. The damage being inflicted upon the dogs of the tribe was appalling. The warriors were doing their best to get a clear shot with bows and rifles to no avail. This thing was brutally savage, shockingly violent and amazingly fast.

As all the tribal dogs took a step back from the onslaught they were suffering, Tristan got a good look at what it was creating all the havoc amongst them.

When he caught sight of what it was, he yelled out with all the voice he could muster, "No! Don't shoot! Do not kill him!" Everyone froze. "He's mine! He is my dog!" It was JoJo!

Old man Ross had told them to take him along with them, but they had left him, thinking it would be too much for him across the desert. Despite the desert, he had travelled some seven or eight hundred miles, on his own, to find them.

The dog stood braced for whatever came next, teeth bared, bleeding from half a dozen wounds. Which was nothing, compared to the damage he'd dished out.

Four dogs lay dead around him and one other would die of his wounds. Tristan wondered at the sight of him if he was rabid. As Tristan stepped into plain view for the dog to see him, he called out to him, "Jojo, Jojo…here boy…come on…it's me buddy…over here boy."

The dog instantly lost all the violence in his face and trotted over to Tristan. Tristan dropped to one knee; the reunion that took place, was what one would expect to see when a dog and his master are reunited.

Everyone who saw, were in complete and utter shock of the outcome. The astonishingly grisly violence, and savagery of this creature was hard enough to accept. Now, not only was it just a dog… it was the pet of their guests.

A pet that had been searching for them, alone, across the most inhospitable desert country and found them.

The prophesies of the spirits had already begun to come true. They had now been joined by someone they had left behind. Someone who truly did have the spirit of the animal within him.

Chapter six

Frying pans and fires

Ariel–None of us were overly excited when the day came that it was time to continue our journey. We had stayed longer to allow JoJo to heal up fully. Tristan, at first, had worried about the dog being around so many people within the tribe. That there might be trouble with him. But there was not even an instant of issue whatsoever.

We were surprised at how his demeanor became so tolerant of everyone. None of us, had ever seen him so happy and content with his surroundings. He even let the other dogs around him, with little more than a snip, here or there.

Tristan–We continued west without incident to San Diego. After spending a month or so in San Diego, we travelled east back to San Felipe and followed the *Butterfield route* to San Francisco. We spent the winter in the city and after one hell of a time, we made our way to Sacramento and waited for the spring thaw to open the mountain passes.

Once we left Sacramento, we decided to take Donner Pass as our route to Salt Lake City. From there we would head for Denver. From there, it was anyone's guess.

We were in no hurry out of Sacramento. The forests and mountains were unlike anything any of us had seen before.

I remember back when we were first heading to San Francisco. In the San Joaquin Valley, you could see the Sierra Nevada mountains on a clear day from tens of miles away at the center of the valley. Now we were entering the heart of the Sierra's. Close to where they meet up and merge with the Cascade mountains.

We had bought another wagon. It was small and without cover, but it would do for our needs. We had the horses tied to the back, as usual, when we were on main paths and stagecoach roads.

Though at least once a day, we took the horses and explored the area.

One thing I recall, as vividly as if it were yesterday, is Trudy, coming back from a little stroll thru the woods. Trudy came riding up after an hour or two with Jo. She had taken a dress and had cut it short, so she could ride better in a dress, when we were out in the middle of nowhere and didn't have to mind travel and riding etiquette.

Jojo was running along beside her. She was riding bareback in her makeshift riding dress. She wasn't riding side saddle either… not that she ever did.

With a little laugh, I said to her, "And I half expected you to be butt naked."

Trudy lifted the front of her dress, up to her neck, to show us she—was—completely naked underneath it. Sticking her tongue out and laughing as she did so. Paris said to her,

"Do you know how bad your backside is going to smell riding bareback like that?"

Trudy retorted, "Do you know… how easy it is to wash up or take a bath?

"Besides, the horse probably needs a wash more than me. I must have had over a dozen orgasms since I rode off earlier." She moved her hips back and forth on the horse's back as if she were performing a sex act on a man from on-top.

I busted out in a full-on belly laugh. Paris tried to hold it back, in an effort, to look disgusted by Trudy's actions but failed. She laughed so hard she lost her voice to a silent laugh. Trudy laughed at us laughing, so hard she almost fell from her mount.

Laughing so hard, I dropped the reins and the wagon veered off the trail. At which point, the horses came to a stop and started grazing.

Ariel told us about a gorgeous lake she had come across not too far away. So, we bridled the horses and rode off bareback too. Just, with a few more clothes on. We left the team to graze with Jojo standing guard over them. It was obvious the dog was ready for a nice country nap. That evening found us at *Pollard's* hotel.

We spent the first few days there exploring the countryside, on horseback and on foot. All the while enjoying the hospitality of the hotel. We didn't expect such luxury in the wilderness.

It was there on the last night of our stay, that an old forty-niner showed up. He was half dead with exhaustion. With a fantastic story of being chased out of the wilderness by demons.

He told us he was the last of a handful of men that had traveled into the mountains with him. Whatever had taken place out there, he was almost mad with fear. Something had scared the living hell out of him. A thing unexpected in a seasoned mountain man. You could almost smell the fear on him. His eyes wide and staring, barely coherent in his jabbering.

I asked Mr. Pollard, "You know this man?"

He told me, "Joshua Clément is his name. Back during the heat of the goldrush, in these parts, he found himself a nice little stake of gold. He lost it all though to his drink... and women.

"These days, he acts as guide for folks still looking to strike it rich. He and six men were thru here a while ago. They were headed north from here to try their luck."

I listened to him tell what he knew of the man's story. After he told of all he knew, I went over to the old man and asked him again what had happened to him.

His story was more coherent this time, but still made no real sense. He said, "They killed everything...! Horses, mules, dogs and men, alike. They didn't want anything except to kill... and eat what they killed. Even the men were eaten.

"We were headed back here. They didn't attack us all at once. They played with us and toyed with our sanity as they took us out one at a time, over the two nights of the last new moon. When there is no moon, these woods become pitch black... you can't even see your hand in front of your face.

"I couldn't see what they did to the other men at first. I could only hear them being ripped apart and eaten.

"After that last night of killing, I was the only one alive. I knew they were on my trail. For the last week or so now, I have been on foot—praying to god—every second... to help me out of this hell hole. Why they didn't finish me off I don't know. I made my way back here by the grace of god and I will never go back. I'm leaving these parts for good and all.

"The devil and his hounds have taken up residence here...."

Mr. Pollard, half expecting trouble asked us to stay on for a few more days. He had never seen Clément in such a fright before that night. Nor had he ever known him to be a liar or tell whoppers just for attention.

If he was lying, then where were the men he took into the wilderness? Something had happened to him out there and it wasn't anything good.

Pollard wanted to be ready with as many guns as possible if trouble came to the hotel. Thinking it might be Indians on the war path. But even they, weren't cannibals, not in these parts for certain. Not man nor beast came calling in any fashion.

The girls were so in love with these mountains, we stayed a lot longer than we had planned. We didn't even realize, or think to concern ourselves with moon cycles, and that a new moon was upon us. By then, old man Clément was back to being, a person not so afraid of the dark again.

We were sitting together on the side of the hotel. Having our way with a bottle of some good whisky. Jo was laying at my feet. Clément was telling me all about the road to Salt Lake City; all the things not to miss of wilderness and towns alike.

Jojo, awakened from his slumber, jerked his head up and sniffed the air, then shined his teeth and growled at the woods. Clément asked me,

"What's he on about now? He looks like he got wind of his arch enemy."

That's when I heard it for the first time. It was long and deep as it echoed across our ears. It was the sound of a man screaming in horror and rage. An agonizing war cry of pain and despair. Blended with the most terrifying wolf howl of all time. The sound was coming from one creature… or two, in perfect harmony. Both being impossible and ridiculous explanations.

Old man Clément turned white as he jumped to his feet.

"They followed me…! Jesus, Mary and Joseph…! They followed me!"

"What the hell is it?" I asked.

"Hell! That's exactly what it is boy…! Hell—come a calling! They are demon dogs straight out of hell I tell ya!

"I've 'eard every sound—every creature makes in these parts…from—rats—to mountain-lions. I have 'eard every squeal and squall—Indians can muster…. I even tracked a Sass-quatch once…high up in the mountains. Although I never did catch sight of the damn-thing. All I ever found was hair and footprints. but I 'eard them screams them sons a bitches' make—though.... Ear'd it good—and I welcome it, to that abomination—just graced itself to our presence."

"Demon dogs...." I said. Thinking out loud more than anything else. Clément took it as a question. Saying,

"Damnit all—I never got a clear look at 'em. I 'eard them mostly. The sounds they make and the sounds of their butchering....

"The glimpses I caught in the dark and the sounds they made... leads me to believe it's... some-kind-of huge... rabid wolves. Way bigger than any wolf I've ever seen or even heard of. Bigger even than them white bastards in and around the Yukon river in the northwest territories."

Paris and Trudy joined us along with Mr. and Mrs. Pollard. Just as, whatever it was, sounded off again. Mrs. Pollard exclaimed,

"That's the most nightmarish sound I ever heard...! What is it that can sound like that?" No one answered her.

We all just sat and listened to it, dumb as to what it might be. All of us were ready to break and run. Even with weapons in hand, I didn't want to know or find out what it was in the dark.

Mrs. Pollard broke the silence again. Saying, "That god-awful sound is coming from across the river not too far from the crossing. That stagecoach that was the last one to leave here should be in those parts about now."

Clément lost a little composure, saying, "They'll not live to tell of it. Someone needs to go after them and with all haste. For just as sure as I am breathing... they are not prepared for what they're up against. You can bet your ass it won't be me going after them...!"

With Clément spooking everyone into action, A handful of men took off after the stagecoach about an hour later. The girls, Jojo and I, left before dawn that morning. Still oblivious to the new moon cycle almost upon us. Hearing no more of those outrageous and revolting sounds that night.

* * * * *

Narration–There were six men that'd left Pollard's that night, armed to-the-teeth and dressed for bear. Riding hard, they had made it to and had crossed the Truckee-river in record time.

They'd neither seen, nor heard, anything out of the forest since the river. No stagecoaches—coming or going…not even a weary traveler. That was strange enough all-by-itself. Yet, unknown to any of them, something critical had escaped them in their haste. Road Markers. They kept travelers on the main path through the wilderness.

The markers had been switched around at the old-road new-road split. Both would get you through the mountains, but the old road wasn't used anymore. It once was a lifeline, now it was just an arduous trek; through what was now, a very remote area of wilderness. In daylight, they would easily realize this. But for them, the coming of daylight was, forever and a day away….

Not yet aware of their perilous mistake, they were figuring, if they hadn't caught up by now at their pace, they wouldn't, and were discussing turning around when something spooked the horses. It was a dreadful foreboding….

Not a bird was chirping. The uneasiness of the horses being the only disruption to the silence.

All of them could tell something was watching them. They were as spooked as the horses.

The rider in the lead looked back at the man behind him. Without words, they both dismounted and pulled rifles from their cases.

The first man motioned the other to one side of the road. Cocking his rifle, he took to the other side. The rest held their place on the horses. The first man had just made it to the tree line and began to relieve himself.

Outside of the torchlight, as his eyes adjusted to the pitch-black, he noticed his piss was splashing back on him. As his eyes focused in on what he was pissing on, he suddenly realized it was a huge mishappen foot. His blood froze, swallowing his fresh chaw of tobacco whole.

He slowly lifted his eyes until he was staring the thing straight in its face. What he saw, took his breath away. It was big as a grizzly standing upright. But a bear was nothing. This was an abomination, far more threatening and malevolent.

He raised his rifle to fire; the creature flashed out an arm and bashed it down, snatching it away from him and tossing it into the torchlight.

All the men saw his rifle flung from the darkness, but none could see what was going on outside of the torchlight.

One of them called out, "What in tarnation Louis? Louis! Come-on now...so-we-can-git!

Before he could yell out, he was struck across his face; the blow killed him instantly. A blow of such force, no one who knew him could have recognized him.

The thing attacked his body as it fell. Both were inside the light of the torches now. It ripped an arm out of its socket and flung it at the others, as it tore free a huge chuck of flesh and swallowed it—whole.

Half of them panicked. It was a moment or two before everyone was trying to kill it.

At first, shooting only at the thing they could see, then in all directions, as they were hit from all sides. The screams and shrieks of horses and men rose to a fever pitch, equaling the sounds of their attackers. The scene quickly became one of nightmare, as the bodies of men and horses were gashed, torn and ripped to pieces.

Guts spilled onto the ground; heads were flung carelessly in the milieu of havoc. Bullets were flying in all directions, causing no real damage to their intended targets. Men slipped on their own entrails and were torn to pieces as they hit the ground. Atrocious onslaught quickly became unspeakable slaughter, with the insanity escalating,

Silence once again gripped the forest. With only the sounds of tearing and rending of flesh to be heard. Mixed with the crunching and breaking of bones filling the dawn air with its repugnant and nauseating racket.

* * * * *

Tristan–We made it to the Truckee river in no time at all.... It wasn't until almost dark, on the following day, when we found what was left of the men, that'd left Pollard's.

Their bodies and their horses were in—shreds. We almost vomited, at the sight of such a ghastly scene. No animal—would do such—horrendous ripping and tearing of flesh on a kill, nor sling guts and body parts so—blatantly.... Only man was capable of such malice.... Thinking aloud, I said,

"All of their belongings are—still—here…. Guns…food-n-ammo…boots…saddles…ropes…. Just—look! There's even—money —on-the ground…!

None of it has-been—pilfered—through. That takes bandits and hostile Indians—right off the list…."

It was upon closer inspection, that the truth of old man Clément's tale, came crashing down upon our senses. The bodies of both horses and men, had been gnawed on. hideous bite marks were plain everywhere. Huge chunks of flesh were missing, from what looked to be single bites, as cause for some of the damage to meat and bone.

Upon realizing this, the hair on my arms and neck stood on end. I looked up at the girls—and as if on Q…that horrifying sound echoed thru the darkening forest. It was not close, but still—it put the fear in—us. Jo let-out a low growl.

Paris said in a low voice,

"Let's go-back to Pollard's. We are—no-match—for whatever did this…. at least—let's go back to Gray's outpost at the river-crossing. Where we can get inside something—and board up. We could be hit from all directions—out here—and we have no experience in this kind-of—terrain."

"No! We keep on ahead. That last scream was between us and the river. It wasn't close enough—for it—to-be—after us. We get-in-the-wagon and haul-ass. We'll keep the horses saddled—and ready to ride…with saddle bags stuffed with all they will carry. Let's gather up all guns-and-ammo we can—from here—and skin-out….

"We'll ride hard-and-fast the rest of the night and—all-day—tomorrow…just as hard. Putting—as much distance—as we can from this place. If we see a need… we'll abandon the wagon and skin-out on the horses. Pick out a couple saddles and bridles for the wagon team. We may need them."

Trudy said to me, "We just haven't got any luck at keeping wagons—do we?"

"So-it-would-seem…. Let's just—hurry up with this—macabre shit —and git-outta-here—"

Paris voiced her disgust. "Are we just going to leave these men—like—this? After we've stripped them like—scavengers?"

"You god—damn—right—we—are! I do not want to come up against whatever did this! Not now, not ever!

"We been here too long already. The thing—or things—that did this is—vicious—and incredibly powerful…to be able to inflict this much damage to the flesh and bodies of these men and horses. As soon as we get to the next town or outpost, we will tell of what happened here."

Trudy said, "Tristan…? I'm afraid…."

With a calmer voice, I told her, "So-am-I babysugar… so am I…."

"Look…. I know this shit is worthy of—freaking the fuck out right—now…. And if it makes either of you feel better to know—I wish we were all in a boat right—now—on the fucking ocean? Then we should all start feeling a whole-lot-better any moment…."

"Let's just get this distasteful and disgusting task over with and skin—the fuck—outta here…!

"Paris my voodoo… I'm sorry…. This is all new to me. And I am man enough to admit it's got my hair standing on end…."

With remorse she said, "Don't be. You're right—about it all. Let's just do what we must and go—"

We gathered what we could and got the hell-out-of-there. Ariel drove the wagon team on with Paris in the back, rifle ready. I rode along beside them on Sarah, rifle in hand, scouting the trail ahead and behind thru the night.

We pushed on hard all night and all day the next day. Switching up so one of us got a little sleep in turn during the day. By nightfall, we were more than exhausted; sleep came fast. What we didn't realize, is that we took the wrong road early-on…and were only heading deeper into the mountain wilds.

* * * * *

Narration–Tristan awoke suddenly, from an awful nightmare. Creepy, to say the least; although, nothing, compared to how creeped-out he felt, now that—he was awake. A thin fog had form; dead silence loomed over the forest, the air deathly still. The girls sat up abruptly, instantly alerted to the threat of impending peril.

Their campfire was struggling to stay alive. Ariel quickly jumped to the task of reviving it. She stoked the fire and stood next to it, shaking out her long black hair. Warming herself as flames blazed-up.

She unfastened her shirt and rubbed her breasts with warmed hands, pinching her nipples to relieve their hardness from the chilly night. She then turned her buttocks to the flames and arched her back as she rubbed them.

Reaching down, she closed a hand on her crotch, acting as one needing to pee. Continuing her pee-dance to the edge of the fire light, she undid her pants and pulled them half off her hips, exposing her rear, as she stepped into the darkness.

Once in the shadows, she quickly pulled her pants up, fastened them, and buttoned her shirt. She hoped her little spectacle had given Tristan and Paris a chance to slip away and fade into the night, unnoticed, like the Apache had taught them.

Instantly, she felt a freakish chill of the supernatural envelop her. Expecting, any second, to see an apparition of a long dead ghost, murdered most hideously, now haunting her, out of revenge. The forest became unnaturally alive, yet, eerily quiet. Every breath, seemed to cast, an echo.

It was behind her now… an icy chill went up her back….

No sound of step, no one else breathing, but clearly, a presence. So close, she thought she felt a breath on her neck, expecting to be touched any second. Dread of the paranormal overpowered her resolve; she darted back into the firelight, snatched up a rifle, and turned her back to the flames.

Tristan and Paris hurried from the darkness as well, faces white with fear. They both took up positions around the fire with Ariel, weapons in hand. Tristan lit one of the makeshift torches they'd prepared, and tried to scan deeper into the ghostly blackness with it, while saying to the girls, "There are some spooky affairs taking place here—"

Paris cut him off, "Well, I'll be damned if I'll chase a ghost thru the woods! Nor will I wait in the shadows for it to touch me again!"

Ariel shot a quick look over her shoulder at her. "Touched you?"

"Fucking touched me!" Paris answered.

"Ariel told her, "I felt a presence too…it didn't touch me though…I didn't give it a chance to…freaked me the fuck out. That's why I raced back beside the fire—so fast."

Tristan followed up, "So-did-I, what in the Sam hell is happening—?"

Just then, the silence was broken, by whispering, and loud movement. There seemed to be people all around them, just outside the light of the fire. Their noises escalating in volume with each passing moment. Taking its toll on the girls and Tristan's fight flight or-freeze response.

Multiple pairs of eyes, with a ghostly glow, then appeared out of the dank darkness. Eyes that were neither animal nor human. They seemed to float eerily—free of an earthly body.

The whispers ceased; silence gripped the forest once again. Tristan was fully in the grip of his own fear, as he forced himself forward, towards those eyes.

Waves of chills ran thru him, as he tossed his torch into the middle of whatever it was, staring back-at-him from the pitch-black. As the torch hit the ground, illuminating the spot filled with eyes, all words were choked back in his throat.

Nothing was—there.... No eyes—no bodies—nothing. Only empty space filled the torch light. The whispers instantly started up again. This time much louder in volume—than before.

Paris felt a deep chill crawl up her spine—yet again. She could feel something, or someone, standing behind her on the other side of the fire. She turned slowly...looking over her shoulder...and was condemned into despair.

On the other side of the fire, stood the ghostly figure of a dead woman. Her skin was—blue with death, her—eyes oozing—from their sockets—with rot. Her body was covered with gruesome wounds, and missing chunks of flesh that looked to have been torn away as if she were eaten by—whatever had killed her.

The woman screamed at Paris, yet there was no sound. No sound at-all.... There was only expression showing desperate need to communicate. As though she was trying to warn her, of some terrible foreboding.

The woman's face went blank, taking on a look of someone straining to hear, then turning slowly to looked over her shoulder, terrified of what she might see...just frozen in place.

When she looked back at Paris again, her facial expression was one of dreadful anticipation. She mouthed—one—final—word. *"Run!"*

The phantom woman turned to run away from whatever was coming. Filling Paris with even more frightful misgivings. As the woman turned, she vanished into nothingness.

Before anyone could blink, a blood freezing howl-scream penetrated the night. Something, big and hideous, jumped out of the darkness and went for Ariel.

Jojo jumped in front of her and leaped on the evil thing charging at her. It grabbed him like a toy, ripped him open at throat and stomach and tossed him like a rag doll.

Now that it was inside the firelight, Tristan could see it plain. It was a demon. Not that he had ever imagined what a demon should look like, it was just the only word that came to him.

He shot at it, but it kept its charge full-on at Ariel. She raised her rifle to fire; it knocked it away effortlessly and gutted her with a swipe of its claw across her belly. Her intestines spilled onto her feet. She looked down at her guts on the ground, then back up at the thing in front of her. Her eyes rolled up in her head as she lost consciousness. It grabbed her and ripped a huge chunk of her throat out with its powerful jaws.

Another one grabbed Paris from behind and twisted her head completely around, one hundred and eighty degrees, and began viciously mauling her face and throat. She was dead before the horrible rending of her flesh began.

Tristan screamed out in horror and disbelief. But before he could charge at the demon closest to him, something grabbed him by the shoulder, stopping him in his tracks. It spun him around on his heals as if he were a child. He was yet again, frozen in place with shock and awe, unable to speak.

It was the ghost of the woman Paris had seen. She was nose-to-nose with him. This time, there was sound. She let out a piercing scream, making him drop his rifle and cover his ears. All he could do was stare, utterly fixated on her rotted face. Before she stopped screaming, something grabbed hold of him from behind and took him to the ground. A multitude of hideous wolfs, began mauling him from head to toe.

He gave no effort to resist. Mentally, he was ready to go to heaven and find his women. For these last seconds of life, all he could do was look on at his lovers lying dead and torn to pieces. He felt no physical pain as he was split open and pulled apart; all he felt was the devastating emotional pain from watching helplessly at his lovers, as their hearts were torn from their opened chests. That was the last thing he saw, of this nightmarish scene, with eyes.

An enormous White Wolf stepped over top of him. He felt it clamp down on his throat, with tremendous force. Blood splattered and gushed as his head parted from his body and rolled to a stop.

Tristan instantly found himself conscious again, seeing from a distance, the scene of insanity still taking place. He watched as his body and the bodies of his lovers were devoured. Something rolled against his foot, then another. He looked down, to see what they were. It was the heads of his lovers. He was swept up with unbridled remorse. A pain, far too great to bear.

Something hit him in his chest with a heavy thump, knocking him backwards and causing him to stumble. The thing that had smacked his chest was now at his feet. It was another head. A head he did not recognize; he forgot all else in that moment, as he wondered about the head. He reached down and picked it up, turning it in his hands to see who it was.

The eyes were still open; it was—his—face. This—was his—head! Terror seized him; he tried to yell out, but as he held his own head in his hands, staring in horror into his own face…the eyes in the head blinked. A bloody smile parted its lips. He shuddered at the sight of seeing that the teeth in the head were fangs.

Then he noticed, his own image, as he stared into the mirrored lenses of those eyes. But the image was confusing, his mouth was blood smeared; his eyes were identical to the demons that were gorging on his women.

A bloody claw clasped his shoulder with a grip that bruised the flesh and fractured cartilage. He looked up to see a hideous face, blood dripping and drool oozing from its jaws. It gave a grotesque smile as it showed him a human heart in its other hand. He opened his mouth to yell-out. As he did, the thing shoved the heart in his mouth. And what frightened him into even greater despair, was the fact that he instantly found the taste, appealing.

The creature continued to stare, as Tristan involuntarily took a bite. He was mortified by his own actions; he spit and flung the heart to the ground. The creature began to laugh.

The world began to rock and spin out of control. As everything faded to black, the demon vanished; the wolves ran off. A blinding white light hit him, like a shockwave. Dazzling his senses before flashing out of existence, its afterglow fading fast, leaving him engulfed in a void of pitch-black. Until…he opened his eyes.

He jumped to his feet, rifle in hand, spinning around, wanting a fight. He could still feel the bites and wounds he had received. Though upon inspection, there wasn't a scratch.

A hand touched his shoulder from behind…he yelled out in surprise and spun around…. It was Paris! She was alive!

Paris jumped back and away from him as she saw the look in his eyes. He was white as a ghost. She had never seen—him so addled.

Physically, he was catatonic; Internally, behind those eyes, were the hysterical manifestations of a soul that'd touched lunacy, and tasted madness, at their most diabolical and debauched.

Ariel and Jojo were up-and-at-attention. Ariel had a rifle in her hands, ready for a fight, same as Jo.

Paris moved toward Tristan again and put her hand on his cheek. "You have had a nightmare—my love. It's alright. Nothing is here. We are ok. You, are ok…."

Tristan dropped the rifle and snatched her up in his arms. He cried as he held her tight.

Trudy began to tear up at the sight of him. She walked over to them; and as Tristan saw her, he grabbed her too, and began to cry, all over again.

"Jojo! He exclaimed. "Where is Jojo? Jo!" The dog came over to him. Tristan looked at him and then back at the girls, then he cried out, "Thank god it was just a dream! A nightmare—I never want as a reality! Gather-up—we're out of here—right now!"

They quickly gathered themselves and got underway. Riding hard again thru the night till the sun light was cresting the mountains. Exhausted, they finally stopped to rest the horses and have a bite to eat. Tristan told the girls of his nightmare in full detail.

"Who do you think the woman was?" asked Paris.

"I am sure, I have no idea. It all seems silly now. I think all the spooky shit we've been confronted with got the best of me—is all. I feel fucking stupid now that the sun is up."

They blew it off and got underway. Feeling less and less anxious about all that had happened, as the day grew shorter.

Towards late afternoon, exhaustion overtook them again. While the girls set up a camp and got a fire going, Tristan cleaned and prepared a deer he'd killed with his bow, earlier that morning.

After some good food, wash-up and clean clothes, they broke out a bottle of whisky and poured some in their tin-cups. Tristan filled each of their pipes (gifts from the Apache), from his pouch of strange tobacco, he had bought in Sacramento. He couldn't remember what it was called, but it gave off an awesome feeling of content and relaxation to anyone who took a puff-or-two....

Less than an hour into their little party, they were startled out of their high. By the last thing, they ever wanted to hear again. It wasn't far-off in the distance—this time. It was close.

The sound of those demonic screams—so close, were hauntingly unnerving. More terrifying than anything else—thus far—they had ever dealt with before.

Tristan grabbed up his repeater-rifle and cocked it, saying, "That was no ghostly sound... it was real.... Real means it's of this world.... No matter how demonic or diabolical its origin—if it makes sound—it breathes air...which means—we can kill it—"

Saying it out-loud, restored his confidence a little. Tristan was mentally preparing himself for a fight of which he had no idea on which front it would be fought. Mental, physical or all the above.

The girls grabbed the other two rifles and rushed over to Tristan. Putting their backs to each other, they all slid down onto one knee, with rifles aimed, and ready for a fight.

After a short drink of silence, a lone wolf howled far off in the distance. As it did, Tristan was struck with an epiphany. His inner voice spoke of it—as he said it out-loud.

"That's what it is, that sound...sounds kind-of-like a wolf's howl. Only much more sinister and—terrible. A sound outside of what earthly nature—conjures...but that's exactly what it sounds like! A howling... evil demon-wolf, and a screaming man, of diabolical insanity...merged as one.

"Like the sounds in my nightmare. Oldman Clément wasn't crazy—after-all.

Another voice was added to the horrendous chorus of sounds. It sounded—exactly like—a woman sounding-off an unnerving scream—of horrible—bloody-murder... at the top-of-her-lungs, over-and-over-again. It echoed through the forest.... But they were all familiar with that—sound.

It wasn't a woman; it was a mountain lion. And, that last howl, was a wolf of nature. What those howling-scream sounds were made by, none of them had the slightest idea.

Tristan went on. "It's like a human screaming...and...a wolf howling.... Fused... into one-long-screaming-howl. Actually..., it begins—with a howl, then it ends—with the scream trailing off... but the howl and scream...are one. One of the scariest damn-things—I—ever heard...let alone the fact it's coming from one throat....

"It has to be Indians...or some other men, trying to scare the-shit-out of us. Some kind of—sick joke maybe... before they move in for the kill. Figuring—if we are petrified...we won't be able to defend ourselves."

Ariel, her anger beginning to overcome her stark fear, exclaimed, "Well it's—fucking—working...! I'm beyond scared! I'm scared-shitless...! And not by some stupid fucks running around out there with sheets over them either....!

"That screaming howl...? I know it's a howling-scream.... Scream-howl just—rolls off the tongue better for me—But...but...no human or animal I've ever heard... or heard of... is capable of—that shit....! Could it be that Sass-Crotch creature? We heard them talking about...? In Sacramento? They said—they're all over these parts...."

Tristan looked back at Ariel. Staring at her in wonder. Saying to her, "You mean, Sass-quatch...,"

Could it be...? this Sass-quatch creature...? Spoken of throughout these parts? By Indian and Whiteman all? Tristan thought on it for a moment. Then he remembered what Clément, the old forty-niner, had said that night at Donner pass. The first-time they heard this god-awful sound.

He said, "Old man Clément told me... that first night... he had heard the screams of those Sass-quatch more than a few times. He had even tracked one deep into the mountains... he said, it was a welcomed sound, compared to that horrifying squalling we heard that first night—together.

"Sooner-or-later, we will learn the truth of what it is that's making that noise. Whatever it is, it—will—come for us… It's hunting us—

"Stalking us like prey… then toying with us. To scare us like one would do children in the darkness…. Only the psychotic whims of murdering lunatics and madmen are capable of such malevolence.

"Don't fire any shots, until whatever it is out there…steps in here—to the fire light…and shows us—the whites of their eyes…or you see the muzzle blast of enemy fire. The second step it takes toward any of us… Light the fuckers up….

"Just—don't empty your rifles at just one…in case there actually is…more than one. God-help-us-this-night…."

Guessing, that whatever was after them, knew right where they were, they stoked the fire, so that it was blazing.

Maybe—they were afraid of fire like most wild creatures. If not, at least they would see what was trying to terrorize, kill and eat them. Just as the bastards had done to everything else, so far.

Jo, silently, slinked off into the darkness. None of them even noticed that he had left.

Something huge was moving around not too far outside the light of the fire. They all heard its guttural growls and rattle of breath. Whatever it was, it was not on all fours. It was bi-pedal steps they heard crunching the ground as it moved around them.

Tristan grabbed up a torch from the fire and told the girls to do the same. He held it high, hoping to shine some eyes out of the dark. His patience getting away from him, he said,

"Motherfucker…! This is intolerable! If you're going to attack us, then do it god damn-it—!"

Something came thrashing towards them from the opposite side of the camp. It was the side Ariel faced and was defending. Tristan and Paris spun around, ready to unload on whatever came at them. A huge black body came into the light. They drew their guns back and let out a simultaneous sigh of relief. It was Jojo.

Ariel said, "He is on about something! What is it boy? What do you want us to see?" she asked him, then she quickly realized, "He wants us to follow him!"

Paris yelled, "look…! Look there…! Thru the trees and down the slope!" It was a cabin with lanterns burning in the windows.

As Tristan and Ariel caught sight of it, Ariel said, "Do we jump on the horses and make a break for it...? Or face this thing here, on its own—terms?"

Tristan told them, "We go for the cabin. When I say...we run for the horses and head for the cabin."

He looked at both the girls in turn. Seeing no doubt in their eyes, he started counting. "One, two... three! Skin out! go—go—go!"

In the blink of an eye, they were on the horses and hell-bent for the cabin. The horses sprang into a gallop and then took off into a full run; the scream-howl sounded off again. This time, it was right behind them.

The sound of something running thru the woods behind them, panicked the horses even more. They broke-out into an almost uncontrollable run. Not that any of the three wanted control. They let up full on the bridles around their horses' necks, holding on for dear life.

They raced passed trees, under low hanging limps and branches. Letting the horses do what they do best when spooked, run like the wind.

The horses, by the grace of god, ran straight for the cabin. It took all their strength to rein them in before crashing into the front of it.

As they jumped from their backs, Tristan smacked his sweet Sarah on her ass as hard as he could and fired a couple of shots from his pistol, into the air. Screaming as he did so, "Hyah—girl! Hyah! Get-the-hell-outta-here! Hyah!"

She broke and run like her ass was on fire and her head was catching; the other two were fast behind her.

The cabin door almost burst from its hinges as they flew through it. Tristan spun and slammed it closed, locking the bolts down. He was surprised it was unlocked and a little open in the first place. After bolting the door, they looked around...it seemed to be, no one was home.

Howl-screams sounded off again. They were just outside now... and there was more than one. That much was now clear. At least, two distinct growls and guttural sounds were coming from out of the darkness. It was Jojo again who queued them in, to a next move.

He was sniffing at the floor. Tristan saw it was a cellar door. He ran over to it and yanked on it. It was locked from the inside.

Just as he realized that someone must be down there, bullets began flying up through the floor all around him. He dove aside to escape the onslaught of bullets that buzzed around him like angry bees. Slamming himself against the wall and yelling out. His words sounding more like single syllables then whole words. "Son—of—a—bitch...!

Believing that any second was his last, unconscious of what he was saying, in the Cuban tongue, he screamed at whoever was shooting, "Pas Cone Tu Madre Cojone Chico!"

Which by best English translation means, "*Motherfucker—the balls on you!*"

The bullets ceased and a voice rang out from below.

"Who's up there? Get away from here damnit? I swear...I'll kill you!"

Tristan exclaimed, "You open this fucking-god-damn cellar door! Now! Or its you who will die this night! Right along with—me!"

The sound of a heavy bolt sliding back caught Tristan's ears. The door flew up and a man stuck his head up out of the opening. Rifle butt to his shoulder, aiming right at Tristan. After a short stare down, the man said, "Fuck you!"

As he cocked the lever and prepared to fire, his actions were halted abruptly as he felt the cold steel of a pistol barrel touch the back of his head, then heard the hammer cock back.

In a low voice of deadly intent, Ariel told him,

"Hand me the rifle, real slow... or your brains come out thru your forehead...."

Paris shouted, "Tristan look...what are those!"

She pointed over to the fireplace. In front of the blazing fire were whisky bottles, with strips of rags hanging out of them.

The door almost burst into splinters as something hit it with a massive impact. The growls and roaring coming from the other side of the door was deafening, terrifying and discouraging—coupled with the door being beat and scratched at, about to be torn from its lodging at any second.

Paris and Tristan fired at the door. Sending splinters of wood flying. Hoping to kill the thing or things trying to break it down.

"Bullets won't kill them! They only back them off for moments! Soon they won't even care! The bottles of kerosene! They're our only chance!" said the man with Ariel's pistol to his head.

"Let me help you? We either help each other or we all die… Just like you said."

Trudy drew her gun away from his head and he climbed out of the cellar.

"Quickly now, grab a bottle in each hand fella. You girls light those two torches next to the fireplace and get ready to light these wicks."

"Wait…help me with this table!" Tristan shouted.

The man knew instantly what he wanted to do and grabbed one side of the table. They slid it up against the door. It was a huge heavy oak table. It would supply some counter to the terrible thrashing on the door, but not much.

Both men quickly snatched up a bottle in each hand. The girls had already lit the torches and stood beside them as they each chose a window. The door assault stopped as suddenly as it had begun. There was a haunting silence, it seemed to last forever.

Tristan said, "As much as I hate stating the obvious…the windows have boards across them. How do you pur-pose we throw these at them without setting the whole place on fire?"

"They will bust thru those boards like kindling. When they do, light the bastards up!"

Everything was all silence now. Tristan moved a little closer to the window in front of him, trying to see into the darkness outside. The fire burning inside the fireplace made it impossible to see anything. As he took a step closer, Jojo growled and shined his teeth.

As Jo's growl hit Tristan's ears, a monstrous set of hands with huge claws burst thru the boards in front of him. Followed by two more doing the same on the other window.

"Now! light the wicks!"

The girls lit the wicks and both men thru them through the windows with all their strength.

The bottles busted against something just outside of each window. The outside in front of the windows filled with fire light as the kerosene in them began to spread and burn. The screaming howls quickly changed to agonizing cries of pain and anguish. Human cries....

Of that, there was no doubt in anyone's mind. Tristan caught a glimpse of something big running away, trying to put out the fire that engulfed it. The other man ran to the window in front of him and tossed the other bottle he had in his hand that Paris lit for him.

He tossed it out the window a few yards in front of the cabin into a depression in the ground. Fire blazed up as the bottle burst on the ground and quickly spread in a straight line in both directions. Encircling the house with one unbroken flame of fire.

"I dug a trench around the house and filled it with all the kerosene and pitch I could spare for the first burn. That box over there has dynamite sticks in it. Those bastards don't like the bang they make. Not one bit. There are a few barrels of kerosene and pitch outside. We'll need to stoke the trench fire when it starts to die-out.

"Or they'll be back as soon as it does—"

Tristan looked at him cross. "Back...? They just ran off burning to death! Are there more than two of the damn cursed things...?"

"I don't know how many there are! All I do know is, they'll be back as soon as that fire dies down much or goes out—all together.... Sunrise is what we got to hold out for. At all cost."

Tristan looked at Paris and Trudy.

Both were scared out of their minds, but no-worse-for-wear. He picked up his pistol and checked it for bullets. Realizing as he did that his hands were shaking uncontrollably.

Seeing Tristan's hands shaking, right along with his own, the man of the house set the bottles on the table and walked over to the cupboard. He brought out a bottle of whisky and four glasses. He poured everyone a drink and sat down.

Saying, "Forgive me for trying to kill you earlier. When those creatures are about, I don't think to straight...and you three—busting through my door was the last thing I expected tonight. When I heard the sniffing on the floor from your dog...I panicked.

"If you hadn't rattled off in that Caribbean tongue...I don't know...it's gotten so crazy here before when those damnable things are a bout...I don't know that I'd have opened that door or even stopped the shootin had you not spit that Caribbean lingo and accent.... What dialect is that—anyway...?"

"Cuban—" ... Tristan told him.

"That's not something you hear around these parts. Accents' way different than Mexican...." Then he noticed, their inability to take their eyes from the window or stop checking that their pistols were fully loaded. Telling them,

"Ya'll can set down them—bags of nails—you're carrying around like monkeys on your back and let your insides simmer down a little, if you won't to.... Till that fire dies down a little you ain't to worry about them getting in here...they don't test that fire...and they don't go aces high for big bangs either...like dynamite and nitro-glycerin...wish we had some nitro....

"So that was Cuban dialect you say? You speak it good for a—Florida Cracker...." He put up a hand to refrain Tristan from asking the question now burning his lips.

Saying, "I've cracked a whip or two in my time...you have to forgive me if I'm babbling on.... I ain't seen hide nor hair of another person since been so long I've plum forgot... but I can tell your all balled up...I spect you got questions about these damn hell-spawns...."

Ariel asked, "What are they? Where do they come from?"

"I don't know what they are or where. They've plagued me here for some two...almost three months now. Before then I had neither seen nor heard one before. They only attack when there's a full moon or no moon out....

"On the nights of the full moon, they will kill one or two things, eat most of it and leave...when there is no moon— like tonight, they maul and shred anything that moves...you can beat your head against the barn...I just caint figure 'em...I swanny I caint.... I thought they were gone when the last two nights passed without incident. I guess I was mistaken.

"They were just busy with you folks.

"They murdered my wife and ate her as I watched...before dragging her body off. I've not been able to find any remains of her.

"They snatched my little boy and girl right out of my arms thru the window and left their guts and brains on the ground right outside the door as if to taunt me.

"That portrait painting on the wall and a few belongings is all I have left of them."

Tristan looked up at the painting on the wall of the man's wife and children, noticing it for the first time. His face went white, as he turned and mechanically walked towards the portrait. Unconsciously dropping the gun in his hand as he did so.

Paris asked, "What is it…what's-the—matter?"

"The woman. The—woman—in this portrait…. It's the—dead-woman—from my dream."

Both-the-girls felt a chill run-up their backs as their skin crawled….

Ariel, talking-to-herself, said, "As-if—demon-monsters—weren't—bad-enough…. No…let's—shove- another-cock-up-our-ass….! Let's add—ghosts—to-the—mix….

"Am-I—gonna wakeup in my bed…? I'm—going-to wake-up—in—my—bed…! this all can't really be happening to us…. God please, let me wake up in my fucking bed.…"

The man asked Tristan, "You've seen—my-wife…?"

"Only in a dream…. She was dead and half eaten…facts that are only—now—becoming clear."

The man said to him, "She had the-sight…. She'd see things that would come-to pass….

"If-I-know—my—darling-sweet—Emma…she was trying to warn you…or fetch you to-my—aid…. Or both.…"

Ariel chimed-in again, "Well—fucking—mission-accomplished—!

"Why-have-you stayed here with all—this shit—happening—to you?"

He looked at her with cold eyes and said, "Where—am—I…to—go…. How…am I…to go…. They've killed all my horses…and I wasn't about to try my luck on-foot…. Not with them—hellion's—playing patty-cake out there…

"No… I hunkered down here, asbest I could, on my own. Fire seems—to influence-them. So, once I realized their pattern of full-moon—no-moon attacks…I'd light the fireplace…set lanterns in-front-of-the-windows…and lock myself in the cellar.…

"Keepin-the-noise-down…whether I'd—heard-them—or not. They'll go after even the—slightest—sound.…

"I leave the door—ajar…so they won't bust it down if they got brave—enough to come-in here-with the fire—crackling.

"All—my—supplies is-about—plum-out.... I-got-no—hankering—what—um-gun-do—after they've—hit-me—a few—more—times."

Tristan responded first, "You'll come-with—us.... Safety in numbers—my-friend... 'We head for the Truckee and back to Pollards hotel."

With despair in his voice, he said, "Weeol-never-make-it-there... Not—on—foot....

"In-you-can—bet-your-ass...they've—killed—the-horses—I heardja-ride-up—on...and anything else—with a heartbeat—

"Tonight was-the first time, I's able-to defend against them, to the point of them runnin-off.... That fire shore-did put ahurtin on their ass!

"With your help...we can kill these things—once and for all."

Tristan snapped back angrily, "Fuck...that!"

"I'm not willing to throw away our lives—in some mad—hair-brained attempt at—revenge—for you-or-your place.

"If we survive this night...we leave with the dawn—and make a run for it—" ... The man cut Tristan off,

saying, "You're down-by-nine feller, I'mma tryin to—"
Tristan cut him-off. "No—I ain't—missing the god damn point...! You—"

Ariel broke-in. "Tristan...he's right.... Without the damn horses, we don't have a chance at making it back to the river—from way-out here...let-alone Pollard's.... And then what? We hide behind the Pollard's...?

"What I'm trying to say is.... are you fucking—stupid...? We barely out-ran them on the horses.... Another minute-or-so...and they'd a caught-us.... So, we barely escape on the horses...and—now—you-wanna—play—tenderfoot—with—these—wacked out fucks? ... Help me here...."

Tristan exclaimed, "I don't know—god-damnit...I don't know...! All I do know is...staying here and duking-it-out with these—demented fucks—is more than—fucking stupid, it's downright fucking suicide...!" There was silence.

Ariel knew he was right, but she needed to vent. Saying, "Deciding to come on this—romp—across the country was hard enough—thinkin I might die.... If you'd told me I was going to be shot at....and had to kill people.... I might've reconsidered.... And let's not leave-out these mean ass bastards…. No-no. Can't—leave—out—those mad fucks!"

Tristan jumped in, "How's I suppose to know any of that shit was going to happen? Or this…this stupid fucking shit?"

Ariel kept on, "Everybody—always leads with…this will be fun…. How-bout…Ariel….? If you go-on-this-trip with us…you—will—fucking—die…. And…you will be—shot-at…. Be forced to-kill—mother fuckers…. And—you'll be chased thru the woods by hell-raising-demons—that aren't supposed to exist…. But-they-do…! Oh Yeah! An—you might-have to watch—Paris and I get eaten—too—"

"How was I—" She cut him right off.

Instantly retorting with, "How-was-I—how was I—how was I…. Why don't you-just go—fuck yourself…!"

"Ok children… let's just stop the caterwauling—shall-we…?"

"And you can—fuck off—too! You simple country-fuck!"

Tristan told him, "You're not helping…stay out of it."

Then he turned back to Ariel. "Ariel…baby sugar…. I'm sorry? I mean… what do you—want— me to-say…?"

Paris countered. "Why don't both you—shut-up? Pisces-women and Aries-men…why me…?"

The man of the house butted in, "This is the last night of the new-moon phase. They won't be back till the full moon. Not to attack anyways. That is how it's been so far.

"That would give us plenty of time to outsmart these bastards and be done with it."

Paris retorted, "Full moon - blue moon! They've been after us for days…! And what if it's more than just a couple responsible for this ruckus? What if there are dozens more?

"We've seen firsthand their destructive power. They tore six men and their horses to pieces like they were pinatas! Why—would you even wanna—stay—in-this—insane asylum—of forest…?"

Tristan cut all-of-them off, "Look, lets worry about surviving the night. Then we will figure out our best course of action. Until this night is over, it's all a moot point…."

Chapter seven

Out of the fire and straight into hell

The night was desperate, and fright filled. Instead of battling fires all night to keep safe, they eventually retreated into the cellar, and kept the noise down. There were a few more intense encounters, before and after they locked themselves down in the cellar, but come the morning sunrise, they were all still alive.

Everyone had fallen asleep from exhaustion. When they woke up and realized it was already midmorning, they began at once to assess their situation.

Looking outside, they were surprised, and elated, to see the horses had survived the night. They were grazing in the field in front of the cabin as though it was just another day.

After proper introductions, during the night, they learned that the man's name was Horace Franklin.

Horace and Tristan wasted no time in mounting up and riding out to see if the wagon and horse team had survived the night. They rode back to the camp Tristan and the girls had escaped from.

After about an hour or so they found the wagon in a small glade. To their surprise, the horses were still alive. They were spooked out of their minds, but with a little coaxing, they were able to retrieve them and the wagon, back to the cabin.

Paris and Ariel were relieved to see them return safe. They couldn't help letting out a few hoots and hollers as they saw them returning with the wagon and all their supplies still in it. It seemed God and his angels were listening to their prayers after-all. Now they had a chance for all four of them to make a break for civilization.

They took a few minutes to eat what was left of the deer meat from the night before. With full bellies, they all took up tasks. The women stoked the fire in the fireplace and sliced up the rest of the venison for beef jerky, all the while, fast cleaning and loading all the guns and counting bullets.

The men had been planning strategies since they woke-up and were now putting plans into action. They cleared and stuffed all the saddlebags with essentials only, checked and cleaned the horses' hoofs and shoes., prepped dynamite for fast use. Trying their damnedest not to miss any critical items or preps that might slow their pace or weaken their response-times to threats.

They'd decided the wagon would only slow them down; horseback would be their best bet. No nighttime breaks, except to cool and water the horses. Sleep would be obtained in the form of alternating catnaps on horseback, during the day.

Tristan, curious about what was harassing them, took of few minutes to study their tracks. They were footprints in-as-much-as they were animal tracks.

While he was examining the prints, Horace said to him, "They leave a trail that is dadburn easy to follow. Though I've never had the sand to track them on my own. Their tracks have always led off in the same direction. That direction leads up the mountain. Up close to the summit is a large cave system. I'd bet my last dollar that's where they're hold up—"

Tristan put a hand up. "Let me just stop you right there… we have no clue as to how many there even are—as if one ain't enough…. I don't want to hear any more of this honor-glory-revenge—till the last man standing—bullshit…! You have a death wish? Be my guest—

"If you want, I'll shoot you right now … if it's a death wish you have….

"It would take—fuckin armies—to storm those bastards…. And if there are more than a few—it would be—leading lambs to the slaughter. So—focus please…? On the tasks at hand…. If we work together at one agreed on purpose… We'll make it back to civilization in one piece. Then you can muster all the fools and armies you want…come back up here and see which side gets massacred."

Tristan saw his face light up at the thought of an army of men at his back. Horace spoke no more of going after the beasts. He doubled his efforts in prepping for getting out of there and back to the world of men. There he would gather a force and return to exact his revenge.

* * * * *

The team of horses from the wagon gave them the extra horse they needed for Horace, plus an extra horse to pack supplies onto. Most of what they packed on the extra horse was for defense against attack more than any other necessities. Though Horace had told them they would not attack again for a while, Tristan wasn't taking any chances.

The things he had seen, heard and been confronted by were straight out of monster legends and Dante's Inferno. If someone would have recounted this tale of horrors to him, he wouldn't have believed them. He barely believed it now, but facts were facts. He couldn't deny his own senses.

What was happening to them, here and now, was as real as real gets. If he were to die and get his women killed in the process, it would be on his terms. With everything done to prevent it that he could muster.

They left the cabin late in the day. The girls and Tristan were wary of the nighttime travel but chose swift travel over fortification.

Horace found it difficult to keep up with them. He wasn't the accomplished rider that the three of them clearly were.

He could think of no one who rode with their skill, save for a few Indians. They rode in a unison that was remarkable to him. It was as though they were thinking all from the same brain.

Tristan, he understood easy enough. A man in charge and fully capable. The women, on the other hand, had him a little vexed: the way they carried themselves, their abilities under extreme pressure, able to think on their feet, their skills on horseback and with weapons, were as uncanny as anything else he had witnessed these passed months. He had seen highly trained veteran war soldiers, during the northern aggression, buckle under lesser conditions. Not to mention how drop dead gorgeous they both were.

* * * * *

It was another starless night they rode through, in their haste for the river. Sacramento was the planned destination. Come hell or high water—that was the plan.

It was a little after midnight when they stopped for a rest in a small clearing with a creek running thru it. They had barely got the horses watered and sat down to eat a bite, when their ears were blasted by multiple scream-howls.

They were barely able to grab the horses before they broke and ran. Ariel was the first one with words for Horace. "So much for your extraordinary theory of moon cycles." All three were staring now. Horace said,

"I never claimed to be an expert. I can only go off what I've seen them do so far. I can't explain it, nor do we have time to debate it. We're sitting ducks out here in the open like this!"

Tristan could make out shadows moving in the tree-line. Holstering his pistol, he turned and shouted, "He's right! No time to argue! There was a trail about a quarter mile back the way we came. It looks like it winds around the summit.

"We head for that and—pray they don't cut us off."

Paris reached for the rifle on her horse. Tristan was running now towards the packhorse as he yelled to her, "No!

"We ride, and we ride hard. This is about escape, not confrontation. If we have—to fight—we do it on horseback with pistols. If we must fight, don't shoot blindly. Choose your targets and conserve your ammo. At least—until we can get to cover that won't allow them to *git* around-back of us."

The others were mounting up as Tristan told them the plan. He pulled out his knife and cut the straps that held the packs on the back of the packhorse. He threw the saddle bags across his horse's butt and secured them to his saddle.

He then said to the pack horse, "Good luck boy." He then slapped him on the ass to put him in motion.

As he mounted Sarah's back, he said, "No matter what, no one gets left behind.... Now let's go! Skin-out! Hyah!"

Horace was worried he wouldn't be able to keep up with them. It was Tristan's words of no one left behind that gave him the courage to try. And try he did. They rode like the wind for the trail.

Horace knew that cutoff. It was a treacherous trail that quickly narrowed into a skinny pass that run along the side of a gorge, barely wide enough for the horses.

Hard enough to traverse in the daytime, leading a horse. In the dark, on the run, it was a death trap.

Better to die that way than to be eaten by these unnatural bastards he thought.

The scream-howls and growling behind them, let them know their flight wasn't a waste of time. The girls and Tristan were side-by-side as they raced for the trail. Horace was close on their heels.

They made the pass in no time. Horace was flabbergasted as he watched the three of them make that sharp turn off the road and up the trail. At a full speed run they made the turn, not breaking an inch of their formation. He fell behind just a bit, unable to make a skilled cut to the left like they did.

It wasn't long until the path narrowed. Forcing them to fall into a single file formation. At first, they barely slowed the horses. As the path became more and more narrow and treacherous, they were forced to slow down.

Horace screamed loud, "They're right behind us! Go—Go God-damn-it—Go!"

They spurred the horses back into a run; giving them full rein to navigate the path without interference; praying the horses didn't slip up and fall, and none of them, fell off.

Falling was not a preferred choice.

On their right side was jagged rock face, threatening to tear them from their saddles. On the left, a drop off, that had no bottom in the darkness of the night.

Tristan was in the lead and shitting bricks. He knew Sarah could make it thru without fail, but it still spooked him giving up all control to her. *And what about the others?*

His real worry was more for the rest of his team than himself. To lose one or both the girls was not an option. He loved them both more than his own life. At present, all he could do was stay positive that it was not their fate, or his, to die here this night.

He noticed just ahead of them, a humungous rock, hanging over the trail. Above it was stacked with tons of rock.

He screamed back frantically, "Duck! Fucking Duck!" Almost having his own head splattered against the rock in due process. A looked back, let him know, he had time.

The other three almost crashed into him, and each other, as Tristan reined-in Sarah to a full stop on the other side of the overhang. Jumping off her in a hurry, he almost went over the side of the cliff. "Careful getting off the horses." He told the other three, as he scrambled for footing.

"Horace! Matches—quickly! Get ready to light this wick!"

Tristan whipped out a bundle of dynamite sticks from his saddle bag and made his way past the girls to Horace. Horace was pulling out a match as Tristan reached his side. Like a gift from God, the match burned first strike and lit the wick to the dynamite.

"Take Sarah and move up the trail—all of you! This blast might bring down half the mountain on top of us but at least these fuckers will go with us!"

Horace shouted, "Tristan! that's way too many sticks! There is no—maybe! You will bring down the mountain—on us all!"

His words were too late. Tristan was standing at the overhang and the wick was burning too fast to stop it now. Nor would he have stopped it, had he heard the warning. Fight fire with fire, was his only thought.

Paris had already grabbed the reins of Tristan's horse and started running up the trail with everyone else behind her.

Tristan ran under the overhang and quickly found a niche; he was drawn from his task, as he saw the shadowy outlines of three huge bodies running toward him on all fours.

As they caught sight of him, they halted and stood up on two legs like human beings. Seconds were stretched to breaking; then time stopped, as he glared in astonishment.

His resolve cried, *Real!* His reason shouted, *Impossible*!

Still unable to see their bodies or faces clear; all he could make out of them, were shadowy outlines.

Time blinked again, and he snapped out of it, hurriedly placing the dynamite in the crevice. Then he shot his pursuers the finger, and shouted, "Fuck You! Then turned and run. That was the last thing the girls heard him say....

As he ran, the beasts let out roars that almost froze him in his tracks. He heard them start running towards him again; he marshalled all his strength for one more burst of energy, desperately trying to put distance between himself and the dynamite. Time stopped again in an everlasting pause…. Then…Boom!

The blast of the dynamite was felt and heard for many miles in all directions. The shockwave felt like it shook the entire mountain. Tristan's eardrums almost burst in his head.

The whole side of the cliff above the overhang, came crashing down, with a sound even louder than the blast.

Tristan launched himself against the cliff face and curled into a ball with his arms covering his head. Rocks and debris came down all around him. Hitting and bruising his body to the point of crushing him. He thought to himself that this was the end for him.

As he waited to be crushed and swept into the gorge by the avalanche of rocks and boulders; he prayed that his girls had made it to a safe distance and were not dying with him this night. He even prayed for Jo. But Jojo, had decided, fuck this stupid shit…. He was in an all-out run, up the path.

Both the girls were truly panicked. The mountain pass shook under their feet like a large earthquake tremor.

They covered their ears from the resounding booms, screaming as the sound deafened them.

They weren't sure they were far enough up the pass to not be concerned with falling debris; although they expected, any moment, the pass would collapse under their feet and drop them into the gorge.

Horace was doing the same when his luck, winked out.

Ariel screamed, "Horace! Look out!"

Horace had already heard the huge boulder coming down. He cried out, "Jesus Mary and—"
his words were cut short.

As he flung himself from his horse, to cheat death, his foot got caught in the stirrup, slamming him face-first to the ground. The boulder came down with a momentum of maximum crushing force, hitting the horse square on its back, right where Horace was sitting a split second before.

Sweeping the horse over the side of the cliff and dragging Horace over with it. He screamed out, "No Not— "… And his voice was silenced.

Both the girls were in shock. Unable to move or even speak. After several minutes, the mountain finally settled down and all was quiet again.

As they gathered their wits, they ran back down the pass to look for Tristan. They started calling his name and peering over the side of the cliff, crying as they did.

It was Ariel who noticed his foot sticking out from under a pile of rocks against the rock face. They tore skin and meat from their fingers and hands, as they frantically tried to dig him out from under the rubble. Tears were streaming down their faces, as they dragged his body out and onto the pass.

Ariel was hysterical, "Oh, my fucking—god no! Tristan! Tristan! Don't you leave us you crazy god damn bastard! Not now! Not after all this! Tristan! *TRISTAN!!*"

Paris couldn't even speak. She was crying uncontrollably as she tried desperately to wake him. She put her head to his chest. Her own heart started racing even faster now.

"He's stopped breathing—and his hearts not beating, but he's not dead. I can feel it—he's not dead yet. What do we do? We can't just sit here and watch him die!"

Ariel told her, "Remember what daddy did once? trying to save that newborn kitten? What about trying that?

Paris pulled his jaw down, opening his mouth. Taking a deep breath, she covered his mouth with hers and blew into it until she saw his chest rise. She continued this for some time with no luck. Just as she was about to give up, Ariel cried out again, screaming his name, hard and loud.

"Tristan! Tristan! Don't you die you son of a bitch! Come back to us…please…come back to us…*TRISTAN!!*

As she screamed his name that last time; lightning-fast thoughts then an uncontrollable urge, came over her. She came down hard on his chest with both fists! His body jerked and convulsed.

Tristan started coughing, sucked in and expelled a huge breath of air, and laid still again. Ariel thought aloud, saying, "What was that? What just happened? Is he breathing again—is he breathing?" Her hand involuntarily went to her mouth. She herself stopped breathing.

Paris put her ear to his chest, and said, "It's beating!"

Then sat up and stared at her sister as she cried out, "Trudy its beating—and he's breathing... he—he's breathing!"

Ariel began crying even harder, but now her tears of sorrow were tears of joy. She said, "Thank-you god thank-you god thank you—god! I will be a good girl from now on I swear! Tristan, you insane crazy fuck! When you wake up—I'm going to kill you." She bent over and touched her cheek to his, then held her puckered lips to his forehead for a moment, then kissed him on his lips.

Paris was crying and laughing out loud, all at once. She checked his body for any broken bones or dislocations.

Finding none, she ripped off a piece of her shirt and began soaking the blood from the multitude of superficial wounds he had gotten.

Ariel was wiping her eyes and calming down her crying when she heard something.

"Listen... What is that? She whispered.

They both heard it the second time.

"Help... Help me somebody!"

It was coming from over the side of the cliff.

They both said at the same time, "Horace!"

Ariel told Paris, "Stay with Tristan." She ran over to the edge of the cliff where the pleas for help was coming from.

She dropped to her knees and leaned over the side. There was Horace! Not ten feet below her, on a small ledge.

"He's alive! No way to reach him though! Hold on Horace! Stay still—and we'll get you out of there!"

Paris shouted, "Trudy! Get a rope off one of the horses and throw it down to him."

Ariel hastened to the horses and grabbed a rope, then she walked back to the edge and tossed some of it over. Hitting Horace right on his chest with it. Though it was only a rope that landed on him, it hurt none-the-less.

He was having trouble breathing. Barely able to speak, after calling out like he did, which was ungodly painful. He forced out some few words to Ariel.

"My leg is broken up pretty bad. I can't move my left arm. I don't know if I can tie the rope around me. I—sure-as-hell—won't be climbing up it—you can believe that."

Ariel pulled the rope back up and tied a bow-line knot. She had looped it out large enough to fit around his body and tossed it back over. The impact on his chest shot pain through him again, so intense he—almost—blacked-out.

Ariel yelled down to him, "You're going to have to try to get the rope around you—so we can pull you up. Paris! I'm going to need your help."

Paris came over to where Ariel was looking over and down at Horace. With much pain and effort, he managed to get the rope around him. Ariel began unspooling the rope.

Paris backed up to the rock face and sat down on her ass, with the rope around her waist, digging her boots hard into the ground in front of her, then shouted, "Ok Trudy. Let's do this."

Trudy ran back and threw the rope over the saddle horn and drew it taut. The second the rope went taut with his weight; Ariel coaxed the horse slowly forward.

Paris instantly began to slide towards the edge. She called out to Trudy, "Trudy! I'm slipping! Wait! I got a bite in the ground with my boots now. Keep going!"

Horace was screaming out in agonizing pain. Paris called-out to Ariel. "Trudy—wait! Something's wrong—I think were killing him. Come check and see!"

Trudy went to the edge and peered over, calling out to him. "Horace! Horace! Are you ok?" He didn't answer.

"I think he's out cold. Or we killed him when we moved him. His feet are up off the ledge. I can almost touch him.

"We have no other choice. We have to get him back up."

Paris told her, "There's nothing else we can do but keep doing what we're doing. Hurry—before he does—die! If he's not dead—already...."

Ariel coaxed the horse on up the trail until they could see the top of his head. As they tried to pull him further up and over the edge, his body got stuck against the ledge, just as his shoulders had almost crested the top.

"Trudy honey, you're going to have to try to pull him over onto the road. If I move, the rope is going to shift and swing him out and back down the cliff-face."

Ariel went over to him, grabbed him under his arms and tried with all her might to pull him up and over, with no luck. "He's too heavy—hanging over—the way he is. I'm going to end up over the side—myself and—"

Paris cut her off, "What'll we do now then?"

All seemed hopeless until they heard, then saw, Jojo, trotting down the trail towards them.

The dog, as if he knew exactly what to do, grabbed the rope in his jaws just behind Horace's head and together, he and Ariel were able to pull him up and over, onto flat ground.

Both the girls collapsed onto their backs with exhaustion. They didn't know if Horace was alive or dead. They didn't know if the blast and avalanche had destroyed the beasts that were chasing them. Nor could they do anything else about any of it. They were both mentally and physically burned out. They just laid right where they were… and passed out from the extreme fatigue of all that had just happened. The night drew quiet again.

Chapter eight

Dog Soldiers

Ariel and Paris awoke from their slumber at the same time, lying side by side on a bed roll, a blanket over them, and saddlebags for pillows. They were under a tree on a grassy slope. The sun was shining beautifully; the morning air was crisp and fresh. Their horses, and Tristan's, were grazing a few yards away. Jojo was at their feet, watching over them.

Horace was sitting up against the tree, not looking too good. Tristan, after a moment, came hobbling into view; he wasn't alone. A half a dozen or so Indian warriors were walking up with him.

He approached the girls, seeing that they were awake, smiling he said, "Well, good morning sleepy heads…I thought you might sleep all day. The whole time we were moving you here, neither one of you, even twitched.

"I couldn't even guess at what went-on—after the mountain came down on us. Until Horace came-to…and filled me in… and told me—what you did for him.

"It had to be the two of you that pulled me out from under all that rock I was buried under. I thought I was a goner—"

Paris cut-in, "Who are your friends?"

"They found us on the pass among all the rocks. I was the only one that came-to when they shook me. They helped me get the three of you here. Their leaders name is Flying Eagle. They are Cheyenne Dog Soldiers.

"Flying eagle speaks a little Apache. It's very broken, but we've been able to talk to each other. Horace speaks their tongue and has helped much with us communicating.

"Horace is busted up pretty bad. He has some fractured ribs, a big gash in his skull and his leg is shattered in two or three places. I'm not sure—but…to look at his hip—I think its dislocated. After he told us how it happened, I was surprised it wasn't torn from his body. He's one, tough sum bitch. His shoulder was dislocated too, but we managed to put it back in place. How he is alive, only god knows.

"He said the worst of it all, was when—you two—pulled him up from the ledge. He said—him passing out was god sent. And that you two girls were in his will now."

Both the girls chuckled at that last statement.

"What are Cheyenne doing this far west? Paris asked.

Tristan told her, "They're tracking these fucking things that have been chasing us all over these mountains. They call them, Wendigo.

"From what little Horace was able to tell me, Dog soldiers are known as the elite warriors of the Cheyenne. The military and other white folk think they are bred and trained to fight their enemies. Though this has been the case of late, fighting and killing other men and warriors is not their true purpose.

"The best and bravest warriors from every generation for as far back as the Cheyenne can remember, have been trained in the skill of hunting and killing the wendigo. That's their true purpose and skill.

"There hasn't been any wendigo for hundreds of years. When they were around back in the day, they were so deadly, only the absolute best seasoned warriors and elder medicine men were able to figure out how to hunt and kill them. The rites and skills have been passed down from generation to generation ever since.

"There are over thirty Dog Soldiers with Flying Eagle. Not including a hand full of elder medicine men that are with them also. They've been trying to hunt down these wendigos—and kill them—ever since they attacked and slaughtered a Cheyenne village last year. Their trail has led them into these parts.

"Flying Eagle said that ordinary spears, knives, arrows, tomahawks or any other weapons won't kill them. Not even bullets.

"He said whatever weapon you use to try to kill them must first be dipped in or coated with a potent mixture of herbs and powerful magic. Their skin is too thick to puncture deep enough to kill them. The only way to penetrate their bodies deep enough to have an effect—is to hit them, in their eyes, ears, mouth, nose or asshole.

"Which, is damned near impossible, given their supernatural strength, speed and adept abilities of anticipation. It is said they are as smart as any man and smarter than most.

"Making them very formidable adversaries against anything that lives.

"Without the potion on the weapons they fight them with, even hitting them in one of these vital points won't bring them down. Even with the potion, it will slow them down greatly, but it won't kill them outright."

Tristan chuckled and continued, "I told them, bringing a mountain down on their heads seems to work pretty well too. The bastards didn't look to happy when we set them on fire either. Flying eagle laughed at my words and said again, it may slow them down, but it won't kill them.

"How they're going to push a shit-ton of rocks off their heads is beyond me, but then again, how can we know any of them were hit by the avalanche. We stopped them from getting us, and that's all I care about. For me, even my life is expendable when compared with the two of you living to see another day."

His eyes started to well up as he stared at them. They were banged-up and bruised all over. Turning his head and wiping his eyes, he quickly changed the subject.

"One of the flowers used in this mix grows in these parts in abundance. Look, this is it."

He pulled a stem with flowers from his back pocket. The flowers were a deep purple color. Ariel instantly recognized it and said, "I know that flower. It's Monkshood. It's deadly poisonous. Our daddy taught us how to spot them. That's only one kind. There are a half a dozen others that grow in different terrain from coast to coast."

"Smart girl." Tristan told her with pride in his tone. "Horace said that in Europe it's known as wolf-bane.

"If I understand them right, it takes most of those different strains, put together, with a whole bunch of other poisonous plants and flowers. And Slime from a frog that lives on the other side of the southern desert, in the jungles of Mexico. Where the Azteca live.

"After its mixed and properly boiled down into a thick salve, it has to be buried and dug up and rituals performed over it. Then, reburied and dug up and blessed by the spirits of the ancestors and a dozen other things before it can be used to hunt the Wendigo with any real affect.

"Like I already said. Even then, it won't kill them. Not the older ones anyway. It only incapacitates them long enough for them to shove some special magic stones through their eye sockets and shit. Keeping them from ever rising again."

"Sounds like a bunch of horse shit to me but after what we've seen… What do I know?

"He wouldn't show me the stones. He said, only a Dog Soldier is allowed, to see, touch or use the stones. Or it destroys their power to kill the Wendigo.

"One other thing he told me was, they've been tracking them, but have yet to find or see, even one. A trail and their howl-screams have been their only signs of them.

"A trail that they have lost time and again. As if these things know they are after them. I told him we should trade places because, I'd had my fill of the damn things.

"So, to sum all this up. All their knowledge and skills to fight these Wendigo, is all just theory. If they see or kill one or all of them, they will be the first, in hundreds of years, to do so."

"Oh yea, and they told me they have seen, Sass-quatch. They are everywhere. It is forbidden to harm them as they are gentle creatures of the forest and avoid contact with humans. He said they are masters of disguise and could be standing a few feet away from you and you'd never know it. And—"

Paris cut him off, "Ok… You need to take a breather mister. You're making me tired. You are wound up tighter than a dick's hat band… So please, take a break and shut—up?"

Ariel looked at Tristan and said, "Wow… that's quite a bit of knowledge they dropped on you in such a short span.

"Especially when you consider barely being able to understand them."

"Well." Tristan retorted solemnly. "It is almost noon… I mean… What else was there to talk about. Plus, Horace translated a good part of it for me. An—"

Both the girls yelled as one voice,

"TRISTAN!! SHUT UP!!"

"Ok, Ok, just this last thing. They know who we are. They've heard of us. From what I understand, all the Indian nations know our story. They all know we are son and daughters of the Apache people. We are known as and called, The Children of the Wolves…. Don't ask me to say it in Cheyenne."

Paris and Ariel, both laughed aloud and then Paris said to Tristan, "You're so full of shit."

Tristan, with a bewildered look on his face told her, "Your Apache speech is as good as mine. You can ask him yourself."

As Paris and Tristan eye balled each other, Ariel said,

"You two can figure all that out… without me. Because, to tell the truth, I could care less—and right-now—could give two shits what they call us…." She paused and then continued, "The last few days have been too twisted and fucked, to be knit picking.

"Right now, I'm going to find me a private spot in these woods—where I won't be disturbed, and take me a nice, long shit—"

Paris and Tristan fell into a belly laugh. With Paris saying as she laughed, "You sick nasty bitch! There is just no shame in your game—"

Ariel laughed back and said, "Care to join me?"

Paris pretended to think about it, then said,

"Yea… Why not… Let's go."

* * * * *

Tristan–The Cheyenne had heard the scream-howls of the wendigo the past few nights. They were heading towards the pass along the gorge as it was the shortest way through the mountains. It was over a week, by any other route. Now that I had made the pass impassable; they would be forced to take the long way around.

They had all felt the mountain tremble in the night, and they were awestruck, that it was a man that had caused this to happen. Even more amazing to them was the fact that us *four-white folks*, had battled the wendigo, and won, not just once, but multiple times. Flying Eagle himself, told me he could see what the Apache saw in us.

The Cheyenne grew extremely excited when Horace told them of the cave system, he thought the wendigo were using as a stronghold, and how there was only one way up to those caves and only one way out.

These facts gave them an advantage they had yet to be afforded in their task of destroying these monsters. Without the pass though, it would be more than a week to get there, but that wasn't the immediate concern of the day. The real concern was for Horace.

The medicine men of the Cheyenne could help, only a little. His wounds and broken body would take his life eventually. To give him their herbs and medicinal substances, would not save his life and restore his health, it only gave him respite.

The Cheyenne had a man of the Washoe tribe with them as their guide. The Washoe were the native inhabitants of the land we were in. The guide told them: *he knew a white man that lived near Carson City. He was well respected by his tribe and knew the white-mans' medicine. If Horace were beyond the man's help, and could be helped at all, he would know where to take him.*

So, it was decided, the Cheyenne would take him to the doctor near Carson City. Horace was a good man and worthy of the effort. Also, that would put the dog-soldiers on the right side of the mountains for reaching the caves.

But Carson City, was a much more treacherous and dangerous trek than back to Sacramento. I told them I was done with my overland adventures in these parts; I had seen enough. I was not willing to put the girls in any further danger with those creatures running around.

We were heading for the coast. It would be an ocean adventure for our return trip home. I was done with murdering marauders and deep forest monsters. Although I've never shared this, I pondered thoughts, with great anxiety; that, if these things were real, what if sea monsters were next?

With everyone prepped, we said our farewells to the Dog Soldiers and especially, to Horace. He and I had forged fast bonds in our death struggles together against a common foe.

He was formidable in a fight: his courage was boundless, and his loyalty came honest and without fault.

Horace was given means to reach us through letters. The girls made him promise to write them. That it would be great a day; indeed, a celebration, to receive news he was alive and well. He swore, to do just that. *That they were each,* **his favorite person.**

The Washoe guide explained to me how to get around the gorge, to make it back to the Truckee as swift as possible; also, he told me, that his people were at peace with white-folk, and we should have no trouble if we ran into any of them. We were each given a talisman to wear around our necks: to ward off evil spirits, bring safe journeys, good fortune and most importantly, would show us to be friends, respectable of the native culture.

It would take us more than a few days to get back to the Truckee from where we were in the mountains. As long, as we didn't lose our way. Not a hard thing to do in these mountains. Even seasoned men to these parts, are often claimed by the Sierra Nevada's.

The Washoe guide, also, gave me one last bit of advice: to mark our trail well, as only we would recognize, so, if we did get turned around, we could find our way back to a proper starting point.

Deciding it to be sound advice, I excepted it with genuine gratitude and a gracious smile. With no more words to be said, we parted ways, and all went in their own direction.

The girls and I didn't say it aloud, but I knew we all were wondering whether, we had put the worst behind us, or not.

Chapter nine

Destiny calls, Fates merge

Paris and Ariel both, tried to tell Tristan for the better part of a week, that they wanted to turn back, catch up with the Cheyenne and go to Carson City. He let their pleas go in one ear and out the other.

None of them realized that it was fate that was leading them to a destiny unknown. No matter which way they went or what they tried, they would not escape the events now in motion.

Although they were heading in the right direction, they had gotten off the track the Washoe guide had laid out for them.

It was more than a few days before they realized they were off course. Tristan was beside himself with frustration at the fact he had gotten turned off their proper path to such a degree.

During their trek back to the river, a company of wolves showed up.

A healthy and strong pack, well over twenty. They had never got to see them all in one place long enough to count them.

The girls and Tristan felt like strays that had been rescued… and now had their own personal chaperones across the wilderness.

The wolfpack stayed not too far behind, at times. Other times, they were out ahead of them.

More times than can be called coincidence, the wolves frolicked right around them.

Tristan just couldn't figure out why, wolves from everywhere, loved those two girls—almost as much—as he did.

The wolves interacted and played with the girls often: when they stopped along the trail, or outside the campfire light at night, or running along beside their horses.

The girls and Tristan were comforted by their howls, and all other manner of sound made by a wolf pack. Knowing they were patrolling all around them, was a blessing for a good night's sleep.

After a week or so, of their company of wolves traveling along with them, the wolves disappeared in the night, like ghosts. The same way they had showed up....

The girls seemed a little glum after they left. For the better part of the morning, even Jo—seemed to miss them.

Tristan had marked an easy trail to follow back as they had been told to do. They were confident they would get back to the proper path. Ending up so far off track, had cost them quite a few days.

Yet, Somehow, they got off track, yet again, following their own trail. Tristan wondered if some supernatural force wasn't at work.

Swinging way out and around the way they had come and had marked; they found their trail again. Finding their old tracks, they noticed tracks on top of them. After closer examination, Tristan realized, he knew these tracks.

They were the same prints he found outside of Horace's cabin; the morning after they were attacked. They were the tracks of the Wendigo. Putting two and two together, Tristan concluded that getting off track, this last time, was a fortunate thing. If they hadn't, they would have run right into them.

How long they had been following them, he didn't know. Guessing they had been behind them all along. He wondered why they hadn't attacked them and got it over with.

Tristan kissed his talisman and told the girls to do the same. Because now they knew they were being followed, and that could be turned into an advantage. The spirits that were watching over them, were to be blessed.

He deduced, that the creatures must not have realized, they had, inadvertently, circled around them. How far back up the trail they were? Or how far behind them were they now? those were the real questions.

They hastened their pace, hopeful that an opportunity would present itself before circumstances became even more estranged.

After traveling a short distance, not able to keep his eyes off the ground from their pursuer's tracks, Tristan noticed something peculiar.

The wendigo tracks had ceased. In their place were human tracks, the bare feet of human beings. As he and the girls sat on their horses with their minds blown by this turn of events, Tristan exclaimed,

"What the fuck is going on here...!

"These tracks make no sense at all....

"Did they change from men to beasts? I know we've seen some fucked up shit...but you're not going to make me believe that men can change into beasts."

Then it hit him. Tonight, was the second night of a full moon. Horace had been going on and on about moon cycles.

Looking back up the way they came, on their return to their original path, he realized that where they had made camp last night was only a short distance away from where they now stood.

He reasoned, that right where these tracks stopped being tracks of men and became tracks of the wendigo, was where the wendigo were the night before, when the moon rose.

Also putting them in easy ambush range from their last camp. Why weren't they attacking? What was their game?

With a grim tone, Tristan told the girls, "We're not being chased or rundown... We're being stalked and hunted again...."

A cold chill climbed up his back. He looked around him like an animal that just realized it was being watched. He said to the girls, "There are some spooky affairs taking place here." His hair stood up on the back of his neck, realizing those were the exact words, he had used in his nightmare.

He quickly shook off all chills and notions of supernatural suggestion. Knowing, that if they were to survive, he could not let any fear creep up into his head. After an intense moment of silence, he said, "If I'm remembering right, there is a lake with a huge clear open space leading down to it, not too far from here. We need to get there before dark and do some prep work. I'll fill you in as we ride."

They reached the clearing with just enough time to put his plan into action.

* * * * *

They decided on a fireless camp. With the full moon rising soon, and the big open space that led down to the water's edge; the moonshine and it's glimmering off the water would be bright enough for their needs this night.

They had found the perfect place, to try and get a look at these things and figure out a way to outsmart them. Tristan had figured out, that whether it be men, beasts or both, they were tracking him, and the girls, more by smell than with any other signs him and the girls were leaving. Tristan used that knowledge for the premise of his plan.

They got out of their sweaty, filthy clothes and stuffed them with grass and such, so it would look like them from a distance. He would make it look like they had fallen asleep early that evening, without making a fire.

They bathed themselves but remained naked. Then caked themselves completely over with the stinking putrid mud and muck that was around the water's edge where the animals came to drink. It was a well-traveled spot and a good mixture of mud and animal excrement. It would hide their human scent, quite well.

* * * * *

It had been many hours since they had executed their plan. Each one of them were in their own hiding place, waiting almost breathless, for something, anything…. To show itself, so this flirt with death could begin.

Each of them, had taken a position that was far enough away to gain access of viewing these creatures without being seen. With luck, one of them would be close enough to see what the hell it was. Was it a man, or was it a beast?

Not too long after midnight, something or someone came into the clearing and started down toward the water, then stopped. It was too dark in the shadow of the tree line, to see what it was that stepped into the open from Tristan and Ariel's vantage points; however, Paris, got a good look.

She had picked her spot in a high crotch of a tree, on the edge of the tree line. From her vantage point, they had come out of the forest about thirty feet from where she was.

Two of them had stepped into the clearing. She only caught a shadowy outline at first, but as her eyes focused in deeper on their mark, her heart began to race.

Her mind told her they were wolves. They were walking on all fours, but something didn't seem quite right. Were they two humans, walking on their knuckles, like apes?

Their heads were like nothing she had ever imagined. They were macabre and beautiful, all at once. The front legs were a little longer than the back legs. Allowing for the shoulders to rest a bit higher than their hindquarters. Unlike the level backs of wolves. As she looked closer, she realized the front legs were more like arms than legs, and the shoulders were most definitely human. The hind legs were harder to discern, but the was a slight humanish quality to them, as well.

Clearly, the sway of their back from neck to buttocks were of human beings. One of them had the chest of a man. The other one, the smaller one, had a chest that narrowed, more like an actual wolf's chest.

What happened next took her breath away. The larger one, stood up on its hind legs. Then, the smaller one did the same.

They walked around in a circle, on two legs, with no trouble. As though it was meant to be.

To her utter amazement, the big one had the genitals of a man. Though she hadn't seen many, she had seen enough of them, to know a man's cock and balls. A quite impressive one too, she thought to herself.

She did not see the same appendages on the smaller beast, giving her the assumption, that it was a female. A male and a female... whatever these things were.

As they moved into the clearing a little more, she could see the legs better. They had the same blend of human and wolf that made up the arms.

They had hands that were also humanish. With palms that were padded like canine paws. Nails that seemed as long, as bear claws.

They were morphed in a perfect blending of a human and a wolf. She had heard bedtime stories about these creatures. They were called, Werewolves.

Half man, half wolf, make-believe monsters to scare children or so she once thought. Now, two were standing a few yards away, larger than life. She was convinced.... They were Werewolves, breathing the same air as her.

The absolute beauty of these creatures was mesmerizing, so erotic and neurotic, all at once. They were both as white as the purest snow.

Their heads and snouts were those of wolves, without doubt. With a sinister appearance, not present on the face of a normal wolf. Their eyes almost glowed. Though they were calm, the eyes resembled those of an infuriated wolf.

The hair was like wolf fur: though shorter, except the back of the head and neck, which was thick and long, running down their backs, kind of, like a mohawked horse's mane. It narrowed as it went down the back. Tapering into a thin strip, the entire length of the spine, down past the waistline, to the tail bone. This strip was thicker and longer than the surrounding hair on the rest of the back, legs and other body parts. They even had what looked to be tails. They had to be close to seven or eight feet tall, standing upright.

Her mind was swimming in thought, desperate for answers. What was the history and evolution of these abominations of nature? That blended wolf and man, so perfectly?

Then she realized, there were no vibes of wild murderous intent coming from these creatures. They weren't hunting prey or stalking enemies. Were these the werewolves that had been terrorizing them in past weeks?

They looked around and twisted their bodies like humans, yet they sniffed the air and stared like wolves, switching between standing on two legs and dropping to all fours. Cautious, yet poised for action at the slightest sign of anything. So beautiful! So quick! So extraordinary!

Suddenly, their demeanors changed to an aggressive posture. Becoming very tense and alert. They had caught the scent of the camp. Another clue that they were not, nor had they been, following them, or they would have already been aware of the camp. These were not the creatures that were stalking them, Paris was sure of it.

They were still the beautiful creatures they were a moment ago. Now though, there was a vicious malevolence about them. Even so, there was no fear being generated from these beasts upon Paris. Tristan and Ariel also felt something different about them.

They did not do what Tristan thought they would, poke at the camp trying to trap them as they slept. Instead, they turned and darted back off into the woods, as silently as they had come.

All three spies stayed in their spots. To see what might show up next, and they were not disappointed. Not long after the first encounter, two full-fledged wolves came into view.

They were at least four times bigger than the biggest wolf any of them had seen so far. Both were solid white.

They came out of the tree line at the exact same spot the werewolves had come from. Paris thought she recognized something familiar about them. Were they the same pair, she had seen earlier? Only, now, transfigured into common wolves? Then she noticed something that was a dead sure giveaway.

The big one, had a huge pair of human balls dangling between his hind legs, and after inspection of the smaller one, there was no doubt this time. On its backside, was clearly a human vagina, where a wolf vagina should be. The smaller one was a female.

They were the same creatures. Only now, fully transformed into actual wolves. All but the reproductive organs.

They were massively larger than normal wolves by three or four times, but wolves none the less. Seeing them as werewolves was hard enough to accept. Seeing them again, transformed from werewolves into natural wolves, frightened Paris. She was struggling to keep her sanity. What sort of sorcery or conjuring of dark arts allowed such things to happen? Where did they fit in to the nature of things?

They put their noses to the ground and then raised their heads to stare at the camp and sniff the air. With the cautiousness of the wild, yet the simple actions of curious wolves.

They made their way down to the camp. Approaching it with no sign of stalking or hunting for prey, only a curious nature of the unknown was their persona. They sniffed every inch of the camp site, including the fake humans that were staged on the ground to mimic real people.

When they got to Ariel's clothes, they sniffed them up and down, turning them over repeatedly. Then they walked a circle around her clothes, noses to the ground.

With a suddenness, which was more than abrupt, they both looked up from the ground, and straight in the direction of where Ariel was hiding. Noses to the ground again, they tracked her scent, as only wolves could do, straight to where Ariel lay in the bushes, stopping only a few feet away and staring right at her.

Tristan was ready to jump up and run straight for Ariel, but he hesitated. Intuitively knowing, it would provoke a disastrous outcome for them both. Plus, there was something about these two giant wolves; they weren't threatening in their bearing, not yet anyway. Deep in his soul, something told him, she wasn't in danger.

Paris didn't share his sentiment. She was already coming out of the tree she was in. As quietly as she could, as fast as she could. She wasn't losing Trudy to fucking werewolves.

Her already decided upon plan was to wait at the base of the tree and at the first sign of danger, for Ariel, she would yell out, turning their full attention on her. What she would do then, she hadn't thought that far ahead to know. Her feet had just hit the ground when she glanced over at Tristan.

He motioned for her to stay put.

The wolves just stood there, staring at Ariel, intensely. The smaller one, which to Ariel seemed to be the female, started towards her. Then quickly stepped back and began whimpering and hopping on her front legs as canines do when they want something.

Ariel was stricken with fear at the size, and proximity of the beasts, but her courage and avid curiosity, proved stronger than her fear.

Sensing the same benevolence that her companions were, about these two creatures of the moonshine; she rose out of her hiding place and stepped into full view for the wolves to see her. Keeping her hands at her side and making no other movements once she was standing on her feet in front of them.

The wolves instantly took a step back. The big one's ears flattened as he shined his teeth and growled at her for an instant. Then, as suddenly as he had taken on an aggressive posture, it changed back to a curious one: ears perked up, tongue lolling out of his mouth, and ever so slight, wag of the tail.

Ariel didn't move a muscle. She was even holding her breath a little. The size of these creatures up close and in her face as they were, was daunting. She instantly was unsure she had made the right choice to confront them in the open.

The two beasts moved closer to her. Sniffing the air between them and Ariel, as they approached her. After what to Ariel, seemed an extremely long minute, they were close enough to touch.

The smaller one was more daring. Touching her nose to Ariel's hand first and then moved closer to sniff at her face.

Though she didn't know how she knew, Ariel instinctively knew, the smaller one was most definitely a female.

They were both staring at her now, right into her eyes. As their eyes met, all of Ariel's fear and concern for her life disappeared. Tristan and Paris were both awestruck at what she did next. She crossed her legs and sat her bottom upon the ground. Putting herself at the complete mercy of these creatures.

Tristan whispered to himself, "if they don't kill her, I'm gonna...."

They didn't kill her though. Nor did they try to harm her at all. With her at their mercy, they willingly and calmly, approached her. Smelling every inch of her. The big one, that Ariel was now sure was a male, stuck his nose into her naked crotch and sniffed her female part most intensely, licking her there once, before quickly pulling away and staring at her from a short distance, just out of her reach.

She was compelled to smack him, for the tongue lick he had given her in her most coveted body part. But was thankful that he had withdrew far enough away that she could not reach him without effort of moving and upsetting the balance of what was turning out to be, an unexpectedly pleasant meeting. Except for the cunnilingus that had just been administered to her.

The female wolf walked around her. Sniffing her backside from top to bottom, including her neck, ears and hair.

The she-wolf continued her sniff inspection as she came back around to Ariel's front side again. Ariel bit the inside of her lip, preparing herself to take another sniff and lick to her vagina. To her relief, it did not happen so. Instead, the female wolf went nose to nose with her and after a moment, licked her face from chin to eyebrows.

The female moved away to the side of the male and after sharing a short glance at each other, both started hopping and dancing, all around Ariel, like two simple dogs whose master had returned.

As the wolves did this, Paris and Tristan were amazed, and sickened, in horrified bewilderment, at what they saw and heard. The sound they made as they danced around Ariel was not the sound one would expect from happy wolves. It was human laughter, coming from them both. As clear as bells ringing, these two animals were throating human laughter.

The laughter of a human male and female. It was an eerie sound; a sound that made the skin crawl and blood freeze.

After their moment of joy, they stopped and stood motionless in front of her. Then both turned their noses up to the full moonshine and let out a gut-wrenching howl-scream.

It was the same screaming howl the three companions had come to recognize. With the male sounding male and the female sounding female. Both were even more horrendous and heart stopping to hear so up close and in Ariel's face as these two gargantuan wolves were. So deafening was the sound, that she involuntarily covered her ears, from its resounding effect.

As they howled in her face, she couldn't help pondering the fact that she was no longer frightened in the slightest bit; instead, she was awe-inspired to be able to interact with such extraordinary and mystifying creatures. To be this close to them was exhilarating. Realizing all of this as she covered her ears; she began to laugh aloud as tears rolled down her face. This was real, it was really happening. Taking place right in front of her. A thing that excited her beyond belief. Indeed, the world was a miraculous place.

Both creatures approached her again, and gave her a kind, farewell lick to her face, and started off toward the tree line.

As they approached the edge of the clearing, they were startled by Paris's presence at the base of the tree. Paris didn't know whether to freak-out or go-blind. Everything was so terrifying and exhilarating, happening so fast. She hadn't realized, she had put herself into visible sight of anything that looked her way.

The werewolves sniffed at her and approached, though much less as cautious, than they were a moment ago. They walked straight to her and stuck their noses directly in her crotch; then walking around to her backside together, each stuck their nose up her rear end. The male, going as far as to lift her onto her toes as he drove his nose deep into the crack of her butt. Making direct contact with her vagina, same as he had done to Ariel.

The two wolves returned to her front side and sat down, ears up. The male made sounds at her that were eerily human, just as before. But this time, it was as if he were trying to speak directly to her. She was astonished that she thought she could have made out human words with a little more time and effort. Before she could though, the sounds ceased.

Both wolves stood and turned their noses towards the ground, showing the top of their heads to Paris. As they did this, they each lifted one front paw, and leaned back deep and low, in a bow. Bowing to Paris as one would a queen.

Tristan's senses had flown. He was completely overwhelmed by the displays he was seeing. Not only was he seeing the biggest damn wolves he thought ever existed, they were playing with and kowtowing to his women. He thought to himself, what in the fuck kind of place, was this part of the world they had ended up in? Where reality was twisted and warped into some fiendish fairy-tale….

When the wolves finally disappeared into the tree line, they didn't just get lost from sight as they entered the woods; they seemed to vanish as they reached the edge of the forest, like ghosts. All three companions were stuck in place for a moment. Wondering what was next in this deranged tale unfolding before them.

It was obvious, that the creatures they had just encountered, were not the monsters that had mauled and torn apart the people that they had come upon, nor attacked the cabin, and chased them through these mountains.

If they were, they sure didn't have the same mind towards any of them now. At least not towards the girls anyway.

As they gathered themselves and returned to their fake camp, it took a moment before any of them could find their voice. Tristan was the first to speak. Saying,

"What in the hell was that all about? I don't think those were the ones responsible for the mayhem that we've been exposed to in these past weeks. But if they weren't?

"Then what were they? Who were they? Where on earth did, they come from?"

Ariel said, "Did you see how they vanished like ghosts—more than flesh and blood beasts?"

Tristan continued as though he hadn't heard her words.

"Wolves with human laughter? Playing with Ariel was shocking enough, but did I see right? Did I see them take a bow to Paris? What kind of shit—was that all about?"

Tristan's next words began calm, then escalated to shouting. "If I appear to be freaking out right now, it's because—

"I am fucking freaking-out right now! What in the fuck—is the world coming too! What's next? Unicorns and fuckin Leprechauns?"

Ariel and Paris remained silent as Tristan had his minor breakdown. After he calmed himself, Paris told them,

"I'm not sure what just happened or who or what exactly they were but, what I am—sure of is, they are not the things that have terrorized us since Donner pass. They were benevolent. They are not the vicious killers that have been chasing us across these mountains."

Ariel added, "I agree. I got the impression they were some sort of wolf royalty or spirits even. Given the way they vanished into thin air at the edge of the clearing.

"They sure didn't seem like spirits when they were in my face though. This whole night has done nothing but produce more confusion and even more questions."

Paris said, "I know that the Indians call these things, Wendigo, but when I first saw those two tonight, I got a real good look at them when they first entered the clearing."

"When they stood up on two feet, I saw human male and female parts—"

Tristan cut her off, "Parts… What do you mean, parts?"

Paris shouted, "Tallywacker and Kitty! Cock and Cunt!"

"The big one had a huge cock and balls on him! A human cock and balls…! The female had a human pussy….

"Now that I have seen them in full view, out in the open, I know what they are – they are Werewolves…."

Tristan and Ariel remained silent. Paris continued, "I know that sounds like madness but… the howls, and the growls, and everything else—fits this puzzle perfectly.

"And those two that came in after the first two left, were the same pair, changed from werewolves into wolves….

"When I saw the human balls on the big one, I knew it was them – it was then that I saw the smaller one had a human vagina and knew she was a female."

Paris's words rang like bells to Ariel and Tristan. That was it, beyond doubt. What they were dealing with were, Werewolves.

Things supposed to be of myth and legend. But they weren't creatures of myth and legend. They were as real as all three of them. Terrorizing the Sierra Nevada and Cascade mountains.

Tristan asked, "Werewolves! Are we all in agreement, that what we have encountered, these past weeks, are werewolves?" Both the girls nodded in reply. Tristan continued,

"And we all agree? That what we met this night, were not the creatures responsible for all the carnage and horror we've endured, since we got into these mountains?"

The girls both nodded in reply again. Everyone let what they all had just agreed was the truth, sink in. Of at least that much, of what was happening to them, was no longer a mystery.

Then Ariel said, "I don't pretend to be an expert on werewolves but, the savageness of the killings and attacks, on horses and people, makes a lot more sense to think werewolves are responsible, than anything else we've thought it could be. Wendigo is what the Indians call them but, in our world, they are known as werewolves. At least both names begin with double-u I guess....

"But what doesn't add up, is those two we just encountered. I was scared to death at first. But that was quickly replaced with thrill. Once I realized the nature of those two. Their visit was just that, a visit.

"I'm convinced—that it was as much a surprise for them to see us—as it was for us—to see them. How it all fits together I can't even guess. So, the real question is, what do we do now? This has all been weird and entertaining but, those other bastards are still out there. We are no better off now than we were when we planned all this."

After a moment of thought, Tristan said, "It'll be daylight in a few hours. Let's get back in our spots and see if anything else comes calling." They all agreed to that strategy.

Tristan and Ariel were about to head off towards their spots. Paris turned and headed for her tree, but she never made it there.

Just as she got close to the tree line, another werewolf stepped out from behind it and let out a roar that froze them all in their tracks. This one was not benevolent by any means.

Tristan yelled, Paris! Run!"

His words snapped her out of her fright, and she bolted. As she moved out of the way, Tristan got off two shots with his rifle.

Hitting the beast in the side of its face as it turned its head to watch Paris run away. The shots distracted it only for moments, doing no real damage, except to make it even more enraged.

Yet the distraction, did give Paris a small head start. The beast looked at Tristan and roared. Then, turned and took off after Paris.

Paris knew she couldn't outrun it. She zigged-zagged in and out of the trees, running wild with no pattern. She was so terribly afraid, she had to yell out loud to herself to keep running.

After many minutes of exhausting chase. She noticed an outcrop of a rockface that was the sheer side of a hill she was running parallel too. There was a huge tree in front of it with low branches. Behind the tree, she saw a ledge in the rock face that she might be able to reach by climbing into the tree.

She prayed aloud that the werewolf on her heels couldn't climb trees or was too heavy for the branches.

She ran toward the rock face, running for the only tree, she could get high enough in to get away. With all the strength she had left, she leaped for a branch to pull herself up. As she grabbed it, she heard it crack and felt it break away. Sending her crashing to the ground and knocking the wind from her lungs. There was no time to catch her breath; death was knocking at her door.

Instantly, she was on her feet again and backing against the tree. The creature was right in front of her now. She was within reach of its grasp.

She thought to herself; finally, this thing that had been terrorizing them, was in full view, from head to toe. She was getting her first good look at the damn thing, at last.

If she was about to be ripped up and torn apart, at least she knew what it was, once and for all. It truly was, a man-wolf, or wolfman. At any given moment you could see both the man and the wolf as one.

This really and truly was, a goddamned Werewolf.... Hideous, brutish and menacing in its every sound, look and move. Close to twice her height, weight and size. Its claws alone were each as long, as her fingers. The stench of it was overpowering. Its breath in her face was sickening. The sinister snarls and growls were terrifying to hear, and heart-wrenching, at so close a distance.

The teeth in its jaws, were long and massive, and fascinating to behold, as it shined a savage grin just inches from her face. Preparing to leap upon her and tear her to pieces.

She set her jaw, looking it straight in its eyes. She was determined to die with no fear in her bearing. Determined, to die on her feet, or so she thought.

It wasn't fear; it was exhaustion that took her over. Her legs gave way to the extreme output she had engaged them in. They buckled beneath her. As she fell, her movement caused a lightning fast strike from the werewolf.

The strike missed her head by mere inches, as she crumbled to the ground. Its long claws taking out a large chunk of the tree behind her. Shaking its upper branches from the impact.

There was a crack and crackle of branches from above, followed by a loud whining cry. Something was falling from the upper branches. It hit the werewolf square on top of its head and tumbled to the ground.

There was a split-second pause from all sides, as the newcomer rolled over onto its butt, and began crying out with its screeching whiny voice again. It was a bear cub.

The werewolf was instantly back on the offensive. Paris knew it would go for the cub first, as it was closest. She didn't think about what she was doing. It was pure autonomic response that sent her grasping for the bear cub and pulling it to her, trying to protect it from the savage and inevitable onslaught.

Then, out of nowhere, **BOOSH!!**

The sound of the impact was like two Oaktree trunks being smacked together like a pair of shoes. It was the mother grizzly, and she was unamused, playing no games.

Her rush and impact threw the thing hard against the rock face. The crack of bone and expulsion of air could be clearly heard. The werewolf had no time for reprisal. The grizzly was on it instantly, as it slammed against the cliff.

Ripping gashes where claws met skin and meat. Hooking the creature under the arm, she flung it into the air. The werewolf flew thru the air and fell to the ground on the back of its head and neck. Rolling and flopping uncontrollably for another yard or so before it could halt its forward momentum and regain its feet.

Her attack was instant and strong yet again. The mother grizzly bellowed out a tremendous roar and launched a full charge at her adversary.

The werewolf gathered itself in an instant. It was now in an all-out rage, and it was not intimidated. The bear leaped through the air, with the force of a locomotive behind her.

The werewolf dealt her a crushing blow to the side of her head, stopping her in mid-flight and slamming her face straight down into the dirt.

The momentum of her charge carried her hind-end over her head. Sending them both toppling back a few yards and separating them as they rolled across the ground.

Both were instantly up and facing off at one another. The werewolf let out a roar of roars, lips peeled back to a sinister shine, revealing ferocious teeth and fangs. Its full fury backing its actions. Its highly tuned senses causing everything around it to seem in slow motion.

The grizzly was not cowed in the slightest bit by this stunning display of werewolf. She rose onto her hind legs and let loose a roar of equal fright. With a display of tooth and claws that was every bit as formidable. Both made a terrifying sight to see, for all creatures unfortunate enough to bear witness to them.

Ariel and Tristan had joined Paris under the tree. They were about to find out what happens when one of nature's finest top predators with unstoppable force, meets an unassailable nemesis of equal savage retaliation and strength.

The werewolf was an impressive size. Well over seven feet in height. The grizzly was pushing ten feet in height at the minimum. The bear had her great bulk and girth of fat, meat and fur protecting her vitals. The werewolf countered all of this with unnatural stamina and freakish ferocity.

Was this the first meeting of these two titans? It was any bodies guess what was about to unfold between these two powerhouses.

The two adversaries circled one another, trading snarls, growls and roars. With blinding speed, they both launched their attack simultaneously. The impact of which, yet again,
seemed to echo thru the forest.

Their massive sizes bulldozed one another backwards and sideways, in struggle for a dominant position. The speed and agility they were showing, seemed too great for such size and bulk. Even so, most of their deadly confrontation was a blur to the eyes. Claws were tearing flesh; teeth were taking out chunks and ripping into blood vessels.

Their bodies twisted, turned and spun about in a blinding momentum. Temporarily being pulled apart by centrifugal forces of such mass of bodies. Only to clash together again, with deadly intent.

Both were trying desperately not to go down first. Trading blows, bites and gouges in an unrelenting match of damage causing calamity.

The werewolf would only become more and more enraged. While the grizzly would not tire or go down any easier. She also had a reason backing her ferocity. A motive that is primal to all mothers of this earthly world. Protection of her offspring.

This fact would see her give her life and die if needs be, which is what made her such an aggressive and formidable opponent against a werewolf with only one forever premise, kill everything that moves, and dying was itself beyond its comprehension. A killer that would never stop, never break and run. Death being the only way to stop it.

As this epic confrontation went on, it became, more and more, clear to Tristan and the girls that momma bear was losing. Try as she did, the malice and craze of violence of the werewolf, was too much for her. She wasn't backing down though. She charged again, only to be met head on and stopped in her tracks once more.

It was just then that Tristan, seeing an opportunity, made a daring move. The two beasts had fought their way to the edge of a slope that got steep fast, not too far past the edge.

Tristan darted from the tree, picking up a sapling that had been knocked over as casualty of the battle. He fought with its balance and weight, then turned it cross ways to his body and charged toward the two beasts. Intending to push them over the edge, in a hope to send them tumbling down and over its steeper decline.

All his strength was mustered for this, last ditch effort, to gain an advantage over this thing.

At that very moment, the werewolf planted its feet hard, sunk its claws deep into both armpits of the bear, lifted her off her feet and spun her around in a circle. Flinging her out over the embankment, and tumbling end over end.

As she was swung around, her butt caught Tristan full in the chest. His forward momentum was stopped dead; the impact of which, fractured ribs as he was tossed backwards thru the air and slammed into a tree. Fracturing his back ribs upon impact with a crunching sound the girls heard clearly.

The bear cub took off after its mother, as Paris released her grip, and jumped to her feet at the sight of seeing Tristan tossed, like a rag doll, against the tree. The creature had now turned its full attention on Tristan.

Tristan's will to protect his women was greater than the pain he was in. He was on his feet, completely unaware of the internal damage that had been inflicted on him. Pure adrenaline was his only fuel.

Paris saw the werewolf turn its attention on Tristan, and though he was on his feet, he was unarmed and defenseless against this spawn from hell....

The belts that held the knives old man Ross had given Tristan, were lying on the ground in front of Paris.

As she grabbed the big one from its sheath, the werewolf charged Tristan. Sinking teeth and nails in deep, and mauling him, like a pup being mangled by a full-grown wolf.

With the blade raised over her head, Paris screamed her war cry. Mustering all her strength, as she rushed in to save her lover. She was caught with an abrupt back hand that crushed the bones in her cheek as it hit its mark. Her feet kept their forward movement, causing them to fling into the air as she was stopped in her tracks by the force of the blow to her face. The blade was flung from her hands to land yards away from her.

As her body hit the ground, the werewolf was on her. It grabbed her up in its jaws with a mutilating bite, deep into her stomach. She screamed in agony as the beast lifted her off the ground and shook her violently; all but fully disemboweling her, slinging her through the air as it released its hold, to hit the ground flopping and rolling uncontrollably, coming to a stop as she slid into Tristan, who was barely conscious from the devastating thrashing, he had received.

Paris was out cold as her body came to a halt. Tristan, with an unbelievable showing of resolve, strength and will, dragged himself over Paris's body so that he was between her and the werewolf. He forced himself onto one knee, pulling from all his reserves with enormous effort to stand and fight, but before he could stand, the beast was on him again.

Driving him backwards on top of Paris; ravaging his body with devastating affect and terminal repercussions. Tristan would not survive this, and he knew it, though he was desperately fighting back, till the bitter end.

*****

Everything happened so fast, Ariel barely had time to process any of it. For what was only an instant, she witnessed what was happening to her cherished companions.

All the rage. All the sadness. The pain, all of it. Came to a single point in the center of her soul. The raw and primal scream that came from her was a sound not human.

As Paris lay dead or dying and Tristan fought tooth and nail for his life, every ounce of what he had within him being sacrificed; Ariel's fight-flight-or-freeze kicked in. And it was – fight!

All thought and process left her. She was as elemental in her instinct as the first age of mankind. Her movement was all one motion as she darted forward, grabbing up the blade Paris had dropped.

Then, with an inconceivable leap into the air, she twisted her body as if her feet were on the ground; causing her legs to shoot out in different directions, with both hands on the hilt of the blade. She screamed a bloodcurdling war cry in mid-air, as the huge blade came down at a perfect angle to the beast's neck, severing through brain stem and skull.

As the creature's face hit the ground, so too did her feet. The blade continued its path through flesh and bone, to lodge into the jaw.

As she pulled back on the blade, drawing it out of the creature's head, she brought it back in an arc and brought it down again and again, into flesh that was inanimate before it hit the ground.

She continued her war cries as she chopped. Releasing her emotions full blown on to the world of all that had happened. She had never let go of control on this level before, few humans have.

The adrenaline rushing through her was off the charts compared to the normal bursts.

She couldn't bring herself to look over at her lovers. All she could do was release all that built up rage that had been building up inside her since the day of her parents' death.

The day the world became real and dangerous, and full of pain, interplayed with wonders, forbidden in their unbridled pleasures.

You could no longer tell what the lump of flesh had been that she continued to chop-up. As the blade rose and fell, it flung blood and gore all over her from head to toe. Covering her matted hair with thick clumps of meat and clots of blood and brains. Blood clot and gore oozed and dripped from the blade in her hand as well.

With a final encore draw of all her strength, she threw her gaze to the **Moonshine!** And let out a final scream of rage, pain and frustration that was more bestial than human.

It was… A Scream Howl! That scream howl, brought fates hammer crashing down upon Ariel.

All her senses intensified instantly. With percentages enhanced far above normal. She felt the strength swell within her as if she could pull a tree up from its roots and toss it with ease.

She knew what she was doing but had no control over it physically whatsoever. Nor did she care too. The feeling of freedom and power from the release of all the rage built up inside her was coming out now – and it felt—good.

She could feel her blood pulsing through her arteries and veins, muscle and brain. Hot burning blood. She knew everything and nothing, all at once. Everything appeared to be in slow-motion, except for her….

The rush of untamed savagery and primal thought processes were overpowering her with their intensity. Creating a cascading effect on her processes; pulling her deeper and deeper into its inescapable vacuum.

As she breathed in, she could feel the outside air around her expand, compressing in again with her exhales. Then reversing, sending waves of unseen energy pulsing from her as she exhaled.

She could smell the animals that were all around her, which no human could've smelled; she could hear their hearts pumping blood. Yet she cared for none of that. All she wanted to do was act upon the impulse to run, run, and run, and just keep on running.

She was about to leap across this insane horror and just forget it all. Just let go and run, with the freedom of Mother-nature impressed upon her, calling to her, with a booming inside her head.

But before she took a fateful leap into oblivion, she heard her name called out, "Ariel." It was Paris's voice.

It called to her, from across gulfs of time and space, tugging at her mind. Drawing her back from the precipice of madness, she was ready to leap from, and disappear into the darkness of what her now primal instinct was telling her was freedom.

As fast as it had come upon her, it was leaving her. She felt as if she was in a transition or transformation. Unable to object or prevent any of it.

Paris was using all her strength to look-up at what she thought, was Ariel. As their eyes met through the blood and gore, completely covering Ariel's face and body, Paris saw Ariel's eyes flash for an instant. Yellow, white, blue and then to a cold shimmering black. Then, just as suddenly, they flashed back to their normal green.

Paris also noticed that Ariel was standing in an abnormal pose as she turned her head to look back. Her face and body contortions conveying the primal instinct of a predator, lost in a murderous rage.

It reminded Paris of how the werewolf moved and reacted. It scared her, giving her hair-raising chills even as she was about to die. Paris knew her body was bleeding out fast, so gave it no more thought than a hallucination of her condition.

As Ariel stared at Paris, everything faded into one big blur of tunnel-vision, then expanded back into focus. With it came her reason and humanity. The reality of what was taking place took hold of her again. She ran over to Paris's side. Stabbing the knife into the ground beside her.

Both were still alive but not for long; their wounds were proof of appalling violence, beyond the grasp of most common men.

Tears poured down her face as she looked at them. Wishing she knew what to do. That's when she heard it.

The voice of a stranger sounded-off, it was only a few yards away. It said,

"So, it's true… A daughter of Talb, exists…."

* * * * *

Desperate for a way to save her lovers, knowing they were beyond conventional medicine and doctoring to save them, she screamed to the stranger with tears rolling down her face and crying, "Help us! Please!"

She would have begged the devil himself, to save Tristan and Paris. Anything, rather than sit there and watch the life bleed out of them, as she was being forced to do.

The stranger then said, "I mean you no harm and will do what I can if that is your wish, but we must act fast and I will need your help, without questions."

"You have it... Hurry, they're dying!" Ariel told him.

The stranger was dressed in clothes that looked like pajamas to Ariel. With what looked to be a robe over them that was split on the sides from the waist, down to the length it fell, to the knee, tied at the waist with a golden sash.

His pants and shirt were large and baggy on him. A deep shade of green in color. Making him look to be a priest or monk. Except for his astonishingly perfect English, he was clearly, of a Chinese descent; although, there were also clear signs of Caucasian lineage.

He hurried over to her and her dying companions. He pulled the blade from the ground next to Ariel, grabbed her hand and told her, "You must trust me now. This is the only way to save them."

She nodded her head in reply; he took her by the wrist and wiped the smeared blood and guts from her skin to expose her bare wrist. He cut it, then held it over each of their mouths, allowing her blood to pour from her into them. As he moved her bleeding wrist over Paris's mouth, he paused for a split second. With a look of astonishment on his face, he exclaimed,

"Never in all my days did I suspect one, might exist! Now all in one instant, I have found two!"

"One, a pureblood of the Talbodai – the other, of the ancient Royal bloodline. This will accelerate her healing, but she doesn't need saving."

After a moment, Ariel drew back her hand. Realizing the absurdity of his actions. In a frank tone, she exclaimed, "What the fuck is in your head!"

He told her, "Do you want me to explain everything to you, as I do it, or do you want me to save their lives, and give you an explanation when they are out of danger?"

She provocatively retorted, "I want both at the same time, and if you're incapable of walking and whistling, it's high time you learned."

As he looked over at her, with a look of surprise, a smile of admiration moved his lips. He admired her love for her friends and her strength of will that kept her mind sane and in the moment. Instead of losing touch with reality, like most would have done, after being exposed to the horrors she was experiencing. He told her,

"An explanation of why is not as easy as walking and whistling. I can help you save them. I can't focus on anything but saving them if you want me to succeed."

He looked straight into her eyes and spoke with a voice that was dead serious. Saying,

"But I inform and warn you. The decision to save them comes with a high price. They will not be the same. Their fates—and yours—take a turn this night that will not be ignored or denied. Live through this night they will. Survive the consequences of it, they still may not, and that includes you too."

Without even the slightest of pauses, she said to him, "Whatever the price, I will pay it."

He replied, "then with God as my witness, I will do all I can.

As he turned to continue his efforts, she grabbed his arm. As he looked back at her, she looked him dead in his eyes, and told him, "You say you are here to help us. I have no choice but to trust you. But know this … —*God* … *Is*, *your witness*…. And so-am-I…. And may he—have mercy on me—for what I do to you, if you're lying, or fuck this up."

He was surprised, yet again. The sublime seriousness of her words while staring into the depths of her green eyes, were unsettling in their dead certainty and exacting tone.

He was never easily moved and rarely surprised or impressed all at once. Yet this young girl had delivered both to him in just moments. He also knew truth when he heard it, and he had just heard it.

He grabbed her other wrist and cut it the same as the first. This time he held it mostly over Tristan's wounds first. Then let it pour into his mouth. Tristan unconsciously swallowed every drop. Moving his mouth directly onto her wrist and drawing it out of her to the point of Ariel almost passing out. just as Paris had done.

They both went into a shudder of convulsions and died.

The was a long drink of silence. Before Ariel could say anything, they each took in a deep breath of air and started breathing normally again.

"That is normal," he told her, "they have died of their old bloodlines and been reborn into yours."

Ariel asked him, "Am I going to bleed out and die now from saving them? With both my wrists cut so deep?"

He smiled big and said "I think not, daughter of Talb.

"You have no reason to fret in the slightest bit. Neither does she. But for him, it will be a close call. He has died once and still may die permanently. I hope he is as strong in spirit this close to true death, as he was when he willingly sacrificed himself to save the two of you without even a second thought about it."

"Against two beasts that he had no chance against separately, let alone both together. Trying to push them down the slope with a tree sapling he could barely lift.

"I've never seen such bravery and stupidity—intermixed—in such a daring display before this night.

Ariel looked down at her bleeding wrist and her eyes went wide in amazement. Right before her very eyes, the cuts on her wrists sealed themselves up. Leaving neither a scab nor scar in their wake.

She looked at Paris's wounds to her stomach. They were healing right before her eyes. Slower than her wrists but clearly improving with every passing second.

The stranger told her, "I should have known what she was, when she was able to consciously call out to you with such terrible wounds. Her calling your name is what kept you from making the shift."

"No pureblood human being would have even still been alive. The fact that—he lives, is something I've never beheld before in a human."

Ariel looked at him as though he was speaking in tongues, saying "What she is… Make the shift… Pure blood human… What kind of babbling bullshit are you going on about?"

He said, "there's no time to explain now. We need to get a fire going to keep them warm. Especially him. Like I said a moment ago; the fact that this man is alive at all is a miracle of the Gods."

Ariel's thoughts were shattered by those words, *miracle of the gods…miracle of the gods….* As it repeated in her head, Ariel's thoughts flashed back to what Tarak had told them that night in the dragoon mountains.

Through this entire ordeal of terror that had transpired since Donner pass; none of them had made a connection to, or even thought of, what they were told by Tarak, and the spirits of the ancestors of the Apache.

With that thought burning in her mind now, she stopped all questions and concern of this stranger's actions and hurriedly scrambled to gather wood to get a fire going like he had said.

There would be plenty of time for questions and answers when her lovers were wide-eyed and bushy-tailed, is what she thought to herself as she labored with the fire. Though, what she didn't know, was just how literal wide-eyed and bushy-tailed, would be….

* * * * *

With all the noise and confusion taking place, no one noticed what happened to the horses and Jojo. The horses had been tied off away from the fake camp, with Jojo commanded to the charge of protecting them. Until help could arrive, from one of his human companions if needs be.

As his human companions disappeared into the forest to deal with their death struggles with a werewolf, taking all the commotion with them, everything fell to a dead silence all around Jo and the horses. An eerie silence, transmitting a vibration of dark and sinister energy.

Jo looked like the Sphinx, as he sniffed and listened for an answer, to why all his other senses would not, or could not, confirm what his sixth sense, was screaming at him.

The only feeling, for Jojo, of any danger, was the hair that autonomically raised across his back and neck.

The horses then began jabbering to Jo, of the stalkers that were close now.

Two werewolves leaped from the shadows and went straight for the horses. Jojo leaped at the closest one. He was no match for it. Jo was snatched from midair by this calamity of nature, like a bulldog would a chihuahua.

With its powerful jaws and fangs, it ripped and tore bloody flesh and bone with deadly effect. Ripping into him as if Jo were a stuffed animal. Tossing him to the side as one discards trash onto the ground.

The werewolf at once joined the other in shredding the horses to pieces. Only seconds had passed since their initial attack and already, all three horses, and dog, were down and dying.

Out of the dark, abrupt and suddenly, the wolfpack that had joined the girls and Tristan along the trail, attacked the werewolves. With the same silent degree of stealth, the werewolves had used upon their friends. Once more, attackers became the attacked.

The werewolves fought desperately just to stay on their feet. Knowing that if they went down, it was over.

Just as suddenly as their attack began, the wolfpack withdrew. Keeping the werewolves imprisoned, in a circle of wolves. Wolves of nature, at one with the Earth Mother.

The imprisoned werewolves caught a flash of light from the corner of their eye. As they looked to see what it was, the light flashed brighter into a flashbulb of blinding light. Causing a momentary blindness to the werewolves.

In the middle of the now dimming afterglow, stood two formidably sized wolves. Both white as the purest snow.

They both stood up on their hind legs. Shifting from wolf to werewolf in the time it took to stand. A silence ensued.

All eyes were fixed on the male and female werewolves with snow-white color. With a dim glow, emanating from all around them.

The male stepped forward and passed his left hand thru the air and back down to his side. As he did this, the eyes of all the wolf pack turned blazing red. The teeth and fangs in their mouths growing instantly to twice their length. The wolves themselves doubling in their size.

They all turned slowly back to their prey and began to taunt the werewolves, with snarls and growls foretelling of a deadly notion.

The werewolves tried breaking free and escaping. Doing so to some small degree. Then suddenly, they were free of the pack and on the run.

As if for the thrill of the chase, the wolf pack let them escape. Chasing after them, to school them in the art of, all for one and one for all. Nothing beats ***the thrill of the chase***.

The white werewolves moved toward the horses. The female went first to Jo. She knelt beside him and put both her hands on him. Jojo instantly sucked in a huge breath.

A glow of magnificent light, of purple-green mix, shined from the center of her chest. It travelled in a spiral out from her center and down her arms. It went into Jojo, swirling in and around his whole body. Turning into one solid glow of brilliant white light.

As the energy she was giving him, began to feedback on itself, it spiraled back up her arms to the center of her chest again. Taking a different spiraling path of return than it did initially while going into Jo. Even Jojo's eyes shined like prisms of colored light. As she disconnected from him, the light encompassing his body flashed like a flashbulb and disappeared completely.

A voice implanted itself in Jojo's mind. It was hers, and he understood her perfectly, she whispered, "This will sustain your life but a little longer. I cannot save your life, for it is not for me to decide if you live or die. It is for another to decide whether to try and save you. Safe journeys my child."

She stood and watched her mate remove his hands from the second horse and move to the third and final one. She joined him in the effort.

It was Sarah, Tristan's horse, that they combined their energies upon. As they finished, they removed their hands.

The flashbulb of light was so energetic, it caused the horse's body to come off the ground high enough to have passed a hand underneath it.

Now that all four animals had been dosed with a sustaining shot of the divine matrix' light and energy, they both shifted back into pure wolf form.

Their eyes turned an amber color, as they gave a telepathic smile to one another, and took off, into the woods, after the wolf pack.

To perform… let's just call it, a final rite of no return, upon the werewolves, they could clearly hear, the wolf pack finishing off in the distance.

* * * * *

Ariel had gotten a strong fire going. The stranger had moved Paris and Tristan close to the fire. Ariel moved their fake camp to where she had built the fire. It felt safer to her to be up against the rock face. At least nothing could get behind them. If any more surprises were in store for them tonight, it would have to come from the front.

When she went for the horses, she found them and Jojo, lying in pools of their own blood. Ripped up far worse than her lovers.

Though they were not dead yet. Even so, it wouldn't be long before they succumbed to their wounds in any case. Why hadn't their attackers finished the job?

Jojo looked up at her and whimpered. He made a great effort to get up but could not do it. Ariel dropped to her knees in front of him with tears in her eyes. Dropping the blade, she was carrying, onto the ground beside her. Jojo dragged himself over to her and laid his head in her lap.

She stroked his head and spoke to him softly to keep him calm. She picked up the blade to give him the honor of a quick death. She looked up to the sky, her chin quivering as tears rolled down her face. Unable to speak without crying it out, she said, "God… please come take my dog home with you… Show him how to get to my mom and dad."

She looked back down at Jo and said, "Never forget that I love you Jojo. Please forgive the pain I cause."

She was hesitant. Unable to bring the knife to bear on his throat as she stared into his pleading face.

When suddenly, she recalled how the stranger used her blood to try to save her lovers. Ariel thought to herself, "Why not? What is there to lose?"

She quickly used the knife to slice her wrist again. She repeated what the stranger did. Letting her blood pour over his wounds first. Then put her bleeding wrist to his mouth. He licked it up as if he were drinking water.

She laid his head softly on the ground. Then went over to the horses and cut her other wrist deep. Using both her bleeding wrists, she repeated her actions over each of their wounds. She knew she wouldn't be able to get them to drink her blood. So, she pulled their mouths open and just let the blood pour into them.

She barely got her blood into the last horse's mouth, before her wounds closed, as they had done earlier. She couldn't believe her own eyes, as she watched them close again. Even more surprising to her, was the fact that she wasn't freaking out about it.

She didn't have a clue, as to why or how this was possible. The stranger, who appeared out of nowhere had answers though. She assumed, that his presence, and her knowing he had answers, were the reasons she was not in hysterics about all these screwed up events that were taking place this night.

She finally noticed, with her tasks completed for the moment, that she was still covered in dried and caked mud, blood, guts and gore. Not to mention she was still completely naked. She didn't want to keep running around the stranger butt ass naked. Not that he seemed to care or even notice really. But before clean clothes, a bath was in order.

She went down to the lake and waded into the water. The cold water on her skin felt amazing. She thought she would be freezing in the water, as she washed herself, but it felt wonderful.

She swam out a short distance and dived under. Swimming down until she hit the bottom with her belly. She had never been able to hold her breath for too long, nor was she ever any good at swimming underwater.

Now though, she felt like she could hold her breath for days; felt like, she could swim all the way across the lake without coming up for air. She released a little of the air in her lungs, so that she could remain on the bottom, and explore her newfound ability, for a moment.

The water was so crystal clear, the moonshine made it possible to see under the water. She played with her newfound ability for a while, and then she returned to the surface.

With a huge burst of energy, she shot up out of the water. Half her body came out and above the water's surface. As she crested the surface, she instantly remembered Paris and Tristan and swam for shore.

She was a little perturbed when she realized; although she was now clean, she was still naked, with the saddle bag that had fresh clothes in it, sitting in the camp.

With nothing to do about it, she walked back into camp as if it were perfectly normal to be naked in the woods, with a weird and spooky stranger.

She did her best not to look his way as she got dressed; Although, she couldn't help noticing he didn't even give her a side glance. Admittedly, she knew she looked a little ruff when they met, but damn…!

Paris was awake and smiling at her as she walked over and knelt beside her. An astonishing thing, given only a few hours ago, Paris's guts were expanding out of her stomach.

"Hi Chica!" Ariel said. "You're looking quite chipper for someone who was all but dead, only a short while ago."

Paris's smile widened on her lips, saying, "Care to explain how that came to be? Last thing I remember is being shaken like a chew-toy, by a werewolf.

"No! That's not the last thing I remember. I remember seeing you…. Looking like you were half a werewolf yourself. Did I imagine that? Or was it real?"

Ariel told her in a somber tone, "I'm not sure what is real anymore…. As if being chased through these mountains by evil creatures wasn't twisted and fucked up enough, this fucking guy shows up and turns the entire world of reason even more upside down. You know me. Normally I wouldn't have pissed in his ass if his guts were on fire.

"But if it weren't for him, we wouldn't be having this conversation. He seems, to know what he's doing…
"He has also promised answers. So, for the time being, we have no choice but to trust the weird ass bastard."

The stranger looked over at her and shook his head. "Good gracious, the mouth on you. You sure like airing them lungs, don't you? You are a rare and wild one indeed. As wild as the animals that inhabit these forests, I'd presume…. Have you ever even had a spanking in your entire life?"

She quickly retorted, "Only when I'm getting fucked….

"By the man you're supposed to be saving. Why isn't he conscious and talking like she is?"

He said, "I told you he might not survive his wounds. It is an exceedingly difficult thing to explain. Be patient, let me tend to him for now... while you sit over there... and shut up." He looked away, shaking his head, and whispered under his breath, "crazy—bitch...."

Tristan was still unconscious and not looking to well. The stranger had laid him so close to the fire, it's a wonder his hair wasn't singed. Even under a blanket and beside a blazing fire, he was freezing as his body burned with fever. The stranger had cleaned most of the grime from his face and body. Keeping his wounds clean as could be done in the wilderness.

The stranger was presently crushing up some herbs against a rock. Herbs he'd gathered from the forest, along with others he already had with him.

Paris asked the stranger, "Will he make it? He doesn't look too good...."

After a silence, he said, "If his fever breaks within the next few hours, he has a fighting chance at making it through this. These herbs should do just that for him.

"His will to live is impressive. He has a strong and powerful spirit and heart. I honestly did not expect him to survive this long. I've not met many men in my time of his strength and willpower. Though I guess he'd have to be this strong—to put up with you." He looked directly at Ariel.

Ariel responded instantly to his insult. Saying, "I'll come over there and shove this blade so far up your ass, it'll be easier to pull it out through your mouth. So, keep it up."

Paris chimed in with, "do you two need a room?"

"Hah!" Responded the stranger. "That'll be the day...."

Paris grabbed Ariel by the wrist, as Ariel grabbed the blade up in her hand and started to rise. With Ariel saying to him, "Oh—you motherfucker. I'm gonna stab you...! Before the sun rises...."

Paris said to them both, "If I didn't know better, I'd swear you two are related."

The stranger jerked his head up and stared at her for a moment. Then gave her a little smirk and continued his efforts of giving Tristan the herbs he had prepared.

Chapter ten

Who are you? What are we?

The she-wolf had her nose to the ground. Trotting up the path with a strong scent to follow. The freedom of the wild and exhilaration for the hunt belongs to the wolf by nature's grace. She was thrilled to be on the trail of prey. If successful, she would live the next so many days free of hunger pangs and fear of starvation.

To hunt to keep from starving is driven by instinct, but instinct is not what drives the greatest thrill—no-no.

The real exhilarations, come from the cool ground against the pads of her feet; the wind blowing across her face and through her majestic coat of fur, blasting her superb senses with a myriad of smells, each with its own distinct aroma.

There were also the sounds coming into her first-rate hearing, telling her of the little critters scurrying in the bushes near-by, and all the other creatures, near and far.

All this combined with her other quickened and heightened senses: of speed, agility, stealth, her fierce defense and attack method... these were what drove her ambition. She was a wolf in her prime, and she was proud to be such.

The scent veered off the path, into the bush, she turned to follow it. She could feel the leaves and twigs of trees and shrub brush her body, moving through and between them without any sound of step or breath. The soil was soft and moist here, rocky and dry there.

She could hear the prey she was tracking now. The smell of it becoming overpowering in her nostrils, slowing her to a walk, then to one step at a time. Choosing her steps cautiously and carefully.

She could see her victim now, just a few yards away. The blood began to race thru her veins. The muscles in her body tensed. All senses were online, as she prepared for the attack.

Her blood pumped; her heart raced, coursing vital energy through her, as she charged her prey. Her abilities of silence making her exceptionally deadly.

Her victim jerked its head up, alerted much too late. The wolf used her sound now, to freeze her prey, for a split second, in its tracks. She quickly locked onto it from underneath, by its throat.

She felt her teeth sink deep into the neck: blood pour out into her mouth, dripping down the sides, splattering her face and head. The taste was warm, sweet and delicious as the blood poured from her victim and over her tongue.

She held it in her grip, sinking her teeth deeper and deeper. Violently shaking her head side to side until she felt the blood from the jugular spurting out in hot pumps into her mouth, in unison with her prey's heartbeat.

This was the law and call of the wild. She felt the rush double inside her as she flung her prey to the ground, gasping for air as it bled-out. She savored every drop of blood, and every moment of its despair. It was in its death-throes now.

A spasmodic shudder coursed thru its body, then went limp. Telling the wolf of its final demise. She quickly and anxiously ripped it open and gorged herself on its meat and entrails. The raw bloody meat and organs she tore out in chunks and swallowed, dazzled her taste buds.

She reached her head deep in under the rib cage she had broken into, and joyfully ripped the heart free. Tasting the sweet blood of the organ squirt and spit into her mouth and down her throat as she bit into it, blood gushing out all over her. She loved her life, and hoped it was never-ending.

With her belly full, she licked her face of blood and gore as best she could, lying down beside her kill to let her meal settle. After a short rest, she rose and trotted towards a small pond that wasn't too far away.

The moonshine came out from behind the clouds, as she stopped next to the water's edge. She pointed her nose to it and let out a long and melodic howl, paying her respects to the light-giver of the night.

She was estranged by the sound coming from her throat; her howling voice didn't sound like it should. It sounded like something else, not her own. She dropped her head and stepped to the water's edge. She was startled back, as she saw her image mirrored in the water.

She tried to bark and growl at the image, but only grew more frantic, terrified by the sound that came out. It was the cry and then scream of a human, as was the face in the water, covered with blood and gore and staring back at her. It was right then, as the face in the water screamed in horror, that Ariel woke up.

She darted to her feet and looked around, feeling her face and hair for blood or guts, but there was nothing to see or find. She could still taste blood in her mouth, yet there was none. She touched her teeth with her fingers. They felt normal to the touch, though to her senses, they felt like fangs were in their place.

Her heart was beating fast. Her fingertips and toes all pounded with a pulse so strong, she thought it should be visible.

What freaked her out the most, was that instead of being horrified and sickened by a revolting nightmare, she was intrigued. Mystified and adrenalized by what was a delightful dream experience to her.

Her thoughts raced, as to why all this was so thrilling to her. It wasn't only the dream she thought of, it was everything going on. But what was going on in her head? Was she going crazy? Why were all these insane and frightful things, and such a vivid dream, so fascinating to her?

Though she wished she were upset by it all, she couldn't deny the fact that she wasn't, in the slightest bit. Was she losing her touch with reality and going insane?

She decided to keep all this to herself for now, and after checking on Tristan, whose fever had broken and was sleeping restfully, then glancing over to see Paris was sleeping just as soundly; she took a walk down to the lake.

Settling down at the edge of the water, she watched as the sun rose over the high peaks of the mountains in the distance, becoming lost in thoughts of a dream, she hoped she would have again.

She wasn't there long when she noticed the stranger on a small hilltop overlooking the lake. He was also facing the sun rise. Doing some sort of, slow dance, that she had never seen anyone do before.

She made her way over to him, and asked, "What are you doing?"

Without stopping his movements, he replied to her, "It's an ancient practice from China. It's known as Chen Family Tai Chi Chuan Fa. This is form practice, it is part of a system of self-cultivation, which is also a very efficient and complete fighting system. It aligns mind, body and spirit with the Dao, and circulates your chi, keeping you strong and alert."

She asks him, her interest genuinely peaked, "The Dao? What is the Dao?"

"The Dao is a word used to describe how everything your senses tell you is there, and everything that they do not, is bound by an all-encompassing, divine cosmic web of energy.

"How it's all connected. From the earth, air and sky, to the Sun, Moon and stars…." He paused for a moment, in thought. Ariel watched him; she was compelled, to see and hear more.

Sensing her interest, he continued, "We are also a part of its energy web. Your Chi, which is described, in your tongue as our breath and life force energy, is what connects us, to the Dao. These practices not only enhance your ability to protect yourself and loved ones from harm or danger, they enhance your ability to tap into the Dao. In ways, that most men and women never even imagine is possible; let alone, believe it exists in the first place."

Ariel walked closer to him and asked, "Are you speaking of—the Ether?

"Ren responded instantly, "Yes…. How do you know that—young one…?

Trudy told him, "My father taught us – shoved it down our throats—more like it…. Will you show me how to do this? May I—dance with you?"

He stared at her for a moment, then said, "Yes! I would be delighted to show you. For now, follow along with me, as best you can. Do not worry about being perfect. Just get a feel for the movement. That's it…. Good….

"Always keep your eyes looking forward. Move your foot out first, like this… then—gently- set your heel to the ground—before shifting your weight onto it…. That's very—good…."

With a delighted smile she did her best to follow him.

He was surprised to see how adept she was at picking it up and following along. She was doing quite well for a first timer. He was a grandmaster, and he could see her potential.

He was intrigued; overcome with a feeling that she was one of the souls, for which he was meant to pass his teachings on to. Had that day finally caught up with him? Were the paths of his life about to come-round full-circle?

·After finishing a short set, he told her, "Let's get back."

They walked back to the camp together in silence. Ariel was delighted to see that Tristan was conscious, and Paris awake again. Tristan, now that his fever had broken, looked much better. Paris's wounds to her midsection had closed-up quite nicely; although, they were nowhere near fully healed. Her cheek had recovered itself though. It was impossible to tell it'd been crushed so very recently….

She tried to get up. Saying, "I Have to pee—"

The stranger promptly told her, "Wait, let me help."

After gently lifting her up in his arms, he carried her over to where she could do her deed and set her down, leaving Ariel to help her with the rest. After she was finished, he carried her down to the lake, so Ariel could wash her naked body of the grime, dried blood and gore that still covered her from head to toe.

After helping Paris bathe, then aiding her in putting on some clean clothes, Ariel called for the stranger, who graciously came, and took her back to her bedding, which he had freshened-up for her.

He grabbed all the canteens and headed back to the lake. Before he took a dozen steps, he was stopped in his tracks, astounded by what he saw.

A humungous black dog was approaching the camp. Behind him, a few hundred yards away, were three horses grazing in the sunshine.

Looking straight at Ariel, he snapped out, "You insane—crazy—little bitch! What—in all hell—did you do?"

After seeing what he was on about, Ariel quickly turned her head to the side and looked up at the top of a tree, as if she were casually studying it for a science project. Paris and Tristan, looked to see what he was pointing at, but couldn't see anything out of the ordinary.

Although, knowing Ariel as well as they did, they knew she was guilty of something.

Paris asked her, "Ariel? What is he talking about?

Ariel not looking at anyone, chuckled with a sly smile and said, "Ah... He's just a—crazy old coot. Don't listen to his dumb-ass."

He retorted, "An old coot I may be... but I know for a fact I saw that dog and those three horses—dying from their wounds last night."

Tristan butted in, "Dying? They look fine to me.... Even if they were, what could she have done to help them?"

His gaze shot from the man to Ariel and back to the man. Both had a look of guilt on their face now, yet neither had anything to say.

After a brief and uncomfortable silence, the man said, "Never mind. There was a lot happening... I, maybe—I saw it wrong. It's possible. He looked at Tristan and said, I'm glad to see—your looking much better...."

As he turned and walked away, Tristan and Paris looked at Ariel again. She just shrugged and smirked while shaking her head a bit.

Trying to take the attention off herself, Ariel called Jojo over to her. After first paying his respects to Tristan, he walked over to Ariel. She grabbed him by the sides of his face and kissed his nose, hugging his neck until the awkward moment passed.

Her mates were perplexed but knew they wouldn't get anything out of her. For now, they dropped it. Both thinking, how they would revisit this little incident soon enough.

Paris and Tristan's thoughts burned with the question, of how they were alive and healing so fast. The fact that they were not dead, being foremost in their minds. For now, both were content, for the moment, just to be breathing.

The stranger returned with the water. He sat down and glanced at Ariel; she was staring at him. After a shared gaze, he smiled, shook his head and continued his labors, saying,

"You're going to make interesting companions, the lot of you."

Ariel then said to him, "My name is Ariel. My friends and family often call me Trudy. It's a nickname. This is Paris.

"We were raised together as sisters. And sisters, we are. And this... is Tristan Eli Jonas."

He responded with a smile, "Pleased to make your acquaintance, Trudy or Ariel, Paris, Tj. My name is Tsui Yuanli. From Shandong province in China. You can call me Ren. That is—my—nickname...."

Ariel asked him, "How long have you been here?"

He replied, somberly at first, "Long enough.... I came here on a ship loaded with my countrymen and women. After we arrived, we were Shanghaied, pun intended... into building your railroad. I killed a few of the men that were brutally mistreating the workers and raping the women. After eluding the posse, they sent after me, I found my way into these mountains. I've been happy and content ever since, living here in quiet solitude."

"How is it that you speak such perfect English? You even use our slang and curse words in context as good as we do... and you look far more Caucasian than you do Chinese for a fact." Ariel asked, and stated.

He said, "My mother was American. My father was a general in the Chinese military. We lived in Jinan, the capital city of Shandong. Also known, in the western world, as the Spring City. Because of all the natural springs in the area.

"I was afforded a good education. I have a gift for syntax and linguistics in general. I speak several languages without a discernable accent—"

Tristan broke in, "How did you know—how to save us? And heal us of such severe wounds so quickly? How come we're not—pushin-up-daisies—right now?"

He replied, "My father and mother taught me the old ways; an ancient art, passed down by healers through the generations. It just comes natural to me. I—"

Tristan cut him off, "What do you know about werewolves?" Tristan spit on the ground.

The stranger stopped his labor and looked at Tristan. Saying, "In China, they are known as Langren. I never knew they were real—until I came here to these mountains...."

Tristan continued questioning him, asking, "How—have you avoided being eaten – by these death-dealing bastards...?"

He answered, "When you're a famous general's son, you learn a few things. Stealth being one of them. Although it's not an easy feat with these damn things – they can smell you from miles away."

"What's a famous general's son—doing on the equivalent of a slave ship—bound for America?" Tristan inquired, with a note of sarcasm.

The stranger told him, "That's personal, and I might tell you one day, but not today. Besides, we have bigger fish to fry – night will be upon us soon. I thought we might have to fortify this camp, but with you two doing so well in your recovery, and now that we have horses….

"I think it best Trudy and I get—those horses—saddled… and we—get on the move. I know a few tricks to cover our tracks and scent." He looked at Tristan and Smiled, "Without caking mud all over us, which was quite ingenious. What did you hope to accomplish though?"

Tristan told him, "We wanted to observe them, maybe get a bead on how to ambush them—"

Ren laughed out loud, exclaiming, "The cock on you! And these two gorgeous anti-prims and proper's…! Especially—that—little spitfire…! If she had balls—they'd drag the ground….

"You do know you can't kill them with bullets or any other normal weapons, don't you?"

"Yes," Tristan told him, "the Cheyenne Dog Soldiers we met, explained that to us."

Bewildered, Ren asked, "Cheyenne? This far west? What are the Cheyenne doing this far west?"

Tristan answered with a perplexed tone, "Hunting werewolves… wendigo as they call them. You're pretty—damned—well informed for a Chinese immigrant…."

Ren put on a poker face and replied, "The Washoe have educated me, a little, on some of the indigenous tribes of the west. I'm a quick learner. It's not like I'm inventing the wheel to pick up information and knowledge."

Tristan had a gut feeling of mistrust. Though he was sure Ren wasn't telling the truth, not the whole truth at any rate, he dropped it and said, "Well, either way, I guess it doesn't matter. Besides, us here and breathing, means you know how to kill them."

"I didn't kill it! She did! Chopped the thing into minced meat," retorted Ren.

Tristan and Paris both jerked their heads towards Ariel. Ariel pulled her lips in between her teeth and rolled her eyes up, as if she were trying to see her eyebrows, then turned her head to the side and stared at the ground.

"Yes!" said Ren, "Impressive to say the least. But it wasn't just her doing alone. It was also the short sword you have with you. It's made of a metal that is thought to be a myth.

"It cut through that thing—like hot butter. Where did you get it? Did the Cheyenne give it to you?"

"No. There is also a big hunting knife made of the same metal. Given to me as gifts. The metal has a special property to it that helps keep a blood disease—that Trudy has—from getting out of hand," answered Tristan.

With his interest peaked, Ren now asked, "Blood disease? How does a piece of metal that was gifted to—you… help her – with a blood disease?"

"A whole other tale all its own…." Tristan replied.

Ren then asked, "Where did you get them?"

"Their grandfather gave them to me. His son, their father, found them on his journeys in the old-world countries… and brought them back with him."

In a low voice, devoid of any tone, Ren asked him, "What is their father's name?"

Ariel answered him, saying, "Our parents were Charles and Jenny Ross."

Ren lost his poker face. Turning pale white as he involuntarily jumped to his feet, and exclaimed, "Charles and Jenny Ross!"

All three looked at him in surprised. Ariel found her words first. Saying, "Yea…." Then, squinting her eyes, continued with a reverent tone in her voice. "Why…?" What do you know of—my parents?"

Ren gathered his composure, reseated himself, and responded with, "I've heard those names before. I think—my father knew them."

Ariel knew he was lying, and she was about to get to the bottom of it, when… A howl-scream echoed into their ears. Her and Ren both, jumped to their feet.

"What in the fuck! It is broad-fucking-daylight!" Exclaimed Ariel. "I thought they were night beasts only!"

Ren said, "Not entirely true. These things have a big bag of tricks. You must really have pissed them off—when you killed one of their own.

"I thought it would scare them off for a while. I guess I was wrong. That came from more than a few miles away. We need to pack up and get on the move and fast!"

Tristan bellowed, "I don't think so! Not until I have a few more answers! Both of you sit your asses right back down! First one to try to leave this camp gets a bullet in the ass!"

Ren turned to him and said, "We both have unanswered questions. They will have to wait though. We need to put as much distance as possible from here as we can. They are fast! And the fact that they have one or more among them, able to change at will in the daylight hours—makes them even more dangerous. You two are barely well enough to ride. The last thing we need is to be backed into another corner and forced to fight them. The only reason they've tipped their hats to us from so far away is because they know, they are faster than us, and hope to scare us out of our wits…. He paused, then said, with a little more conviction,

"Causing us to make foolish choices. We are in this together now… we have to trust each other if any of us is to survive…." Ren stared on at him.

Tristan nodded reluctantly. There was hard truth in Ren's words, and Tristan knew it; he was confused, not stupid.

Ren and Trudy quickly snapped to it. They gathered the horses and brought them into camp. Ren saddled them, while Ariel packed.

* * * * *

Tristan had made it onto his feet and was able to dress himself. Ariel had to help him with his socks and boots. Other than that, he managed.

As they were finishing packing the horses, Ariel asked Ren, "You want to double up with me on my horse?"

Ren said, "Not my first choice…. You've already threatened to shove a knife up my ass… and stab me…."

They both looked at each other, trying to hold back a smile. Then ren told her, "I suggest I ride with Paris. She shouldn't even be off her back yet. I'm a little concerned at what this hard ride—we're about to take—will do to her.

"She won't die—but the pain—could cause her to pass out and fall from her horse. You're going to have to stay real-close to Tristan—for the same reason. We will all trade up mounts from time to time, so we don't wear out the one carrying two of us."

Ariel told him, "You and I can do that. Nobody can ride Tristan's horse but Tristan. She's getting better at letting me and Paris on her back sometimes but, other than that, unless you're a small child, she'll throw and stomp you before you can fully mount her."

Ren nodded his head and replied, "that's good to know." He stepped closer to her and in a low voice asked her, "How do you want to handle telling them the parts we have left out about last night?"

She was silent for a moment. Then she turned to face him, looked into his eyes and asked, "Am I a Werewolf?"

Ren simply replied, "Yes—"

She let that sink in, then asks, "And they are too— now?"

"Yes. Tristan became a werewolf last night when your blood entered his body and he drank from your veins....

"Paris was already a werewolf—. Is this truly your first knowledge of this? And hers too? Neither—was aware of any of this?" He waited for words, as she pondered silently.

She shook her head, and sadly, said, "I don't know… I think my father did—and somehow… —was able to hide it from us. I think that is the reason for the—bullshit story—about a blood disease. I don't… I don't… —it's all happening so fast…. Much too fast!" She fought back a panic. Then looked up at him again, with the saddest eyes he ever saw.

She buried her face in his chest and said to him, "Ren… I don't want to be some—evil thing. Murdering and eating people…innocent people – little children and the like. What the hell are we? What exactly does it mean to be a werewolf? What are we going to do?"

He pulled her in tight to his chest, his lips went to the top of her head, and he held her until she let it all out. Telling her, "It may not be—as bad as you think. Not for you, or them. Besides, it's never a bad thing to realize you don't have all the answers. It is only then that you might start asking the right questions."

He released her only when he felt her calming some. He then put his fingers to her chin, and gently moved her face up to look into her eyes, and said, "I cannot explain now. But there is a good chance you won't become what you are afraid of becoming. There is a way. It's not a simple thing. but I swear to you. We are in this together now, to the end. Don't give up hope just yet—baby-girl."

She smiled and hugged him. He knew, as he held her, that he would protect her with his life, at all cost. He would never abandon her, or her lovers.... For good or bad, they were of one common goal now. Until the bitter end... or a happy end... he knew not. Nor did it matter to him, either-way.

He changed the subject to try to help keep her mind off things beyond any of their control at present.

"These are Arabian Horses, aren't they?" He asked.

Ariel told him, "Half Arabian... Arabian and quarter horse. Can you believe Tristan had one as well as Paris and me? Without ever meeting each other. Us girls chose them same as he did." She paused again in thought, then went on,

"This is Duke. He's mine. He is a gelding cause, grandpa swore if he hurt me one more time, he was gonna shoot him.

"That's Bella, Paris's mare. I think her and Paris have conversations when nobody is looking. And that's Sarah, Tristan's pride and joy. I think he'd fuck that horse if it were humanly possible.... He loves her more than he loves himself. He's almost got himself killed, more than once, protecting her."

Ren smiled at her wit, and said, "Let's hope you all love them, and very much. Because they are going to be with you now, for an exceedingly long time. You'll have your work cut out for you too, for the next month or so, trying to control them. And if it's even possible, training them back down to ridable horses again, once they've changed. Now that is going to be hard pressed. And wait till that damn dog—makes his first shift.... He might put us all on the run. Especially if it's during a black moon."

"Black moon?" Ariel inquired. Ren told her, "That's what is known as new moon, in your culture."

She looked at Jojo and said to Ren, "We'll just have to cross that bridge when we get there. I know you don't approve of what I did.

I know I shouldn't have played with something I don't understand... But—but look on the bright side. My actions have already proved helpful. Now we have horses to ride out of here on, instead of fighting a hopeless battle on foot...." She had him there.

She continued, "As for Jo, that's the meanest dog you've ever seen. When he gets riled up, there is no stopping him. His violence is nothing new to us—but it shocks the shit—out of everybody else...."

Ren looked over at the dog and smirked, saying, "You haven't seen what shocking is yet.... Give it a month or two. Do you know what breed of dog he is?"

Ariel shook her head in reply. Ren told her, "That's a Tosa Inu. They are Japanese fighting dogs. Bread solely for war and fighting. 'One of the meanest damn dogs on the planet' indeed. It scares even me, to think of what he will become."

Ariel looked at jo with loving eyes and said, "We love him, and he loves us. He has saved us more than once. When you see him and Tristan together you will understand the bonds."

"You know, Ren, I have yet to thank you for what... what you did... and still are... doing for us. What you did for me.... So, from the bottom of my heart... thank you."

Ren touched his forehead with both hands and brought them out and down to signify, your welcome. Then asked her, "So, the three of you are... all lovers...?"

"Yes, we are... and don't give me any crap about how it's not proper."

Ren smiled at her and said, "The first emperor of China had a thousand wives. It's only your race that's hung up on just one mate. Even then, it's not all your kind, which think that way. Even the Indians of this country, often take on their wife's sister... or sisters – if their husbands are killed."

Ariel didn't reply but her body language spoke volumes as she walked away, looking over her shoulder. Saying to him, "I still might stab you." She winked at him and walked on. Ren said under his breath, "Tristan Eli Jonas, you're one lucky—bastard....

Chapter eleven

No second chances

Tristan tried to mount his horse's back, on his own, and fell right off on the opposite side.

Paris's eyes watered with tears from physical pain as they put her on her horse.

Ariel decided to lead her horse along beside them and ride in front of Tristan, so that he could just hold on tight.

Ren climbed up behind Paris. Falling off horses would not work with the speed of travel he was counting on.

They made their way, into the deepest and uncharted parts of the mountains. Keeping a beeline as much as possible in one direction. Even though, to overcome obstacles, their trail led them to many different points on the compass.

Where Ren was taking them, there was no going the way the crow's fly to get there. He took them deep into an isolated region that only few men, including Indians, had ever traveled.

Every single day and evening, at least once, sometimes two or three times, they heard the disturbing howls of their pursuers sounding off through the mountains. Echoing their macabre song into their intended victims' ears. Even though they were still many miles behind them.

They had managed, so far, to keep a steady distance between them and that sound. Given their disadvantages, none of them had expected keeping such a good lead.

It didn't take long before those sounds became a comfort, instead of a fear factor. It set them all at ease to know there was still many miles of distance between them and their stalkers. Or so they thought.

On the fifth day of their arduous and painstaking travel, with only a few hours of daylight left, Ren came riding up fast. Reining in his horse to a sliding stop, that almost tumbled man and horse over backwards, he told the three of them, "They have fooled us! The howls we've been pacing ourselves to has been a decoy... for a larger number that are behind us less than a half a day. I caught outlines of several bodies dropping down into that last valley—right where we came into it.

"Those sounds have—easily been ten or more miles in the distance –but has never been more than—three or four different howls. I counted—at least—ten – on the other side of the valley. These bastards are—clever….

"I'd guess—they are over twenty or thirty strong... —all gathered up together and in one place – maybe—even as many as forty. We need to make some highly intelligent moves on this—*Chessboard of Death*—we've found ourselves on... and do it now... —we need to ride hard! Harder than we've been doing by thrice the effort! Or they'll be on us by nightfall for sure…!"

Ren paused his words and sniffed the air. Looking back at the trio, he said, "Scratch all that! We've got company now!"

Ariel told him, "Let's ride! Lead the way!"

Ren said, "You and Paris on one horse will never be able to keep up... Tristan isn't even well enough for the ride I suggest—"

Ariel shouted at him, "Are you going to lead us out of here or complain all day. Let me worry about—us – while—you—lead the way."

Tristan chimed in, "I'll take the rear. We can do this. Show us the way. I can almost guarantee, these girls doubled up as they are on one horse, could keep a hand on your horse's ass no matter how hard you ride."

Ren did not believe him for a minute. He had yet to meet anyone of his riding ability since he first arrived in America.

Though he did not say it so, as he told them, "Well, I guess this will be the test."

He gave Paris's horse the reins. She reared and lunged forward with all four hooves off the ground as she took off like lightning up the slope, with the other two horses close behind.

Ren truly was an exceptional rider. When they made it to level ground of the trail they were on, he lit-out with his horse in a run of all she could give. Turning this way and that, shifting his weight in perfect unison with his horse's actions.

As horse and rider reached an open clearing in the trail, keeping his full run pace, Ren glanced back to see how far he had left his followers behind.

To his astonishment, Tristan was on his right side; Trudy and Paris were on his left. Both were close enough to slap his horse's ass. Ren realized just then that they could over-take him if they chose too.

Tristan looked back across the clearing as they left it. He saw three werewolves, entering the clearing opposite them; they were on all fours at an incredibly fast run.

He shouted, "They're close enough to see! Coming up on us fast!"

Ren guessed the clearing to be about a quarter of a mile across. If they could keep that lead a little longer, there was a high probability his plan would succeed.

This was their only shot at escape. There would be, absolutely, no second chances.

Making the shift in the daytime, made a werewolf less in charge of full ability and strength. Werewolves exert incredible amounts of energy in the daylight just holding form.

Ren knew they were convinced of their superiority over their prey, to try such a drastic measure. A mistake he would make them regret. All he needed to do was to keep the distance between them constant for another mile or so, and he would make them pay, for their arrogance.

The horses were cut hard and ran on straight, until their riders were forced to rein them in fast, to keep from running headlong into a huge cliff face.

Tristan shouted, "You dumb fuck! You have led us to our deaths!"

Ren acted mechanically, as he searched the surrounding woods for unwanted guests, spinning his horse in a circle on her hind quarters to do so.

"Not yet my brother," was his reply to Tristan.

Ren jumped from his horse and ran to the rock face. Feeling around on the smooth surface of the rock, his fingers found the indention they were looking for. He recited an incantation and pressed-in with both hands against it. A large section of the cliff made a cracking sound, moved inward and slid to one side to expose a large tunnel with daylight showing its other end in the distance.

Ren shouted, "Dismount and get your asses—in there…. Leave the horses—I'll need them to lure them away from the entrance."

Paris shouted, "They will kill the horses… —and you! Why not just come with us now?"

Ren pulled a bag of powdered herbs, he had prepared, from the saddle bags and began spreading it, all over the ground, in front of the entrance. Answering Paris as he did this, "At all cost, they must not be allowed to discover this entrance. They're not hunting horses, they're after—us—

"Besides, after what Ariel did for them and Jo—the other day to save them, the horses won't be so easy to catch or kill… if not all together impossible at this point. Take Jo—"

They did as he bid them do and called Jo into the tunnel with them. As the entrance closed again, Ariel called out to Ren. Saying, "Ren! Don't fuck around! You come back to us… and I mean it!"

"Don't you worry about me—baby girl… I promise, you will see me again. Wait for me in the clearing at the other end of the tunnel." The entrance sealed itself with his final words.

He stared at the door as it closed. His mind wandered with thoughts of the future… and seeing them ever again.

In a little prayer under his breath, he wished them well. Asking that he be allowed to watch over them, after his death.

Then he snapped out of it and snapped to it. He leaned toward the horses and said something to them in a strange tongue. They understood his words perfectly, responding instantly, and bolted off in different directions. With his bag of herbs exhausted, Ren removed himself from plain view and simple discovery.

There was no audible sound of steps, as three werewolves came to a stop and stood in the middle of the clearing, at the rock face. Walking in on hindlegs, then dropping onto all fours, to sniff the ground for a trail to follow.

The herbs on the ground baffled their sense of smell. Forcing them to track by sight for a trail that would lead them to their intended victims. They were incredibly intelligent creatures. Yet, they were a little confused on whether to split up and follow all three tracks leading away or stay together, to chase after them one at a time. As they hesitated, they were confronted by something they never expected.

A huge—jet-black—werewolf stepped into view. A full head higher than any of the three. Ferocious and formidable; its lips peeled back in a snarl that even his adversaries found disturbing. This was the quintessence of all Werewolves.

The outraged monstrosity was in its victims' midst before they could blink. Tearing and rending, with tooth and claw, with an extreme prejudice and hate that fueled it. Biting the nose off one; slashing gashes that went to the bone across the chest of another.

The three werewolves fought frantically for an upper hand on this savage opponent. For savage and violent, this werewolf surely was, even by their standards.

Their attacker gave no ground at all as it bit, tore and flung them around like playthings. Slamming them into each other and to the ground. Sidestepping their onrushes easily. To it, they moved in slow-motion.

The werewolf continued its onslaught, grabbing the one missing a nose by the back of its neck with one hand. Tearing out a huge chunk of its throat with its teeth and fangs.

Delivering another strike to the head that crushed its skull and brains before the thing could fall to the ground to choke on its own blood and lack of breathing functions.

The other two withdrew from the fury of its rage. Attempting to flee with their lives, to no avail. This jet-black werewolf's attack was so savage and violent, that even hell was ill equipped to conjure such ferocity.

It was in-front of them before they could make it to the tree line of the clearing. Its roar froze them in their tracks with fear; fear of the awful ways it was about to subdue them to their deaths.

It rushed in on them before they could make a move to escape again, which was now their only thought process, knowing, full well, they were no match for this thing.

What ensued was no longer battle, it was butchery. Butchery, in its most awful sense. Even the evilest of demons, would have found this scene unsettling, in its relentless brutality and awful cruelty.

The werewolf continued to shred them, even after they were, without doubt, dead, and no longer able to be recognized, for what they ever were, in the first place.

The newcomer stood on two legs and threw its head back. Sounding off a horrendous, god-awful howl-scream. Scattering wildlife in all directions.

As it calmed itself, with its task completed, it stood staring; sniffing the air for any others that might be lurking.

It wasn't even breathing hard from the exertions of its murderous attack on the other three werewolves.

Finally convinced there was no other werewolves to murder most heinously, this magnificent specimen of werewolf, made its way on two legs into the woods. After it did so, it began to travel with incredible speed; using two legs and all-fours, to make its journey through the woods. Making a huge circle around its starting point, re-entering the clearing next to the cliff face. It sniffed what was left of the werewolves it had committed such horrible atrocities against. Then it casually made its way back into the tree line. After a short distance, it stopped beside a pile of clothes.

There it began to morph back into a human form. Its transformation was almost effortless. With his transformation to his human image complete; Ren – took in a deep breath.

Stretching and flexing his body like someone who had just got-in a good pump. Then he grabbed his clothes and stepped back out into the clearing.

He called the horses back to his side with the same sounds he used to send them away. As Bella, Paris's horse, that he had become most accustomed to and her with him, came to his side. He reached in the saddlebag and pulled out some cloth to wipe himself of filth, then put on his clothes.

The other two horses walked up to him as he finished dressing. Tristan's horse, Sarah, rubbed her head up and down against his chest. He smiled and stroked her gently, as he spoke to the other two. Telling them to stay put until he returned. Then he effortlessly jumped into the saddle on Sarah's back, and rode out of the clearing. Laying to rest Ariel's theory of being hurt by Tristan's horse, even though she had not made-it-up, and she wasn't exaggerating.

He rode off to confirm, one more time, that there was nothing close enough to see him reopen the portal. Horses hoofs splashed through pools of blood as they took off. Satisfied that he was alone, with not even a bird within a mile of him, he dismounted Tristan's horse and gathered the other two. Taking the reins of the three horses from around their necks, he led them to the side of the rock face. Finding the indention, he had previously used, he repeated the incantation, he had muttered earlier, and pressed in on it. After it opened, and he closed it behind him; he led the horses into the tunnel. It would be dark soon, and he was anxious for some company, beside a nice warm fire.

Chapter twelve

Answers

Ren walked out of the tunnel with the horses. When Ariel saw him, she jumped to her feet and ran over to him. Smiling from ear to ear, she jumped into his arms, Rapping hers around his neck.

Tristan and Paris gave each other a look that spoke volumes between them. With their eyes, they said to each other in unison… What the hell is that all about?

Tristan whispered to Paris, "What's gotten into her—about him? She is usually the first one—wants to kill everybody. She is acting like he's some long lost—family member…."

Paris whispered back, "You've got me bound and gagged…. One thing that is—clear though, is they are bonding. That's been obvious to me since he showed up."

Tristan said, "Well, that's all well and good. I'm not going to get dead in his shit tonight. Cause I don't want my anger and frustration being mistaken for jealousy.

"But it is high fucking time he lets us in on what he knows and what exactly is happening to us."

Looking for recognition in her face, he then said, "I know you've been feeling the same weird sensations I have. I can see it."

They dropped their conversation as Ren and Ariel walked up. Ren said to them,

"Let's camp here for the night and get some rest. We still have a good ride ahead of us before we get where we are going."

Paris asked him, her tone filled with frustration, "And just where exactly, is here? And where, exactly, are we going? And don't keep trying my patience with telling me to be patient!"

Ren smiled at her and said, "This is a hidden land locked valley. Unless you can fly, we just used the only entrance.

"Where we are going, can only be explained by seeing it firsthand. Only then will any answer I give you make any sense.

Tristan told him, "Fair enough…. But before we leave this spot, you're going to show all three of us how to use the only door that leads in and out of here, complete with those words you muttered. And only after all three of us have opened and closed it once and are convinced we all know how to use it; will we be leaving this spot."

Ren was already shaking his head before Tristan finished.

"That's not a good idea Tristan. We start playing with that door—we could be discovered by whatever is lurking—"

Tristan cut him off, "Don't give me that shit! Nobody capable of making such a contraption, would do so without being able to see what's on the other side before they opened it. I understand you don't make a hidden door, to a hidden valley and stick a welcome sign on it. But you damn sure make a peek hole somewhere."

Ren took a deep breath in and sighed. Sitting himself down beside Tristan, he said in a calm voice, "Yes. There is a way to see out. But these things have proven they are very smart. If my decoy of herbs and tracks leading away fails, we are in a world of shit. They could be hiding where we couldn't see them. Then what? We'll be right back where we started."

He dared not to tell Tristan: that he had also changed into a werewolf… and scattered the blood and guts of three other werewolves in front of the portal, in an attempt, to throw off the scent and tracks leading through the portal, to keep them from being at risk of simple discovery… and that was why he didn't want him looking out there.

Tristan was showing his anguish now, openly. Saying,

"I don't give two fuckin shits! Eaten by those things out there…! Or stuck in here with only a lick and a promise that we're safe with you…!"

Those words winded Ren for a moment. Tristan got a feeling, a strong feeling, that he was getting excited over nothing. He felt something, as though some unseen spirit was whispering in his ear. Telling him his concerns were unwarranted. That Ren could be trusted. With those thoughts in mind, he said, "Look…. trust must flow both ways, or there is no real trust or cooperation between us. We've followed you without question for days now. Throw us a bone here…."

"Ok...." Ren responded. "None of us are going anywhere before morning. Let's just agree to disagree for now. Get a good night's sleep. And tomorrow, we can go around and round until one convinces the other that they are right. Deal...?"

Tristan was silent for a moment, then nodded in agreement. With that settled, Ren asked Trudy to get the horses unsaddled and set loose to graze while he got a good fire going.

Tristan and Paris were sound asleep before the fire was burning. Ariel and Ren followed suit as soon as they laid their heads down. None of them had slowed down enough in past days to realize just how exhausted they all were.

* * * * *

It was after noon by the time any of them started to stir and wake up, except for Ren. He'd gone hunting that morning. By the time they were all up and about, he had fresh meat just coming off the fire, ready to eat.

"Go easy on the water. We are a good-ways away from a fresh water source." He told them.

They ate their meal over some light conversation. A good night's sleep had cheered all, of their sour moods. They talked and joked, laughing and carrying on with one another.

It was past midafternoon before any of them spoke about trying to make-do with what was left of the day. It didn't take long for them to all agree, that they had enough water to stay put for another night. Another good night's rest would be good for all. After what they had all been through in past weeks, it was a relief to be able to just sit-around.

Getting familiar with how to open and close the portal entrance would be the only task for the day. Before they ever walked back into the tunnel, Ren had already taught them to pronounce the incantation for opening the door, perfectly; he complimented them for being good students and quick learners.

Paris asked Ren, "How does saying those words out loud effect its opening or not?"

Ren told them, "Sound creates waves in the air like ripples in the water. Only difference is, sound waves are invisible.

"The higher the pitch of the sound, the closer together the waves it makes are." He paused, then said,

"Just like ripples can encompass an entire body of calm water, so too can sound waves travel through the air for long distances. Echoes through the mountains, are the result of sound waves, bouncing back and forth between mountain valleys and canyon walls.

"The ancient race who built the entrance, understood how to manipulate this law of nature. Each syllable you speak in a word creates its own unique vibration with its sound. The incantation is worded, so that each syllable increases those vibrations. As they increase, they become strong enough to influence the ingenious locking mechanism of the door.

"Causing it to vibrate out of its resting place long enough to work the portal open. When the vibrations stop, the lock will slide back in its place when the door closes."

"How did cave men figure that out?" asked Trudy.

Ren laughed hardily. Saying, "There have been civilizations that have existed for thousands of years before they collapsed back into the dust of the earth. Taking all their knowledge with them, including all knowledge—of them.

"After tens of centuries, knowledge would be rediscovered again by the next civilization to come along, only to be lost again and again in the vastness of time. Your world is on the verge of rediscovering things left behind by the last race of intelligent people. A few races—to be more precise—that documented all their knowledge on stone and papyrus, for the generations that would come after them.

"But there exists, a far more ancient knowledge that is beginning to be uncovered, from a race that existed more than ten millennia ago. One the world is not ready for, in any form. What is fortunate for your people, is that it wasn't so long ago, that everything has turned into dust. There have been a few men, which have rediscovered some of these secrets, in Europe, in the last few hundred years. They were burned alive by religious fanatics, as heretics and pagan witches for their troubles. The inquisition is an example of such bloody times....

"Just like it was once heresy to believe the earth revolves around the sun and not the other way around, only a few hundred years ago. What started in Europe, and made its way to America, will make this land, a land of freedoms like no other land in history.

You will see these wonders come to life soon—if we all live long enough—that is."

Tristan asked him, "How is it you know all this?"

"My father taught me. China has five thousand years of recorded history. It's only been a little over twice that time, that the last great civilizations before ancient Greece and Egypt, were destroyed by a great cataclysm." Seeing he had their full attention, he went on,

"A great flood... that wiped out an ancient and highly advanced race of people completely out of existence—almost overnight—in terms of time passage. They were called the Atlanteans. Of the great and powerful, Atlantis."

The Atlanteans! That name rang bells in Tristan's head. He remembered, after a moment of thought, where he had heard it before. Old man Ross, the girls' grandfather, had showed him books their father had acquired, that belonged to that race of people. He didn't divulge what he knew just then. But he did begin to trust Ren just a little bit more, in speaking the truth of what he was talking about.

He was showing them how the door worked (without opening it) when Ariel stumbled upon the peek hole and looked through it. She instantly drew back from it and exclaimed, "Shit! There is guts and body parts laying all over the ground out there. Just like those we came across back near the Truckee river!"

Tristan darted over and spied thru the hole. After taking a good long look, he pulled his face away from the hole and asked, "How did shit—end up out there—all torn to pieces like that? Were they coming here?"

Ren said, "No one else that knew of this place is alive. I alone... know of its location. The larger group of werewolves must have killed the three that were chasing us when they caught up with them. When they figured out, they'd lost our trail."

Tristan rebutted loudly, "Those are men out there!

Ariel broke into the conversation, "After I killed the one that attacked you that night... and looked at it the next day, all there was in its place was a body of a man. Or what was left of one."

Tristan looked at her, clearly perturbed by the fact she was only now speaking of this, saying to her, "You didn't think that to be something to share before now? How about leading with—that shit—next time!"

She quickly retorted, "I thought I was going in-fucking-sane! I wasn't sure if anything was real or just my imagination! Fuck you!"

Tristan was oblivious to her words, while asking Ren, as he looked him in his face, "What happened out there last night? After you closed us in here—"

Before Ren could respond, Tristan continued, "That sure is fucking coincidental that they killed them right in front of where you were supposed to lead them away from...."

Ren stumbled in his answer, saying, Well, I, they must have.... Shit—I have no earthly idea—what went on—after I snuck back in here. They must have back tracked us back here. You know yourself they are incredibly smart. Without me having to recount every step I made—to throw them off—long enough to get in here!"

All three were looking at Ren now. He knew his bullshit answer wasn't flying with any of them. He also knew, none of them were ready to hear the truth. He thought Tristan would try to kill him just for holding back. God forbid he found out he was lying outright to their faces already. No matter how good of a reason for it. Not to mention his and Ariel's shared lies and withholding of information.

Suspecting wasn't knowing; he prayed under his breath they wouldn't press him further or get indignant. He didn't want to hurt any of them in any way. He would tell them the truth before it came to that, but he still didn't know if that would help his case.

He was relieved when Ariel came to the rescue, thinking to herself if she didn't, he was gonna blow-it, being such a terrible liar.

Winking at him, she said, "Well... I think we will have to take it on faith—that the damn door will open for us. I would rather be trapped in here with Ren—than have to take on—those radical—fucks'—again...."

When Paris and Tristan looked to Trudy, then the door, Ren winked back at Ariel. She gave him a little smile. She knew he knew more than he was claiming, but she trusted him. Whatever his reason she thought, it must be a good one. She felt nothing sinister about him. She knew Tristan didn't either nor did Paris. Or he'd be dead already.

After a little more talk back and forth, they all went out of the tunnel. Not twenty paces out of the tunnel and into the clearing, a huge bald eagle swooped down to fly just over their heads.

Without thought, purely on a reaction of instinct, Ariel jumped into the air with incredible agility and caught it by one of its legs.

Before her feet were even back on the ground, she had already turned it loose. The thrashing it gave her was not worth the act of catching it in the first place. Not that she meant to. Her reaction was quicker than her thoughts. Both of her companions were looking at her in complete and utter astonishment.

Tristan's anger got the best of him. In his confusion of how she did that, and at just what the hell was going on, he yelled at her, "What in the mother fuck was that? You just—fly ten-feet in the air now? Catch eagles out of the sky? In mid-flight? Who the fuck—are you? What have you done with Ariel?

She was frightened, as she stood there; not understanding herself, just how she did it. Tristan knew she didn't have a clue by the look on her face but knew she was holding something back. Just like he knew Ren knew more than he was saying openly. He looked back and forth between them both.

Saying, "You two—motherfucker's—know more than your saying! When we get back over there… and get another fire going… both of you are going to fess-up or I'm going to empty my revolver—in your fucking forehead—Ren. And as for you Ariel, do not fuckin piss me off—"

"I'm a Werewolf!"

All was silent. She did not mean to just blurt it out, but it was too late to worry about that now.

"What…!" Paris said, more than she asked.

Ariel's knees were shaking as she told them, "I'm a werewolf. And so are the two of you now…. They hid it from us somehow—Paris. Mom and dad did. They kept it from us for all these years.

"I don't have a blood disease. I'm a fucking werewolf. I always have been since I was born. Apparently, so are you Paris. You were born a werewolf too—

"Ren used my blood to save you that night. Both of you.

"You were dying right before my eyes. I begged Ren to help you—"

Ariel's face went blank, as she relived those moments, mumbling brokenly, "Cut my wrists, let my blood pour into your wounds, then you drank from them, till I almost passed out—then you – died… —and came back – a werewolf.…

"We did the same for you both—but you Paris, you would've healed without it. Because you were already a werewolf. It'd have taken you months but.…

"Jojo! The horses… all dying—too…can't…tell Ren I saved them…same way he saved you.… What have I done…I don't know—what they are now…yes, I do…they're alive…? But-how-do-I…? What-do-I…more time."

Paris had stepped close to Tristan and had grabbed him by his arm with both hands.

Ariel's chin began to quiver profoundly, as her face became the most grief-stricken face, they had ever seen on her, saying to them as best she could, choking out her words with tears, "I'm sorry… I'm so sorry… You were dying… I didn't know what to do… —I was afraid… I was so afraid.

"I was watching you both die… right there in front of me. I'm sorry… I didn't know what to do.…" She collapsed on the ground and continued to cry uncontrollably. Paris, knowing she was telling the truth, as only she would know, feinted. Falling to the ground at Tristan's feet, at the same time Ariel dropped to the ground.

Tristan was struck dumb. He couldn't move, speak or even turn his eyes from side to side, from the shock of her words. Tristan knew he had just heard the truth from her too.

The reality and gravity of what he had just heard was devastating to hear.

As he regained his senses, his first thought was to shoot Ren, just for the hell of it. In the years to come, when he spoke of this moment, he would swear he reached for and grabbed the butt of his revolver, though he did not.

What he did do, was ask Ren to get Ariel… and bring her over to where they had made camp. He reached down and picked up Paris. Carrying her over to her bedding and gently laying her on it. Then fell backwards with unbent legs straight down on his rear… and stared in front of him.

The climax of Ariel's pain and sorrow for not telling them sooner, had not yet reached its pinnacle. She had kept the biggest news of all their lives inside her and secret for days, without letting on as best she could. Not knowing how or when the best time would be, to tell them the truth. Now that she could deal with it openly herself, she was overwhelmed by it all, way more than she thought she would be.

From being lied to all her life, then lying and hiding the truth from the two people she loved most in all the world, to being, a werewolf....

And not just being turned into a werewolf... no-no. She was born a werewolf. Which meant she comes from a family of werewolves.

And then, to top it all off, she had condemned the only man she'd ever genuinely loved in this whole wide world, into being a murderous evil spawn from hell along with her.

She tore herself free from Ren's arms and screamed as she ran off into the woods. Tristan was shaken out of his stupor when he saw her running away and jumped up after her.

"Let her go," Ren said to him calmly, "let her get it all out. There is nothing out there that can hurt her now. Not even herself."

Tristan looked at him and said, "Why don't you go fuck yourself! And when I get back—I'm gonna shoot you!"

With that said, he went running after Ariel, without waiting to see if Ren had anything else to say. Knowing he would surely shoot him if he did.

Ren, not the least bit bothered by what Tristan had said to him. Said out loud, though there was no one to hear his words, "You go and make your peace too... my newfound brother. I can only imagine what it is like, to believe you have become a monster. Condemned to kill and cannibalize your own kind. Not knowing that even now there is still some hope, that you may not be so condemned."

* * * * *

Many hours had passed before Tristan returned with Ariel. She was calm, though anyone could have noticed, she was a mess. The fire was well stocked with wood and burning strong. No one was around it though. Tristan called out for Ren and Paris. It was Paris who answered him. Ariel and Tristan walked towards the sound of her voice.

She was a few hundred yards away, lying on her back, staring up at the stars. They joined her, lying down on either side of her. Paris said to them, "In all the many times we've gazed up at the stars, I can't remember a night that they were more brilliant and spectacular than they are this night."

With her last word, a shooting star streaked across the sky, burning long and bright. With its comet like tail, not burning out in the usual manner of most shooting stars, it left a long trail thru the sky. It fell behind the mountain peaks and disappeared. Leaving no trace of its passing, across the brilliance of the starry night.

Ariel recited their favorite little saying, after seeing such a sight. Though they changed it up a lot.

"I wish I may, I wish I might, wish upon a star tonight."

All three of them closed their eyes and made a wish. They never told each other what they wished for. It was taboo to divulge your wish to others. Never knowing that they all wished for the exact same thing, every time they made a wish. To be together, for good or bad, no matter what. That premise was first and foremost to all three of them.

Tristan finally broke the silence, asking Paris, "Do you know where Ren has run off to?"

Paris answered calmly, "I don't know. When I woke up, I was alone. I came over here... and this is where I've been ever since. Are you two alright?"

Tristan answered her, "Trudy had a wee-bout, but we are all alive and together. That's all I will ever need, to be ok. No matter what fate and destiny throws at us."

Ariel sat up and said to them, "Speaking of fates and destinies... has either of you given any thought to what Tarak told us that night on the mountain?"

Tristan and Paris sat up abruptly. Each staring off into nothingness, unable to see anything material of their surroundings. Their minds taking them back to that night, with Tarak and Nantan. Their thoughts, swimming in the memory of what the spirits of the ancestors had told them.

After a long drink of silence, Ariel told them, "That night that we were attacked... and Ren showed up out of the blue.... He said something that made me remember that night with Tarak. They told us, not to search for it, that it would find us. Well, I think what's happening to us... and the fact that Paris and I are just now finding out we are born into this, fits that bill all too well. Ren showing up when he did was no mere chance. I feel that deep in my soul. There is something about him I trust. We all need to trust him...and Jo too. Until they give us a reason not to."

They sat for a long while, discussing all that had happened and how best to continue. They had agreed that night in the land of the Apache; they would not speak of anything they were told, until the future of their fate and destiny, revealed itself to them. One thing they agreed on now, without question was... Fate and destiny had come calling.

After setting a few more things in order, they all laid back and continued their stargazing. After a long period of silence, Tristan blurted out, "So, now we are werewolves.

"Nothing has changed that much. Except now we have official titles to prove rank. I'm the alpha... and you two, are my bitches."

Both the girls sat up and started in on him with insults, letting their disgust for his words be known. He just laid there with his legs crossed and his hands behind his head, looking up at the stars with a grin on his face.

They paused their rebuttals and stared at him. He casually looked at them and said, "What...? I need to get use to this... and that's just what I'm doing. Everybody knows, bitches bitch about stuff...."

They both laughed and jumped on him. Twisting him up, pulling his hair, tickling and punching him. He laughed and begged for them to stop. With them saying, they would stop only when he took back what he said. Finally, he gave in and took back his words.

After they all settled down, Ariel said, "Besides, I'm the alpha. You two are—my—bitches... my blood. Remember?"

Tristan sat up laughing and jumped on top of Ariel. The two of them started back and forth on who held the title of alpha. Paris watched them and laughed at their silliness, saying, "Well, at least we know who the bitches are."

Tristan and Ariel both jumped on her, double teaming her. All were laughing and enjoying their camaraderie.

It wasn't long, before tickling, punching and wrestling became touching, feeling and kissing. They made love, there under the stars. Their passion and love growing ever more for one another.

Afterwards they curled up together. Tied up into each other like a giant pretzel and went to sleep. The next morning, they were up, dressed and finishing up some breakfast when Ren returned.

"We were just about to send out a search party. Glad to see you're alright and returned in one piece," said Tristan.

Ren smiled and said, "I figured I would give you all some space. To sort out all these new things happening to you. I am also not ashamed to admit I wasn't so sure one or all of you wouldn't try to murder me in my sleep... or worse."

Tristan said with a smile, "We wouldn't have been that sly and sneaky about it.... Your safe for the moment."

Ren sat down and grabbed one of the canteens to quench his thirst. Then said, "I guess you guys made up then."

Tristan replied, "There was nothing to make up about... I'd rather be alive than dead. If what Ariel and you did, was the only way to keep us alive, then I have nothing but gratitude for it. We all agreed last night. At least, we are all werewolves together. As long—as we are together and free, the world is still a place worth living in. If we have to isolate ourselves from all humanity for the rest of our lives... at least we have each other."

Ren asked him, "Why would you isolate yourself?"

Paris spoke first, "Because none of us want to savagely murder and eat people. Finding a place where we will never cross paths with other people is the only way to accomplish that."

Ren sat in silence for a good while before asking them,

"What if I can offer you another option?"

None of them said a word, but he had their full attention.

He continued, "What if I can teach you how to control it... and use it? To your advantage.... Instead of what you believe, you will become."

Before any of them could say anything, he said, "Before you answer, it's my turn for confession. I ask only that you give me a little longer. Let's make haste today to where I've been taking you all this time. Once there, what I must tell you, will be easier to swallow and accept as the truth."

Ariel was the one that spoke up first, saying, "We agreed last night. You have given us no reason not to trust you... and that, we can always just kill you, when and if we find out that—we can't trust—you.... We were going to press you for answers now but, I can wait until we get where we're going."

Tristan and Paris agreed and then Paris asked Ren, "How much further is this place you speak of?"

Ren replied, "If we saddle up and head out now—we could be there well before night fall."

Tristan then said, "We'll have to track down the horses. I haven't seen them all morning. I haven't seen Jo either. But I'd bet he's with the horses."

Paris started to get up, saying, "You two stay put—Trudy and I will go find them."

Ren said, "No need."

He put his hands together in a strange configuration. Putting the back of his thumbs to his lips, he made a loud, ear piercing, whistling sound, which made them cover their ears.

The sound echoed far out into the distance. Where no echo should have been able to manifest. After a minute or two, three horses and a huge black dog came running into the clearing and stopped in front of the campsite.

After a moment of wonder, questions and answers, followed by feelings of sheer delight at the prospect and then promise, that all will have these skills, the girls took the horses and began prepping them for their journey.

Ren watched them as they walked away. Admiring their extreme beauty and gorgeously perfect female frames. Then he looked at Tristan with a sly smile and said, "Got yourself a little harem going, I dare say...."

Tristan returned his smile, saying, "It's not like that—"

Ren cut him off, "Tell that to someone who hasn't been with the three of you, like I have in past days. I see how you covet them... and do everything possible to ensure their safety... and they, do the same for you.

"Those girls could shove hot pokers in your ass... and you would still be glad just to be near them. What you three have is a rare thing. Not the fact of two women and one man. I speak of the unconditional love and devotion the three of you have for one another. The three of you are as one in all things. That commitment to each other is the greatest strength the three of you have. It will serve all of you well in the trials and tribulations that lay ahead of you now."

Their conversation was interrupted by the screech of a bald eagle. It swooped in low, circled the camp, then landed on a small boulder laying just outside the inner circle of the camp. Almost close enough for Ren to reach out and touch.

"This is king," Ren told Tristan, "I'm surprised he came back so soon after Trudy plucked him out of the air."

Tristan was mesmerized by the eagle's magnificence. Ren said to the Eagle, "Good morning old friend, come to meet our guests?"

The eagle spread its wings out full and screeched again. The girls were watching in the distance. They were as mesmerized as Tristan was. The eagle's wingspan was every bit of ten feet across. Standing over four feet to the top of his head. A truly magnificent specimen of a flying predator if ever there were.

The eagle closed its wings and sounded off a short number of squeaks and squawks. Ren returned his squeaks and squawks in kind. Tristan realized after a moment that they were speaking to each other.

"You have got to teach me how to do that," he said to Ren.

Ren replied, "I will. Although as time passes you will come to realize speaking to all animals is part of the abilities you now have. As you mature, they will come to all of you naturally. I think it safe to say Paris will be the stronger of this skill at first. What I can teach you right here and now is... All animals, of the natural world, communicate through a mind connection of thought. Even the trees have this ability. Although they don't have much to say to our kind. With all creatures, big or small, every look, sound, and movement is language. This will all become clearer to you as your training and skills progress."

Tristan started to probe him as to how he knew all this, then decided against it.

King flew back into the sky as the girls approached with the horses. Ariel asked Ren, "Is that the one I caught?"

Ren smiled, "Yes! Lucky for you he didn't hurt you."

"Didn't hurt me? Have you not noticed the cuts and scratches all over my arms and face?" Ariel retorted.

Tristan laughed a jolly laugh.

Ren replied, "lucky for you he realized your innocence and didn't kill you."

Ariel asked him, "How do you know?"

Ren said, "He told me so, just now."

Ariel turned away smiling and shaking her head. Saying,

"You are—one weird—motherfucker."

Tristan laughed again. Ren turned to him and said,

"Motherfucker.... This is not the first time she has used this insult on me. Even you called me this yesterday. Why does she insult me now?"

Tristan laughed yet again and said, "She wasn't insulting you just now. It was meant more as a form of endearment. Whereas yesterday, I was insulting you...."

"In the southeast region of this land, where I am from. It is a title given to black slave men—used for breed stock. It progressed from there, into an insult. We would jokingly call each other this and after a while, if you were among friends, it was used the same as she used it just now. As a term of endearment and admiration. Few people used it in this manner besides my blood family... and the black folk I consider family. The girl's picked it up from me. I think Trudy has improved upon its use somewhat...."

With a solemn tone, Ren asked him, "You owned slaves?"

Tristan quickly replied, "No! We freed slaves... and protected them on and around our lands and property. I have not... and will not... ever condone the slavery of any man, woman or child. Even Sarah and Jojo are free in my eyes."

Ren then asked, "You fought in the war of the states?"

"No... I wasn't going to fight for the south and kill for a cause I didn't believe in. Nor was I going to fight against my southern brothers. Not every slave owner was hostile towards their slaves or mistreated them, except in their owning of course. Even so, for the slaves blessed with gentle masters, it was safer than being free, to roam a land that has not yet grasped the concept that all men are born free... and should remain so all their lives. Call me a coward if you want. That is my take on the subject... and I stand by my conviction."

Ren looked him in the eye and said, "Tristan my brother… I may call you many things… in days and years to come. Coward… will not be among them…. Motherfucker…."

* * * * *

They got under way and pushed through the thick forest of trees that had been blocking their full view of the valley, they now found themselves in. It was a spectacular scene.

So large, you could not see the other end except for the tops of the mountains that contained it. Even the sides were barely visible. From where they sat on their horses, on the slope of the mountain they were on, they could see the huge lakes and water ways that wound through it.

Even Tristan was crying and laughing simultaneously at its beauty.

Paris cried out through her tears of joy, "I could live here the rest of my days and never walk out that portal again."

Tristan put his arms above his head and yelled at the top of his lungs, "I love you Earth Mother! Yeah!! What a privilege you have afforded us!"

Ariel, unable to hold in her excitement upon hearing his words, began to cry and laugh even harder. "WOOOOOO HOOOOO!!" She exclaimed.

Ren, who was intimate with this valley, was moved by the admiration and respect they were showing for it.

"It's like seeing some prehistoric land that time has left alone!" exclaimed Tristan. Not even trying to hide his tears of joy. Completely enveloped in his merriment for such an extraordinary and miraculous sight.

They could have reached their destination within half a day. Less, if you knew the valley as well as Ren did. Though he also knew, of his trio's childlike wonder for all of nature's beauty and gifts. From the highest peaks to the smallest flowers and grass. Stopping even to inspect small insects, spiders, snakes and bugs. It would be after night fall before they arrived at where he was taking them.

If they thought what they had seen and witnessed thus far was, off the map. They would be blown away by what they didn't know they didn't know, that still lay before them.

They rode on through the day. Completely enveloped in the beauty all around them. As Ren had predicted, it was after night fall before they got to where he was taking them.

Ren bid them, to set up a camp and fire. While he freed the horses from their saddles and tack. Then went off, with Jo at his side, to fill their canteens with water from the nearby creek.

You would have never known the horrors and terror they had faced in weeks passed. Not by looking at them, as they joked and laughed around the huge blazing fire they had created. None of them were even hungry. Something Tristan spoke of, after a time. Saying,

"You know, I'm not the slightest bit hungry. Even after such a day. I can't recall many days as wonderful as this one has been. I thought being a werewolf would make me dark and evil. If anything, it has increased my own personifications tenfold. The colors of the mountains and forest, even the water, seems more incredibly beautiful than I can recall them ever being.

"There is a glow around everything. Each with its own separate sphere of glowing shine around it. From deeply colored, to bright silvery white. Like surrounds you—Ren.

"I don't want to kill anything in this valley. Not now, not ever. The fuckers we've seen, want to kill everything… Will I lose this feeling as a werewolf? When I am in the form of a werewolf?"

Ren told him, "Yes and no… you will see all the colors even more vividly, as a werewolf. But you won't give a shit… without a doubt. But it is possible to reclaim your humanity during a shift. Then you will have the power to choose again." After a short pause he continued. "If left untrained, the werewolf within you will consume the humanity of your being.

"A wolf of nature is no-more-evil, than the rabbit. It's only its nature, and its place in the food chain of the web of life.

"Nature has a perfect balance for all living things. It is only humans that have forgotten… and lost their place within it. Forced to cast it aside eons and eons ago when evil found a foothold in this world through mankind.

"There are men, with an evil side to them, that is far greater than any werewolf, will ever be.

"Mankind was once the fairies of the forest. Using its intelligence to help all lesser animals and living things to live and grow in harmony. Then they were captured and enslaved, by beings of another world. When they finally freed themselves from their bonds and overthrew their masters; they had forgotten who they were, and why they were here in the first place.

"A thing that has been slowly correcting itself through the ages ever since. Less than a century or two from now; if evil does not take over, humans will remember and realize their place in this world once again. They will take their place in the web of life and become more powerful, intelligent and protective of this Mother Earth than can be imagined in their present state of growth."

He allowed them a long drink of silence, to absorb what he had told them. When they looked at him again, he continued, "Only man, as you well know, is capable of diabolical things outside of his nature. If you see a man eating another man, you say that's evil. Yet, bears, mountain lions and wolves do it. Is that evil? No... it's just their nature. The call of the wild. The law of the jungle.

"It's simply how mother nature keeps the balance of all living things from stagnation and decline. You will not lose your newfound insight and gifts that have yet to come into full fruition. If, you embrace and love what you now are.

"You must realize that the wolf you perceive, as only now existing within you, has been there all along.

"It has only now been unleashed to form a duality within you that must be reunited with your humanity. Or you will lose yourself to it and become the things that you have seen thus far as werewolves.

"The first werewolf wasn't part of the natural order of this world. He was above it you might say. An ancient protector of the angels of the one god. Always here and never here, all at once. The angels were sent to teach man his place in the new order as protectors of this earth mother... and give him the gift of knowledge of the Ether. So, that he could do the tasks placed upon him."

"One day, not too far in the future, all men and women will remember this knowledge and once again be the protectors of this precious Mother Earth. There are many like this Earth Mother. But this one is ours... and we are hers. To love and cherish her is paramount to the future.

"You may or may not be hungry. You may or may not be thirsty. Cravings are all they are now. You will never have to eat or drink again to sustain your life and energy.

"Food and water will now only be something you do, as when you smoke a cigar, or drink some really good whisky.

"Only when you are severely injured and close to death, will it become necessary to consume, to heal quicker.

"The glow you are now starting to perceive, comes from all living things. Even inanimate objects have it. It has always been there. You are just now finally able to perceive it.

"For men and women both. When all things are happy and positive, they glow brighter with what has recently been coined, an Aura. When they are in negative feelings and emotion, it dims. It will dim... and they will not be able to perceive it around others.

"When there is danger, yours will at once clue you in to its presence. Danger and evil will no longer be a thing able to hide itself from you ever again. No matter what mood you are in.

"Most people see all this as magic, that only a privileged few are born with, which could not be further from the truth.

"It is a birth rite of all humanity. That has been forgotten by most and suppressed by the ones who have knowledge of it. Holding knowledge of this power only for themselves. So that they can continue to repress the masses and keep them in their grip of enslavement without any one ever being the wiser to this fact.

"All men and women are capable of this. They need only to be taught how to cultivate it within them to understand its mystery... Be it towards good, or used for evil, is a choice.

"Great knowledge and power corrupt... and turn into great evil only when a few possess it, and the wisdom to wield it is cast down. They only way to thwart this travesty is to teach and give it to everyone.

"Then it can no longer be a foot on the necks of the uneducated. When everyone has access to cultivate and own this great gift, Mankind will be, united... and all poverty and sorrow will disappear. Creating a wonderous world that is not even imaginable thus far.

"Though it will take the arrival of beings from another planet to show up and attack, for mankind to see that all races of men are of one blood, and brothers as such.

"All of this I speak of, that is to come, will not be a new discovery. It will be a rediscovery….

"But I have regressed greatly. Werewolf…. the Greeks call us Lycanthrope. In ancient Egypt, we were worshipped as Wepwawet and Ophois. The Chinese call us Langren.

"The Franks called us Garulf, and now the French, call us Loup-garou, the Cajuns call us Rougarou. The natives of this land call us Wendigo. The most common term from Europe today is, Werewolf.

"Our true name, from the time of the first werewolves, is impossible to pronounce with a human voice and tongue.

"The earliest pronunciation and meaning in human tongue, came long after the first werewolves. The first and oldest name comes from the time before the lands of Atlantis and Lemuria. It is … The Talbodai….

"It means, protectors of the light within all things good… and the messengers and executioners of destruction. Ponder this… Evil spelled backwards… is live. That's the yin and yang of things—"

Tristan stopped him there. All three had the same question on their tongues. Tristan just spoke first.

"Why do you keep using the reference, we and us?"

Ren looked at him and the girls. Not realizing, till that very moment, he had said as much. Then he said,

"I promised you a confession when we arrived here. I guess now is as good a time as any. But It will be easier to show you than to tell you."

He undressed himself completely and stood naked before them. "Do not be afraid, my little trio, who possess three hearts that beat as one."

He closed his eyes. When he opened them again, both of his eyeballs were jet-black. Within a minute's time, he transformed into a Werewolf and stood before them in all his glory. They all thought him, magnificent… and fierce.

Tristan was on his feet instantly. Instinctively reaching for his pistol, which was not on his side. The werewolf snarled and growled at him. He stood frozen in place as one does to keep an angry dog from biting or outright attacking.

The werewolf now before them was well over eight feet in height. Paris noticed that he had a human cock and balls, even though he was not human. They would later find out that Ren was a werewolf first and a human second. A true shapeshifter... An original Talbodai....

The werewolf threw its head to the sky and delivered a tremendously loud screaming howl that made the onlookers cover their ears.

It then looked again at Tristan. Its demeanor and look on its face, especially in its eyes, were both menacing and threatening. Never once did this change. Was it still Ren inside this monstrosity? Were they safe? It stepped toward Tristan.

Tristan took a step backward. The werewolf was in his face before he could take another. It shined its huge teeth and fangs. Making a hissing and low growling sound. Then, the werewolf took its hand, with its long and sinister claws protruding from its fingers, and caressed Tristan's head from back to front.

Tristan expelled a huge breath of air from his body. Sucking in another and expelling it the same. His adrenaline was pumping through him on an astronomical scale.

He found himself, once again, laughing with tears rolling down his face. His heart filling with joy from the knowledge of this new reality, no longer to be misunderstood or not believed. He could feel the tremendous power and strength coming from the werewolf as a tangible thing. Emanating from its hand with every stroke to his head, yet the strokes were as gentle as his own mother's touch.

Tristan spoke to the werewolf before him. Saying, "You can control it. And you will teach this to us. I can see my family again without worry of hurting them. We are not condemned to be a plague to mankind."

In response, the werewolf through his head back and howl-screamed again. Tristan fell to his knees. Relieved he was not to be the things that had chased them through the mountains. A huge weight was lifted off his shoulders.

His tears were the cleansing agent for the dark cloud he had been slowly creating above himself. The fear of being an evil spawn of hell being erased with each teardrop.

The werewolf stepped to Paris next. She stood up and looked him in his eyes. No fear was in her of any kind. She was spellbound by the awesome creature before her.

Its breath rattled with its inhales and exhales. Even such a simple and innocent thing, seemed menacing by its very nature.

Paris's misgivings and misunderstandings were being eradicated and irradiated, simultaneously, here and now.

Then, with a movement that was a blur to normal vision, grabbing her by the sides of her head, it instantly put its face beside hers. Snarling and growling as she smelled its breath mixing with hers. She did not flinch or show any sign of fear because there was no fear in her. It stood upright again towering over her. Still holding her on both sides of her face. It then took its huge thumbs and stroked the sides of her face. From the edge of her eyes to the back of her head.

Then it moved away and stepped in front of Ariel. She was already on her feet and staring up into his face. The werewolf's head moved from side to side. Snarling and growling a low growl as a dog would when something is too close. Ariel said,

"I feel like little red riding hood. Except you are not ugly to me. You are the most beautiful creature I've ever seen.

"I'm scared and exhilarated at the same time. You truly are a gorgeous spectacle...."

The werewolf shined its teeth and let out a roar in her face. Its breath blew her hair back as it did so. Ariel stood as one who had just been blown a kiss. Saying,

"I thought your breath would stink but it doesn't. It's an alluring odor. Quite pleasant. This is your true form isn't it?

"Your human form is your mask, huh? I bet you can assume the form of any human you want, can't you? You are him, aren't you? You are the first of our kind. Or one of them anyway. I don't know how I know this. It's as if I have always known. Even before I was born and couldn't remember until right now, at this very moment with you in my face."

The werewolf roared in her face again. Lips peeled back in a snarl that would have sent most into cardiac arrest. But not Ariel, she laughed and said, "That's how a werewolf smile's, isn't it? It's like I can read your thoughts. Change back now."

The werewolf, with a sudden abruptness that made the trio jump back, roared an immensely powerful roar in their faces.

They were startled by its suddenness... and humored by its reality at the same time.

Then, the werewolf stepped back, and as quickly as it had transformed into a werewolf, it changed back. After a half minute or so, Ren stood before them once again and began putting his clothes on.

The trio were full of questions and inquiry. Asking multiple things all at once.

"Enough for now." Ren told them. "I will tell you no more tonight. Rest now and absorb what you have learned about what and who you are. There will be ample time to teach you what you need to know—my Trio. You've done very well with your first up close experience with a Talbodai. Rest and sleep now. We have a lot to do tomorrow. This isn't the end... It's only the beginning...."

* * * * *

The next morning, Ren woke them up early. "Gather yourselves and do what you must to be fully awake when the sun rises over the mountain tops. All of you need to know this and how it works," Ren told them.

They got up and were ready when the time came, he spoke of. The morning light had showed them that he had brought them to the base of a huge rock face again.

They were at the base of the mountains that made up the north side of the valley. An enormous protrusion of rock stuck out about a hundred yards at a right angle from the cliff face. In its face was carved out a gigantic platform some ten feet from the ground. It stretched the entire width of the protrusion. It was open on its east and south sides. With its north and west end making up the side and back walls. It went back into the rock face some 150 feet or so from east to west.

The wall at the back or west side of the rock face, and the north wall, was carved into beautiful, intricate patterns and faces from a time long past. Precious metals and jewels decorated both walls. The roof of solid rock, some twenty feet above the platform, was held up by tremendous columns, staggered across the platform. The roof and columns were also, intricately carved and imbedded with jewels.

Steps were carved into the front, or east-side, of the platform. With another set of steps carved into the south side, that also led to the top of the platform. Carved into and out of the bedrock, the whole thing had been chipped out and polished to an astonishing perfection. The west wall looked to be the front of a temple or fortress.

There was a huge door at the back of the platform that faced east. Or what looked like a door at any rate. There was no visible way of opening it that the girls or Tristan could see. The entire thing looked to be ancient, as old as time.

The sun finally rose high enough above the mountain peaks for its light to shine upon the entire platform, and shine upon the back wall with the door imbedded in it.

As it did, a keyhole began to glow in its surface. Ren quickly approached the keyhole and pulled a key from a pouch he had taken from its hiding place under a fake rock against the cliff face, at the side of the temple fortress.

He inserted the key and turned it in an exact combination of turns from side to side.

Tristan recognized that combination, as the exact one used to open the entrance to the underground chambers that the girl's grandfather had shown him. He assumed it had similar determents as the chambers on the ranch. A question he wouldn't forget to ask Ren later.

The door opened inward, swinging in on huge hinges. Ingeniously fabricated to a fine precision. A precision that seemed impossible for even modern building. Let alone seemingly stone age peoples.

Of course, then again, this entire temple was carved into and out of solid granite. A thing not easily done even in this modern age. Impossible without the use of explosives and modern powered machinery. Its construction and completion must have taken decades.

The outside was crude in comparison to the inside. The inside walls, floors and ceiling were overlaid with slabs of marble of all colors. Inlaid with patterned lines of silver, gold and jade. There were many objects within the structure made from obsidian. Some small and some large.

In the main chamber, there was nine daises with throne like chairs upon them. Tristan and the girls looked like children sitting in them due to their large size. The thrones were made of the same metal material as the miniature pyramid that was in the hidden chamber back at the double R ranch in Texas. Black in color, with the same dull green glow emanating from deep within it, from no discernable source.

There were hallways that led deep into the mountainside.

Even Ren had not yet explored every chamber and passage, nor had he discovered, every hidden chamber or secret passage, which led to places, only ghosts from a time long forgotten, knew their purpose. The bed chambers had cushions and mattresses that were untouched by the passing of the ages. Tapestries that looked like they were hung yesterday, yet they were thousands of years old.

Ren avoided their questions of how this was possible, telling them that, for now, to just be satisfied with knowing they would live in the comforts of the temple while he trained them. Instead of on the ground and smelling like the campfire every morning.

He told them that the properties of this place and its power source, would accelerate their mental capacities to master disciplines of the mind and body in weeks and months, which would normally take years.

"Come with me, the three of you," Ren told them. "There is something I want to show you. And something else I need to confess."

With their interest peaked, they followed him over to the wall that was directly behind the nine thrones. He took a small statue from its pedestal at the far corner of the wall. He then shoved it into a hole in the wall where it fit like a key.

He turned it to the right and pulled it free from the wall; the entire wall began to move down until it was flush with the floor. The chamber he exposed, was large and spacious, with many couches and chairs, made for comfort. In the middle was a huge bed. Fifteen or twenty people could sleep on it without ever feeling cramped. He told them it was the orgy room.

Though this was easily the most beautiful room he had shown them so far, they didn't seem to notice. All three, had their eyes fixed on the back wall. On that wall were two large paintings. The colors used were vibrant and pure, giving them a 3D effect. It looked as though you could step right into them. They were both so large, you couldn't see any of the wall they were attached to.

They looked like they had been painted and hung only a few days ago, their colors were so rich and bright.

It was the images within the artwork that had them staring as though they'd saw a ghost. One painting was of two White Wolves. The other, was of two White Werewolves.

The girl's and Tristan, all recognized them as the pair they'd seen that night at the lakeside. Just before the attack and Ren showing up.

Ren wondered why the paintings had them so enthralled, finally saying, "Those two are the father and mother. The first of the Talbodai to walk in the flesh.

"They are, Tal, the father and Tatyana, the Mother. It is all written in that codex right over there."

"The very first of our kind were demigods. When they first appeared on this world, they were in the form of what is known today as werewolf.

"The first two Talbodai were male and female. Both were as white as the purest snow. They were sent here as guardians of the nine angels. Sent here to establish and teach humans, whose time it was to rule this world."

"Bringing balance to all its creatures that were here and had survived the great catastrophe; that happened many tens of thousands of years before the time of the cataclysm that sank Atlantis and Lemuria.

"After the nine angels returned to their plane of existence, the white werewolves chose to stay and continue the care for this Earth Mother. For them, she was a paradise and they fell in love with her.

"Through the eons, they learned to change shape into any living creature that had a heartbeat and pumped red blood.

"Heartbeats and red blood are unique to this world.

"When the time of Atlantis came to be, they were known as, The Taobodhi."

He took out writing material and wrote out the spelling, T-a-o-b-o-d-h-i. Then said, "After the cataclysm, its pronunciation changed and is better spelled this way."

He wrote, T-a-l-b-o-d-a-i. Then said, "Through the ages, the E sound at the end has become an A-or-I sound. Use which ever you like."

"The male was called Tal, messenger and bringer of balance by death and destruction. The females name was Tatyana, which means, Fairy Queen and keeper of the balance of life according to the nature of this world. Tal and Tatyana were the first werewolves as they are known today.

"During the time of Atlantis, they were still worshipped as demigods of the creator. During that time, they had two twin boys. These boys were born in the form of werewolves as their original form but had the gift of shapeshifting, like their parents. They were named Ren and Jinn. One of the brothers, Jinn, fell in love with an Atlantean woman.

"Against royal decree, they secretly chose to be together anyway and had a son. They named him Thorax.

"He was born a human. He had the ability to change to a werewolf but, he would only change according to certain cycles of the moon. He had no control over when he changed nor did he control the werewolf during these cycles. He was wild and terrible in his wrath.

"He accidently murdered his own beloved wife and child, because he refused to let his father, teach him anything about his true nature or how to manage it.

"What his father didn't know was that a demon had possessed him. Turning him and twisting him into a malevolent thing of the darkness.

"Full of grief and hatred, he killed his parents and ate them. Doing so, completed his transformation to a spawn of hell. Turning him into the evil thing that werewolves are known to be today. He eventually learned thru dark arts how to control the werewolf. But by that time, he was evil to the core. He is the descendant of every werewolf that exists today, except for the three of you and me…. We are the only offspring of the true Talbodai."

Paris said, "We have seen these werewolves… or Talbodai. They played with Trudy… and after smelling me up my ass and everywhere else, bowed to me. Then they just, walked away. When they got to the tree line, they just disappeared. Vanished into thin air like ghosts. Though they were most definitely not, ghosts. The cold noses up my ass, and the sounds they made—are still fresh in my memory as if it happened yesterday."

Ariel said, "Me too. When they interacted with me and Paris, they looked like that." She pointed to the painting of the two images that looked like wolves. "When they first came upon us in the clearing, they looked like, that." She pointed to the werewolves.

"We were hiding in wait to get a look at the fuckers' that had been chasing us; they, showed up first. They came into the clearing as werewolves, spied our fake camp and left.

"Not too long after, they both returned looking like real wolves. Except for how humongous they were.

"I realized, after they sniffed me out of my hiding spot and started playing with me, they were not the ones stalking us. So did Paris, after they treated her like a queen.

"We had all just agreed they weren't the bad guys... when the bad guys showed up. The same night you showed up."

Ren almost fell over. He turned white and then beat red.

He was speechless as he stared at the three of them. He wanted to speak but could not.

His mind was racing trying to make sense of what he had just been told. His first thought was they were lying. But how could they be? Why would they be? His legs began to give out from under him.

Tristan, being closest, ran over and grabbed him before he fell. He asked Ren, "Are you alright? What's happening to you?"

Ren muttered, "I need to sit down. And I need you to tell me everything you remember. I want to hear from all three of you exactly what you saw, and what happened."

They recited their tale with no detail left out. The whole time they were telling him their story, Ren never looked at them once. He just kept staring at the paintings of Tal and Tatyana. They had finished their tale for some time before he took his eyes off the paintings. Saying,

"You have just recited, in exact detail, word for word, the beginning of a prophesy fulfillment. A prophesy that was written down and documented in two books that are exact duplicates of each other. Books that were written and bound over twelve thousand years ago. Before the ancient cataclysm, and still look like they were written yesterday.

"Pages and bindings that wouldn't come again before mankind fell back to writing on stone, clay and papyrus and would take thousands of years before books as we know them would reemerge."

Knowing by the looks on their faces, they didn't believe him. He walked over to a bookshelf on the side of the chamber and pulled a book from it.

Tristan instantly recognized the binding and cover as identical to the one Richard had shown him. He held his tongue for the moment. Too curious to know what Ren was on about before changing the subject.

Ariel was standing next to Ren as he thumbed through the pages of the manuscript. She asked him, "What language is this thing written in?"

Tristan, unable to hold back, though he wished he would have, blurted out, "Atlantean." They all looked over at him.

"Right?" he continued, "Its written in Atlantean."

Ren quickly responded, "That wasn't a guess. How do you know this?"

Tristan said, "Because I've seen the twin to it you just spoke of."

"Their father brought it back from his travels overseas. He was in the middle of trying to translate it when he was killed—"

"Charles? Found the other book?" asked Ren, a look of excitement on his face; before Tristan could answer him, he started talking again. Talking to himself more than to anyone else.

"That crazy son of a bitch! He went back there after they almost killed us the first time. Well him anyway. He was right.... It was there...."

He looked at Tristan and asked, "The treasure... Do you know if he found the treasure too?"

Tristan said, "Which one? If all that was down there came from one place, that's an amazing amount to find all at once."

Ren, really excited now, responded, "Ingots! Gold and Silver ingots, with strange writings on them. And statues! Life size statues made of Imperial Jade."

"You mean the beautiful green stone statues?" Tristan asked.

Ren said, "Yes! And a black-metal pyramid!"

"Then, yes. It's down in the hidden underground chamber with the rest of the valuables and artifacts he collected and stored down there."

Ren jumped to his feet, "Hot damn! He was right! He was right all along! I should have listened to him. I never should have left his side. But we were at an impasse in our search.

"I never figured on him being crazy enough to go back on his own." He looked at Ariel and said, "Though I suppose he had good reason."

"Ariel asked, "So, you knew my father?" Her question was a statement in as much as it was a question.

"Yes, I knew your father, and your mother. They were the best human friends I can remember ever having. I loved them like family. I saw them as a brother and sister to me.

"I'm sorry I denied it that night. You weren't ready to hear all or any of this back then. Even now, some hard truths are about to come to light. Though I guess, there will never be a time where they won't be. But first… Come over here, all of you."

They came over to where the book lay open with Ren standing before it. He had opened it to the pages he had been looking for. There on the pages were drawings.

Though they were crude, they were easily discernable. One showed a woman, standing in front of two wolves, who were bowing before her. The other, was of another woman sitting on the ground with two wolves playing with her.

On the other page was a picture of two wolves again, with a man half hidden in the bushes, staring at them.

The only difference from that night by the lake being, the man on the page hiding in the bushes had red eyes. The red of the eyes being the only color on either page. All else was devoid of such vivid color.

After he was sure they got the point. He turned back one page. On that page, were two werewolves. There was a lake; beside which, hid two human figures. With a third figure in a tree staring at two werewolves from above.

"It says," Ren told them, "three will be their number. They will arrive when the great evil once again tries to reinsert all mankind into the bonds of slavery. Plunging the world into a darkness from which it will not recover if evil triumphs. It will be known that they are the chosen, when the Talbodai greet them and bless their task. The one who will make the sacrifice, will be known by his eyes that blaze Red…."

Tristan chimed in, "Red eyes? I don't have red eyes."

Before he could say any more, Ren said, "And I've never known of any werewolf whose eyes burned red."

Paris, showing agitation, said, "Really…? We are looking at a scene that happened to us only days ago… in the pages of a twelve-thousand-year-old book… and all you two can talk about is—who has red eyes?"

Without thinking, Ren replied, "closer to thirteen thousand."

Paris balled up her fist and turned toward Ren. "Ooh!" She exclaimed. "I can put up with a lot of shit… but your about to get a bloody nose—smart-ass!"

He told her, "Hey, trust me… I get it… I thought this all to be bullshit ages ago. Now… here it is in my face. Those two on that wall right there, haven't been seen for a thousand years before Atlantis was wiped off the planet by the cataclysm. Now, I stand here—with two females that didn't know they were werewolves—and a turned human… who have seen them up close and personal, and are the embodiment of a prophesy that's over twelve and a half thousand years old. So, don't fuck with me—right now. I think a little patience with me is in order."

Paris huffed a breath of disgust and said, "Unfucking believable! Me-me-me… my-my-my… Go fuck yourself!"

As they went back and forth, Ariel drifted into her own little world. She wasn't interested in any of their nonsense.

Wheels were turning in her head about a different subject that was foremost in her mind presently. Snapping back to conscious thought, she rudely interrupted their squabbling, saying, "Back to you and my father. That night you showed up out of nowhere. Your first words were… *So, it's true, a daughter of Talb exists.* What did you mean?"

He sighed deep and walked over to the bookshelf again. After a minute of searching, He pulled out an envelope, brought it over, and handed it to Ariel.

"Charles sent this to me in, Paris-France in 1839. It's a wonder I received it at all. It arrived the day I left Paris for China. For many reasons—I won't get into now, he could not put a return address on it. Read it out loud... Please."

Ariel looked at the page for a moment. It was her father's handwriting. Even Paris confirmed that. The letter read...

Hello, Langren, Tsui Yuanli,

Ren, my friend. We have made it safely back to America without incident. I want to thank you again for saving Jenny's life. I know you may still not be happy with me for convincing you to do so. There will be time to figure out more later. I know we will meet again. Especially when you read my next few words. Jenny is with child. We became aware of this not long after we put to open sea for America.

We are most certain that she was with child prior to the vicious attacks upon her person by some few weeks. You know what that means now that Jenny has your blood in her veins. When your blood reached the baby at such an early period of growth, I think it safe to say, what was mine is now yours in every way that matters my trusted friend.

Looks like Paris already has a sibling to love and cherish. I know I shouldn't have sent this by mail. I had no other way of letting you know these facts. It may be hard to track me down these next couple or so years. We will have to both make it priority for finding each other again in the future.

Especially if one of us should succeed in finding what we've risked so much for. Stick to the plan as will I, should it become imperative we should require contact. You have all our love always. Safe Journeys Lang Ren – Charles Ross – 1839.

"1839.... I was born in 1840. What does that mean exactly? What does he mean by, what was mine is now yours...?"

"Your mother was attacked trying to help Paris's parents escape execution. Her parents were killed and burned that day. Jenny was about to die. We had no idea at the time, she was carrying you when she was attacked. When I fed her my blood... She became a part of my blood line.

"Your mother became a Talbodai the second my blood entered her body through wound and ingestion. By the time her werewolf blood passed through you, it had already been purified into my line."

Ariel at once responded, "You take so fucking long to say anything. Let's just cut the chase. Are you, and this letter, saying that I'm your true blood daughter because you did the same thing for my mom that I did for Tristan and Paris?

"That all this happened after I had just been seeded by my dad?"

Ren said, "Yes! That is exactly what I am saying."

"But his seed. I'm from his seed, first and foremost...."

Ren told her, "Wrong. You are first the embryo of your mother. When you are seeded you become active.

"The strongest seed always wins over the lesser. This is known. In this case, even more so. Your mother became a werewolf by a pureblood descendent of Tal of Bodai. When my blood passed into you, it killed the seed and took over the embryo utterly. You are my daughter. My only child.

"God bless Charles and your mother Jenny for taking such good care of you. But you are more mine through my blood than even my own semen could produce. Even I can see you look nothing like Charles."

Ren stopped talking for a moment. Everyone was quiet for some time. He thought it best to change the subject.

He said, "Those annoying bastard's have been tracking me... not the other way around. It was easier to let you believe otherwise until this moment; until this very moment, when enough had happened, and I could show you enough evidence to prove testimony.

"I was staying a step ahead of those bastards as best I could while picking off a few at a time.

"I caught Ariel's scent back in the mountain's and recognized the scent of a true Talbodai descendant.

"It never entered my mind that the child of Jenny and Charles was in these mountains. Not even when I came upon you.

"I found you when I did because I heard the werewolves after something and zeroed in on you finally. I had been tracking your scent to find out who you were. Up until I first caught your scent, I was the only one who has that smell.

"Now, there are four of us, three horses and a damn dog but, I had no idea of your connections to Charles and Jenny.

"How could I have known you were there daughter?

"Here… in the middle of the wilderness. I said *daughter of Talb* that night because of your scent. The circumstances of how we've all been thrown together, still boggles mind."

Ren drifted off in deep thought. No one bothered him while he was in his recollections. He was a little somber in the tone of his next words. "I have been alive for so long I can't remember most of it. Most everything before the great cataclysm has been lost and is now just forgotten memory.

"Every now and then I will have my memories jogged… and rediscover or recall something. I remembered this place in a dream. It took a great amount of time to recover its location from my mind and return here. I was about to go looking for your father and mother, to bring them here.

"Though it was taking far longer than I wanted because of these infernal night fiends. There were too many to just be a social gathering. I had to figure out their game before—even considering—contacting Charles and Jenny. That was just before the war of the states began. I've been in this game of cat and mouse, ever since.

"Whoever it is, that leads this pack of werewolves, is unclear. I have been unable to learn, to any degree, who is behind these offenses and atrocities. They want me for my knowledge of the location of this Temple and all its treasures stored within… and because they think I know where Charles and Jenny are hiding. More so now that they are dead. If they found them first and killed them, they must believe I have all the answers they seek."

As Ren and Tristan, shared their knowledge with one another, Paris listened intently. Not Ariel though. All she heard was, womp…womp-womp.

Ariel's thought processes were completely scrambled. Fighting frantically to answer all the questions popping up. What the fuck had just happened to her quaint little upbringing?

Ren was the first to speak to her again. Saying, "There is no way this can all be summed up in one sitting. There are many blanks to fill in, before all how's and why's become clearly understood. So, let's just do this as we go? Slowly."

That was something everyone was unanimous about. Ariel wouldn't give back the letter. The day went on without further talk of the matter. They all turned in early that evening. The next day, training of their human side began.

Chapter thirteen

Taming Werewolves

Ren's training was intense and brutal. He trained them in a fighting system known as praying mantis. A very intense training method of self-control and incredible physical abilities. An unforgiving fighting art with devastating effect on the bodies it is used against.

An art that launches defensive and offensive attacks simultaneously. Leaving the person, it was used against, maimed, broken and/or crippled for life. He also taught them the Dim Mak. Known in English as the death touch.

As far as Ren knew, his little trio of disciples were the first white folk to be taught its discipline. Let alone master its mysteries of touch. It is the highest form of praying mantis, from a fighting perspective.

Although, Ren told them all, more than a few times, fighting is a byproduct of Tong Long Chuan Fa (Praying Mantis Kung Fu). Ren had his flaws and vice's. But he was a damn good teacher.

What took most people years to learn, the trio mastered in weeks. Due to the magic of the temple and the processes taking place inside them that would turn them into werewolves soon enough.

They trained from daylight to dusk. Day in and day out. Once one system was mastered, others were picked up quickly.

After mastering the praying mantis system, he taught them a system known as Hsing-yi, then Pa Kua. Then another system closely related to praying mantis called Bah-ji.

He then taught them the art, which would tie and combine all the others into one. Chen Tai Chi Chuan Fa. A very advanced system that blended perfectly, all the others, into its technique. They also delved deep into the mysteries of stealth and anti-personnel, of Japanese Ninjutsu, most ancient and wicked, in its dastardly deeds. Then it was weapons: spear, sword, staff, and bow.

Tristan wielded a nine-ring broadsword better than anyone Ren had ever seen. The girls were deceptive and evil with spear and staff.

All of them noticed how all the different styles were remarkably similar and wondered if they had not all come from one source… once upon a time.

Most people could not have mastered all these disciplines without a lifetime of dedication. They did it so quickly, due to their incredibly unique circumstances.

Ren wished they would be well into the meditations that followed the physical disciplines before they made their first shift. That did not happen.

When the time of their first change got closer. Ren showed them another hidden chamber. This one, was underneath the platform of the temple. The entire platform was hollowed out beneath its floor.

There were a dozen or so steel cages to one side of the huge chamber. Ren told them they would use them to try to tame and train the werewolves they were about to become.

Tristan was reminded of the big steel cage that was in the cellar chamber back at the double R ranch. Now he finally realized, its purpose.

The entrance to this training area, was a trap door in the floor of the upper platform floor. There was a side door in the south wall that could only be opened from the inside.

Unless it was open, you could not detect it was even there from the outside.

For Ariel and Paris, the fact that they were born into it made their first shift a little easier and intensely more pleasurable for them, than as it was for Tristan. As a full human, turned into a werewolf, his first changes would not be as pleasurable as they would eventually become. It was Ariel who experienced the first shift.

* * * * *

Ariel–The first thing that happened was, I thought I had started a menstrual cycle. Something I had never had before. I now know, that is because I was born a werewolf. Still, it was strange to bleed down there for no reason.

It was heavy bleeding that only lasted for an hour or so, then it stopped. When I told Ren what was happening, he made me take off all my clothes. Then locked me inside one of the cages. Said my first shift was about to start. About thirty minutes later, I had a strong and powerful spontaneous orgasm. I remember telling Tristan and Paris,

"Oh my god! I'm cumming! Right now! Ooooooh! It feels sooooo good!" That first one was followed by multiple orgasms exploding upon my senses. Ren told me my shifts, would include orgasmic pleasures. That for the first shift, at least, I would experience nine levels of orgasm before the change went into overdrive. Every woman is capable of nine levels of orgasm. Though few ever experience it.

Ren made Tristan and Paris go into a chamber where they could see me, but I wouldn't be able to see them. The first changes of any werewolf are wild and unpredictable as to what they will do. Too many people around, only serve to create more tension.

I remember looking down and seeing my hand had changed. It looked like Ren's did when he changed into a werewolf in front of us. I was staring at my hand, when that ninth level of orgasm hit me, and ... —**Oh My God!!**

It was one long, continuous orgasm, that just kept increasing, and never did stop, until I blacked out.

I made my first shift during a new moon cycle. Ren told us, that the new moon cycle was known to all werewolves as the black moon. Whatever you want to call it… it made me one evil bitch. Pun intended. They said all hell broke loose when Ren opened that cage door.

Tristan and Paris said I tried to kill Ren, right off rip. That I was vicious and terrible in my rage. They said that Ren did what he said he would do with us all. Let us fight with him, until we showed signs of tiring a little, and drew back from him. As soon as we did that, he would run out the opened south side door and let us chase him through the wilderness. Ren told me I chased him only for a short time.

He said I stopped chasing him, to tear a moose to pieces and devour it, before taking up the chase again. Stopping again to kill a few wild pigs, not eat, just kill. Then chased and fought with him until I changed back the next morning as first light came around. I felt like a freshly fucked fox.

I couldn't remember anything but the orgasms. I thought I would be tired the next day; I was far from it. I could have fuck-started a hibernating bear; I was so full of energy.

* * * * *

Paris–There wasn't much difference between mine and Trudy's experience of our first shift. Except, I could remember small parts of my time as a werewolf.

Like running through the forest on all fours at incredible speed. Darting past things and missing them by millimeters, getting faster as I went. Only flash backs more than full memories.

It felt like a dream of seeing through the eyes of a real wolf. Head low to the ground. Sniffing out all sorts of smells.

Ren said I killed too, though I wasn't as blood thirsty about it as Trudy was.

One thing he did note as extraordinary about my first shift, was the unbelievable strength and savagery I possessed when I attacked him. He thought he was going to have to hurt me, to keep me from killing him. He told us all we would get stronger as we matured, but he never expected me to be so aggressive the first shift.

He said Ariel had incredible strength and skill. He could even detect that, somehow, she was holding back on him. A prospect that spooked him. For if she were already in possession of human faculties during her first shift, the probabilities of what she would mature into were astronomical.

He told me, she might have held back, I did not. He also said he could barely keep me from catching him during the chase. It was all he could do to stay a step ahead of me. That I didn't just chase him, I predicted his moves and hit him from the side a couple of times. Bowling him over and forcing him to get rough to keep me from seriously hurting him.

The most exhilarating part of being a werewolf, that I can recall, was how everything around me moved in slow-motion. The worst of it for me, was waking up after it was over; the feeling of ick on my body was unbearable. It's like what you could imagine feeling like if you'd run around in the woods all night. Butt naked and covered in crude-oil. Then falling asleep before washing it all off you.

I also remember still having blood in my mouth. With raw meat between my teeth when I changed back to human form and woke up. Ren said I was still eating a fresh kill when my shift back to human started. Ren said I was the super bitch. Tristan and Trudy have never stopped calling me that, ever since.

* * * * *

Tristan–The beginning of my first shift was far from pleasant, nothing like it eventually came to be. Because I was born a human, it was different for me than what the girls experienced.

The first thing I felt was my saliva become very thick in my mouth and throat. There was so much, I started trying to burp it up. But the more I burped up, the more I produced. Making it exceedingly difficult at times, to swallow or breathe. Causing great gasps for air that only intensified.

I ended up having to let all that drool just pour from my mouth, to keep from choking on it. Trying not to consciously interrupt autonomic responses that were causing the drool in the first place. Being forced to open my mouth wider and wider to keep it from running out of my nose.

I was compelled to open my eyes and mouth as wide as possible. Doing so, gave me a sensation of my face and teeth swelling and growing. I could feel it, but to the touch, they were normal. Then, I felt my face pushing outward; Though as I looked down with my eyes to see these things, there were no such physical changes.

I farted and shit saliva. I vomited-up saliva. I was sweating fucking saliva. Drool… like a dog has never experienced.

The feelings of pleasure, I finally began to experience, are indescribable. I remember ejaculating all over the place but when I looked down, it was blood.

After a moment or so, all I wanted to do was be as still as possible and take in all feelings my physical body was emitting. They were extreme waves of euphoric ecstasy.

I didn't want to move. I just wanted to keep experiencing the ecstasies of all that was happening to my body. The physical changes on the outside and within me.

It was like the ultimate indulgence of psychedelic phenomena. At any given moment, I was falling, rising, flying.

I just floated thru dimensions of fractal imagery. A kaleidoscope of light and vision… and then, I just drifted away into everything and nothing.

When I came out of it, like a free diver breaking the surface, desperate for air; I couldn't seem to catch my breath.

My heart was beating to a point of bursting. The flashes of memories and/or hallucinations hitting my brain were so chaotic, I tried just closing my eyes and slowing my breathing. All that did was make it worse. Then, the multitude of memories slowed to a menagerie of twilight zone type visions. A playback in my head. Like puzzle pieces, scattered upon a table. With no connection yet to be conceived.

As it picked up pace… and began to fast forward thru my head. I couldn't help, involuntarily pulling my knees to my chest and rocking back and forth. Because I had no memory of what I was seeing so vividly now play by play.

It was as though I was seeing the thoughts and recollections of someone else's deranged and psychotic brain patterns. Visions of horrors and insanities no human should ever see or conceive.

As it became more and more clear that they were my own memories, I began to laugh aloud. A maniacal laugh, of comic relief that quickly escalated to the hysterical ravings of a madman. For whom sanity has been lost, to what had been seen.

Followed abruptly by screams of sheer and utter horror as my mind forced me to watch a play back of butchery and inconceivable violence committed.

I fell onto my side and cried, like a child who had figured out its mother wasn't coming back.

Was this the price for the incredible places I had journeyed to? That's when it hit me….

I thought, wait a minute… I went to a psychedelic reality as real as anything and everything. I have a memory record of it all. Including the feelings of ecstasy, joy and pleasures beyond words to describe them. That's when the moment came that I finally looked down and noticed my body.

I was filthy, covered in bloody gore: my hair felt like matted dog hair, skin felt sticky from head to toe, like something was dripping off me, though nothing visibly was.

My fingernails were caked with half dried blood clots and skin. My hands and feet were covered with dried, bloody chunks.

Upon inspection, I realized my chest was also smeared with clotted blood, half dried and caked. Becoming sickeningly clear that it was not my own.

Right as my reactions turned into, What the Fuck! I felt something ooze out of both of my ears. Dripping onto my collar bones and chest. It was blood. With a strange florescent pink color to it, instead of red. With crystals sparkling and shimmering all through it. It then started from my nose, pouring out like mucus from a bad cold. As it hit my lips, I was elated by its taste, and disgusted by the fact I liked it, all at once.

Then, I started to feel an orgasmic sensation. Welling up in my stomach and guts. It felt so good I began to smile and giggle at its prodding's. Until, out of nowhere, the involuntary reaction to vomit became impossible to prevent.

I puked until dry heaves took over. Every time I heaved, I was bombarded with feelings so wonderful, I didn't want them to stop.

After a time, it ceased. For the next few seconds, I felt like a junkie in need of another fix. Which was quickly replaced, with a profound blankness. All senses falling into a tunnel vision of almost complete blackness. As everything came back into vivid focus. The feeling of emptiness was replaced with feelings of fulfillment and content. That is, until I looked down again.

As I looked down and saw what had irrupted from my body, I shouted, "What in the mother fuck?"

There were pieces of bone and teeth. Half of a digested ear of some animal. Chunks of jelly like goo and bile that were a myriad of colors. Intermixed with a dominant red, darkened to a rancid shade, with a putrid milky mucus like fluid, running through it. A most unpleasant sight.

I closed my eyes and just looked away. My entire being was awash with every emotion that mankind is capable of.

Any given moment, feeling guilt stricken and justified, simultaneously. Horrified and amused. I could no longer perceive a barrier between these opposing extremes.

At that point, I was overtaken with a rush of overwhelming exhaustion. Mind, body, and soul had all reached their limits. I rolled over onto my side again... and fell into the deepest realms of sleep.

Awakening after only an hour or so, refreshed and energized. Far more mentally stable as well. Surprised that the feelings of remorse had subsided and were no longer even detectable. A strange thing, given the still vivid recollections stored in my head.

I was told I was the worst one to deal with. That I came close to killing Ren out right more than once. A thing that astounded him.

He said never had he seen a first timer, especially a turned human, be so vicious and diabolical in their intent. He said I tracked, chased and killed. With savage butchery, so violent, even he was taken back. He told me, I puked up all that shit, because of all the carnage I left in my wake, killing everything I saw, from rabbits to moose.

He said if I could be tamed down enough to control the shift, I would become one of the most powerful werewolves that ever lived and breathed. If not, I would be the most dangerous evil and savage bastard to exist for an age. If I wasn't put down.

For my next few shifts, they locked me in the dungeon beneath the temple fortress. Until Ariel and Paris were able to control themselves well enough, to help Ren keep me at bay.

Though I must say, given all that, none of us were prepared for what happened when Jojo made his first shift.

Thank god it was during moonshine and not a black moon.

We were so into our own concerns we had forgotten about Jo. The only change in him was, he grew to the size of a Siberian tiger. Five times as fierce as a tiger to boot.

He did not recognize any of us. We all begged Ren not to hurt him or kill him. He promised he would do his best, just before he shifted. Although, subduing Jo without harming him, turned out to be impossible. Thank god we hadn't shifted yet.

The battle that took place between them was long... and terribly violent. Ren and Jojo's battles were epic. We finally screamed for Ren to break away and run inside the temple with us. We barely got the door shut and secured, before Jo got in. He had put us all on the run....

Why he didn't attack the horses, we guessed, was because they had always been his companions and they had all been turned together. We will never know for sure. We found dead things for days after that night.

Jo had inflicted so much damage to Ren in werewolf form, it's a wonder he wasn't killed. It took him two days and nights to fully recover after he shifted back to his human form. Which he was unable to even do, until late the next morning. Being too weak to make the shift.

We felt bad for asking him not to hurt him. He wouldn't have gotten his ass tore up so bad if he hadn't started out trying not to hurt or kill him.

He told us, that next time, if we can't figure out how to tame and handle him, he would be forced to kill him. He said that when he told Ariel, "if you think he's violent now just wait till the shift," he had no idea just how bad it would be.

When I said to all of them that the thing that freaked me out the most about Jo's shift was those glowing, burning, red eyes. They said, how funny it was I said that. Beings the most disturbing thing about me as a werewolf was my glowing, burning, red, devilish eyes.

* * * * *

Narration–When Ren felt well enough to be back up and at it, his first decision was to put Jo down before he killed one or all of them.

He grabbed the short sword from its case and told Tristan, "We have to put him down while he is just a dog… and I'm going to do it, right now."

Tristan had his pistol in his hand before Ren could turn completely around to walk away. Standing with the barrel to the side of Ren's head, hammer cocked fully back. Telling him, "That's as far as you go you—ruthless bastard!"

Ren stopped in place, knowing Tristan would empty every chamber into his head. Too much healing time involved with that sort of thing, he thought to himself.

Ren exclaimed, "He will kill us…! All of us…!"

Tristan told him, "Take another step toward my dog with that blade Motherfucker! And I, will kill you all!"

"He's my dog… my affair! He didn't ask for this, any more than any of us did. He will have his chance, just like the rest of us."

Ren replied, "I hope you're the one that he kills first. So, you don't see any of us die."

* * * * *

The rugged and ceaseless training was paying off. Within several changes during moonshine, the girls were already able to control themselves well. Their human side had not awakened yet, but they could understand, and did listen some, to Ren's telepathy. They were also showing signs, they were understanding his words.

Tristan was wilder than Jo. Ren stopped letting him out of the cage after only a couple of shifts. Whether it was black moon or moonshine, didn't matter. His rage and intent were more savage and relentless than Ren had ever seen in a werewolf that could not be awakened. Try as he might, he couldn't get Tristan to settle down in the slightest bit.

Ren finally threw his hands up. With Tristan frantically trying to tear the cage apart to get at him, Ren told him,

"Fuck you! You hard-headed savage bastard! I'm going to put you on a leash with all the other dumbass dogs of the world, you—untrainable prick!"

Ren left the room and walked around to where the girls had been watching, through the slit that allowed them to see Tristan, without being seen by him. Ren told the girls,

"Eventually he may come around but, that's going to be a long time from now. If we could just get him to recognize one of us even for a moment, It's all downhill from there."

Ariel was listening to Ren and Paris while still watching Tristan. She interrupted them, saying, "Hey, hey guys, come here… look at this…."

Tristan was standing at the cage door with his fingers rapped around the bars. He had stopped trying to tear them out. He wasn't screaming and roaring anymore.

He wasn't even shining teeth, just to be shining them. He shook the bars once. Then sniffed the air as if he recognized a scent. He shook the bars again. This time it was more like a frustrated human would shake bars of imprisonment.

Then, with a body language that was more human than werewolf, he looked at the ground in disgust and kicked the bars with his foot. A human like kick. Then he raised his head and howled the saddest, loneliest howl-scream.

When he looked back straight ahead where they could see his full face, he had the face and eyes of a dog, pleading to be set free. It was only there a split second, before he was back at it, trying to tear the cage apart.

Paris said, "Tell me you saw that too…." She didn't wait for either of them to respond.

She turned to Ariel and said, "Come on! I have an idea."

Ariel and Ren both followed her into the chamber, in front of Tristan's cage. Tristan went insane with rage with all three of them in front of him all at once.

Paris told Ren, "Turn around… and stay that way until told different."

She then whispered to Ariel, "Trudy, take off your panties and wipe yourself with them really good. Wipe your ass… and kitty… and get them good. Then rub yourself all over your face and neck with them."

Ariel did what she was asked. Paris did the same. She then grabbed Ariel's panties and rubbed herself with them, telling Ariel to do the same with hers. She then took the panties and tied them together around the end of a pole and laid the pole across one of the cross bars just inside the cage.

Tristan stopped his ranting and moved over to the panties. His ears lifted in curiosity. His face instantly went to that of a wolf that had caught the scent of a female in heat.

Ren had already turned around and was watching as the girls slowly approached the cage. Tristan didn't pay them any mind at first. All his attention was on the new smells.

When he did see them. He didn't fly into a rage. He just shined his teeth and gave them a menacing growl.

Paris quickly took two fingers, she had saturated well, in her female juices, and ran them under her nose. Then held them straight out toward Tristan.

She told Ariel, "Do the same."

Ariel said, "I didn't wet my fingers, just my panties."

Paris told her, "well do it quick and put them up here next to mine. We have to approach together as if it were one hand in his face."

Ariel reached down into her pants and jammed two fingers in deep and quickly removed them. Then went to stand next to Paris, hands side by side. Tristan instantly stopped growling and started sniffing. As slowly as they could, and still be moving forward, they approached the cage.

He was now sticking his nose through the bars to sniff at their hands. They put their hands up next to the bars. As they looked down to avoid direct eye contact for the moment, they noticed that he was becoming aroused as his penis was half erect.

What happened next, Ren never expected to see so soon. Tristan calmly closed his eyes and licked the girls' hands.

Before morning, they were able to hold hands with him through the bars. Even Ren was able to get close. He was quite content with the progress the women had made that night. With Tristan's human side awake now, it was just a matter of time.

* * * * *

Ren and Ariel's bond grew with each passing day. It didn't take Ariel long to realize the truth of everything... and embrace her true father. Not holding him to blame for anything that happened. Knowing he was innocent of anything she might try to pin on him. They spent a lot of time alone together. As Father and daughter. Happy in their new rolls to each other as such.

As she got to know him, she started to understand just how much she had in common with Ren. He told her, she had a lot of her mother in her, that he could see. She still loved and cherished her memories of Charles, she always would. Now that she was getting to know her real father though, a lot of blanks were being filled in about who she truly was.

Ren was as proud of her as any father had ever been with a daughter, since the dawn of time. He saw so much of himself in her. Since the first night he laid eyes on her and spoke with her, she had impressed him. Those feelings for her only grew deeper as the days and weeks went by.

After a few more months, the trio was able to choose not to change during both moon cycles. With that skill in his back pocket, Tristan doubled his efforts with Jojo.

He worked with Jojo from the moment he made his changes, until he changed back with the dawn. The dog was so powerfully strong, he left many teeth marks in the steel bars, and on Tristan, as testament to such strength; although, his were not the first marks on the bars.

Tristan wouldn't let anyone in the chamber with them while he worked with Jo. During black moon nights, he did not even bother with him at first. Not until he made his first real breakthrough with him **under the Moonshine.**

Chapter fourteen

Werewolf and Were-animal College

The first Moonshine that Jo showed promise was purely by accident. One of the wooden poles Tristan had been using through the bars with pieces of his clothes tied to them was splintered into pieces by Jo yet again.

This time, a huge splinter became lodged deep into Jojo's eye socket. Buried deep, just under the eyeball. Jo instantly shut down his savagery and began trying to dislodge it with his paws. In his agony, he had completely forgotten about Tristan next to him outside the cage. After a minute or so of useless effort to remove the splinter himself, Jo whimpered as he would do when he was still just a dog.

Tristan's love and compassion for the dog took over within him. Before he realized it, he stuck his hand through the bars and pulled the piece of wood halfway out before letting go from fear of losing an arm.

Jo remained calm as he looked at him. For the first time, Tristan saw recognition in the weredog's eyes for him. He slowly reached in again. Jo growled low but did nothing else.

Tristan pulled the splinter all the way out of his eye socket. Then as Tristan stared on to see what was next, he saw Jo's tail wag slightly.

"Jojo…?"

Jo's tail wagged again as his eyes filled with recognition and remembrance. He stood up now onto all fours. Acting as he did that day in the Apache camp when he first heard Tristan call his name and come into view.

Tristan knew right away all his hard work had paid off. It was downhill from there with Jojo's taming and training.

Although Tristan would say, forever more, that tame is not the word he would use in description of Jo's new temperament, he also wouldn't use it for himself, his women or Ren either.

Tristan entered the cage and greeted his old friend. Jo laid down in front of him and as he did; he licked Tristan's arms and hands.

After a few moments, Tristan heard a voice in his head call his name. He looked over at Jo, who was staring straight at him.

"Was that you just now in my head?" Tristan asked the dog.

Without a word said aloud, Jo spoke again into Tristan's mind. "Finally, you've learned to hear me. All dogs learn human language as pups. It's your dumb asses that never realize how to hear us and talk back. Every look, movement and sound we make is speech. It's a crying shame we had to become monsters to communicate, on this level. For you to realize that all animals are telepathic and so are you, once awakened to it. Your kind, fucked up everything when you disconnected from the mother and attempted to take her place."

Tristan asked him, telepathically, "The mother?"

Laughter filled his head. Tristan intuitively knew the dog was laughing at him.

Jo told him, "You call her Earth. Just another name for dirt. A dumb fucking name for our mother if ever there were.

"You and the babes weren't so bad at communicating with me before all this happened. At least you cared enough to try. I'll give you that. The one thing that makes me love the three of you is, you never treated me like a dog."

Tristan, his mind blown, said, "How is it you can talk so intelligently?"

Jo replied, "I'm your dog… I know everything you know. My speech patterns take after yours and the babes."

Tristan quickly barked out loud like a dog. Jo's dog instinct followed suit… and he too, barked. Tristan laughed hard, saying through his laughter, "I'd say there is still a little dog left in you."

Jo shined is teeth and growled. Then jumped up, stepped closer to Tristan and licked his face.

When the others came down to see why everything had gotten so quiet, fearing Jo had killed Tristan. They found Tristan sitting crossed legged in the cage with his pet weredog. Luckily, Tristan had closed the cage door behind him when he went inside. Jojo instantly went into protect mode and got between them and Tristan. He still didn't recognize any of them.

Before the morning came, they were all outside with Jo, sitting by a fire. Ren said he was enormously proud of Tristan and the progress he had made. His progress was an impressive feat, given he had no experience with such a beast.

From then on, Ren would work just as intensely with Jo. Realizing what a powerful and formidable ally he would fast become. Next, it would be about interaction with Jo. While they are all in werewolf form.

First, The Trio, as Ren now called them, needed a lot more work before they were ready to be doing anything in werewolf form. Other than fighting, feeding or... you know.

* * * * *

They finally tracked the horses down during a shift. The horses always disappeared into the wilderness during the shift. They weren't attacking or killing anything. They knew this because they never found anything dead that was clearly killed by them.

Except a mountain lion that must have attacked them. It took some time to figure out it was a mountain lion from what was left of it. It was torn to pieces... and was burnt and charred. They couldn't figure how the body had been burned.

When they found them, they were impressed to say the least. Even Ren was amazed. He had never seen a Werehorse before.

Their eyes glowed red like Jo's and Tristan's. They had grown teeth in their mouth's that resembled those of the ancient, saber tooth cats from prehistoric times. The insides, of their nostrils, glowed with a dim reddish orange glow.

When they saw the Trio and Ren coming up to them, all three of them took on a defensive posture. As they whinnied, a quite scary whinny, fire shot out of their noses. Everyone was awe-struck by that unexpected display. Now they knew how the mountain lion burned.

Be as it may, the horses allowed them to approach them. It didn't take long for them to realize that, though their physical appearance had changed, their mental faculties were still intact..

Tristan and the girls each went over to their horse and were greeted in kind. Except for their eyes, teeth and given the fact that they breathed and snorted fire from their noses, they were still the same horses in appearance. Except for their hoofs that had changed only a little but were now razor sharp around their edges and hard as steel.

Ren, most impressed, said, "I should have turned a few for myself through the ages. They are astonishingly beautiful.

"Not to mention, their appearances would send anything that didn't know better running for the hills. If only we could train them as war horses, we would be in real business."

Tristan told him, "During the time we spent with the Chiricahua, they trained them for their style of warfare.

"Teaching us at the same time. My horse, Sarah, inadvertently got a taste of war during our travel from Florida to Texas before the war ended. The Apache had all three of them in superb condition before we left."

Ariel had heard enough. She looked back at everyone and said, "Well, no time like the present to find out if they are still ridable in the shift. This, will be the test...."

Before anyone could open mouth to protest, she jumped onto her horses back. No bridal, blanket, saddle or lead rope.

Duke reared up as she jumped on his back. She grabbed a handful of his mane… and leaned up as he reared, staying on his back.

The horse bolted as his front hooves hit the ground. Ariel yelled out, "Wooo!! Hooo!!" As Duke showed her the incredible speed and power he had as a Werehorse.

Tristan and Paris followed her lead. They jumped to their horse's backs and took off after Duke and Ariel.

Ren said to himself, "Hey, don't worry about me… I'll just walk back to the temple. You inconsiderate—"

"Need a ride old-man?" asked Paris, as she came back around and offered him a hand up.

* * * * *

They stayed at training themselves and their animals ceaselessly. They worked and struggled hard at getting control of the beast within.

Ren also made them fight each other while one was a human, the other a werewolf. This was one of the main reasons for all the hard training in different fighting styles. To be formidable as a werewolf or a human, against a werewolf or a human.

The first time the girls tried staying in the cage with Tristan during a black moon, while they were still in human form, with Tristan changed to werewolf, it didn't go so well.

Tristan had become angered when they moved while in the last spasm of his change.

Once a change is fully made, a werewolf has a massive rush of adrenaline that must be released like bubbles in a syringe. Before it can start choosing who or who not to attack and/or kill.

Being real still during those few moments is imperative when dealing with even the most mature werewolves, when standing up close and personal with them as a human. Not heeding this unwritten rule can make your worst nightmares come true. A fact Trudy and Paris were finding out the hard way.

Paris was the target. As she was slowly backed into a corner of the cage, she said, "Trudy... I think I'm in trouble...."

Ariel wasn't sure what to do. She was afraid that anything she did, would only make things worse. She cried out to Ren. "Father, what do I do?"

Ren told her, "Throw some chi into his balls!"

Ariel, looking confused, said, "Huh? Do—what...?"

Ren yelled out, "Kick him in the balls! Hard! Do it Now!"

Ariel came up behind him just as he was about to jump on Paris and delivered a kick from hell. Lifting him up ever so slightly. Her shin bone contacted solid against his ball sack.

He let out a howl of agony and almost buckled down onto his knees.

Just like what happens with a kick to the groin of most blood pumping animals; so too, did this phenomenon happen to a werewolf. If you had the balls to do it.

He closed his eyes for a brief second and made a sound that was more human than werewolf. Paris wasted no time, she darted around him and headed for the cage door that Ariel had already opened and was standing ready to slam shut.

Tristan still managed to snap jaws so close to her face, he sprayed her with drool, as his teeth and jaws clamped together. He did manage to tear deep gashes in her arm and shoulder, with his claws, as she ran past him. Tristan was livid. It took two shift cycles before they felt safe to go back in the cage with him again.

As time passed, Ren, satisfied they were ready for the next phase of training, began their internal mind training. Meditation didn't come easy… for any of them.

*****

The sun was about to rise over the highest peaks to the east. Ren was well into his explanations. "What you don't know, is always far vaster, than what you think you—know. To travel down the path of enlightenment, you must first travel down the path of awakening.

"When you have fully awakened to the truth, only then, will you find yourself at the crossroads where awakened path and enlightened path meet."

"One who looks externally, sleeps. One who looks internally, awakes. You're not human-beings about to have some spiritual werewolf journey; you are light-beings about to embark on a human-werewolf experience. We must open and awaken your mind awareness and belief to this truth."

Ren paused to see who would speak first. It was Ariel who spoke first, saying, "Sounds like a load of horse shit and magic. Are you going to teach us magic?"

Ren smiled and answered her, "Magic, as some would call it, is not, by definition, magical. Once you understand it. There is a process by which all things happen. Each process, for each thing, is not always identical in its procedure of steps from beginning to end; however, the baseline from which all things happen is fundamental.

"What's the most powerful force in this universe at man's disposal?" He got no answer.

"Anyone? Don't be shy. Just spit out whatever comes to you." Another long silence. "None of you dumb-asses are even going to guess at it—are you?"

They just looked around at one another, Ren continued. "Thought…. Thought is the most powerful force in man's possession. Everything ever invented, created, discovered or resolved, first came from a thought to make it so.

"Everything that makes our body and brains, everything you can see with the eye, and everything you can't see, is all made of the same baseline material…. Atoms…."

"Vibration is how all of us—atoms, become animate. Atoms and vibrations are the fundamental baseline of physical reality. Light-being reality is what you must understand as just as real.

"Do trees move? Trees are constantly growing and renewing themselves. They're alive, just like you and me."

"If, you can quiet your mind and body enough, you can feel a tree's vibrations through touch. Vibration does not always make a sound. A thought is nothing more than a vibration in, itself. With what I'm going to teach you now, you will become aware of these subtleties."

"First, we must destroy all the negative influences, which are buried and trapped, within you. Clearing out the blockages of the energetic cosmic force that is—you. To rebuild or remodel a temple, you must first reassess the old temple."

"Your first meditation will be on the things you fear the most. What are you truly afraid of? Bring all your fears to the surface and dissolve them in the cosmic fire within you.

"During this meditation, chant the words: I am alive, safe and unafraid.

"You must enrich your own potential for cultivation, interpretation and understanding. The desire to want to learn all this, must come from—within you."

After many days of intense recollection, reflection and reorientation. Ren felt they were ready to move forward.

"Your second meditation will be about your guilt. What do you blame yourself for? What guilt, do you carry around with you? Suppressed and holding you back with the weight of it upon you. Let it all dissolve in the waters of your essence, by forgiving yourself for what you think you've done.

"We feel guilt when we betray our love for something, or someone, including ourselves. It is usually for our self, that we find it hardest to forgive. Work on this through your meditation. Free yourself of the burden of guilt. Your chant will be: I forgive myself and all others; I am filled with joy and gratitude."

After progressing quite rapidly through the guilt meditations, Ren pushed them on.

"The third meditation is about confronting your shame. What are you ashamed of about yourself? That you hide from everyone else. Push it out of you, by chanting: I'm enough just the way I am. I am able to succeed in anything."

After considerable time on this, they were finally ready to move on.

"The fourth energetic center we must open through meditation, deals with your love and compassion for yourself and all things. It is blocked by grief.

"Let go of all grief locked away inside you, by knowing that the ones you grieve for, would not want you to suffer, in this way, for them. The moment you let go of your grief: you will be able to see—all the good and joy—you shared, with what you now grieve for; realizing that you never lost them in the first place. That they have always been with you, in your heart. Use the mantra: I am loved by many… and my love for all things, radiates from my heart.

"Your greatest strength, and most valuable—asset, that each of you possess is the love bond you share, with one another, equally. For I have never seen such a bond between souls as strong as yours—is. Pay attention now as one and you will succeed in achieving all of this in no-time.

"When compassion comes easy, it is a benefit to all mankind. For those who find compassion impossible, there is a rot at their core that must be countered.

Be as it may, it is easily countered. Provided, there is a will to do so in the first place. Otherwise, you lose your human soul and death becomes the only recourse for a werewolf gone bad."

After many days on this subject matter, they made enough progress to continue forward and so, Ren pushed them on.

"The fifth energetic center is in your throat and deals with communication with others, yourself, your higher self, and the celestial beings that guide and govern you at times of honest need. For now, our focus will deal with—truth.

"The truth… will always set you free, spiritually.

"The energy center in the throat gets block and choked by the lies we tell ourselves and others.

"Uncover and admit to yourself—of everything, you have ever done, that brought on feelings of a dishonest nature.

"See yourself as you truly are; knowing that—imperfection—is the point. The true beauty of living as a human is its imperfections.

"Finding it hard to confess a hard truth, can be as detrimental as the evilest acts. Especially, when you are unable to confess it to yourself, let alone others. What a person cannot do for themselves; they often time, cannot do for another.

"Every soul must choose to cross those lines on their own. You can take them to the race, but you can't make them run it.

"Only you, can know the truth of your soul. You are also—the only one—you cannot lie to.

"When we stare at our reflection and look into our own eyes. The eyes in the reflection—are the eyes of your confessor. They are the only eyes you cannot lie to.

"Confess your sins to your maker, the source of all things.... Confess to yourself, while staring deep into your own eyes, and be freed of the bondage that ties and weighs you down.

"Use the chant, I speak the truth with confidence.

"The one thing that should be clear by now is, there are no secrets or secret ingredients. To make yourself special, you must trust-in, you are special.

"People fear what they do not understand… and they hate what they fear. By removing hate and fear, with understanding; we open a door for all, who step through it, to realize how special they are. Open your minds. Believe… and imagination can become reality."

Time passed by more slowly now for the three pups in training. It was refreshing to see things with the clarity they were opening-up to.

Now came the most difficult to fully understand. The energetic centers that only metaphysics spoke of, until modern quantum physics exposed their truest realities.

"Next is the opening of your third eye. A quartz crystal is imbedded in the middle of your brain. When glowing brightly, insight and intuition will be yours.

"Your chant will be, I see clearly in all dimensions of life."
Considerable time was spent on this one.

"The last energy gate to open, is the Celestial Crown center. It is your connection to the spirit realms; the collective conscious and the cosmic divine web that connects all things.

"When this center is opened, your spirit will connect with you in a way you have never even imagine was possible.

"Energizing your mind, body and spirit into the realization that—all is one, and one is all.

"Your concepts, of heaven and hell, exist right here on this earth. It's your state of mind that constitutes, which one you experience at any given time. Your thoughts, actions, feelings and emotional state of consciousness is what governs it.

"Hell begins, with not knowing what you genuinely want.

"Heaven is just the opposite. Once you have achieved a cosmic consciousness, these truths' will be fundamental.

"Everything you are, from your thoughts to your most basic body functions – is a process of vibration and your bioelectric energy.

"When you are truly calm and quiet, without and within yourself, you will begin to feel your own subtle vibrations that exist within you. Your own vibration is formed by what you think… what you feel… and what you do.

"More times than not, our heart tells us, in seconds, what it is we need to do, to stay in balance with the cosmic nature of things. Just as, more times than not, we are either too lazy or too chicken shit scared to do it. Most times we can't hear—it… because we're not listening for—it….

"A lazy person – is a person with too small of a vision of the future. A worrier – is a person who has allowed dark thought processes, to overwhelm. Everything they think, is disconcerting… and nothing, adds to a solution. Good intentions help, some, but won't solve problems all on their own. The road to hell is paved with good intentions.

"The first thing a person must do if they genuinely want to understand who and what they are, and what they want – is to admit—they don't have all the answers.

"Figuring out you don't have all the answers, and admitting it to yourself, will allow you to start asking the right questions. Wishing and wanting, without doing, is just a foolish waste of everybody's time and effort."

Tristan broke in with a question, "A werewolf is a raging beast in today's world. No matter their origin's. How is the rage of the beast suppressed?"

He told them, "By not trying to suppress it. You must accept and embrace it with your humanity. You must fully awaken the human locked away inside you during the shift.

"You have already achieved an awakened state, to a small degree, of your human self, while in werewolf form. Now we will complete this process.

"There is no duality between you the human, and what you call the beast within you. You are one with each other.

"Good and evil is a human concept only. There is no good or evil in true nature… only harsh realities. The will and ability to be good or evil, exists in all human beings, at all times, simultaneously. Which one you give the most attention, is always the one that dominates your life."

"When you can accept and embrace the fact that you are a werewolf by understanding and accepting the reality of what that truly means. You will become a powerful weapon against all adversities. By driving out all blockages of guilt, shame and so forth from your past, you rid yourself of unconscious motive and self-sabotage. Once you achieve this, you will be in proper balance with the cosmic nature of all things. You will be at one with what the ancient Chinese named, The Dao… The cosmic web of all life and matter.

"In order to do that, you must forget everything you think you already know, and relearn it all, from inside yourself.

"If you tell a child what something is, say, a tiger or ape, and they believe it without question; they will be limited in understanding how special these things really are. Unless they open themselves to new possibilities; they will never see past what someone else told them of the way things are—despite the truth of it"

"The only way to realize cosmic truth, is to seek for the answer deep within your own mind.

"When I say mind, I don't mean your brain. I mean your higher self, your spirit, your subconscious. That part within you that speaks with and is eternally connected—to what you understand as God. The Divine Source of all things, which created this Universe, and breathes life into being.

"There is the light… and then there is the source of the light…. You are all a light of the source, and the source of the light, exists within you. As it does in all men and women… and all living things"

"The three of you must unite all your resources. Within yourselves first… and then, between each other. This singular task carried-out, will make you invincible as a team.

"Rage—Tristan – can be an asset, when properly channeled. Having to let off steam – is nothing more than having a buildup of too much frustration and anger. When you can harness the emotional energy of rage, and put it to use for a greater good, it becomes a powerful asset.

"Just like a train harnesses steam to move tremendous amounts of weight and cargo, so too, can aggressive emotion be harnessed and channeled.

"Love is much easier to harness and channel. But we are fucking werewolves…. Mastering love—never comes easy for us.

"We are all the offspring of the demigods, called the Talbodai… All is attainable and obtainable, once you channel and focus your aggressive and negative emotions, so they don't overpower your resourcefulness.

"Channeling your thoughts, emotions and feelings into one single vibration, is how you unite with spirit…."

"You do that, by bringing your brain, heart and gut minds back together into one mind. There is no duality between them. It is only a perceived illusion. They are one. All is one and one is all…

"Some believe they must be turned on, but they only need to be perceived. They are already on; they just need to be harnessed. They are yours and you… just-as-much-as your hand is.

"Believing yourself unable, to manage whatever comes before you, or to achieve what you want, will limit your ability to realize the absolute truth.

"But finding love for yourself and all things, is not the endgame. Love is a cure for all things; in as much, as it is a disease. A maddening distemper that strikes down all levels of human being—from kings to peasants.

"If let go and unchecked, unharnessed or worst of all, invested in someone who doesn't deserve it. Love will become its evil counterparts. Which is obsession and hatred.

"It's not a hard thing to take true love and fuck it up royally. But nothing, is ever a fuck up; until you cannot, will not or do not—try to fix it. When it does become impossible to fix, it is still not a tragedy. Unless you let it destroy you in its process, and do not learn the lesson of what went wrong, so that you can prevent it from surfacing, in such a way, ever again.

"You cannot spend all of your time, learning a little bit about a lot of things. If you are sleepless, drunk and scatter brained all the time, you will never learn how to manage your time wisely.

"Managing your time so that you can progress and advance on an ascending path, is one of the absolute, and most important things that must be conquered. As if it were the only thing you need do. Do not be the creator of your own limitations. We all must suffer one of two pains in life. The pain of discipline or the pain of regret.

"The pain, of discipline, weighs on you far less, than the pain of regret. Regret can devastate everything you strive for if let build to a size that is unmanageable.

"There is a big difference in knowing the path and walking the path. Knowing is always, half the battle in any situation; although, it's not what you know that makes you strong and powerful. It's what you do with that knowledge that produces the potential for great power and strength. As long, as your knowledge is from a limited view, there can be no real or true progress.

"You must find yourself limitless, if you wish to do all the things you wish to do, so you find happiness and peace within yourself.

"Will power and discipline, leads to faith and belief in oneself. Faith and belief lead to hope and desire. Hope and desire induce proper motivation. When you are properly motivated, you will find purpose and self-respect. Motivation is not a solution—in itself. It is a symptom. Brought on by the root cause.

"When you find your true purpose and fall in love with it, and yourself, you will be in alignment with self-mastery. Mastery of yourself brings forth true peace and joy.

"Peace and joy bring love into your life. Love for all things.

"Your inner, sub self, is always searching for familiar vibrational patterns to lock onto. Whatever your feeling, whatever emotion you are giving off, it will always search for more of the same in all things.

"An example of this is when you watch passing clouds on a lazy day. Looking for the images they create and mimic.

"Whatever your emotional state is will usually determine the sort of cloud images you see. If you are angry, you will notice like imagery and so on.

"The turning point is realizing, your thoughts can produce who you presently are, but you are not your thoughts.

"You—have the ability—to choose your thoughts. Once you realize this, it simply falls back to knowing what you want… and doing something to make it happen."

Trudy interrupted, "I get it… And that's all well and good but, how does all this crap make us badass werewolves?"

Ren retorted, "It doesn't. The werewolf will take care of itself. What this will do is make you able to visit friends and family without wanting to eat them. To control your negative emotions so they don't pour out into your werewolf… and create havoc without reason.

"So that one day you will have full control over the shift even during a black moon. And most importantly, so that when you are, a werewolf… you have control over what you do. So that you don't end up doing things you may regret.

"Trust me, there will be a lot of times when all the training in the world will be useless….

"These teachings will help you to forgive yourself. So that you don't become a guilt-ridden sack of shameful shit and end up mindless and one tracked. Like the bastards we've encountered outside this valley."

Ariel smiled her little sly smile at him and said, "It doesn't seem to help—you—from getting all—riled-up."

He laughed and said, "Hey, this isn't about me; besides, we are fucking Werewolves! Nothing will stop us from getting riled up. I haven't killed you yet though.

"I haven't even entertained the thought—of killing you. That's saying something, for any werewolf.

"If your humanity goes dark, your werewolf will go pitch black.

"Human beings weren't meant to become werewolves. Werewolves were never meant to become human hybrids.

"I am not a human being. I was born a werewolf, a Talbodai….

"The man image you see before you is the shape, I chose for the past five hundred years. I can shift, or shapeshift, as it's called by most, into any sizeable form of any blood pumping animal of this Earth Mother. My original name is Ren, and I'm the thing the Chinese saw all those centuries ago and named Lang Ren, their name for a Werewolf.

"Ariel, you are my only living pure-blood relation. Yet, you had a human mother. Paris was born a human but, her parents were werewolves. Tristan is a human who has been turned. In human terms, Tristan and Paris are my grandchildren, because your blood now flows in their veins Ariel.

"I am the son of Tal and Tatyana, the first Talbodai. I'm a shapeshifting being whose original form is what is known in this time-period as a Werewolf—"

Paris interrupted Ren, "Speaking of my birth. Please tell me what happened to my parents."

Ren went quiet. They could all see the pain in his eyes as his thoughts drifted off. After a long moment, he told her,

"Your parents were each the last of an ancient line of werewolf. Now you are the last one of those two bloodlines.

"But you are also a daughter of Talb now. When I used Ariel's blood to heal you faster, you became both your parents' daughter and mine. My granddaughter at any rate.

"Your parents were royalty as far as werewolf bloodlines go. They were also the most famous werewolves of their time. They were the first to rediscover and learn how to control the shift and become the guardians once again that the Talbodai were meant to be.

"They began teaching others how to do the same, and built-up a small army of followers. They were very gifted both. Lavish and rich in their human existence. Eccentric as werewolves.

"They were murdered because they were becoming too powerful. No one realized, not even me, that they had been targeted, until it was too late. I'm not even sure who's responsible for their deaths. Charles and I killed all those who were sent to take them out but, I was never able to learn who was the architect."

"There is a powerful evil, that for many eons, has plagued all living things, with its filth and carnage. Every time I get close to exposing them, they disappear for decades or centuries. The trail goes cold before I can figure out who is the mastermind behind it all.

"I am almost positive, whoever it is, is now the one behind this latest outburst of werewolf attacks and killing across this country. The casualties of the war are what brought them here in numbers initially. War makes it easy to cover up and hide the carnage left behind by werewolves.

"But as I've already told you, I am now the hunted, not the hunter.

"I have become a fugitive myself. Your parents and their followers... and Ariel's parents were my only allies.

"The day they were killed, was also the day Ariel's mother Jenny was attacked and almost killed. Both of you girls' parents were as close as it gets to what true family means. Love makes family, not blood.

"When I became the hunted that day, Charles and I separated, in hope of, they would follow me and not them. When he went on and recovered what he did, he painted a fresh target on his back."

Ren covered his face so they would not see his tears. Tristan said to him, "let it out my cherished friend. Someone once taught me to let tears fall when your heart tells you of its sadness. Tears are the cleansing agent for the soul."

Ariel touched his shoulder and he looked up at her startled. The pain in his eyes made her own tears fall. She smiled at him through them and he lost all control. He put his head to her shoulder and balled like a newborn baby.

After a good long cry, he lifted his head and wiped his eyes and face. Telling them, "This is the first time I have cried in ages. It is also the first time I have let myself mourn the loss of your parents Paris. And now your parents too, Ariel.

"The three of you are having an effect on me... on my compassion. It feels good to have it exist in me once again.

"Let's call it a day. We will begin again tomorrow. Let us all let the information sink in and get some rest.

"But first, I want to tell you something Paris. Something that I have wanted to tell you for many months and could not find it in me to do so. Until this very moment.

"Your true birth name is, Rachelle Paris Martin. Your parents were Victor and Madilyn Anne Martin. We called them, Vic and

Maddie... and you look just like her. And I have much to tell you of your mom and dad both...."

Paris put her hands to her face, covering her mouth and nose, as she smiled big with tears rolling down her face. She had just been given the only gift she had ever wished for herself, her whole life. It was a moving experience for them all, especially for her.

* * * * *

Over the next few weeks, Ren turned them all into Bodhisattva's. For those who do not know what that means, it is a name given to a person who is able to reach nirvana, but delays doing so, out of compassion, to save suffering souls and beings. One can't help noticing the similarities in the name Bodhisattva and Talbodai. Especially when one considers the ancient pronunciation and spelling, Taobodhi.

When they asked about it, Ren just smiled, saying, "I have been alive for an awfully long time... and Gautama Siddhartha was a life-long close friend and brother to me."

Again, they had learned in months, what took years to achieve without the powers of the Temple and their newfound existence. Granted they were at it day and night. Lost in themselves inside a pitch-black chamber, deep under the temple, where no light could reach, and the walls, floor and ceiling, was of bare natural granite. For most of their meditations, this was where they trained.

Tristan gave Ren every detail of the chambers in the ground back in Texas. He even told him the combination for the opening. Which turned out to be the same as the one for the Temple. He also divulged more about the Pyramid of dull green glowing metal in the lowest chamber. How the girls' father had rigged it with the batteries from Bagdad to create an energy field that, he now knew, was to suppress the shift from happening to Charles' wife, daughters and boys.

They determined that the reason Jenny and the boys had died so easily was a result of that energy field. Their regenerative capabilities were just too weak. The boys mainly because, their throats had been slashed so violently. Almost severing their heads from their little bodies.

Ren took them all into a lower chamber of the Temple. There was a hidden door with another elaborate opening mechanism.

Inside was the exact duplicate of the pyramid Tristan had seen in Texas. It was the source of the temple's power and mystique.

Ren told them that for a person who knew how to wield it or had the text that taught how to wield its power, they could do great or terrible things. Especially if both pyramids were brought together into one place.

Ren told them, "If both pyramids are rejoined and used for dark intentions, those who are in control of their power would be almost unstoppable.

"When one is placed next to the other, they align with each other magnetically through an energetic charge of energy.

"They will levitate into the air. One will stay right side up, the other will turn upside down. They will align, one above the other, so that they are all but touching at their points.

"They will then start spinning. One in one direction, the other in the opposite direction. As they spin in midair, they will tilt to align with the axis of the Earth Mother. My two blades that you now own, I named after these two pyramids of grand ultimate power. They are known as, The Twins of the Nine."

"Brought here by the nine immortal angels that build this temple and one other just like it in another part of the world.

"They were a source of much of their power while on this plane of existence." He explained more about the immortals and the pyramids as they returned to the main chambers of the temple.

When they got to the main room, Tristan, now knowing that the blades belonged to Ren, offered them back to him.

Ren refused them. Telling Tristan, he wanted them to stay in his and the girls' keeping. He prayed they would bring them good fortune.

As more time passed, Paris picked up the language of the ancient Atlanteans quite well. She had also learned to read and interpret the words and symbols of most of the other ancient scrolls, texts and manuscripts. Ren was ever the more impressed with how intelligent she was. If only her parents had lived, Paris would've made a fine queen.

They got Jojo trained to a point where he was himself again, no matter what mode he was in, mostly. During black moon though, he was not to be trifled with.

They did the same with the horses. Ren, with Tristan helping him, trained the horses more for warfare. It took no time at all to finish training them into full blown warhorses; the Apache had done a fine job with them.

Another perk was, they were still ridable as just fun-loving horses. But in werehorse form, they were formidable killers. With or without riders on their backs. During black moon, they were sketchy at-best, as unpredictable as Jojo.

Ren wondered often about how the girls, Tristan and he had come together. He often gave thought to one or all, of the girls' parents, having something to do with it, from the spirit realms.

He also felt deep within, that there was a greater power at work. That his Trio were here by destinies grace, and fates kiss; the prophesy said that much. He was hopeful, they would bring back the glory day of the Talbodai tutelage. To protect goodness through destruction of wickedness.

The fact that they had seen Tal and Tatyana, the mother and father of all werewolves and wolves alike, was of a great significance. He had not seen them in ages, and he was their offspring. Only father time would reveal the truth of why and what. No one can rush father time. You can be rushed for time, but you cannot rush time.

He watched all three of them as a proud father watches his children play, work and grow into something greater than himself.

There was no doubt that Ariel had accepted him as her father. They had become closer, in their short time together, than she had been with her human father.

She called him Daddy now. He thought that word and her voice was the most beautiful sound he had ever heard in his entire existence. He would often say to himself, "and I thought Tristan was the luckiest man in the world. How is it, that I have been granted such fortune."

The girls and Tristan wore their hearts on their shoulders. Making it easy to know they were the perfect choice to carry on the charge, should he fall. He also wondered if they would be able to keep their happy go lucky attitudes in years to come. The werewolf will tax a heavy toll on their souls.

Keeping from losing the goodness and reason within is a hard thing for any shifter, including himself.

* * * * *

Tristan–Days rolled on into one another. No one was even sure what day it was any more, nor did we care to. Winter and spring had come and gone once again, and the beginning of a great summer was upon us. During our stay in the valley, none of us had given the slightest thought to leaving it. Subconsciously, we were content to stay there forever.

After much time and effort, we were all fully conscious during the shift. During a moonshine that was a powerful thing; it wouldn't be long before we would be able to shift at will. Free of the moon's cycles.

We still needed a lot more time to control ourselves during black moon shifts though. We were already able to choose, not to change during black moon, but all of our moods during this time were soured, and it took great effort to suppress the change; however, controlling ourselves if we did change was even more difficult. Ren told us, *control would prove easier in a century or two*.

We also learned that full control, compassion and empathy did not exist for a werewolf, fully shifted during black moon, and no matter what cycle the moon was in, during a shift, the very real aspect that the situation could get ugly, fast when in werewolf form, was always a very real and present danger, filled with many pit-falls.

A werewolf is never fully tamed, only a little more aware. It takes an exceptional mind and character to achieve control in any form or fashion. In ten thousand years, there have been no others, who succeeded where Ariel, Paris and I have succeeded. It's never just a walk in the park, but control is doable. Still, it was never truly about taming the flesh and blood werewolf, as much as it was about conditioning the human host to its highest level of humanity and existence; where as such, anything was possible, even controlling and – Taming a Werewolf.

Taming a werewolf takes place at the beginning of every shift. And is never successful every time. If a mind is not superbly fine-tuned, coexistence with the werewolf during shift is near impossible. Even in full control, little things can easily upset the balance and give the werewolf full rein to wreak havoc, free of the human hosts influence. A precarious tight-rope act, with a clumsy step at best, for the uninitiated. For them, the bloodlusts of the werewolf will always win.

But for the keen and enlightened mind of an already exceptional human being, the possibilities are endless. A werewolf with such a human host, during moonshine, free of any distraction of taunt to rage, is a breathtaking and spectacular sight to behold, and an even more marvelous and incredible thing to be, in the still of the night....

* * * * *

Narration–Tonight, would be different than the trio had grown accustomed to. It was the first night of a moonshine, and what a gorgeous moonshine it was, Ren thought to himself. A perfect night to show his three pups what all this hard work had been for. They all walked out onto the platform of the temple, naked and already feeling the shift coming on, without any interference on their part.

Once all were shifted into werewolves, Ren took his motley crew out into the wilderness of the valley. Not to hunt or kill this time. This time would be about seeing the wonder of the Earth Mother, through the eyes of a werewolf. As a werewolf was truly meant to experience her awesome nature. All four of them, were psyched and pumped for this.

On all fours they ran. Running with tremendous speed and agility, they ran through the thick forest of trees. Dodging this way and that. Going between and around obstacles at a blinding speed. Barely missing tree trunks and the like.

Going faster and faster and then faster still. Making astonishing leaps across ditches and streams.

Jumping twice higher than necessary to clear fallen trees and long dead trunks and stumps. In the clearings they would zig-zag and circle all around it before returning into the forest, fighting playfully with one another.

With their newfound power and strength, also came the instinct and cunning of the Werewolf. Not to mention an overwhelming thrill for mischief. They played heavily with these new gifts of magical ability and extreme power and strength. Just to feel the heart pumping and the blood flowing, at all times, was adrenalizing.

To see as a werewolf sees, in the first person, thru its own eyes: being close to the ground while running at speed through the forest and underbrush, the feel of all fours gripping the ground, springing the body forward with amazing agility, turning on a dime and launching through the air in great leaps and bounds. To look at the image staring back from the surface of the water just before taking a long cool drink, to feel a long wolf tongue lapping up water and splashing them; taking big bites out of the water to quench their thirst.

Running together, they could feel the heart align and pump in unison with their companions' hearts, receiving huge blasting bursts of energy when this happened.

Ren had told them it was known as the quickening. All wolves, werewolves and even dogs feel it when running together or in a pack. Werewolves experienced the quickening best when the rage is subdued.

They came into a large meadow with a gentle slope. Ren stopped in the middle of it and stood on two legs. He looked up at the moon shining her glorious shine and let go a scream-howl in honor of such magnificent majesty. The trio joined in with him.

The four of them howled at the moon for some few minutes. Their harmonic vibrations and monstrous voices echoed out across the valley in waves of sound. Reverberating back to their own ears, sending waves of adrenaline rushing over and through them. As the resonance of their howling increased into one harmonic of vibration, they were pumped with more and more tremendous energy, to the point of bursting. They could feel their strength and power getting stronger and stronger.

Right at the point where they were ready to explode, Ren roared, dropped to all fours and charged out across the clearing like a raging bull.

Charging out a short distance, and showing unbelievable control, as he stopped dead in his tracks, and simultaneously spun around to face the others before being followed.

He stood there on all fours, snarling and growling as one preparing for a charge and attack. The trio's ears all went flat as they dropped to all fours and braced for it.

Fangs shining in the moonshine, under peeled back lips. Saliva drooling out from their jaws. Then, Ren did what no four-legged dog like creature could ever resist. He took off like lightning, in the opposite direction.

The Trio leaped twenty feet across the ground before their feet touched after their launch. They were a blur as they raced after Ren. Chasing after him back into the depths of the forest. Feeling again the empowering rushes of adrenaline course through them.

No words can clearly describe what it truly felt like to run with a pack of werewolves on the chase.

Now that they were feeling it, they didn't want it to ever stop. That is the addiction. A deadly adversary to be sure.

After many hours of play, they made a big arc through the wilderness and headed back toward the temple. When they cleared the tree line of the temple clearing, Ren ran toward the sheer rockface behind the temple. Picking up speed as he got closer to it. He then made an insanely high jump into the air and grabbed onto a high hand hold in the cliff face.

From there he swung himself up to another and another. until his hand holds were also foot placements. Scaling the cliff as a skilled climber would, coupled with the strength, power and agility of a werewolf. Moving faster as he climbed higher. Exerting huge amounts of energy without tiring in the least little bit.

The others followed him up the side of the mountain as if they had done it a thousand times. They reached a leveled off outcropping of the mountain where they had ample room to stand, lay down, play fight or whatever else the mood called for.

They were high above the valley floor. The part of valley and mountains they could see from this new vantage point, was absolutely stunning in the clear shine of the moonlight.

They howled at the moonshine, frolicked and fought playfully. Having one or two vicious tangles that went as fast as they came. For what reason was the squabble, no one knew or cared. They were werewolves, free and vibrant with life. Enjoying the one, true gift of this world. The thrill, excitement and joy of just being alive and breathing.

As dawn crept closer and closer, Ren laid down and fell fast asleep. The Trio, after a time, began sniffing and cooing each other. Becoming more and more aroused with each passing moment.

Going from sniff and lick, into a full-blown love making session, werewolf style. They made savage love right up through the shift back to human form, passed out curled up together, and slept like babes.

Ren woke them all up after a while. Saying,

"Let's get going. We have much to do today."

Ariel said, as she yawned, "Oh man, I really don't feel like climbing down just yet."

Ren said, "Who said anything about climbing down. Just close your eyes and let your werewolf instinct take over. It's the cycle of the moonshine. Your werewolf is just as conscious now in you, as you were in it, last night."

The trio knew right away what he was getting at, though Ariel questioned him further, "You mean, jump down? From this high up? In human form?"

Ren said, "It's Moonshine. For the three days of the shine, your human side is just as powerful as your wolf side. Consider this your lesson for today. You might get hurt. Most do their first jump.

"Remember this – only a werewolf can kill another werewolf. The only other ways you can die… is burn to death, and by the metal of the twins of the nine. Other than that, your immortal.

"Besides, it would make my day if all three of you land on your back. I would consider it proper payback for this morning.

Do you know how sickening it is to awaken to hearing your daughter having sex? And have to smell it? Thanks to you, I do…. So, fuck all of you, and good luck…."

Without another word, Ren jumped far out and over the edge of the outcrop. Falling from an incredible height at an incredible speed. Landing on his feet as though he had only hopped off a bar stool.

His Trio hesitated for a long while. But when they finally came down, they landed all at once. Deciding to make the death-defying jump together.

Ren said, "Well I'll be…. All of you… first time jumpers, from some three hundred feet, and you do it, holding hands."

Chapter fifteen

Can't Say I'll Miss You

Many moons had passed since entering the valley. Tristan and the girls sensed something in their minds. It was coming from Ren, calling for them. They walked outside and joined him. He was standing at the edge of the clearing that encompassed the temple. Ren said to them,

"I'm not sensing anything sinister, but something has entered the valley and is now right out there—not too far away. Whatever or whoever it is—give off a friendly vibe. It's not just one either. There are many."

Then he asked Tristan, "Where is that damn dog? I'm sure he's in weredog mode around here somewhere."

Tristan called out, "JoJo!"

All heard a deep growl and then a half roar. It sounded like five tigers all at once. They all looked up towards the sound as Jo dropped out of the tree beside them and sleeked over next to Tristan. He gave a low growl as he crouched down at Tristan's side and looked up at him. Tristan patted him on his head and said something to him. Too low for anyone else to make out.

They all turned their heads quickly from Jo, back to the woods. The Trio felt it now too. The wind was blowing wrong to catch a scent, although now they could hear whatever was coming.

None of them felt threatened in the least little bit. It was a vibe a lot like you get when you know you're about to meet someone you've sorely missed. The wind shifted and broke the tension abruptly.

Ariel exclaimed, "It's the wolfpack!"

She ran into the woods. She didn't get far before being hit solid in her chest. Stopping her forward motion dead in its tracks, sweeping her feet into the air in front of her and planting her on her back to the ground.

It was the alpha wolf, standing on her chest. She laughed as he licked her face in happy greeting. She reached her arms around his neck and hugged him deep. The rest of the pack dashed past them and ran into the clearing to greet the others.

The wolves all stopped suddenly, as they came into the clearing, as if they'd hit an invisible wall. Bundling into a tight group to stare over at Jo.

Jojo didn't react at all. He was Jo again, more-or-less, on the inside anyway. He just looked like a beast from a time long gone. As big as a prehistoric bear dog. Tristan had brought him a long way, despite the unchecked savagery he displayed during his first shifts. Only now, when he was on about something, shockingly violent was a huge understatement.

Tristan and Paris greeted the pack with open arms. Ariel and the alpha walked out into the clearing together. After explaining to Ren who the wolfpack were to them, Ren told them, "I saw this pack the night of the attack. They were attacking the werewolves that were after the horses and Jojo."

Paris asked Ren, "I thought you said the valley was land locked on all sides. With the portal being the only way in or out. If that is so, how are they here?"

"There must be a passage that they know of and I do not. A curious thing, but I'm not surprised.

"At any rate, their presence is welcome here. This valley and temple embrace all of Earth Mother's wild nature folk." Ren told her.

The day was spent happily playing with the wolves. The wolfpack was not afraid of any of them when they changed into werewolves that night, at will, free of moon-cycles.

They ran with the pack; hunting and playing together with them as werewolves was a thrill, they thoroughly enjoyed. They did not challenge the alpha male. They let him do his thing. Although, he did not challenge them either.

The day after the wolves showed up, Paris got the itch to ride off alone on Bella and explore some of the valley that she had yet to visit. No one questioned her motives. She rode off alone often. They bid her a safe journey as she rode away.

The wolves and Jojo went with her, so there were no needs for concern. Besides, she was fully capable of taking care of herself.

The day after she left, Ren caught a bad vibe. It wasn't long before the others felt it too. Tristan asked Ren,

"What do you suppose this is all about?" Do you think Paris might be in trouble?"

Ren responded, "No…. Something has come into the valley. Something not welcome. I don't have a good feeling about it."

* * * * *

Paris rode south through the valley for some few hours and then turned and followed it east. She had made it back around close to the portal when she decided to camp for the night. The wolves disappeared off on their night stalking.

Jojo was with her though; she was stroking his back as they both sat with no fire. She wanted to star gaze and a fire only hindered that pastime.

Close to midnight, she was suddenly startled up from her stargazing. She had a sickening feeling in her stomach but wasn't sure why. After a short while, something told her to get up and head for the portal. Still not in full understanding of what she was feeling, but deciding to trust her newly blossoming instincts, she decided to check into it.

The portal wasn't too far at all. She left Bella where she was, and her and Jo went to check it out. As they got within sight of the portal, Jo stopped in front of her and growled low. She quickly hushed him to silence and got down on her belly to the ground.

The portal was open. Men were pouring through it in droves. There must have been close to a hundred already grouped on the valley side of it. With more still coming through. There was no wind, but Paris knew in her soul, they were werewolves. They had to be the ones that had chased them through the mountains.

Paris watched on as the last one came through. He was a werewolf, of outstanding and tremendous stature. Impressive to say the least she thought. Except for the diabolically evil vibe she got from him. They didn't close the portal as they all traipsed off silently into the valley.

She was still laying on the ground, her mind swimming with thoughts. Struggling to organize them into a coherent idea of what the hell was happening. She felt the snort of Bella's breath on her back.

She quickly climbed up on her and rode to the front of the portal. She knew she had to get around this small army of werewolves somehow and beat them back to the temple to warn the others. She just wasn't sure how she was going to do it. As she considered options, she heard a loud screech above her. She looked up to see King, the bald eagle. He landed in front of her and they shared a stare.

She was amazed that she could hear his thoughts in her head. He told her that her plan to save her loved ones, would mean death for them all, including herself. Without ever laying eyes on them again.

He then told her of her only choice now, for staying alive. As the eagle finished his last thought to her, which was **follow me now**, he lit off the ground and flew through the portal with Paris and jo following.

* * * * *

It was midday on the following day when Ren, Ariel and Tristan, from their hiding place, caught sight of the multitude of men crossing a creek that wound through the valley from the main lake. Ren saw one of them who, appeared to be, the leader. With dread in his voice, He mouthed one word, a name, "Thorax—"

Tristan and Ariel both looked at him questioningly. When he finally noticed them staring at him, he said, "Remember the bastard I spoke of? The one that killed and ate his parents in the days of Atlantis? Who is the father of all werewolves except for us? That's him…."

"The one that stands a foot taller than all the rest. And to answer your next question, I have no earthly fucking idea how they found this valley and got in here. Even if I did know, it's now been rendered academic, beings they are already in here. Let's get back to the temple. We are in a world of shit—"

Tristan exclaimed, in a whisper. "What about Paris? She has no idea what's happening. She could run right into them. If they don't have her already!"

Ren responded, "I don't see her, but that means nothing. You can bet your ass he has scouts scattered all over the valley, Looking for the temple. We will be lucky to make it back there ourselves."

"You got that right old man!" Exclaimed a voice behind them.

As they all turned around and started to their feet, the man said, "Now!"

A huge steel mesh net flew into the air and spread out full above their heads, coming down over top of them. They were jumped from all sides and beat with club's unconscious.

* * * * *

Ariel thought she was dreaming, at first, hearing strange voices as she awakened from the beating, she had endured.

As she raised herself to her knees, realizing the reality of what had happened, she found herself outside the temple.

A humongous fire was blazing in the clearing. A full moon was shining. Tristan was on his knees beside her. Men and werewolves surrounded them.

Tristan had had, the living shit beat out of him, but he seemed alert. His hair and body were crusted with his own dried blood. One eye was completely swelled shut, proof of a fresh beating. She might not have recognized him had she not known him so well.

"What's going on?" She asked him in a low voice.

"I'm not sure. I have been knocked unconscious half a dozen times since we got back to the temple. Not to mention the beatings I endured getting here. I've only recently regained senses once again. You've been out a full day and half since they captured us. This is the second night since they hit us."

"Where is Paris…? And my father?" she asked in earnest.

"I don't know…. I haven't seen Paris. You and I have been right here since we arrived back at the temple. I haven't seen Ren either, but something is happening. They haven't said a word to me or asked me any questions. Only beat me back unconscious every time I've opened my mouth." As if on que, a fist was driven into the side of Tristan's head.

Some men came out of the south exit of the training area under the platform, dragging Ren behind them in chains.

When they stopped and dropped his chain, he managed himself up onto his knees. Only to receive a massive fist in the side of his head for his trouble. Knocking him back to the ground.

He stayed down until the powerhouse of a man that had delivered the blow, walked away. He then struggled back to his knees. He was naked, with dozens of deep cuts all over his body that were not healing like they should be. He was struggling desperately just to hold himself up on his knees. He didn't notice Tristan and Ariel, until Ariel cried out, "Daddy!"

He closed his eyes and prayed he was hallucinating. Because if not, the torture that was about to take place upon him and his daughter would be the end of them both.

"Daddy? I could smell the stench of Talbodai on the two of you, but I never even thought to hope I would hear Daddy...!"

It was Thorax who stepped into view atop the platform as he made that statement. He was a huge brute of a man, not too unattractive, curiously handsome in a sinister sort of way.

He was muscular from head to toe. He stunk of evil. The devil's right hand if ever there were one.

"Bring my uncle up here to me." He told his men.

They picked Ren up off the ground and carried him over beside the platform. Tossing him the ten feet or so into the air to land on the platform at Thorax's feet.

"Have my men been mistreating you Uncle?"

He helped him to his knees by grabbing a handful of his hair and pulling him up.

"They must have beat you all day for you to be healing so slowly Uncle..."

"Now, back to this daddy business. Bring those two over here closer to the platform so I can see their ugly faces better."

They started manhandling Ariel and Tristan to the platform and he yelled at them. "Stop! Let them get up and walk if they are able. I want to savor every moment of this. I've dreamt of this moment most of my life. I don't want anyone expiring before I'm ready for them to.

"I thought you told me there were four of them, including my uncle?" Thorax said to one of his men.

His man responded, "He said she was killed outside the valley in front of the portal the night they butchered Drasos and his brothers."

Thorax shook his head as he said, "What a shame. I was hoping to fuck them both in front of their boyfriend. Before he parts to the never lands beyond. I wasn't even going to kill the girls if they pleased me. I could use a couple of good fuck slaves. But with one gone and this one the daughter of my uncle here, I'm thinking up new ideas as I speak."

He seized Ren by a tuft of hair again and pulled his head back to stare down into his face. Saying to him,

"So, daughter huh? I thought that was a taboo for you?"

Ren told him, "Go fucking fuck yourself! Motherfucker!"

Thorax slammed a hammer fist straight down into his face. Licking the blood from his fist that splattered all over it, as Ren's nose burst from the impact. Thorax cleared the angry look from his face and said, "Fuck me? Huh! Look at you....

He pulled the Atlantean long blade from its case at his side and examined its bloodied blade with a lust in his eyes.

"You're about to go to the one place you've haven't been yet. But you go there this night. Death has finally arrived for you. Not before a few more evil acts on my part though.

"So, Fuck you! You Om chanting motherfucker! I'm surprised you get around enough to know the meaning of those words. Let alone using them in context." He shoved Ren's head forward as he released his grip on his hair.

Ren, still as sarcastic as ever, spit out a mouth full of blood and said, "How did you become such a prick anyway? What do you do? Eat only the dicks off your male victims? Turning you into the biggest dickhead on the planet?"

Thorax laughed and said, "Cute... Keep them coming. Don't disappoint me after all this time."

Thorax continued, "My men tell me this little girl killed one of my men with this knife. Is that true?

"She wasn't the one responsible for the killing and downright slaughtering of my men outside this valley, is she?

"No... that had your signature style written all over it, Uncle. We might not have found the entrance had you cleaned up after yourself. But then, I suppose you figured there wasn't enough time. Still, I almost didn't find it. I spent months just discovering how to get in.

"My method was, shall we say, rather unique. Someone has some work to do if they ever want to close it again. Unfortunately, that won't be you—Uncle."

Ariel, not being able to stand in silence any longer, with his continued taunts at her father, said to Thorax,

"Why don't you go eat another dick... you piece of chicken shit bastard! You're a real badass with my father in chains and us surrounded by all your little minions...."

Thorax looked down at her from the platform, "Man O Man! The mouth on you. Wouldn't it be fun to break your spirit! Followed by your spine! You little bitch!

"But am I missing something here? You do realize that the three of you are worms on my hook? That you are going to be tortured and killed, most heinously?"

Ariel retorted, "Why don't you come down here and get some—then? You—fucking—little pussy!"

"Thorax was perplexed by her audacity. Saying, "What? Who? Just who the hell...? Do you even know who you are talking to?"

He looked at Tristan and said, "This is your woman? How? Why? Do you even put up with her?"

Before Tristan could respond, Ariel yelled back,

"Because I Fuck him like Cleopatra with her ass on fire! That's why!"

Thorax's anger slipped, "I've heard enough! Somebody, teach this little bitch a lesson."

One of his soldier werewolves stepped up, snarled at her and rushed her suddenly. She never twitched a muscle or took her eyes from Thorax's face. When the thing was close enough, she grabbed it by the balls and squeezed them as hard as she could. Stopping it dead in his tracks. She then hit it in a vital point with a palm strike that stopped its heart; she then grabbed two handfuls of hair at its shoulders and swung herself up. Wrapping her legs around the neck, she seized it by upper and lower jaws, and ripped them apart at their base. Blood gushed as the beast fell to the ground, still caught between her ankles by the neck.

She stared into Thorax's face as she squeezed and twisted her legs. Snapping the neck like a twig.

Another werewolf rushed her. When it was at the proper distance, she leaped into the air and spun herself around in a spinning back kick that caught it in a down angle, square in the chest. Crushing its breastplate with an awful sounding crunch. Bearing him to the ground under the impact and landing with both of her feet on either side of its body. She raised her hand to show it had grown out werewolf claws, without making any other shift to the rest of her body. Then as quick as lightning, she drove it, straight fingered, into the beast's stomach and reached in under the ribcage. Ripping out its still beating heart, she held it up for all to see.

She took a huge bite out of it before flinging it to the ground like a piece of trash. It made a splatting sound as it hit the ground. As it did, she swallowed the piece in her mouth and wiped her bloody lips with her forearm; with her hand already almost shifted back to a human form again.

As a group of men and werewolves rushed in and grabbed her, holding her as she continued to stare at Thorax, Thorax glared back at her. He was astonished by such a spectacle from this young girl.

Finally saying, "Wow! There is a hell of a lot more to you than meets the eye isn't there… it's going to be fun watching you succumb to being raped by all my minions, as you called them, before you die.

"I was going to offer all of you a quick clean death for your compliance with telling me where the chamber that holds the pyramid of the nine is. But I see now it would be a waste of time to even try. Bring her boyfriend forward." His men did as he ordered, bringing Tristan closer.

Thorax turned back to Ren and said, "Your pet human… what was his name? Charles? I know he found the other pyramid and brought it back with him. I trusted in the stupidity of humans to kill everyone but your pets and a few others, so that I could torture them in front of him to make him tell me where he had hidden it, along with the treasure.

"They let their lust for killing and raping screw everything up. I should have done it myself.

"But I couldn't risk being exposed until I found you and the temple. Now that I have, it is only a matter of time before I find the pyramid hidden here. Even without your help.

"I never expected to find your pet human's brats here with you. They will tell me where on that ranch the other one is hidden. It will be fun to see who breaks first as I torture them both in front of each other.

"You should know by now that I am much smarter and wiser than you are Uncle."

Ren said, "A true wiseman would never make such a claim. A man cannot proclaim himself wise. Others can only hear wisdom in his words. Even a young child can speak wisdom if you are listening.

"Just like you say you will destroy me. You can take my life, but you cannot destroy me.

"My objectivity and subjectivity have integrated. I have renounced self and become one with the void. From all points of view, I am at one with the universe. You can never destroy me.

"The very look on your face tells me you don't have a clue of the meaning of the words I just spoke to you... and you call yourself wise. You're nothing but an evil piece of shit that's hungry for gold."

"Gold?" exclaimed Thorax, "I don't give a shit about gold! I take what I want, from the ones I rape, torture, murder, stalk and eat. Eating humans makes me stronger with every bite. My men and I are the top of the food chain. That's why I'm known as supernatural.

"What I search for is the Twins of the Nine.... Once these bastards tell me where your pet Charles hid the other one and I put it together with its twin, here in the temple, I will control this entire world. The entire human race will be my sheep. All will bow and worship me. It is the evolution this planet has always been destined for. And with the scrolls that are here and the ones I recover that your pet stole; together with the twins, I will be unstoppable. I will be invincible in every way you can imagine"

Ren laughed aloud and said, "That'll be the day.... Your anger and hatred have corrupted you... and twisted you to such a degree... you lack the capacity to rule even a small village, without killing everyone off... in some fit of rage, over some slight, against your... self—proclaimed authority. Let alone rule a world.

"You will destroy yourself and everything along with you. Because you do not understand the full power of the twins or how to control them. That's why they were separated. No one, but the nine could wield their power.

"Even they knew no single being can wield them. That's why the creator sent nine. You haven't the slightest inkling of what your tampering with, and it will be your end....

"Listening to your little speech just now has only proved to me that you're a bigger fucking idiot than I've ever imagined you were."

Thorax flew into a rage. He began beating him with all his strength. He snapped the chains that bound Ren with his bare hands and took them up as his weapon of death. Striking him over an over with all his might behind the chain.

Ariel screamed and pleaded for him to stop. Even Tristan, had a tear fall, as he watched the brutal beating Ren was taking.

Then as abruptly as his attack started, Thorax dropped the chains… and picked up the long-bladed knife.

Seizing Ren by his hair on his head again, he lifted him back up onto his knees. Thorax's eyes were mad with rage as he looked at Ariel and said, "Say goodbye kitten—because this is the end. I'm sure if he could speak, he would."

Ariel couldn't even recognize her father through all the blood and carnage: his eye hung from its socket, a large chunk of his skull had broken away, exposing his brain to the night air. It was difficult to tell it was a man.

To every one's astonishment, Ren, looked at Ariel with his one eye that was still in his head, with recognition. He convulsed and spit up gobs of blood and bile.

Then he said to Ariel through crushed jaw, "Do not mourn—… —little pup."

Ariel was crying profoundly. Thru her tears she said,

"Daddy… Nooo… No… Oh daddy…. Nooo…."

Ren tried to smile, and said to her, "The greatest… lessons… learned," he gagged, "and earned in… field… never ready… —first field tes—"

He gagged again, sucked in a small breath, and said clearly, "You go when you're ready enough Sah—"
Slam!! The impact stopped Ren's words…. He turned his eye down, to see a blade, protruding from his chest…. A blade that had just pierced through his heart….

Ariel screamed, "Noooo!!"

Thorax laughed and said, "Oh, did I ruin your little speech. Aww too bad…. It seemed, as though, you weren't finished. Maybe we should have wrote that shit down."

As Thorax opened his mouth to say something else, with all his remaining strength he could still muster, Ren cut him off.

He said to Ariel with his very last breath,

"Sometimes... Death sets you free... Ahhh..." And Ren died....

Thorax was not amused by his uncle's final show of strength and defiance. He pulled the blade from Ren's back and dropped it to the floor, picked up Ren's lifeless body and flung it off the side of the platform where Ariel and Tristan could not see him.

His rage was not quelled in the slightest bit. He grabbed the blade back up, jumped from the platform and made his way over to Ariel. His soldiers backed away as he approached her. She was frozen in place. Not from fear, but from shock for her father.

Thorax slapped her so hard across her face, she was spun around and down on one knee. He grabbed her by her hair, same as he had done Ren. Then snatched her head back to expose her throat.

He looked at Tristan and said, "Don't feel left out. I'll be with you in just a moment. Don't feel bad for them. You will be joining them right away. Can't say I'll miss you."

Tristan didn't give him the satisfaction of begging for their lives. He just stared deep into his eyes and said, "The devil you know.... If you weren't too cowardly to set me free, I would introduce you to a different breed, new and improved...."

Thorax raised the blade above his head. Tristan knew he meant to sever Ariel's head.

Inside, Tristan was screaming with pain, sorrow and remorse for his lover. Yet, he refused Thorax the satisfaction of seeing it.

Thorax raised the blade a little higher to bring it down hard as he could against Ariel's throat. That's right when....

An arrow flew out of the dark and lodged itself deep in Thorax's eye socket. More arrows flew and hit their intended targets. Hitting every man and werewolf around Thorax.

Thorax dropped the blade and let go of Ariel. With both hands, he desperately pulled at the arrow to pull it from his eye socket.

Finally freeing it from his head, he examined it with his good eye. The arrowhead was made from the same metal that the twin pyramids were made of. Lucky for thorax, it didn't penetrate far enough into his socket or he'd be dead. A score of his soldiers were not so lucky.

Thorax looked at his eye still stuck to the arrowhead. He had just lost an eye that he wasn't even sure would grow back. If it did, it wouldn't be anytime soon. Fully enraged he spun back around to Ariel.

She was gone… and so was the blade he dropped. He looked up to see Tristan was also gone. Now he was beyond rage. "Where are they? Who saw where they ran off to?" No one answered him. "They didn't just vanish into thin air! Your telling me nobody saw where they went?"

Tristan and Ariel had made good use of the ninja skills Ren had taught them. They were only a few yards away. Up in the tree that Jojo loved to hang out in.

They didn't know what was happening. All they knew was they had been turned loose of the grips that held them in place and both took advantage. In their dash for freedom they didn't even see the arrows fly in.

Tristan told Ariel, "We are going to die here tonight. There is just too many of them. I don't want to spend my last minutes or hours running like a rabbit to be killed in the end anyway. I say—lets die on our feet and focus on taking that bastard with us. It won't matter what happens after he's dead. The battle is already lost, but if we get—him, I'll feel like we've won."

Ariel nodded in agreement. She grabbed Tristan by his face and stuck her tongue in his mouth and kissed him passionately. He returned her passion with all he had. As they started to shift into werewolves, she told him,

"*I love you*… —Tristan Jonas…"

Tristan smiled and said, "And I love you Ariel Gertrude Ross Jonas… Wherever Paris is, I pray she is safe."

Thorax was already halfway through his shift. His clothes were ripping and tearing as his body grew and transformed.

He tore the shreds of clothes from his body. His insane rage at being made a fool of first by Ren, and then by his pups, had unbalanced him. Making him vulnerable without him being aware of it. Which was Ren's strategy, all along.

Now, fully transformed into a ferocious werewolf, Thorax let out a roar that echoed across the entire valley.

All his men, now changed into werewolves too, gathered around him.

Tristan and Ariel, now fully shifted into werewolves, dropped out of the tree to the ground. With lips peeled back to shine teeth in a menacing and dreadful snarl, they both roared back at Thorax. Taking on the challenge against overwhelming odds.

Thorax, with his soldiers all around him, prepared to rush his enemies, Tristan and Ariel doing the same.

Just before both sides launched their attack, Jojo stepped up between Ariel and Tristan. Fully shifted and ready for a fight.

Behind him, another werewolf stepped up from behind and stood with Ariel and Tristan.

This werewolf stood a full head higher than both of them. As they turned to see who it was, they almost jumped into the air with joy to see Ren standing there.

He was full and vibrant without a scratch on him. Nothing to show for the beating he took before being murdered and tossed aside.

They did not understand how. And they didn't care. He was there. Alive and in the flesh. Ready for a fight. Even though they were still outnumbered, his presence fueled them to even greater heights of enthusiasm for this battle.

Before Tristan and Ariel could turn around to face their enemies, something else came out of the shadows.

Though they didn't know it, it was the answer to how Ren was alive and ready for battle, that stepped into the fire light.

It was the White Werewolves, Tal and Tatyana. Even Thorax was frozen in place for a moment at the sight of them. A streak of dread climbed up his back.

As they walked up directly behind Ren and his children, more bodies stepped out of the shadows.

Scores upon scores of men stepped into the fire light. It was the Cheyenne.

Horace was in the lead row with them.

It was not just the Cheyenne that stepped out of the dark. There were Chiricahua, Mescalero, Lipan, Warm Spring, White Mountain and Jicarilla Apache warriors.

There was also Kiowa, Navajo, southern Paiute and Washoe. They had all gathered to battle the Wendigo and drive them from the lands.

From the woods came the wolf pack, with blazing red eyes and larger fangs and size for wolves of nature. Along with them, were three Werehorses, breathing fire.

The Cheyenne and Horace were completely naked. The reason becoming clear after a moment. All the Cheyenne… and Horace, were shifting into werewolves.

And there it was…. The real secret and reason they were called, The Dog Soldiers.

They were all a shade of gray unique to them and them only. As all sides braced for attack, another werewolf stepped out of the shadows next to Tristan and Ariel.

It was Paris, shining teeth… ready to kill.

The eagle had led her to the warriors, who had lost the Trio's trail. They had been searching for them, and for Thorax's werewolves, the whole time. It was fates kiss to destiny that had them close when the time came.

The Cheyenne never took Horace to the white doctor in Carson City. He never would have made it, with the terrible wounds he suffered. The elder dog soldiers and their chief, Flying Eagle, decided he deserved his revenge and turned him, to save his life. Thirsty for revenge, he happily accepted their offer. He was now a Dog Soldier too.

Three Indian warriors ran up to Ren and his Trio. They tied strips of bright red cloth around their arms so they wouldn't be mistaken for enemies.

The stage was set. The odds were evened up. There was a haunting silence over the valley. A dreadful silence that was broken by the screech of a great Bald Eagle.

King screeched loud and proud as he dove in and attacked Thorax in his face with piercing talons. The eagles attack was the que for the charge. A battle of epic proportion, that no one outside of the Indian nations would ever know happened.

The first clash was thunderous as bodies smacked together and death was dealt from both sides. It quickly escalated into a savage frenzy of carnage and bloodshed.

The Indian warriors were well armed with arrows, spears, knives, tomahawks and warclubs. All were made of the same metal as the twins of the nine, pyramids.

Some even had shotguns and repeaters they were firing. Though bullets wouldn't kill the werewolves outright, they slowed them down considerably when well placed in eyes, ears, and ... you know....

All the Indian warriors were fierce and severe in their onslaught. The Cheyenne werewolves fighting at their side, were even more brutal and vicious. Their enemy was no less brutal and merciless.

The element of surprise had taken its toll on the soldiers of Thorax. Caught off guard as they were, there was no time to rally into proper build up. Still, the battle was pitched for quite some time before lines could be drawn on which side was winning.

The Indians attacked werewolves two and three to one. Trying their best not to be caught one on one with the powerful beasts. The dog soldiers were more than a match for their enemy on a one on one basis.

The horses were in the melee as well. Delivering massive and horrendous wounds with hoof, fang and breath of fire.

Rearing, stomping, biting, kicking and blowing fire into faces and eyes. Sending all that came in contact with them, scattering or dying.

Jojo fought side by side with Tristan and the girls. He even snatched a couple werewolves off Ren that had piled up on him three or four at a time. Ripping their throats out. Tearing flesh and breaking bone just like his family was doing. With no remorse... and mercy, nonexistent.

The fighting quickly escalated into sheer and utter madness. The ground became a slippery mess of blood and guts: arms and legs were shredded and torn from their sockets, faces and torsos were mauled into a mash of meat and bone, werewolves were impaled on spears and driven to the ground, where multiple knives were driven deep into eye sockets and ears.

Tomahawks severed feet, hands and snouts. Knees and ribcages were smashed with war clubs.

Heads were bitten and ripped from bodies. Guts spilled out onto feet as stomachs were disemboweled with fangs and claws.

The minds of the men, fighting in this battle, touched insanity.

Bodies from both sides were being flung into the fire. Not the ones that were fatally wounded and torn apart. Creating a horrible and sickening stench as hair meat and bone caused the fire to blaze out of control. Some lost footing on the slippery ground and fell into the blazing flames.

The wolfpack attacked two and three on one. Never did they go one on one, head to head. Even King continued to take out eyeballs with beak and talon. Causing confusion and disruption as he beat with his powerful ten-foot wingspan.

Darting back out before he could be grabbed hold of and plucked from the air.

Now, in the center of it all… Ren and Thorax had spied each other and squared off.

A large space opened around them. The fierce fighting eased as both sides drew back. Each side taking their respective place behind their champion.

Both werewolves circling in the center, were torn and bleeding from a score of wounds inflicted upon them.

The dead were in pieces everywhere. The ground glowed red in the fire light from all the blood and entrails. Half the number from both sides were dead or dying.

Both combatants now circling each other for a final battle royal, stepped over body parts, and kicked disembodied heads out of their way. Tension now was at a climax.

Just as Ren and Thorax were about to clash… Boosh!!

Ariel hit Thorax from the side with an impact of tremendous force. It happened so fast; Ren wasn't sure what the hell had happened for a split second.

Ariel had an axe to grind. No one treated her and her loved ones raw… and got away with it. Especially, after the way Thorax had treated her Daddy. No-no….

Blood from the ground blinded Thorax in his one eye, as it splattered and splashed his face, as he was driven to the ground, onto his chest and stomach.

Ariel's attack was relentless. She bit into the back of his neck and tore a huge chunk free. Digging in deep again at the same spot on the back of his neck and shaking him violently with ferocious vigor. His growls and roars quickly turned to yelps and howls of extreme pain and trauma.

For the first time in his existence, Thorax was being manhandled by an adversary more powerful and vicious than himself.

Despite his injuries, he managed to get to his feet and fight back. They circled each other on all fours. Clashing together up onto hind legs. Slamming chest to chest and viciously attacking face and neck. Ariel gained the upper hand again, by grabbing him in her jaws by his ear and scalp and slamming him to the ground, onto his back. His ear hanging by shreds.

She didn't attack him in his face and head this time. Instead, she bit deep into his cock and balls and shook them viciously. The screams that came from him were discernably more human than anything else. She tried to rip them from his body. Before that happened, his motley crew of werewolves charged her.

They were met by her allies at once... and the fight was on again. The pile up forced Ariel to turn Thorax loose.

Thorax managed his way to the edge of the battle, where he took a look back. The second round of battle was clearly being lost. His band was dropping like flies now.

He was in bad shape from the mauling he received from Ariel. He knew she would have killed him had the fight continued much longer. He also knew the wounds to his face, neck and particularly his groin, were too great to go on. It wouldn't be much longer before they were wiped out utterly.

Thorax sounded a howl of retreat.

He and what was left of his bunch were chased all the way to the portal. The portal entrance was now the enemies exit.

By the time they reached the portal, less than twenty of Thorax's band remained.

* * * * *

Back at the temple, the White Wolves, Tal and Tatyana, appeared again. They had done the same for Ren, that they had done for the horses and Jojo that night by the lake. Only, they had brought him back to life, and restored him to full strength and power, plus a little more. You could say, he had evolved.

They had only given the animals a jolt to keep them alive for Ariel to save. Knowing full well, what she was going to do, before she did it.

Ren now had powers he wasn't even fully aware of yet. It was his, reward, you could say. For his loyalty to his duty and charge, as a Talbodai, throughout the ages. They told him they were proud of their one remaining son.

That he had done a fine job of raising his three offspring. They were ready for him to continue their work as Talbodai, and he would get to be with his daughter and her mates.

But first, he had to go with them, for a while. There were new lessons for him to learn concerning his upgraded existence. When they reappeared after the battle, they were in wolf form.

The wolfpack, who had suffered only minor loss, fell in behind them, their eyes, teeth and size, normal again.

Everyone watched in amazement, as Tal and Tatyana shifted into Werewolves. A spectacular thing for the warriors who were not werewolves themselves. Ren walked over, greeted his parents once again, and fell in beside them.

All present, heard words in their minds. It was Tal who spoke, "We are both lights of the divine source. Children of he, who breathes life into all things. Children are we also, to this great Earth Mother... whose name was Gaia when we walked this world as our own. The light, of our souls are one with the collective conscious of this cosmos. As are all of you... the same as us. The divine source... of the divine light... exists in us all.

"All of you have fought a great battle this night and won a great victory. A battle that'll be remembered in the legend of the Talbodai... and among your tribes and people forever.

"Your ancestors smile down upon you this night, for your courage and bravery.

"The ones who have survived and the ones who sacrificed their lives this night, for a cause greater than themselves, will forever be marked with the divine light. Immortalizing their deeds here this very night.

"This night, you take your place, among the brave souls who have fought against the evil of this world since a time unremembered.

"Inside the temple, you will find a table of food, water and wine. Prepared and placed for you by powers that be.

"It will revive and heal your bodies, replenish your spirits and minds. Cleansing you of the filth of evil you have fought against this night. Rejoice as you fill yourselves with its divine energy.

"The portal has been collapsed to prevent it's use ever again. The wolf pack will show you how to enter and leave this valley from now on.

"This valley will pass to all the native people of this land who wish to continue their traditional ways in peace. Protected forever from the encroachment of the races who look to drive you from your lands with genocide.

"In time, others like it will be revealed to you. Respect, honor and love this valley forever... and this valley will return your love in kind.

"For the end times, never really are, the end times... And paradise, is forever imprisoned, in paradise."

He waved his hand; a swirling light encompassed everyone in its brilliance. All werewolves, except Ren, returned to their human form, fully healed of all their wounds. The ones who were dying of their injuries, arose off their backs, fully restored. Men and wolves alike.

Tal and Tatyana then walked forward toward Tristan, Ariel and Paris. The Trio knew in their minds to step forward.

When they got close enough, they were shoved together against each other and overpowered to the ground onto their backs. The white werewolves stood over them. Snarling and growling, lips peeled back to show ferocious fangs and teeth. Saliva dripped onto each of their faces.

It was a show of dominance of who the true Alphas were. The Trio knew this... and calmly stared up into the faces of Tal and Tatyana.

Before their very eyes, the white werewolves morphed into wolf form again and licked their faces to mark them forever more... as true blood of the Talbodai.

They moved off and the Trio rose from the ground, back onto their feet. Ren greeted them, in his human appearance. He told them, "Unless they are needed in a desperate time, you will not see them again. They are the old way. You three, are the new way.

"I will now take their place as guide and advisor. You three and I are now, the Talbodai guardians of this Earth Mother. You are the keepers and protectors of the twins of the nine now."

All the warriors were listening intently to Ren's words. He looked at them as he said his next words.

"All the warriors here this night, both alive and passed on... and all their descendants, will be remembered for their deeds this night. For those who choose to be so, will be protected and honored as warriors of the Talbodai and in turn, be their army should they have need to call upon you....

"The animal kingdoms of this Earth Mother, large and small, will also come to your aide should you find yourself in need of them. Just as you will do the same for them forever more. Respect forever, the call of the wild things and laws that govern them."

He looked back at his Trio and said, "You have been given and provided with all you need... to progress to your highest selves. I know, you will do well. And I can tell you one thing about your futures, it will never be boring...."

Tristan said to Ren, "There is one thing that I am a little confused about. Everything that was written in the prophecy has come to pass, except one thing. It said that the one with red eyes, me, would make the sacrifice."

It was Tatyana who answered him, she had transformed into a gorgeous woman. She walked up and touched Tristan's cheek, saying, "You have put yourself in the path of sacrifice your whole life. You did so for Paris and Ariel, before you even met them, and many times since. Countless times for your Sarah, your Jojo.... You fight for what you live for... and believe in....

Ren smiled and said, "I wouldn't have made it past the damn dog, but that's what makes you, you....

"And when you and Ariel decided to face insurmountable odds to protect the sanctity of this valley and temple... and avenge me in the process...

"You knew it was a death sentence. Yet, you chose to do it anyway. In hopes that you would take Thorax down with you. Ending his evil rein. The three of you have fulfilled the prophecy.

"Along with your allies that stand behind you now. For they never gave up searching for you. Knowing you needed them. They stand with you now and always will. Along with others that haven't even been born yet."

Ren looked at his Trio and all the warriors, who he also considered his kin, with the glowing eyes and face of a proud father.

He then looked back at the girls and Tristan and said, "I must leave you now... for a while. I have been granted a new life this night, as you know.

"I also, you might say, have evolved into something greater than I was before I died this night. I must learn to wield these new powers now.

"So that I may assist you and watch over you the same as Tal and Tatyana have done for us all. Even when we didn't know it. Do not worry. We will meet again in the not-too-distant future."

He then looked at Ariel, who was smiling through tears of joy and admiration. He said to her, "Ariel, my lovely sweet beautiful badass—daughter."

He too now shed tears of joy and admiration as he continued with choked up voice, "No father has ever been prouder of his daughter, than I.

"I know I shouldn't, but I will brag about how you defeated Thorax so impressively... for a long time to come.

"Watching you avenge what he did to me, was most inspiring."

He spoke to all three of them now, "If ever you feel need of me. All you have to do is close your eyes, and think of me, in quiet moments alone... and you will hear me—loud and clear."

"When you are quiet, I will speak. As you progress in your meditation, you will be able to see and talk to me. No matter how much space or dimension separate us."

He stepped back, looked at all three of them and continued, "I leave you now to go with my Mother and Father.

"Do not say goodbye. This is not goodbye. It's more like... see you around—motherfuckers!!"

They all laughed. Him and Tristan grabbed each other's forearms in farewell. He then hugged both Ariel and Paris, then walked over to his parents, Tal and Tatyana. The three of them, disappeared into the woods together. The celebration that ensued that night, and all the next day and night, became as legendary as the battle itself.

Chapter sixteen

Present Day

Paris turned off the cameras while Ariel poured everyone a drink. After a long drink of silence… and whisky. Thomas said, "I've got to get this off my chest. So, in human form, Tristan, you're the elder, then Paris and Ariel's the baby….

"But in werewolf form, Ariel's the elder, then Paris and you Tristan… You're the baby…." Thomas started to laugh.

The girls instantly joined him in his laughter, by the time he got his second breath, he was laughing hysterically.

Tristan, trying to look upset, said, "Why don't you shut-the-fuck-up?"

That put the other three in overdrive of laughter. Tristan dropped the facade and joined them in their voiceless laughter. As they were able to calm down Tristan said, "They have never hit me with that before. Now you have planted it firm in both their heads. Do you realize what's about to happen over the next months? I won't live it down…."

Thomas then continued, "So, you guys are like, crusaders… and you think I am worthy to join your ranks. And want to try and train me, same as you were. If I'm to be a crusader too, do I get a cape?"

Ariel rolled her eyes and said, "This fucking guy—"

Thomas retorted, "Are you insinuating—I'm stupid or somethin…?

Ariel said, "Well… if it walks like a duck," she looked at her lovers, "I honestly don't think I can put up with his stupid shit—"

Thomas retorted, "Oh yea? Well, I honestly don't think I can look at you without getting a hard-on! You sexy bitch! Pun intended.

Paris and Tristan laughed as Ariel shot him a bird with a smirk on her face, saying, "Eat-your-heart-out! Or maybe— I'll just do it for—you," she licked her lips. Thomas instantly lost all humor and went blank faced.

"And take your fucking dick off default setting."

Tristan said, "You two should just fuck and get it over with."

Ariel responded, "Oh—I'm gonna fuck him... —in his ass... if he doesn't shut-up—"

Thomas opened mouth to say something, but Tristan cut him off, asking him,

"So, you're in? You think you can survive what we're about to put you through?"

Thomas looked at him and said, "Sure... why not...? You only live once—"

Paris jumped in the conversation, "Wrong.... You only die once. You live every day."

Thomas asked, "So when do we start?"

Ariel said, "Don't start whacking-off to your new assignment just yet—soldier—boy, we've got more important things on our agenda—right now."

Tristan said, "Not today. It's the last night of the moonshine and pismo surf report is claiming eight-footers, at the pier. Shortly after dark...."

Thomas clapped his hands together and rubbed them back and forth saying, "Great! Got a board for me?"

Tristan told him, "I think we can find something to tow you out on...." The girls laughed some more.

Thomas got serious for a second, saying, "before we get off on a different subject, did you ever find the translation to the Atlantean scrolls on how to cure the werewolf curse?"

Paris told him, "It's not really how you cure a werewolf. It's how you can cease to be a werewolf if ever you choose.

"Not an option for just any werewolf, save for the most—elder and powerful ones. You have a long way to go pup.

"One day though, if you make it that far, you can always choose to renounce your werewolf side. If you can refrain from using your werewolf abilities, in any way whatsoever, for a couple of decades, you'll begin to grow old... and one day, die like a human of old age.

"Provided you never use your powers again. Which is like an itch that never, ever, stops itching. One transgression, one scratch of the itch... and it's back to square one, and to answer your next question. We've never known anyone who succeeded. Or anyone who even tried for that matter. But it is written... in the ancient Atlantean texts."

Thomas spoke out again, asking, "How can a human body make such a transformation?"

Tristan told him, "Only in the past few years, has science been able to tell. It's been an arduous journey because of the level of secrecy we must keep. Only after we found a few we could trust, have we started making real progress. What we have figured out so far, from a modern-day scientific standpoint, is,

"The DMT levels at the time of the shift are off the scale. The forebrain, midbrain and hindbrain begin to act as three separate but equal brains. Functioning in a perfect symbiotic unison. With the left and right brain conception of normal function, nonexistent.

"The Vagus nerve is completely locked out, except for full sympathetic nervous function, which is why the human side is completely shut down. With primal instincts and violent reprisal... the very essence, of all it emits."

"The body creates a protein that floods saliva and mucus... or drool, as I like to call it, throughout the entire system. Increasing in volume until it spews from every orifice of the host body. Including tear ducts and ears, genitals and anus.

"Not before red blood of the body is pushed out through them first. The normal red blood of a human host is pumped and pushed out of the body. Replaced by the new proteins, with the production of a bright pink colored blood that is loaded with a sparkling quartz crystalline substance in its matrix. The pink blood ignites the new system of meridian's that were created, once the host became a werewolf, and now coexists with the human meridians in a fused state.

"Born into existence by the fusion of Lyca DNA with human DNA, which is now almost impossible to distinguish between. The new meridian system is dormant while the host is in human form. Coming to life as soon as the crystal quartz blood begins pumping from the heart. Once fully transformed into a werewolf, the blood returns to its normal state and red color.

"The saliva and mucus fill the body, pushing out profusely from all entrances and exits, save for the nose. The whole process, functioning now as one, triggers the metamorphosis. It splits the skin open in places all over the body. Joints begin dislocating and reorienting; bones breaking, growing, shrinking and re-fusing themselves, poking through skin and flesh; to reorient themselves in favor of the new matrix.

"With muscle, ligament and tendon doing the same. There is an acceleration of growth of the hair, teeth, nails and other hormonally controlled systems.

"All the while, the human consciousness, still clinging to threads of the real, is finally forced into sur-real. As it's overpowered by such an influx of DMT.

"The DMT continues to build to such an extreme, it persuades the consciousness, into an out of body experience of astral projections and hallucinations, that completely overtake all human cognition and memory. Until after the shift has completely cycled thru its process.

"Bombarding the senses of the host as soon as they're awake, with all that transpired while the human conscious was in its dream state.

"But the human host's senses can hardly make it out, in a coherent lineal timeline. It's just a jumble of flashbacks.

"That's the process, in a nutshell, for humans that have been turned. The consciousness of the human host is only in a dream-state until fully awakened during werewolf cycle… and learns to stay conscious. Sharing the experience with its counterpart… if the human ever gets that far.

"For born werewolves, they are essentially shapeshifters and have a quite different process taking place. Able to make the shift in less than a minute. But because there are only two, that we have access to, presently," he pointed to Paris and Ariel, "and they won't give-in to being poked and prodded, that science still is a mystery.

"The White Werewolves, Tal and Tatyana, are the original two shapeshifting Talbodai. Their offspring, Ren, being the only other, with no connection to humans. He's a werewolf first, human second. Trudy's mother is the only human he ever turned. Her being pregnant with Trudy when he did so, made her also a shapeshifter over the mucus and drool process. Paris too, because she was born of werewolf parents and then had Trudy's blood fused with her own. I am a pure human turned… so I go through the process I've just explained. Which isn't as uncomfortable as it sounds. It's quite addicting. Eventually, we'll all evolve to shapeshifting."

They filled in a few more blanks before Ariel came back into the room and interrupted them. "It's getting late. Are we going surfing or what? He has plenty of time to learn all this shit. But if I miss the swell, he won't live to fucking see tomorrow. And you can bet your ass on that, poncho's!"

They gathered their things for the beach and the city. Giving Thomas some proper attire for the beach and night on the town… and headed for the car garage
.

* * * * *

When they got home, Tristan and the girls went on into the house. Thomas was slow to get out of the car. He walked around to the side yard, to check out the grounds. A decision he instantly regretted.

As he rounded the corner of the house, a humongous and fearsome creature met him. Bigger than a Siberian tiger, with blazing red eyes. Pissed off and shining fangs from hell, at the presence of a stranger unannounced.

It was Jojo. In full weredog form. Thomas didn't know whether to freak-out and run or shit and go blind. Jo was crouched to give Thomas a solid lesson in manners and etiquette when in someone else's yard.

Just before he launched his attack, Ariel stepped up behind Jo and nailed him in the balls with her shin. He let out a yelp and spun around for a fight. When he saw it was Ariel standing there angry at him, he stood there as if they were talking back and forth, but there were no outward words being spoken. After a few seconds, Jo put his head down and walked off sulking, to tend his ball sack.

Ariel told Thomas, "Hey Yo! You need to be a lot more careful. He'll—fubar-your-ass—in a heartbeat! Just watching him get after something is a shock to the system.

"Even for me and I'm used to him. Jojo… is some-what tame—when he is just a dog, but when he's in weredog mode, dumb-shits like you provoke the-shit-out of-him….

"Once he's in full swing, it's almost impossible to shut him down before the damage is done. By done, I mean dead!

"So, until he gets used to you, don't go wandering around and exploring on your own."

Thomas was still in shock, saying, "That fucking monstrosity is Jojo? I tried picturing what he looked like but – Got-Damn! He's still around? The horses are still around too—aren't they! I fucking knew it...! I just can't get my head around the fact that – That! Is your fucking pet!"

Ariel exclaimed, "Oh my fucking god! You are such a Titty Baby."

Ariel cupped one of her breasts and started petting the top of it. Cooing and blowing small kisses at it as if to a baby.

Whispering, "Hush now. It's ok... you're ok.... Did that big bad doggy scare you?"

Thomas smirked and replied, Ha ha! Have your fun at my expense. But that fucker is a heart attack waiting to happen... for anyone... who just happens to see him."

As she walked off, Ariel told him, "Well, just remember... we love him. You... we'll see.... Now get your ass in the house and out of his yard before I dump some chi into—your—ball sack."

* * * * *

It was mostly Tristan who worked with Thomas. Especially during his first shifts. Paris and Ariel stayed busy trying to figure out the truth behind the night Thomas's team was wiped-out.

They shouldn't have been there. It was more difficult to find out who had ordered them there than it should have been, for people of their clearance level. They still hadn't gotten a clear answer. Which told this whole affair went higher up the ladder than they'd first expected.

Two months of investigating passed by like a weekend; they were no closer to an answer than when they started. The girls decided to start back at the beginning and search the area where it all first took place again.

They were there about ten minutes, before they turned around and left. They both, had caught a scent this time that they hadn't noticed there the first time. A scent that they hadn't smelled in an awfully long time.

The building that was there, was just an old abandoned warehouse, next to just an old dried out ravine, in-reality.

Why the guys have been saying gorge all this time, the girls had no clue.

Yet, somebody had been coming and going, and on a regular basis, for the scent to be so strong. They must have covered the scent the first time, somehow. Not an easy thing to do to a Talbodai. Whoever it was, had slipped up not continuing to do so. Ariel and Paris were thinking, they must have thought they had fooled them well enough, to not be concerned about it anymore.

When the girls filled Tristan in, he ordered surveillance of the place. He told the girls that he wanted them with the team. If suspicions proved true, their days were about to get a whole lot more difficult… and interesting.

It wasn't long before they figured out there was an underground facility at the site. A sizeable pack had taken up residence there, and they were—not too unsophisticated. A little—too highly—organized for just a random bunch who ended up together.

This was not a simple hide-out for strays; this was a gathered and growing force for someone's agenda. But to what end? What is that agenda? Who was cash-funding all of this? And just what greater design was in play?

They were soon rewarded for their efforts when they finally spied who they had expected was playing a role in all of it… Dominique! For many decades, she had been the new mastermind behind the dark and grim goings-on, of werewolf packs of late.

She had figured out a way, or had evolved to a point, where a simple bite from her or one of her direct offspring, was all it took to change a human being into a werewolf.

For half a century, she had been building her forces up, always eluding traps and outright attacks, set for her. The trio would take out her forces and she would slowly build them back up again. If they could be fortunate enough to take her out, it would be a major win.

Thorax had not been seen, or even heard of, since that night at the temple, some hundred and fifty years ago now; yet, they knew he was still out there, somewhere, and he was probably the mastermind behind Dominque's aspirations; although that had not yet been confirmed, they never tossed it out as impossible.

Thinking more of it as being highly probable. Only time would tell.

For now, they would do as they had always done, when they uncovered her and her schemes: take out her pack and hope that they took her out with them. A goal, most difficult to secure. She was no beggar, nor slouch, in her methodical nature. A very evil and dangerous adversary, not to be trifled with.

Thomas was livid when they told him he wasn't ready and ordered him to stay put at the mansion; putting Jojo in charge of making sure he didn't leave the property.

* * * * *

They called in the special teams they had personally trained, for werewolf seek-and -destroy, and were on a majestic level of security, as such. Mostly because of the weapons they were using. Besides being the most advanced technology available, they were also equipped with incendiary weapons and projectiles made of the same metal as the twins of the nine. Courtesy of the Indian nations. The metal, in the present day, had been humorously dubbed, Cryptidimite.

Tristan and the girls had confirmed Dominque's presence at the stronghold, before setting their plans in motion for the night they had chosen for their assault.

The plan was simple: kill everything – then do a full reconnaissance of the compound, inside and out, for intelligence that could tell them what these things were up to; then destroy the facility, leaving no trace it was ever there. Simple, easy to remember.

They always had a contingency plan for traps. On this mission; however, there was no way of knowing that the entire thing: the wolfpack, the compound, all of it, was just an elaborate and ingenious ruse to capture and/or finish the Talbodai off, for good. Exterminating them from existence was the only aim.

Dominque was aware of their surveillance from day one. They had been closely watched since then. Like a fish on a hook that is let run, giving it extra line until the opportune moment, to snatch and set the hook.

Another fact they did not know; Thorax, was the mastermind behind it all. He had one goal that night, and one only; he wanted to kill Ariel, personally. She had made him look foolish all those years ago, during their last confrontation.

Facts they became painfully aware of when they tried to enter the warehouse undetected.

The trio and their company were hit hard at first assault. There were so many, the Talbodai was on the defense for most of the battle. The fighting was fierce, brutal and unrelenting. Tristan and his team were driven back once, twice, and yet a third time.

Because it took Tristan minutes instead of seconds to fully shift, he was in werewolf form when they were attacked. The girls made the shift at their first opportunity.

Thankfully, the enemy didn't have cryptidimite in their possession. Or the battle would have been over before it started. How dominique had produced such a numbered force, under their noses and without sooner knowledge, would be a question they would ask themselves for a long time to come.

Fighting was intense but short lived. With over half their number already dead or dying, Tristan, reluctantly, sounded the retreat. Just as he did, a crossbow bolt, shot out from its hidden location of origin, and buried itself deep in Ariel's head.

Two score of werewolves poured from the warehouse entrance. Instantly adding to the melee. Making it impossible for anyone to get to Ariel. She was at once attacked, from multiple sides, by more than a dozen werewolves. They viciously tore at her, before anyone could draw them off and away from her.

Still unable to get to her, with the multitude of attackers trying to take them down, Tristan and Paris fought furiously, to no avail.

The first order of Thorax's force was to keep Ariel's allies backed away from her. So, her lovers could watch her demise, and it was working.

All Paris and Tristan could tell at present was that she had been severely mauled and wasn't moving, with a crossbow bolt sticking out of the side of her head. They fought desperately to reach her. Being driven back every time.

Thorax was beside himself with joy. He had fired the bolt that allowed Ariel to be jumped by so many at once. Now, he was frantically fighting his way to her. With a torch in his hand to set her on fire and finish her for good. His revenge would be complete, and it would be a sweet taste in his mouth. He had waited long for this moment, which was now upon him.

Paris and Tristan could no longer even see Ariel. Nor could any of their remaining men. They did see thorax trying to get to her though. They drew all their remaining untapped strength to get to her first.

With a bloody and mighty effort, Tristan and Paris pushed their way through their enemies and got in between Ariel and Thorax. There was an instant of pause... then, Whoosh!!

They were hit hard again and dragged out of his way. He rushed the last few steps to the body and poured the gas he held in one hand, all over it. Quickly followed by the torch, which set the body ablaze.

The scream-howling roars that Tristan and Paris let out were awful in their sorrow of sound. There was nothing they could do. They were still being steadily driven back.

They were near to joining their fallen love and fought desperately, just to stay on their feet.

Thorax stood next to the flames and smiled, ever so sickeningly humble, at Tristan and Paris. Waiting for them to receive their final death strokes when,

Whoosh, Boom! whoosh—whoosh—whoosh! Boom—boom—boom! Followed by the buzzing sound of 20-millimeter cannons, mounted on the front of Apache helicopters.

Though they were reluctant to do so, the team tranquilized Tristan and Paris, and they were dragged from the sight by their remaining troops as fast as they could. None too soon at best.

They had barely made it out of the kill box zone before two A-10 thunderbolt jets made a fly-by, spraying everything, with their front mounted seventy round per second 30-millimeter gatling guns. Followed-up by three, seven-hundred-and-fifty-pound incendiary firebombs, dropped from an AC-130 gunship, with two huge blasts from their 105-M102 howitzer cannon as it made its Pylon turn.

Utterly demolishing everything. Creating a mushroom cloud plume that resembled a nuclear explosion, to the untrained eye.

Tristan and Paris were devastated and infuriated. Not only had they lost Ariel and were forced to watch her body burn, while Thorax stood over it and stared back at them with a shit eating grin, there was nothing even left to retrieve of her now. The blasts had seen to that. They had also saw Dominque and Thorax, escape without a scratch, just before the bombs went off.

By the time the fires and smoke had cleared, there was nothing left to tell there was ever a warehouse there at all.

Even the underground facility had been decimated. Leaving a huge crater in its place.

Tristan and Paris refused to leave the site on their own accord. There injuries were extensive.

Their men had no choice but to remove them by shooting them with their own powerful tranquilizers again.

Subduing them away from the site before curious eyes came looking for what all the commotion was about.

* * * * *

The next morning, just before sun-up when they awoke, reality set in hard. They did not speak to anyone. They got straight into their car and drove back to the gorge, arriving just after midday. Once there, they walked to the edge of the gorge. Looking over the edge they tried to see if they could see Ariel's remains. Spying something burned and charred.

At Tristan's feet, at the top of the gorge, was a crossbow bolt. He picked it up, and they made the jump down and stood next to the gruesome sight.

That's when it hit home. Ariel was gone, and she wasn't coming back. The pain of that reality was unbearable.

Paris and Tristan looked at each other. Then locked into a hug and cried harder than they had ever cried in their entire existence. They fell onto their knees, screaming and crying.

Looking up at the sky, Tristan screamed at the top of his lungs, "Why? You tasked us! All we wanted in returned was to always be together! Why did you let them take her away?

"Why didn't you come and save her like you did her father? Fuck you! You ungrateful useless fucks!"

He grabbed two fists-full of his own hair, grit his teeth and tensed his body severely. Saliva was pushing out between his locked jaws. He let go of his hair and roared at the sky again, saying, "Ren! You evil Bastard! Why? You had to know! Why?"

He fell on the ground next to Paris, who was lying next to the charred remains, staring blankly. They laid on the ground next to the ash and bones for hours. Crying and choking on their own pain and suffering. Without ever saying so to one another, they both wanted to lay there until death took them.

But because of their deranged existence, they couldn't even do that. They just laid there in the middle of the desert, at the bottom of the gorge, all night.

They didn't care that it was freezing. They didn't care that they were in pain from their severe injuries, which weren't healing due to the severity and extent of them, weighed down by their extreme sorrow. All they wanted, was for death to take them to Ariel. For the pain of Ariel's loss, to be alleviated with one fell swoop of the Grimm Reapers death stroke. But that, was not going to happen.

* * * * *

The next morning, they rose as the dawn was breaking. Paris asked Tristan, "Now what? What do we do? How do we… proceed from here…?"

Tristan looked into her eyes. The look in his eyes, scared Paris. She had seen him undergo every emotion, from best to worst, throughout their lives together. Never, had she seen such darkness staring back.

Tristan grit his teeth and peeled his top lip back. saying to her, "I'll tell you how we proceed… Let this be Ariel's epitaph… We go to War!!"

"Ariel's name will be our war cry!! We will show them why they should have always feared the dark!! Every—last one of them… good, bad, misunderstood, innocent by oblivion, it doesn't matter!!

"Humans, werewolves… —little dogs and children….

"Anyone and everyone, in-any-way, associated with Dominique or Thorax….

"We Kill Them All!!"

Chapter seventeen

Fates Kiss

Around midmorning on the day following the battle, eyes opened, and were at once blinded by the brightness of everything. Eyes that asked, "What was this blinding light?"

Why were they unable to see through and name the source of the blinding light?

Oh yea, the sun. It's called the sun. Why was it being so cruel to them in this moment? Why weren't the hands, which protect them from such things, doing their job?

Oh yea... hands. Did hands still exist and work? Yes, there were two and they functioned.

Two hands cover the eyes and face to block out the brightness of the sun. Peripheral vision took over at once. Noticing ground, shrubs, rocks and shadows. The eyes then asked their self, "What are we attached to? Why can't we move up?"

Oh yea... We are imbedded in a body.

Why doesn't this body move? Is it no longer able? How does it move? What is the mechanism that induces and produces movement so we can see more?

Remembering after a moment how to move, the body moved and then sat up. Realizing only in that moment that it had been laying down on a huge flat slab of rock.

Body, the eyes thought to themselves; this is our body. Oh, how the body ached and was covered with cuts and bruises in multitude. Most of the wounds looked more like bites, as if by some huge dog. They were all almost healed. Though the body told a different story, through the pain it was still feeling.

The eyes looked down. "What are those? Oh yea... Legs and feet. My legs and feet. My... My... mine!"

They are mine, realized the eyes. The eyes then thought, mine... what... mine... me... We are me... No, not we are me. My eye am me... No, that's not right either. I... I am me! I am... What? What am I? Who am I??

The eyes then looked to where the legs came into the body. What is between our legs? My legs. P... Pa... Pu, Pu, puss, oh yea.... I am a gir, gir, girl. I am a girl!

Now the eyes quickly noticed, I am a naked girl! Why am I naked? The eyes looked around, Wuh, Wuh... Where? Am naked? Where am I, and naked...?

The eyes surveyed their surroundings. Struggling for words and names for what they saw. After what seemed like forever, something clicked. Coherency returned.

I am a girl... Naked, in the bottom of a desert canyon of some kind.

She wiggled her toes. Then felt her hair. Ugh! What a nasty mess! How long have I been laying here? She thought to herself. It's time to go... no matter how long it's been.

Go... Go where? Where do I go? Who do I go to? Who am I? What is my name? What in the mother fuck has happened to me that I have no memory at all, of anything? Not even simple sentence structure is coming easy for me. Makes me want to scream.

Scream.... Voice... I have a voice that makes sound. Then she spoke aloud to herself, "It is one of a bunch of senses that I have. Sight, sound, feel, smell, taste, vestibular and intuition. And I'm particularly good with them all."

Between her and the cliff that made up the side of the gorge, was a body of something that had been burned, leaving mostly charred bone and ash. It looked to be human.

What was it doing there? Why was it laying so close to her? Was she responsible for its demise? It must've fallen from above. She must have fallen from above too. If they fell over together, that only added more questions than it answered.

She noticed there was a creek not too far from where she sat. As she went to get up, her hand came down on a bar of metal. She picked it up and examined it as she walked to the creek. She knew what this was, she told herself. Why couldn't she spit it out.

Oh yea... This is a crossbow bolt. A damn peculiar metal it is made from too.

It was dark, almost black. It seemed to have a green glow emanating from deep within its center.

She set it down beside her, as she kneeled beside the creek and dunked her whole head into the cool, flowing water.

Taking mud and washing the grime out of her hair, and then getting into the creek, she took a well needed bath.

Feeling refreshed, she climbed out of the creek and sat down beside a small calm pool of water that was cut off from the main flow of the creek. After a time, she looked at herself in the reflection of the water. Dark hair and green eyes. Rare but not hard to look at… she thought to herself.

Then the questions of who, what, why, how, when, and where and so on, plagued her mind once again. Finally, she grabbed her crossbow bolt made of strange looking metal, stood up, through aches and pains, stretched her lithe body, and said aloud, "Well, I'm not going to accomplish anything sitting here in the middle of a fucking desert gorge.

"I need to leave this desert, find me some clothes, then figure out just who the fuck I am!"

She made her way up and out of the gorge at its north end and made her way in the direction that she felt might be the shortest way to something other than just more desert.

She was able to walk without limping by the time her first hurdles of leaving the gorge were past her.

Though she was proud of her accomplishments of realizing her senses, getting clean and finding her way out of the gorge… — Ariel's troubles were just piling up….

Epilogue

When Ariel was hit by the crossbow bolt during the battle, it had stunned her heavily. She was hit from all sides violently. So violently she was left for dead at the edge of the drop off into the gorge. When she was hit and mauled so horribly, the heavy-duty crossbow bolt came out of her head.

As ordered, Thorax's werewolves had left her where she lay, ready to be burned.

At one point, when the fighting for who got to her body first, was at its most intense, both sides lost sight of her for a moment. At that same time, one of the trio's men died.

In that instant, he fired a crossbow bolt made of Cryptidimite at a werewolf, penetrating the side of its head. Killing it instantly; causing it to nose-dive to the ground, sliding hard into Ariel's body. Sending her over the edge and assuming a position in her place, which made it look like, it was still her, lying there.

In Thorax's mad rush to burn the body, he never noticed that he was burning one of his own men, not Ariel. Neither did anyone else, including Paris and Tristan.

The still burning body was blown off the edge by the first shock waves of the bombing.

To land next to Ariel at the bottom of the gorge and continue burning up completely.

She had miraculously survived the attacks and fall. Only to awaken with amnesia from her deadly encounter, followed by the fall into the gorge.

For Ariel, who is a natural born werewolf, amnesia of the human host spells disaster.

Because a human host with amnesia…

Is a Werewolf, *Off the Chain*….

Find out what happens in book 2

Moonshine - Off the Chain

Coming soon

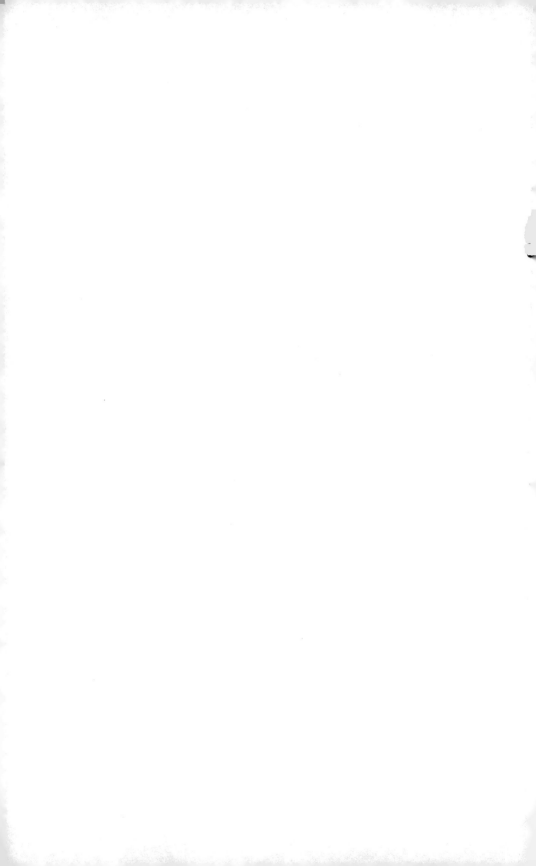

Made in the USA
Columbia, SC
29 September 2020